# The LADY or the LION

# AAMNA QURESHI

# The LADY or the LION

CamCat
Books

**Content Warning:** This novel contains potentially distressing material. Some characters use racist language and/or behavior. Some scenes deal with the reality of sexual and physical assault. This language and these behaviors are elements relevant to the authenticity of the story and in no way reflect the attitudes of the author or the publishers.

CamCat Publishing, LLC
Brentwood, Tennessee 37027
camcatpublishing.com

Hardcover ISBN 9780744303445
Paperback ISBN 9780744303421
Large-Print Paperback ISBN 9780744303889
eBook ISBN 9780744303377
Audiobook ISBN 9780744303940

Library of Congress Control Number: 2021931277

Book and cover design by Maryann Appel
Cover illustration by Asrar Farooqi
Map illustration by Rebecca Farrin

5    3    1    2    4

*For Mama and Baba,*

*Jazakullah Khair for everything.*

*"In the very olden time, there lived a semi-barbaric king . . ."*

This is not his story.

# THE TRIAL

*T*he appointed hour arrived.

From across the mountain, the people gathered into the galleries of the arena. Though considered a barbaric custom in the nineteenth century, the trial by tribunal was tradition. It was with sick fascination that the villagers filled the seats; the overflowing crowds amassing themselves outside the amphitheater walls.

The sky was a murky gray above them; summer was over. A breeze traveled through the air, and the villagers shivered, clutching their shawls and their children close.

The chatter and clamor ebbed to hushed whispers as the Badshah entered the arena at its height, where his ornate throne awaited him. His bearded face was stoic and severe, his lips pressed into a thin line, his eyes sharp.

The onlookers lowered their heads in respect as he took his seat. His wife, the Wali, sat beside him. A low murmur pulsed through the crowd as one more took her seat beside the Badshah.

It was the Shehzadi.

The low chum-chum of her chudiyan echoed through the arena as she moved toward her throne, her blood red gharara trailing behind her. Her golden crown glistened, bright and shining as her blue-green eyes.

She held her chin high, proud as ever, as she took her seat. The villagers had not expected her to come. How she could stomach such an affair was beyond them! To see one's lover torn to shreds or thrust to another was no easy sight.

Yet, there she sat, beside her grandfather. They sat directly opposite the two doors; those fateful portals, so hideous in their sameness.

All was ready.

The signal was given.

At the base of the arena, a door opened to reveal the lover of the Shehzadi. Tall, beautiful, strong: His appearance elicited a low hum of admiration and anxiety from the audience.

The young man advanced into the arena, his back straight. As he approached the doors, the crowds silenced. A crow cried in the distance, and the lover turned.

He bowed to the king, as was custom, but his gaze was fixed entirely upon the Shehzadi. The sight of him seared through her.

He reached for her, she reached for him, but their hands did not touch; they were tangled in the stars between them, destiny keeping them apart.

From the instant the decree had gone forth to seize her lover to trial, she hadn't spent a second thinking of anything else. And thus, she had done what no other had done—she had possessed herself of the secret of the doors.

Now, the decision was hers to make.

Should she send him to the lady? So that he may live his days with another, leaving the Shehzadi to her envy and her grief? Or should he be sent to the lion? Who would surely tear him to shreds before she had a moment to regret her decision?

Either way, they could never be together.

Then, his quick glance asked the question: "*Which?*"

There was not an instant to be lost. The question was asked in a flash; it had to be answered in another.

It was time to seal both his fate and hers.

# CHAPTER ONE

*D*urkhanai Miangul heard the bell echoing throughout the mountains.

Her hand lay atop her grandmother's, the Wali
of S'vat, whose hand lay atop her grandfather's, the Badshah of
Marghazar. Together, they three had rung the bell to alert the
tribespeople of foreign entrance into their land.

For the first time in centuries, the capital city of Safed-Mahal
was opening its doors to foreigners, those from their neighboring
districts.

Coming to harm her family.

The sound resonated through the mountains, in cacophony
with crows crying. It was said that crows brought visitors with them,

and as a child, Durkhanai was always excited to see who would visit her castle in the clouds.

But today, she knew the visitors would bring turmoil. While entrance throughout Marghazar was permissible, sparingly, for trade, entrance into the capital Safed-Mahal had been forbidden for centuries.

Until now.

"It is done," Agha-Jaan said, his old face flushed florid from the wind.

"Yes, janaan," Dhadi said somberly. "Now we prepare."

Durkhanai was clad in a pistachio-green lehenga choli, her ears and neck dripping emeralds and pearls encased in pure gold. The ensemble made her eyes more green than blue and her skin a soft brown. Beside her, her grandparents were dressed in bottle green; her grandfather in a sherwani, her grandmother in a silk sari.

Maroon-red mehndi covered Durkhanai's hands in flowery details of blooming roses. Her curly hair was swept up in an updo with ringlets framing her face in front of her dupatta, which sat atop her head and fell down one shoulder.

She was the essence of a princess, but she would need to be *more* to protect her people.

It was the beginning of April, when the world cracked open its shell to let greens and pinks begin to spool out. The weather was softer, warmer.

Up in the bell tower, there was no spring; wind slapped her cold on both cheeks, turning her nose numb.

From here, she saw the great expanse of lands she was heir to; the jewels of the earth. The palace was on the side of the mountain, with views of both the empty valleys and the populated ones. On one populated mountain, she saw two waterfalls, and while ordinarily the glittering water brought her peace, today the two holes punctured in the mountain flowed water like eyes flowing with tears. In the distance of the unpopulated lands, she could almost see the blue-green S'vat river which protected them in the north from the Kebzu Kingdom.

Now, for the first time, they would need protection from those within their lands.

*Ya Khuda, protect us,* she prayed.

They waited for the bell to quiet, the valley to turn silent. Then, hand in hand, her grandparents made their way to the door to head back down to the palace below.

"Come," Agha-Jaan motioned for her to come.

"Just a moment longer," she responded. "I want to make dua."

Her grandfather nodded, allowing her solace, and she was alone.

"Ya Allah," she prayed. "You are the Protector of all people, so please, protect my people. Bless us, forgive us, let no harm come to us. Ameen."

She blew onto all her lands, the homes that dotted the mountains, praying her people and her country would stay safe from those who were coming.

"I will protect you," she promised her people. It was her sacred duty. With a final glance, she went back down to her palace, to prepare.

A banquet had been arranged for the ambassadors, and Durkhanai had to change to get ready for it. The defenses were up, but their greatest defense was their behavior; they had to act absolutely unbothered by any of this and entirely innocent—which they were.

They were to be kind—but with an undercurrent of cruelty.

As Durkhanai walked to her rooms, she noticed a man walking alone in her hall, his fingers dancing along the windowsill. She paused, blinking.

Who was he? More importantly, what was he doing here?

Durkhanai approached until she stood beside him. Noting her presence, he turned and smiled at her, his black eyes molten and warm, hiding a thousand emotions and layers.

"And you are?" she prompted.

He smiled an easy smile.

"Ambassador Asfandyar of the Afridi tribe of Jardum," he said. His deep voice was stone: ragged and solid. "Pleased to meet you."

He lowered his head with respect, but a smirk tugged at his lips. Durkhanai frowned.

From what she knew, the Jardum people were courageous and rebellious. They were good fighters who were pragmatic in picking their battles and making alliances.

She didn't even know him, but she knew he would be trouble.

Sudden anger flashed through her; she had known the foreigners were coming, but now that they were here, in her home, the irritation was thrice folded. And in her halls!

This would not do.

"How pleasing indeed for you, Ambassador," she said, voice clipped, "that such an egregious occasion has arisen to force Marghazar's hand into welcoming your sorry hides into our pure lands."

He met her glare with an easy half-smile, nearly laughing.

"Forced your hand?" he drawled. "And here we were under the assumption the mighty Marghazari couldn't be forced to anything."

Her breath caught. She had slipped.

She had let her temper get the better of her when she knew she was supposed to be fawning over the ambassadors with sweetness to prove her grandfather's innocence. Her cheeks burned.

Worse still, he had twisted her words and was looking at her like she was as non-threatening as a child. It tore at the insecurity deep within her that told her she would only be a pretty little fool: beloved, yet useless.

*Decorum be damned.* In that moment, she felt less the sweet rose petals and more the deadly thorns.

"Haven't you any manners?" she asked, a bite to the words. She had never been anything but loved and adored, and the way he looked at her made her heart freeze over. "You will speak to your princess with respect, Ambassador, lest I have to cut off your tongue."

"Princess?"

He raised a brow, mock surprised. He cocked his head to the side, looking at her intently. She wanted to point out that she was, in fact, dressed as one, and how daft he must truly be to not realize, but she refrained from doing so. Instead, she lifted her chin.

She felt small, somehow, even though she was far from it; with her tall stature, she was used to commanding the space around her. But somehow, this man was looking at her as if she was as clear and thin as water.

One look at her was proof enough that she was born of the mountains and the rivers: eyes blue-green, her hair as wild as the rustling trees. Soft brown skin like golden earth, she was solid like a tree, but she had the silken stream of the river and the contours of the valleys.

She knew she was beautiful; she twisted her lips.

"Be careful where those eyes travel, Ambassador," she said, saying *ambassador* like an insult. "People have been blinded for less."

"You may blind me, but the truth we shall still see," he said. Whatever humor he had granted her before was gone. Now his voice was somber.

Durkhanai furrowed her brows. This was usually the part where people lowered their heads, excusing themselves. No one liked to be on the receiving end of the Shehzadi's temper.

Yet Asfandyar took a step closer, meeting her gaze head on with a blazing one of his own.

"What, precisely, is that supposed to mean?" she snapped.

"I was at the summit," he said, face hard.

So it was a threat.

Durkhanai did not even bother to check for a nearby guard; she knew no one would have the audacity to hurt her in her own palace.

The summit had been organized by the Wali of Teerza, who had invited the walis and advisors of the other four zillas—or districts—of the mountains to discuss a treaty of unification: To join the tribespeople of all five zillas into one united nation.

The Badshah was adamantly against the idea. Independence was integral to their culture. The other zillas believed in this as well, but with increasing pressure from the Lugham Empire in the east and south, the Wali of Teerza had managed to get four of the five zillas to agree to at least begin negotiation of unification.

That is, until the explosion.

And seeing as Marghazar was the only zilla absent, all fingers were pointed to her home.

"I witnessed the explosion, heard the screams," Asfandyar continued. "I saw the blood and the bones; those leaders were not merely your so-called enemies but my colleagues. Moreover, they were mothers and fathers, wives and husbands. They were close confidantes and friends. They were *people*. And if Marghazar truly was responsible for such carnage—well, then the butchery will be repaid in kind."

"Was that a threat? Don't forget your place, Ambassador."

He smiled that easy smile again.

"I assure you, *Shehzadi*," he said, turning her title of *princess* into the insult. "I know my place quite well."

"Then you know this is my palace and my land, and I can have you killed in a variety of ways without having even a single strand of hair coming undone."

Unfazed, he tsked. "That's thrice you've threatened me. Where is your hospitality?"

She pressed her teeth together and said nothing. He drew closer.

"Anyhow, your threats are empty," he said, close enough to touch. "For if you kill me, you will have the war you so delicately prevented. I assure you my life is very dear to the Wali of Jardum."

It was true; the only reason the ambassadors from the other zillas were even invited to Marghazar was to buy the Badshah time to prove his innocence so that war could be avoided. It was a gesture of good faith.

Her threats were empty. But something turned in Durkhanai's mind as she recalled. The Wali of Jardum was Shirin of Khwaja, a young Wali who had inherited the zilla when her mother was killed at the summit attack.

She looked at Asfandyar then, how handsome and young he himself was, not yet twenty. Her smile was sugar honey sweet but laced with poison.

"I didn't realize they were sending the Wali's whores as ambassadors now," she said matter-of-factly, more than a little bit proud of herself.

Asfandyar offered her a smile just as sweet.

"Of course that's why they sent me," he responded coolly. "We had heard whores were the only company you kept."

Durkhanai couldn't help her mouth from falling open.

Her entire face scrunched with anger, but before she could react further, he tapped her forehead lightly, where her eyebrows were pinched together.

"I wouldn't hold that face for long," he laughed. "It might get stuck that way—and what a shame it would be to ruin such lovely features, Shehzadi."

Her fingers curled into little fists, her long nails piercing skin. She didn't know what to say, but before she could, a boyish grin split his face, setting dimples deep into his cheeks.

How could he turn from grief-stricken and furious to nonchalant and amused so quickly? Surely, there was something curious about such control over one's emotions.

"Excuse me, but I have important matters to attend to," he said, bowing his head with respect and walking away, shoulders relaxed, chin high.

She watched him go, wanting to throw a dagger into his broad back. He must have sensed her watching, for he looked over his shoulder and winked.

Unbelievable!

It was only when her servants surfaced in the hallway that Durkhanai was swept back to reality.

"Shehzadi," one of her maids called. "Your bath has been prepared."

Releasing a measured breath, Durkhanai entered her bathing room, where the tub was filled with warm honeyed milk. Her maids undressed her, then scrubbed her skin with milk cream until she was soft and smooth. Then she transferred to a second tub filled with rose water. All the while, Asfandyar's face lingered in her mind, his words playing over and over: *They were people.*

Surely, such a loss was tragic, but it was not her grandfather's fault. Her family was innocent, and she would prove as much.

After she was clean, she went to her dressing room to see an elaborate, draping suit.

The folds of the brocade lehenga were thick with embroidery, crystal stones, emeralds, and cutwork. The peplum top held the same heavy work, as did the dupatta. It was more ostentatious than anything she had ever worn. Spread beside it were what must be half her weight in jewels and gold: twenty-four chudiyan for each arm, rings for almost each finger, dripping earrings, a wide necklace, thick anklets.

It was florid and ornate, and while she and her grandfather usually adored the extravagant, this was excessive to make a point; it showed the wealth of the capital Safed-Mahal, the zilla S'vat, to foreigners. The power of the Ranizais tribe and the Miangul family.

The might of the Badshah of Marghazar and his crown princess.

Durkhanai straightened her back and raised her chin. She was the daughter of the mountains and river S'vat. She was a princess to this valley and the purest tribe.

She would not let a lowly ambassador faze her.

# CHAPTER TWO

urkhanai stood by her grandfather's throne, waiting to greet the ambassadors.

Beside him, her grandmother, the Wali, sat on her own throne. Already feeling tense, Durkhanai turned to her grandfather. He met her gaze with a warm smile.

"Don't worry, meri jaan," he whispered, squeezing her hand. With his other, he reached for his wife's hand. "The Wali and the Shehzadi by my side—together, there is nothing we cannot conquer."

She knew she was his beloved beyond anything in the world. She was her grandfather's jaan, his very soul. She was loved by him above all humanity. And he was loved by her.

Durkhanai would never let anyone hurt him. Never let harm come to anyone she loved.

The door swung open with a solid thud as the ambassadors passed from the receiving room into the throne room. There were four ambassadors, each accompanied by one servant. There had been requests to bring their own security; those had been denied. There had been requests to bring along spouses; those had been denied. Eight foreigners were already eight too many.

The ambassadors from the four zillas—B'rung, Teerza, Jardum, and Kurra—came close, spreading out until they stood before the Badshah. Three ladies and one man. Durkhanai's eyes immediately went to Asfandyar.

He wore a more formal, black sherwani atop his black shalwar kameez. It looked simple, but when she looked closer, it had fine black embroidery woven into the material.

Subtle but fine.

He looked sharp. When he caught her staring, he smirked. Pressing her teeth together, she turned her gaze to the others.

She would not lose her composure as she had in the hall. She knew her orders: She was to be the sweet and beloved princess and to treat her guests with kindness and respect. She would prove her grandfather's innocence.

The ambassadors all bowed before the royal family. When they rose, the Badshah's eyes narrowed when they fell upon Asfandyar.

"Come now, this won't do," the Badshah tsked. "The Jardum sent their servants to represent them?"

Durkhanai bristled at the cruelty in her king's voice. It was evident Asfandyar wasn't a servant—did her grandfather mean to humiliate him?

Asfandyar was unfazed.

"No, Your Excellency, Badshah of Marghazar," he responded coolly. "My name is Asfandyar of the Afridi tribe, ambassador from Jardum, here to represent Wali Shirin."

The Badshah was unimpressed.

"A Jardumi?" he asked. "One so Black?"

"My mother was from Dunas," Asfandyar responded. He hadn't lost an ounce of composure, but she noted his jaw clenched as the Badshah laughed.

His eyes flicked to the Wali for an instant, almost unintentionally, then his focus was back on the Badshah. It seemed like he recognized the Wali somehow.

"Very well, son of a Black woman, we accept you in this court," he said. "As charity was beloved of the Prophet."

Asfandyar bristled but kept his smile, showing no reaction to the king's cruelty.

Unease needled through Durkhanai. She had no misgivings about punishing him for crimes against her people, but the color of his skin was no affront. This was not the first time she'd been jarred by her grandfather's beliefs. She'd spent the first portion of her life somewhere else, apart from her grandparents. Their gap in age did not help to assuage such chasms.

Asfandyar retained his aplomb, but she could see his smile like a cracked egg: jagged and crooked, hiding everything soft inside.

Asfandyar was Black, no doubt about it. He was different—and being different made you dangerous.

"We accept you all into this court, into Safed-Mahal, the jewel of S'vat and Marghazar," the Badshah proclaimed. "My sincerest condolences for those who suffered in the abhorrent attack on the summit held in Teerza. I promise you, on Allah and his Messenger, Marghazar had nothing to do with such a horrid act, and we will all strive together to uncover who the guilty party is. Punishment will be swift and severe, I assure you.

"You are here in my court as a sign of solidarity and comfort, my brothers and sisters. Stay in our court, eat our food, speak with our people, and learn that the Marghazari are enemies to no one; that we are all brothers and sisters serving one Allah, following one divine message. I extend asylum to you all."

Everyone was smiling, acting like her grandfather's words were sincere, as though they truly were brothers and sisters when in truth, Durkhanai was in a den of snakes, all with fangs poised to attack her family. She would not let that happen. She swore to it.

"You are my honored guests here, in my court," the Badshah declared. "You will be safe and cared for and honored. Protected by the mountains and by my warriors. We are not enemies. We are family."

But Durkhanai heard the threat underneath, as did the ambassadors; that they would be safe so long as they did nothing out of turn, and if they did, the mountains would suffocate them, barring exit, and his warriors would kill them.

"Now," her grandmother said cheerfully, "let's all retreat to the banquet hall for a feast!"

Durkhanai followed her grandparents into the ornately decorated ballroom. There, her extended family and the other nobles were waiting for them, smoking shisha and making light conversation.

The men were dressed in crisp white shalwar kameez and black or gray waistcoats, their heads topped with wool pakols. The women donned clothing heavy in floral embroidery on smooth silk or soft lawn cotton. Thin chiffon dupattas covered their hair, and warm wool or velvet chaadars covered their shoulders from the chilly mountain night. Their hands, necks, and ears were covered in shining gold; their lips coated pink or red.

Durkhanai knew they were all curious and frightened and exhilarated and infuriated by the foreigners. The hall opened into a courtyard where large bonfires lit the night and warmed the cool air.

The smell of food filled the air. Naan cooked in the tandoors, wafting melted butter and garlic, while coriander garnished dishes of butter chicken and large swaths of mutton legs with roasted potatoes. Chapli kababs were stacked high with onions, while carrots and raisins garnished dishes of lamb pulao. The air was full of smoke: firewood, tobacco, and roasted meat, all swirling together to create a sweet charred smell.

This was her castle in the clouds. This was her home. The rubab played softly in the background, the melody as distinct as her heartbeat. The stars glimmered in the vast sky like sugar crystals in black tea.

She looked around, watching the people, those who were hers and those who were not, until her gaze caught on Rashid, the nobleman she was to marry someday. He was the son of the head of the Yusufzai clan, the most powerful people after Durkhanai's own family. After an instant, he caught her glance, his ears turning pink as he quickly looked away.

She wished he would dance with her, do *something*, but he would never do anything so blatantly dishonorable without an official courtship. Their inevitable affection for one another was silent, yet understood and equally understood by both her grandmother and his father.

But Durkhanai had more important things to worry about. She couldn't understand how to exonerate her grandfather when they were innocent.

"Don't fret, gudiya," her grandfather whispered. "All will be all right, my smart little girl."

Her grandparents left her to mingle. Walking toward the familiar faces of her court, she stopped by Laila Baji and played with her cousin's new baby girl—a chubby little thing. Durkhanai rattled the chudiyan on her arm in front of the baby, who cooed and laughed in response.

Feeling a little better, Durkhanai watched the people from the ambassadors' eyes. Her grandfather was eccentric, sometimes unbelievably cruel—as he had shown with ridiculing Asfandyar. Her grandmother, the Wali of S'vat was kind but quiet—stoic. She was always on guard.

And her people? The Marghazari were loud, lively. They laughed widely and ate continuously. It was the semi-barbaric part within them all; the lack of modesty and overabundance of pride. To talk, to dance, and to laugh, all exuberantly, the men and women together. They were entirely unashamed of their culture and had grown even more proud and obnoxious during her grandfather's near fifty-year reign of prosperity.

Durkhanai could tell it bothered some of the ambassadors to see the women so brazen, to see the dancing and the noise and the drinking exhibited by the elite. It was un-Islamic, but some traditions were hard to shed.

"Come now, everyone join us in a dance!" her grandmother exclaimed.

In the background, the dhol and pipes called the people to dance under the stars. She circled with the ladies; the men did the same. It wasn't unusual for the dance to be mixed, but she knew some of the other tribes, like B'rung, were more conservative. All the ambassadors joined the dance except for the ambassador from Kurra.

Durkhanai took the hands of those beside her, and the beat started off with slow steps as they circled. To the rhythm, they clapped inside the circle at the instant the music called for, then brought their hands out again, only to repeat.

The music gradually quickened, as did their motions, adding an extra clap, adding a twirl, between the beats. To show their regard for Durkhanai, the ladies clapped, then touched their fingers to their foreheads in respect to their princess. As they did, Durkhanai smiled, looking away.

Across the floor, she caught Asfandyar's gaze, glowing with firelight.

He grinned.

She averted her gaze quickly, her breath catching. Face flushed, she risked a glance back, and he was staring at her still—and so openly!

She had never known such forwardness. Usually, boys were tripping around her, such as Rashid, always nervous in such a sweet, endearing manner. But Asfandyar—he had no shame.

Durkhanai knew she was beautiful, even more so with the precision that had gone into getting her dressed, and boys usually did stare, though not so unabashedly. She wondered if it was because the Jardum pass connected the east and the west, so its people were known to be more metropolitan.

Whatever it was, she couldn't stand the heat of his gaze.

Heart beating quickly, she danced with the movement of the song, quickening her steps as the dhol intensified, and between the clap and spin, she caught Asfandyar's eyes on her, unwavering, unflinching. As the beat of the drums quickened, so did her heart, filling her with a fiery feeling she couldn't displace.

He was focused more on her than the steps of the dance, which he executed perfectly, even as the beat quickened further. His neck shone with sweat, but it was nothing compared to the glitter in his eyes. Breathless already from the dance, Durkhanai felt there wasn't enough air in her lungs.

He kept staring, easily gliding in and out of the dance steps, eyes never leaving hers.

Durkhanai couldn't stand it.

"I'm going for a drink," she said to her friends, out of breath. They continued on without her as she went to the side, picking up a goblet of shikanjvi. She sipped it carefully, resisting the urge to drink the spiced lemonade in one gulp. She forced her heart to find a steadier rhythm than the quick music and even quicker pounding of feet.

Somehow, she felt him before she saw him.

He slid into the space beside her, grabbing a drink as well. He didn't say anything, just turned to look at her over his goblet as he drank. She watched the long column of his throat. She sensed people watching them, but she couldn't bring herself to move.

He was staring at her lips, which were coated in purple lipstick. She knew it looked as if she'd been sucking on blueberries, her lips plump with stain. He swallowed.

"Shehzadi," he finally said, breaking the silence. He lowered his head in respect. A smile tugged at his lips.

"Ambassador," she replied, unamused, even though she was, ever so slightly, charmed by his infectious buoyancy.

"I had heard you are famed for many skills, Shehzadi," he said, lowering his head close to hers so she could hear him over the music. "But I had not known dancing to be one of them."

Her heart ricocheted against her ribs. Something illicit coursed through her.

"I am a woman of many talents."

"What else can I expect?" He drew closer. She met his gaze; matched his smirk.

"Good things to those who wait."

"But I am not very patient," he sighed, close enough to touch.

"Kasam se?" she asked, voice bored. "Truly?"

"Teri kasam," he replied with a grin.

What a flirt!

He swore it on her name, as if she meant anything to him. She resisted the urge to roll her eyes. She knew she was supposed to be sweet-talking the ambassadors, reassuring them that despite Marghazar's bold customs and manners, they were not cold-blooded enough to plot the murder of their neighbors, but Asfandyar rifled something deep within her.

She bit back a rude retort. She was supposed to be polite.

The banquet was loud, and with each sentence, he drew closer.

"Come now, you are famed for your kindness, yet all you have been to me is cruel." His grin softened into a pout. Firelight danced in his eyes.

"I am kind to my people," she countered. "Not those with ill intentions."

He smiled fully then, drawing close enough to whisper into her neck. His body swallowed the cold space between them, and when he spoke again, his breath was warm against her ears.

"I assure you," he said. "You don't know my intentions."

The words sent a shiver down her spine; he was too close. She wondered if he was drunk, but when she drew back, his eyes were entirely clear of alcohol, simply glittering with mischief.

She narrowed her eyes. She would not be fooled. If this was the game he wanted to play, she would play.

And she would win.

She rested a hand on his shoulder, mirroring the way he had spoken into his neck. They were a whisper away from an embrace. She lifted her chin to speak soft words into his ear.

"Just as you don't know mine," she said, voice husky.

She would dance along the knife's edge of seduction and secrets; she would not get cut.

Durkhanai withdrew her hand. They held each other's gaze.

"A prayer for you then, Shehzadi," he said, raising his glass between them. "May Allah keep your intentions pure as the snow that caps the heavenly mountaintops."

"And may He keep your thoughts even purer," she added, raising her glass to his.

They both grinned, suddenly drunk off the game that had begun.

"Ameen," they said together, and they drank.

With a smirk, Durkhanai flitted away, chin up. She swayed her hips, feeling suddenly giddy. She knew he was watching, but she didn't bother to turn.

Instead, she approached another foreign face, determined to wrap all the ambassadors around her fingers before they could cause any harm. Putting aside Asfandyar, who had already infuriated her, she needed the rest to believe her grandfather innocent of that deadly attack, and people were so much more amiable with a healthy layer of sugar added to them.

But that did not mean she would be feeble or a weakling. Durkhanai was famed for her kindness, as Asfandyar said, yes, but she could be cruel, too. Just like her semi-barbaric grandfather.

Nobody would expect it from the rosy princess, making them all the easier to prick with her thorns. She couldn't afford to slip with them, as she had with him.

The ambassador she approached was a young woman, who had a slight limp and carried a jeweled cane. When she saw Durkhanai approach, she immediately extricated herself from another conversation, taking a few steps forward to meet the princess.

"Gulalai," the ambassador introduced herself. "Daughter of the Wali of Kurra."

"Pleased to meet you," Durkhanai responded, calling information to her mind.

Kurra was a relatively irrelevant zilla, known to remain neutral or uninvolved in most matters. It was famed mostly for its beauty, the velveteen greenery, and colorful flowers and moonlit water. Gulalai came from a land of gardens and orchards, lush greenery, and flowers. The people were mostly nonthreatening, though, that had changed once their wali had been injured at the summit explosion.

"Wondering whether or not to trust me?" Gulalai asked, smiling. "Don't worry, I'm lame. How much harm could I possibly do?"

"Though not lame in wits, I can see," Durkhanai replied.

"Besides, I'm younger than you, and by Allah's command, I must respect my elders," Gulalai said, voice teasing.

Durkhanai smiled. "Younger than me? You must be a baby, for I'm usually the youngest in the room, save for the infants."

"Yes, I know, Shehzadi," Gulalai responded. "But remember: Where the young give the elders respect, the elders must give something in return, as well."

"And what would that be?"

"Sweets, of course!" Gulalai said. "And warm baths and pretty little gifts. You must coddle me."

Durkhanai smiled, taken by this girl's bubbly personality.

"Come now, you must only be a few months younger than me," she told Gulalai.

"That is true," Gulalai responded. "All teasing aside, I know what it is like not to be taken seriously because of your age. Seventeen and eighteen and heir to our family's titles means we are old enough to decide the fate of our people, yet we are treated like pretty little fools by our seniors."

"Yes," Durkhanai agreed. "Pretty little fools, indeed."

"Though not fool enough to believe the Badshah orchestrated the attack," Gulalai whispered, just loud enough for Durkhanai to hear.

"Laugh as though we are chatting about silly little nothings," Durkhanai said through her grin, as though Gulalai had made the most hilarious remark. The ambassador mirrored her behavior, lightly tapping her arm.

"Clever little princess," she said. "My father was injured badly; they aren't sure he'll walk again, but I know in my heart it wasn't Marghazar."

"And how could you know that?" Durkhanai asked.

"It's much too obvious," Gulalai replied, pretending to laugh still. "I'm infuriated by my father's injury, of course, but I believe you and your family. Somebody is trying to frame Marghazar. And I don't wish for my people to die in a false war."

"Frame Marghazar—" began Durkhanai, but Gulalai cut her off.

"Let's chat over chai, sometime," Gulalai said, leaning forward to kiss both her cheeks.

Durkhanai mirrored the action. From the outside, they appeared as two young girls, gossiping about silly things. But Gulalai's voice lowered to a sincere warning, one that sent a chill down Durkhanai's spine.

"Until then, be careful around Asfandyar-sahib," she whispered. "He'll bring you nothing but ruin."

Before Durkhanai could ask for elaboration, Gulalai was swept away by a noblewoman. Heart hammering, Durkhanai tried to understand if she could truly trust Gulalai or not.

She needed to acquaint herself further with both ambassadors before passing any judgments. But there was no time to consider where to place her trust because her grandmother was excusing herself, following a servant out of the room.

*Strange.* Her grandmother never slipped away from formal occasions such as this. Whatever it was, it had to be pertinent. Outside the hall, she followed the barely audible voices to a secret alcove in a darkened hallway. Her grandmother was speaking to a dirty soldier, streaked in mud and blood. But it was his face that frightened Durkhanai; he looked like he'd been kissed by death.

"Dhadi?" Durkhanai asked. Only close family members were permitted to bypass formal titles for more personal names.

Upon seeing the princess enter, the soldier bowed his head with respect and excused himself.

"Dhadi?" she asked, voice low. "What happened?"

Her grandmother placed a hand on Durkhanai's face, smiling a forlorn smile.

"Meri jaan," she said, not to worry her. "You don't fret, go back to the party, attend to those in your court."

"Dhadi," Durkhanai repeated. Her grandmother sighed.

"I had called for soldiers from the front lines to fortify Safed-Mahal with the onset of our visitors," she explained. "But it seems our Lord has taken them back from this world."

"They're all . . ." Durkhanai began, trailing. She couldn't finish the thought, let alone the sentence. Dhadi nodded.

"They're all dead."

"But how—"

"Don't worry, gudiya," her grandmother assured her. "Allah will provide for us."

With a kiss to Durkhanai's cheek, Dhadi left, back to the party, leaving Durkhanai alone with her thoughts. All their soldiers in the north, dead? It would mean sending more from within their lands to the frontlines, thinning the security they had within.

But how could they all have perished? The Kebzu Kingdom had great fighters, but never had Marghazar suffered such great losses. Perhaps—

Something shifted in the air behind her.

"Dhadi?" she called. A shadow flickered beside hers.

But when she turned, she was alone.

# CHAPTER THREE

*I*n her sunroom, the weather was warm, full of birds chirping and rustling leaves. From the window, the land on a mountain cut with vertical slices that looked like fingers reaching toward the sky, toward something unreachable.

But they got close.

Maids entered and set the table for tea. Fine porcelain from the far east was laid out, along with potato samosay and chickpea curry to go on top, along with tamarind chutney. There was a steaming pot of chai and various little finger foods to go along with it: Durkhanai's favorite almond pastries and flaky biscuits.

"God, this place is gorgeous," Gulalai said, entering loudly, her cane clunking against the marble floor. "Marghazar truly has a knack for finery. I haven't seen anything so grand in any of the zillas."

"Shukria," Durkhanai responded. She wondered about the other zillas; she had never been.

But she didn't need to go. Marghazar was enough for her.

"Your wealth is truly astounding," Gulalai said, taking a seat with a labored sigh. "Tell me about your grandfather, the great Ghazan Miangul of the Ranizais tribe, the boy king of legend. It's nearly fifty years of rule now, isn't it?"

"Yes . . . well, what else do you want to know?" Durkhanai responded. "The Luhgam Empires slaughtered his elder brothers and father. That's how he became king. Fifty years later, and here we are."

She didn't want to say anymore. She wanted the truth of her family to stay cloaked for all eternity. The truth of the trauma Agha-Jaan faced—of tragedy and sorrow and sudden power. It was under him that Marghazar came to encompass S'vat, Trichmir, and Dirgara; under him that Marghazar became a hegemony among the zillas.

After his coronation, it was true Agha-Jaan became a little mad with grief and vengeance. The Badshah had been fighting the Luhgam Empire ever since, and no matter how many battles were won, he was insatiable. She knew he needed victory to avenge his family's deaths. She knew he would stop at nothing until then.

And yes, sometimes she disagreed with how hard he pushed, how stubborn he was, but he was everything to her. Durkhanai would do anything for her Agha-Jaan.

"Fine, don't say anything more," Gulalai responded. She set her cane to the side as a servant poured her some tea. "Now, time for some reiterated advice that I don't think you understood the first time: Stay away from Asfandyar-sahib of Jardum. I saw him follow after you when you left the banquet yesterday."

Durkhanai's heart ricocheted against her ribs. Asfandyar had followed her? But she hadn't even seen him. She opened her mouth in protest, but Gulalai put up a hand.

"Oh, save me the excuses," she said, stirring sugar into her tea. "I believe you can handle yourself, but he is handsome and charming. Anyone is capable of being a fool for love, even you, Shehzadi."

Feeling exposed, Durkhanai narrowed her eyes.

"I already know the man I am to marry," she said quickly, thinking of Rashid. She wasn't a fool. "He is the son of a nobleman from our court; he is of good family. And . . . kind and smart."

"You're engaged?" Gulalai asked, biting into a cookie. "Fascinating."

Durkhanai shook her head. "It is understood."

"And what of love?"

"It will come. With time, respect, and effort, I will grow to love my husband, whoever he is. But my duty is first and foremost to my people."

She was a princess; she had to do what was best for her people.

"I would still be careful around that Jardum boy, though," Gulalai advised. "People love to spread horrid rumors."

"Don't worry," Durkhanai told her.

She was unbothered by the thought of rumors. The people wouldn't believe such filth. They knew Durkhanai wouldn't do anything she wouldn't have the courage to admit to upfront. Besides, the people were better than that. They weren't malicious and gossipy.

"Besides, I am sure he is preoccupied with his wali, Shirin," Durkhanai added, gauging Gulalai's reaction. She wished to know if Asfandyar really was involved with Shirin, as Durkhanai had alleged in their first meeting.

"Oh, *her*!" Gulalai said, cheeks turning pink with anger or a blush, Durkhanai could not quite tell. Perhaps both. "I don't want to think about her. We have more important things to discuss."

"You're right," Durkhanai said, biting into a biscuit. "We must stop this impending war before it comes."

The Badshah had three months to prove his innocence or there would be war. Until then, she hoped the ambassadors could be sated by hospitality.

"It is my opinion that somebody is trying to frame Marghazar," Gulalai said. "It's much too obvious for the Badshah to be behind the summit attack."

"Yes, but who?" Durkhanai asked. "I can't figure it out. Who has anything to gain from this?"

"I can't see what anyone has to gain from the summit explosion or the war they are all calling for," Gulalai said. "My father doesn't wish to go to war, either, but if it is what the rest of the zillas have agreed upon, my father won't refuse his allies. And I believe B'rung is the same."

"Whereas, Jardum and Teerza do seem a bit enthusiastic for war, don't they?"

"Theoretically, Teerza and Jardum should be in the clear, since their walis passed," Gulalai responded. "They couldn't have planned the summit explosion as grounds for war because it was their own who were injured."

"Theoretically," Durkhanai agreed, waving for more tea. "But isn't the enemy usually the one in plain sight?"

Which made her think: What made her so sure Gulalai and the Kurra zilla were innocent? Their wali had been injured, yes, but not killed. And Gulalai was making a great show of being her friend.

"A fair point," Gulalai said. "But Teerza was heading the summit. Why attack their own meeting, in their own homeland?"

"Teerza is also conservative, and I know they have problems with some of the Badshah's rulings," Durkhanai added. "But they're the strongest military zilla. If they wanted to fight, they would skip this negotiation nonsense and go straight to war."

They would lose, but wars rarely had any purpose other than harm.

"What would be the point of making Marghazar look guilty?" Gulalai stirred her tea pensively. "Despite how much the other zillas might detest Marghazar, you are still the strongest zilla. We surely hoped to eventually convince your grandfather to join us, once we were all united. It is why the ambassadors have just been negotiating simple things, like goods or more accessibility—we're taking advantage of the three months we are here."

"And even then, on the request of Marghazar," Durkhanai said. "It was the Badshah who offered to accept ambassadors in order to gain time to prove our innocence and appease the other zillas."

"The ambassador from B'rung, Palwasha-sahiba, is a bit elusive . . . I can't get a good read on her. But I don't know where this leaves us." Gulalai rubbed her temples. "I have a headache."

They looked at one another and sighed. They were going in circles with no true evidence. Their biscuit supply had long since dwindled, and the warmth of the morning was thickening with afternoon.

"It definitely wasn't Marghazar," Durkhanai said. "That much I know."

"And it definitely wasn't Kurra," Gulalai added. "That much *I* know."

"I believe you, but Gulalai, tell me this: How can I trust you?" Durkhanai asked. It was just the two of them in Durkhanai's sunroom. She regarded Gulalai closely, staring into her warm brown eyes.

"Simple." Gulalai tore into a samosa. "Because I want your favor, and I intend on gaining it through friendship and loyalty. Kurra does not have want or need for much, and I do not intend to achieve anything through conniving. I wish for us to be sister tribes, one day. Whatever you offer through goodwill is enough for me."

"What if we have nothing to offer?" Durkhanai responded.

"Shehzadi, you mustn't bother with false pretenses," Gulalai said with a smile. "All the mountains know of your soft spots and kindness. Even if the Badshah and my father see no use in an alliance at the present, I think one day, you and I will benefit from it. Besides, I don't think you want war between our zillas, and neither do I."

Durkhanai nodded.

"And to prove my loyalty, here is a secret: Jardum and Teerza have become more brothers than cousins," Gulalai said.

"What exactly does that mean?" Durkhanai asked.

"I can't say more, for Jardum is Kurra's ally as well," Gulalai responded. "And even that I shouldn't have said, but take it as a token of my commitment to an alliance with Marghazar. Keep an eye on Teerza."

"I will," Durkhanai said. "Thank you for the warning. As for our alliance, only time will tell," she added, but she had a good feeling about it. Her gut wasn't very often wrong.

"Have you considered the possibility of it being the Kebzu Kingdom?" Gulalai said after some consideration. "I've given it much thought, and they would have an incentive—keep our zillas weak so that we cannot become more effective at fighting them. It's a similar incentive to Marghazar's."

"The Kebzu Kingdom only pushes on Marghazar's borders in the north," Durkhanai replied. "Why would they care if the southern zillas unified?"

"Perhaps they would see it as a future threat?" Gulalai responded. "If Marghazar joined the unified zillas in the future and pushed back harder on the northern border?"

"Hm," Durkhanai said. "You bring up valid points. But how would they have known about it at all? The summit was only known to the five walis, particularly the date and location."

"So, it had to have been a wali." Gulalai bit her lip. "I wish I had been there. Perhaps I could have gauged something better."

"Do you know all the walis personally?" Durkhanai asked. "I've never met any of them."

"We're acquainted, but I don't know them that well," Gulalai replied. She considered something for a moment, then shook her head. "But do you know who does know them all quite well? And who was at the summit?"

Durkhanai had a sinking feeling that she already knew the answer.

"Asfandyar-sahib."

Durkhanai sighed as Gulalai continued.

"If anybody will know something, it'll be him."

# CHAPTER FOUR

*T*he clouds kissed Durkhanai's cheeks. It brought her peace.

Nature reminded her of the princess that she was. She could handle this and all that was to come.

Some days after the arrival of the ambassadors, she gathered the people at court for a walk through the mountains. When it came to hospitality, what better way to be kind than to show the foreigners the beauties of her lands? She arranged for all the ambassadors to join her, along with some Marghazar nobles and a few of her cousins, though not Laila Baji and the baby, sadly.

Her niece's soft giggles would have pacified Durkhanai's discontented mood, which was even worse because her cousins

Zarmina and Saifullah still had yet to arrive. Durkhanai walked behind everyone, more comfortable with them all in her sight. Gulalai was busy chatting with Palwasha-sahiba—the ambassador from B'rung—about road designs. The ambassador from Teerza, Rukhsana-sahiba, walked alone.

When Durkhanai approached to make polite conversation, Rukhsana-sahiba fixed her with a glare so sharp that Durkhanai spun away with childish spite and refused to speak with her.

That left Asfandyar.

She very purposefully did not initiate contact with Asfandyar, who looked even better against the backdrop of mountains during the soft morning. His wool pakol sat crooked on his head, allowing some curls to sit on his forehead under the cap. He was in black shalwar kameez once more, though this time adorned with a metal gray chaadar. Not that Durkhanai noticed, of course.

She was far too preoccupied with appreciating her beautiful land. Green grass stretched across the hills like plush velvet. The trees looked like little shrubs one could pick from the landscape like flowers from the earth; so soft and small, like moss.

It eased her heart, ever so slightly, until her gaze strayed once more to Asfandyar.

*He'll bring you nothing but ruin*, Gulalai's words rang in her mind. But Durkhanai could handle herself.

Gulalai was *also* the one to observe that he was one of the only people who might be able to help untangle their questions about what had happened at the summit, so perhaps her advice was contradictory.

If somebody truly was trying to frame Marghazar, Durkhanai needed to find out who and why. The Badshah and Wali were hard at work trying to draft negotiations and even harder at work trying to find evidence to prove their innocence, but what evidence would there have been?

If it was the Kebzu Kingdom behind the attack, they must have been informed by one of the zilla's walis. The walis that Durkhanai knew nothing about.

But Asfandyar was friends with them all.

Perhaps she needed to make an ally out of him after all.

If she could get him to trust her, maybe he could give her information about the summit which could lead her to figure out who was behind the attack. He didn't seem bloodthirsty for war—perhaps he wished for peace as well.

What had he said? That his life was of value to the Wali of Jardum—if that was so, he must have been close to the Wali and her family.

Durkhanai looked at him again, this time considering him closely: The way the sun shone off his high cheekbones; the long, curled eyelashes; the plump, soft lips; the thicket of ebony curls. His height, his build. He looked like a warrior, face harsh and . . . sad.

He turned, catching her staring.

Her heartbeat spiked. Durkhanai averted her gaze.

Asfandyar slowed his pace. In a few steps, she was side by side with him. He regarded her with open curiosity, as if waiting for her to speak.

She shivered, then shivered again, suddenly bitten by the cold. Her fingers had numbed without her noticing, her nails turning a shade of lavender blue.

"May I, Shehzadi?" he said, voice low. She blinked in surprise.

He extended his hand. Something sharp turned in her stomach. He smiled in a manner meant to be courteous, but she saw the dare that glittered in his eyes.

He didn't think she would allow him—it was uncouth—but she would not be intimidated.

"How uncharacteristically kind of you, Ambassador."

His eyes glittered, but he did not smile.

She placed her fingers delicately onto his forefinger, and his gaze caught on the family crest ring she always wore on her third finger. Sudden emotion ran through his eyes, but before she could read it, the mischief was back.

Strange.

His hand swallowed hers. Something volatile, something barbaric, ran through her as he ran a thumb over her fingers, his knuckles grazing ever so teasingly against the curve of her palm. Pleasure rose in her throat, but she swallowed it.

"Comforted?" he asked, a small smile tugging at his lips.

She smiled sweetly. "Not quite."

He raised her fingers to his lips, then blew air into her hand. She couldn't help the delicious warmth that ran through her, but two could play at this game.

She lifted her fingers until her nail grazed the smooth stretch of his bottom lip. His mouth parted, releasing a soft sound. Just as his lips closed into the whisper of a kiss, she swiftly pulled her hand away.

He looked stunned—starved.

"Shukria, Ambassador," she said, trying not to smile triumphantly. "I am most comforted now."

She swore she almost heard him laugh, but he withheld, his lips in a downturned smile.

A draw then.

They continued their walk, side by side, and admired the scenery. Below them, they could see a small lake, and the vertical folds of the mountains looked like the ruffles of an extravagant lehenga. Higher, on the land, the roads looked like lightning bolts imprinted into the earth.

Durkhanai reminded herself to focus. She needed to make an ally out of him.

"You are quite the dancer," she remarked. Men were easily placated with compliments. Asfandyar smiled.

"Nothing in comparison to you," he replied. "Tell me, what other skills do you possess?"

"There's too many to count," she replied coolly.

"For the sake of your people and mine, let us hope exoneration is one of them," he said pointedly. "You've three months to prove Marghazar was not behind the summit attack."

Durkhanai bit her tongue. "The innocent needn't worry about the swarming of vultures—the truth always reveals itself."

"The sooner you find out, the sooner we can all leave," he said, voice bored.

Despite wanting that outcome herself, she couldn't stand his indifference to the privilege he had of being in her lands. "Why would you hasten your departure? Was it not you and your zillas that begged for the chance to be allowed entrance into my home?"

"Only to ensure there's no fabrication of evidence," he replied. "The chance to negotiate is a plus for the others, but Jardum and I couldn't care less about the famed Marghazar. We've had great success without you for all these years and have no need of you now."

"Oh, please," Durkhanai said. "Marghazar has twice the resources of any other zilla."

"Yet you withhold," Asfandyar replied.

Durkhanai faltered. "We spend our resources on our people."

"And what of the other tribes?"

"Their leaders should take care of them."

"But you just stated Marghazar has twice the resources of everyone else—don't you think that's unfair? We can't help the lands we were born to, after all. Haven't you considered that trade would help the other zillas and their people as well as your own people? Isolation is a barbaric notion."

"Well . . ."

"No, you haven't considered it. For the same reason you didn't attend the summit; you are a haughty, selfish lot." Asfandyar shook his head. "At least *we* have one another. With our joined forces, we've been able to hold back the Lugham Empire on all of our borders, and no matter how strong Marghazar is, that strength cannot last forever. Especially if Marghazar cannot prove its innocence and there is war. Yes, you are strong—but a triple-frontier war? Even Marghazar will crumble."

There was merit to what Asfandyar was saying. Durkhanai had never considered it like that before. Perhaps he *would* be a useful ally after all, though, she was doing a poor job at trying to make him one.

"Is that why you are here?" Durkhanai asked, keeping her voice level. "To convince Marghazar into your talks of unification?"

"No, that is not why I am here."

"Then?"

Asfandyar cut her a sharp grin. "For you. I came for you."

"What?" She didn't understand, but it didn't stop her heart from racing as the space between them narrowed. Her stomach twisted.

He balanced her chin on his index finger and lifted her face to meet his.

"Of course," he said, voice husky. "I came to see the famed jewel of Marghazar."

His voice split into an easy grin. He was mocking her. She turned her cheek, but she couldn't help her heartbeat.

It was then she realized that they had gotten even further ahead of everybody, no one in sight ahead or behind them.

"You're distracting me," she said, irritated.

"Yes," he replied. Gulalai had warned her, but she couldn't help how much she enjoyed his company. He was surprisingly candid.

She cocked her head to examine him.

"Why are you here?" she asked again. "The truth, please."

"The truth?"

"*Yes*." She was losing her patience.

"I'm a spy." He smirked, drawing closer as she frowned. "Aren't you as well?" he whispered. "Isn't that why you're here? Don't worry—I won't tell."

Her frown deepened.

"I'll give you some advice, spy to spy," he said. "But it's a secret between you and I. Do you think you can manage that?"

He was treating her like a child.

She wanted to strangle him.

"Don't let every emotion show on your face so plainly, little red," he told her.

Her eyebrows furrowed together, her face folding into a frown.

"See," Asfandyar continued, tapping her cheek. "Your face gets florid."

She wanted to scrunch her face up in irritation, but she caught herself, flattening out every emotion she could until her mien was detached.

"That would be good advice if I was a spy," she tried to say coolly. "How unfortunate you lack basic logic. Why would I be a spy in my own home?"

"Okay," he countered, eyes glittering. "If you are not a spy, why are *you* here, talking to me? When you and Gulalai-sahiba seem to be such friends and Palwasha-sahiba is desperate for your help and Rukhsana-sahiba's anger should surely be placated. Why are you here?"

She started, unsure. Nobody ever questioned her. She looked at him. "Because the mountains are beautiful. Because I am a princess." Then, heart hammering, she said, "Because I enjoy your company."

His lips twitched.

"Well done. I cannot tell if you are lying or not," he responded, charmed. She had told him a half truth.

Durkhanai was never good at lying; she was always filled with acid and everything burned for the heartbeat before the lie left her lips. Often, she would feel so guilty, she would concede and tell the truth.

"The mountains are quite beautiful indeed," he said. "The mountains and the river S'vat make a good pair."

"Indeed they do." Durkhanai loved them both—but she couldn't help but sigh in remembrance of the valley in which she had spent the first half of her life.

"What troubles you?" Asfandyar asked. She hesitated, but his face was kind and curious. Besides, she needed him to trust her. Despite their bickering, perhaps they could move forward, reach some sort of common ground, as with Gulalai.

"I wasn't raised here, you know," she finally told him. "After my parents died, I was sent away to a village named Mianathob, far from this place, to be raised by distant family. My father was the crown prince, and after he died . . ." She swallowed. "I am the crown princess; I needed to be kept safe."

"How did they die?" he asked. Something sparked in his eyes at the mention of her father, but it was something she could not place. Everyone knew she was an orphan, but few knew the full story.

Unfortunately, she was not one of the few, either. Her grandparents said there was no use in knowing things that would only hurt her, and after some time, she had stopped asking.

She told him all she knew.

"They were assassinated. I barely survived myself . . ."

"I am sorry to hear that." This time, she knew what was in his eyes: genuine sorrow.

"The valley was the first home I had ever known," she continued. "So, I miss it. Things were so much simpler in the farmlands. Bari Ammi—my grandfather's sister—raised me for the first part of my life."

She had grown in a lush, green valley by a cerulean blue lake, surrounded by golden farms and eternal sunshine. There, her grandfather's sister, who never married again after losing her husband in the wars, raised her. The village had been filled with widows; a sort of safe haven for women with no family and nowhere else to go. When Durkhanai thought of her childhood, she imagined her head in Bari Ammi's lap, the older woman's gentle hands stroking her hair as she told story after story. She imagined a pretty cloth doll that a maid had told her was a "secret gift from her father," that became old and worn because she took it with her everywhere.

She hadn't known any sorrow there, only peace and simplicity. She had been spoiled then, too, but with attention and love; vastly different from the jewels and finery she was spoiled with at court.

Back then, she would visit the marble palace once a year for a few of the hotter months when the mountains were cooler, and she had always yearned to be home in the valley. The mountains had seemed too cold back then—unkind and harsh.

She was adored by her grandfather, of course, and her chachay and phuppo, but it hadn't been home. And while she loved her grandparents, Agha-Jaan would always be busy, and Dhadi would always be reminding her of her duties as princess when all Durkhanai wanted was to play. At the palace, her every choice and her every word were scrutinized.

"It's been years since I've been back at court, and I adore it, truly," she told him. "But I miss home, too. Back then, I didn't even know how to say my whole name. I could only get out Durre, so that's what everybody called me." She paused. "Nobody calls me that anymore."

She hadn't told anyone that before, but there was an easy comfort in talking to a complete stranger. She could be whoever she wanted to be.

She dreamed about and missed the fields, the women, the rivers, the crops, the heat, the sunlight, the golden sheen of it all, the stories, the stars.

Sometimes, Durkhanai ached for that simple life away from court.

"It's horrid because I remember then, I would miss my grandparents and the mountains, and now I'm missing my aunts and the valley," she said. "Always missing something."

Asfandyar didn't say anything, and they continued walking. From here, the mountain was mud brown, but the base was gray-blue where the stones met the river, like the mountain's toes had gone numb.

"Rule number two, if you want to be a successful spy," Asfandyar said, breaking the silence. "Don't give anyone information for free."

She stopped walking, her lips turning down into a frown. She had slipped. Again.

"You've tricked me," she said stupidly. She hated to be made a fool of. She really was going to strangle him.

His smile didn't waver, but it was one of kindness, not malice. He shook his head.

"I haven't," he told her. "For in exchange for your anecdote, I shall share one of mine. When I was a boy, I didn't love the mountains, either. I would visit my mother's tribe in Dunas, where there are no mountains at all. We lived right by the water, and the vast ocean's beauty is incomparable, I believe. There, the horizon stretched for centuries, and at night, there were more stars than I've ever seen here, shimmering in an infinite sky.

"I don't think there is anything more beautiful than the stars and the stories they hold. My mother would craft tales from the constellations; we'd lie on the beach for hours, staring at stars."

Durkhanai made a soft sound. She didn't know what to say. They walked in silence for a bit longer.

"You didn't have to, you know," she finally said.

"I know," he replied. The devilish glint returned to his eyes. "But perhaps I enjoy your company as well."

Their eyes met in an infinite moment. It felt like staring at the sunrise, like being outside of time. She felt a strange softness toward him, the hatred she knew she should feel already gone, and Durkhanai couldn't help herself.

She knew he could be her enemy, could be using her, or distracting her, or making a fool of her, but in the end, she just couldn't help herself.

She wanted to know him. It was as simple as that—she wanted.

"Durkhanai!"

The moment shattered.

She turned to the sound of a familiar voice. Durkhanai grinned.

"Zarmina!"

# CHAPTER FIVE

*T*hey were here! As her cousins Zarmina and Saifullah grew closer, she saw they gave Asfandyar a strange look, glancing between the two of them. Durkhanai put on a smile, masking the slight panic that rose in her throat.

"Where have you been?" Saifullah said, furrowing his brows. "We've been looking for you."

"Why did you stray so far?" Zarmina asked her.

"I didn't realize," Durkhanai replied. "But never mind that! Tell me about your journey!"

The twins whisked her away before she could realize she hadn't said goodbye to Asfandyar. But when she turned around, he was already gone.

Almost like he'd never been there at all.

As they walked along the path, making their way back to the palace, they passed a small river. The water looked like a liquid moon—luminescent white and gray blue. It was beautiful but hazy; she couldn't see what swam beneath the surface, couldn't see anything but the current pulling the water along.

As they made their way back, they passed a group of noblewomen speaking with Palwasha-sahiba, the ambassador from B'rung; Durkhanai caught a snippet of conversation.

"I do appreciate ho-how beautifully managed your lands are," Palwasha-sahiba said. She spoke slowly, with a mild stutter. "B'rung, too, has many . . ."

Durkhanai slowed her pace, straining to listen further, but she could not hear.

"What is it?" Zarmina asked, slowing beside her.

"I'm not sure," Durkhanai replied. "But we're about to find out."

It would be too conspicuous to turn around and follow Palwasha-sahiba, but Durkhanai knew these trails intimately. Saifullah and Zarmina followed her wordlessly as she made a sharp turn, then sidestepped down the steep trail edge. There was a parallel path that ran below the trail the ambassadors were walking, built into the mountainside.

"Come on," Durkhanai whispered. She quickened her pace, holding onto her jewelry so that it would not jingle. Zarmina did the same, and they slipped along until the voices grew louder above them.

This side trail was designed precisely for this purpose.

"Ambassador from B'rung," Durkhanai whispered to her cousins. They listened closely.

". . . I find it mo-most agreeable!" Palwasha-sahiba said, her voice high with enthusiasm.

That did not sound like an ambassador who believed Marghazar to be guilty of attacking her wali.

"How clever, indeed!" Palwasha-sahiba cried. "I would be so grateful if you would consider describing to me . . ."

From the corner of her eye, Durkhanai saw Zarmina slip. She bit back a cry and threw her hand out to stop Zarmina from falling.

But in doing so, the gold chudiyan on her arm jingled loudly. The three of them stilled.

The conversation above stopped. Silence filled the mountains.

Durkhanai pressed further into the mountainside. If the ambassador or noblewomen above looked over the trail edge, they would not see Durkhanai and her cousins, but just in case.

Then she noticed a steel gray shawl lowering into her sight.

It swung back and forth, until it entered the opening of the hidden trail rather than hitting solid mountain.

*Oh no.*

"Dear Shehzadi, I hope that is not you down there," an amused voice called. Asfandyar. "What a nasty trick indeed, though poorly executed."

They'd been caught.

"Fitteh mu tera," Durkhanai muttered. He had not even been with them earlier. He must have heard her chudiyan, as well. Unfortunately, she was the only one obnoxious enough to be wearing so much jewelry.

"Zarmina!" Saifullah hissed.

"Shut up!" she snapped.

The conversation above had truly ceased, and there was no point listening further. Cheeks burning, Durkhanai motioned for them to retreat. They made their way back, pace quick so as not to be truly caught red-handed.

Ashamed by their lackluster performance, Durkhanai rang for tea and changed her clothes. Only after being placated by biscuits and samosay did Saifullah breech the subject.

"Foreigners, conspiring in our own mountains! How could Agha-Jaan have let it come to this?" Saifullah sighed, running a hand through his wavy black hair. "It hasn't been done for centuries!"

They were angry at her grandfather for allowing the ambass-adors to enter Safed-Mahal in the first place. For the people of Marghazar—for her family—tradition was everything.

"It isn't so simple," Durkhanai argued. "Marghazar looks immensely guilty right now. To appease the other zillas, it had to be done."

"But what precisely are the ambassadors *doing* here? What were those two discussing?" Zarmina asked, dark brown eyes confused. She played with her long braid of thick black hair. "It is clear they do not simply wish for a view into the land of legend."

"I doubt it's so simple," Saifullah countered. His eyes matched Zarmina's. They looked so alike to one another and nothing like Durkhanai, who everyone said looked just like their mother, her Nazo Phuppo. The twins resembled their father, while Durkhanai was all her grandfather.

"The other zillas have never had the opportunity to negotiate with Marghazar," Durkhanai explained. "This is the first time any of them have been allowed a serious audience with the Badshah, and while Agha-Jaan won't be bullied into any sort of agreements, he is open to negotiation in order for appeasement. Nobody wants war. And it's buying time to prove our innocence."

"We shouldn't have to prove our innocence," Saifullah said. "The other zillas should accept our word."

"I suppose," Zarmina sighed. "I still don't like it, nor do the people."

"What do you mean?" Durkhanai asked. "Have you heard of unrest?"

This was new.

The twins nodded.

"When we were traveling from Dirgara into here, along the way, many seemed disgruntled," Zarmina explained. "They don't understand why foreigners are being allowed entry into S'vat when for centuries, they have been turned back. Marghazar does not need to prove anything to anyone."

"If the Badshah was a strong leader, he would see that," Saifullah said.

Durkhanai stilled.

"Mind your words, Saifullah," she warned, voice deadly. She straightened to her full stature, which was broader than her cousins' wirier builds.

The transition from cousin to princess was seamless.

"Pardon me," Saifullah said. He met her eyes with a hint of anger and frustration, as if she couldn't see what he saw. Regardless, while disapproval and discontentment were bearable, outright criticism was unforgivable.

"Acha, bas," Zarmina said, breaking the silence. "How are the ambassadors, Durkhanai? Any we can possibly trust? That Palwasha-sahiba seemed awfully elusive."

"Gulalai-sahiba of Kurra is nice," Durkhanai said, steering the tension from her tone. She discussed her thoughts regarding the ambassadors with her cousins, the same way she had with

Gulalai yesterday. She was left with the same frustration at the end. Durkhanai groaned.

"Nevertheless, this is a puzzle for which we don't have all the pieces yet."

But she had a sneaking suspicion Asfandyar knew more than he let on.

"Teerza is the worst, of course, because of their insistence in establishing a united nation," Saifullah said. "Especially because of their disapproval for the Badshah's semi-barbaric ways."

"But they don't understand him," Durkhanai argued. She hated anyone to disapprove of her grandfather.

They didn't appreciate what it meant that he had been a boy-king, given the throne at fourteen when his father and three elder brothers had been slaughtered by Luhgams.

Of course he would be eccentric, a little bit overzealous—a little bit unhinged.

"I wouldn't trust Jardum, either," Saifullah added. "I haven't heard good things about Asfandyar."

He gave Durkhanai a pointed look.

"By the way, what *were* you two doing earlier?" Zarmina asked, eyebrows raised.

"Nothing!" she said, a little too sharply.

The siblings exchanged a glance.

"That was entirely unconvincing," Saifullah said. "But we've more important matters to attend to. Just be careful around him."

The twins were eighteen, as well, only six months older than Durkhanai, but they sometimes spoke to her like she were a child.

"He isn't so bad," she replied curtly.

Zarmina raised a brow, giving her a look that said she saw through everything.

"Don't worry! I'm only searching for weaknesses," Durkhanai said, but it tasted acidic, like a half lie.

She wasn't a fool. She could handle herself.

"We shall *all* search for weaknesses," Zarmina said.

"We will protect our people," Saifullah said. "We will protect the mountains of our home . . . even though we are not heir to it."

His voice was strange, as though he knew something Durkhanai didn't; nonetheless, he sounded . . . bitter. She gave him a glance, but he didn't notice . . . or pretended not to.

It was true Saifullah and Zarmina were not heir to any part of the mountains, but it had always been that way. They and their younger siblings were born of Agha-Jaan's youngest, her Nazo Phuppo, the youngest of her father's three siblings.

Zmarack Chacha, the eldest after her father, was the Wali of Trichmir. The next of her father's siblings was Suweil Chacha, the Wali of Dirgara. They were obedient branches in the tree of her grandfather's domain—a bit distant from the trunk, but connected all the same.

Marghazar encompassed the three smaller regions of S'vat, Trichmir, and Dirgara, and each family stayed in their own ruling region.

Nazo Phuppo and her family, without a region to rule, lived in Dirgara, where the twins' father was from. She was a sapling that had spread her roots elsewhere and did not visit often.

"Dirgara is too far away," Durkhanai sighed. "I am cross with you for not bringing Nazo Phuppo along to stay."

"Uff, the way Ammi dotes on you and forgets us," Zarmina said, "you would think you were her child and not us."

"You know that is only because Ammi and Wakdar Taya were exceptionally close," Saifullah said. Durkhanai's heart squeezed.

"And I adore her so," Durkhanai said. "I wish you all lived here permanently, with me."

Zarmina laughed. "You call me here every few months anyhow, and my stay is always for another few. Are you still not content?"

"No," Durkhanai said, voice purposefully petulant. "I want you all to myself, always."

Durkhanai grabbed Zarmina and hugged her tightly to her chest. Laughing, Zarmina struggled, but Durkhanai held her close.

"All right, all right," she said. "I'm here, may I breathe?"

"No," Durkhanai refused.

"You're such a baby," Zarmina said, pinching Durkhanai's chubby cheek. With a laugh, Saifullah pinched her other cheek. Durkhanai pouted.

"Aw," Saifullah teased. "Are you going to cry now?"

"Yes," Durkhanai responded, swatting both of them away. "I am going to cry to Agha-Jaan, and then you'll both be sorry."

On either side of her, Zarmina and Saifullah dropped her cheeks and pulled her into a hug.

"No, no!" they said. "We'll be good to you now!"

"Fine," Durkhanai said with an elaborate sigh. "But to make amends, you must never leave my side!"

The twins laughed.

"We'll never leave you," they said. She smiled and held them close.

"Good," she replied. "Now, let's play some games!"

They moved to her game room and immediately set up a game of kadam board. The next few hours passed in the bliss of laughter and competition and games. The mockery and teasing that belonged to family.

That night, as Durkhanai and Zarmina climbed into bed, Durkhanai was grateful the emptiness was filled. Zarmina had her own room in the marble palace, but tonight, they would stay awake until fajr talking and talking.

"My heart has longed for you in this time apart," Zarmina said, holding Durkhanai's hands. Durkhanai squeezed her hands and was glad her cousin was finally home. She felt safe, more like herself. Stable.

"Finally, Saifullah has left," Zarmina said, snuggling in. "I can ask: How is the kind Rashid?"

Zarmina wiggled her eyebrows.

Durkhanai laughed. She'd almost forgotten about Rashid. Though as son of the strongest nobleman, he would make a good ally . . .

"Quiet, as usual," Durkhanai replied with a sigh. "I wonder when he'll gather the courage to talk to me."

"Not all are as courageous as you," Zarmina teased. "Besides, it is good to have shame."

*How boring*, Durkhanai thought to herself.

"Any new gossip with you?" Durkhanai asked, changing the subject.

Zarmina sighed. "Mama showing me this nobleman and that, but they're all too old or too stupid for me to consider. I yearn for love, just as you do."

"But duty must always come first," Durkhanai said, reminding both Zarmina and herself.

"Yes," Zarmina agreed. "Or I told Mama, I'll just stay with her forever, and she said she would like that, to keep me all to herself, but such is not the way of the world. When she and Baba have passed, what will become of me?"

"You could stay with me!" Durkhanai said. "I'll take care of you, always."

"Mm," Zarmina said. "That would be nice, wouldn't it? Just you and I."

"It would," Durkhanai agreed.

Durkhanai knew one day she would be Badshah, and she would fulfill her promise to take care of Zarmina, to take care of everyone, from her extended family to all the families that lived in her mountains.

It was her sacred duty.

# CHAPTER SIX

*S*ome days later, Durkhanai made her way down the mountain, enjoying the view: the emerald green mountains, the tufts of trees, the cerulean blue sky. The thin streams of a waterfall looked like the white strands of an old man's beard. On another mountain, clouds hung low in the sky like smoke, making the mountains look like they were on fire.

Here, nature was an entity of its own, and to Durkhanai, it was the loving presence of the parents she had never known. The trees had supported her when she had learned to walk, the air had kissed her cheeks every morning. The rain had softened her angry tantrums, the sweet hum of birds had sung her to sleep.

It warmed her heart. This was her home.

She was on her way down to the villages. Durkhanai, the devoted princess, tried to spend a few hours with her people every few days, at least. There were various villages scattered along their main mountain, and she tried to visit different ones on different days. She'd been neglectful with the arrival of the ambassadors and wanted to investigate the unrest her cousins had mentioned.

Today, she went to Kaj'li, her favorite village. Besides, a little love from her people would help assuage the shame she felt at her failed espionage attempt. It might clear her head a bit, too, to be away from the palace. Give her more time to consider her conversation with Gulalai and consider allyship with Asfandyar.

Today, she had tried to get Zarmina to accompany her, but Zarmina had been busy with something. Durkhanai had asked Saifullah then, but he was suspiciously quiet and busy as well.

Durkhanai set out anyway and let the hours spool away, listening to the villagers' grievances, quelling their qualms. Durkhanai would read books to children in schools or help the women cook or go on walks with the elderly. It made her feel less lonely . . . most days.

Today, she knew it would ease the tension she felt from the ambassadors' arrival and Saifullah's strange distance.

Above all, she reassured her people that the Badshah and the Wali and the Shehzadi would not let them down.

"Shehzadi Durkhanai Api!" a little boy's voice called. She turned to see Mahmud, a five-year-old village boy.

"Hello, guddu!" she replied, crouching down to catch his running hug. He wrapped his arms around her neck and squeezed.

"Look, look!" he said, bringing a piece of paper before her. He unfolded it to show her a drawing he had made. It was a drawing of the pointy mountains with clouds on top, and standing atop the clouds were two figures.

"Wow!" she enthused. He smiled, proud of himself.

"Will you come play cricket with us?" he asked, grabbing her hands. With a laugh, she nodded, allowing him to bring her to the rest of his friends.

They all cheered upon her arrival, crowding her, waiting for hugs and kisses. She was smothered by them all; her heart felt full.

When she tired of playing, she went to where one of the elderly women of the village was sitting, stitching embroidery onto a little kurta.

"Nano, how are you today?" Durkhanai asked. "Did the salve I had sent help at all?"

"Ah, my Shehzadi," the nano responded. Durkhanai lowered her head to allow the old woman to hold her face. "Yes, the salve helped, but my blasted knees . . . I am too old."

Durkhanai waved a hand. "Tch, nonsense! Come for a walk with me; they just need to be put in use."

Durkhanai took the woman's hand, and they began a slow walk. This was what it was to be Shehzadi: to spend time with the people, to be their princess, their daughter, their sister, their friend. To be everything, for everyone.

They walked past a little creek, and the whitewater looked like a stream of luminescent milk.

"Look, Nano," she said. "See how beautiful Allah has made our world."

"And He made our Shehzadi most beautiful of all," Nano responded, kissing Durkhanai's face. "But how I miss my Hussain."

The old woman spoke of her son who had died in the ongoing war against the Kebzu Kingdom.

"He died with honor," Durkhanai reminded her, but she knew it was of little consolation.

The people were too heartbroken over those lost to the endless wars against the Kebzus and the Luhgams.

The war against the Lugham Empire was the only thing keeping Marghazar safe from becoming a colony. Their imperial-minded neighbors had been expanding for decades, and the Lugham Empire had the advantage of size and resources. The only reason Marghazar had remained unconquered was because of their ability to fight in the mountainous terrain.

The wars had become worse in the past few years. She knew it was because the Badshah was getting closer and closer to defeating the Luhgam Empire once and for all and was thus disbursing all his energy and resources to the eastern front.

But she couldn't tell the people as much.

Losing their men was tough on the villagers, not only emotionally but economically. With fewer workers in the field, they couldn't keep up with the crops. Durkhanai tried to think of solutions. The women could work in the fields, but the children would need to be watched. Perhaps she could establish centers for the children to go after school or extend the school hours in order to give the adults more time to work?

But as Durkhanai continued on through the village and met with more and more people, war wasn't the only grouse the people had. Everyone was in a mood because of the ambassadors: from the women tending to the grain to the men cutting and cleaning meat.

"The ambassadors are only here for a little while," she tried to explain. "And it's in the best interest of Marghazar. We wish to avoid war at all costs. Especially with our men already fighting the Kebzu Kingdom and the Luhgam Empire."

She could tell they were angry with the Badshah, that they disagreed with and resented what was going on, but they would never say as much out loud. They were discontent, not dissident. She listened attentively to their grumblings.

Always the devoted princess.

"I will speak with the Badshah," she assured them. "Don't worry."

Durkhanai tried her best to dim the people's worries, yet she could tell they listened only for her happiness. This was the part where they thought she was silly, pretty and young, to be doted on and adored, not capable of true action, not capable of *really* understanding their grievances.

Beloved yet useless.

Durkhanai was adored and loved being adored, but sometimes she wanted more.

She didn't know how to appease the unrest growing through the villages. At the very least, everyone disagreed with allying with the other zillas.

Something flickered in the corner of her eye. Durkhanai glimpsed a shadow somewhere, a tall and lean man. For an instant, she wondered if it was Asfandyar, following her.

Perhaps she was imagining things.

Nonetheless, it made her sharper, even though she knew there were guards silently tailing her, ensuring her safety. She was more on guard as she walked through the silent trail.

Durkhanai stopped in her tracks when she heard something. Muffled voices ahead. On another occasion, she might have ignored it, but her sharpened attention refused to let it go. She approached, then stopped when she saw a young man and woman pressed against the side of a house. Lovers.

Her heartbeat quickened, and she averted her gaze quickly, but something wasn't right. She could hear the girl whimpering as the boy's mouth moved across her neck. Durkhanai cleared her throat. The girl met her eyes and gasped.

The boy, however, was preoccupied until the girl tried to shove him off her. Unrelenting, he held her in place.

Durkhanai picked up a rock and threw it at his back.

"What—?" The boy turned and immediately paled. "Shehzadi!"

He released the girl and took two steps back, lowering his head. The girl scrambled to retrieve her dupatta from the floor while the boy had the good graces to look embarrassed. When Durkhanai looked closer, she noted the girl was crying, her mouth swollen.

Durkhanai narrowed her eyes.

"Come here," she commanded the girl. "What's your name?"

The girl came close, wiping her cheeks and sniffling. She couldn't have been older than fifteen.

"I-Inaya," she stammered.

"Was this boy hurting you?" Durkhanai asked. Inaya looked back at the boy, who answered with a sharp look of his own. "Don't look at him. Answer me."

Inaya lowered her head, then nodded slightly.

Anger burned in Durkhanai's chest. She rounded on the boy, who was staring at his feet. He seemed a year older than her, just nineteen. "Come here," she demanded.

He shot forward and stood before her, though he wouldn't meet her eyes.

"Do explain," Durkhanai said.

His cheeks burned red. "I-I didn't mean to," he said pathetically. "My hands slipped."

"I see." The woods were silent around the trail, no one else in sight.

The boy mumbled an apology, but that wasn't good enough.

"On your knees."

The boy had no choice but to obey. He went to his knees.

"Hands forward."

Hesitantly, the boy put his hands forward, and she saw angry tears glistening in his eyes. He apologized again, his voice clipped. Inaya shifted uncomfortably, still behind Durkhanai.

"Inaya, hand me those rocks," Durkhanai said, pointing to two large stones. She obliged, one by one. They were heavier than they looked. Durkhanai took one and held it at her eye level above his hands. The boy whimpered, understanding. But he didn't pull away.

It was not in the Marghazari to be cowards in the face of punishment. Moreover, he knew doing so would insult the Shehzadi, which would earn him the Badshah's wrath—something nobody in their right mind would solicit.

Durkhanai forcefully dropped one on each of the boy's hands.

The crunch of bones was loud in the quiet. He cried out in pain.

"Oh dear," she said. "Looks as though my hands have slipped, as well."

The boy was crying now, hands still beneath the stones. She kicked them off and saw his fingers were bloodied, the bones at strange angles.

How gruesome. Guilt panged through her, but she could not have the locals thinking she hadn't inherited anything of her grandfather's spirit. The guilt gave way to anger. She would not be underestimated, considered silly and frivolous. She could be just as quick and clever as her grandfather.

"Get up," she snapped. He did as he was told. With one finger, she tilted his chin so he looked into her eyes.

"Let us hope such a mistake won't reoccur," she said, voice sweet. "Tell your friends as well."

Where there was one scoundrel, there was bound to be an entire herd. He nodded, face wet with tears. Fear and pain shone in his eyes as he fled.

Durkhanai turned to Inaya. "You have nothing to fear from him, anymore," she said, voice soft with kindness. Inaya nodded, wiping away her tears.

"I thought he loved me," she said.

*Poor fool.* And how Durkhanai hated fools and scrupulously avoided becoming one herself. She gave Inaya's arm a pitying squeeze. "Let me walk you home."

Inaya lived in a cluster of homes that seemed eerily silent. Usually, the women here would be out hanging laundry at this time. When Durkhanai followed Inaya into one house, she heard a cacophony of coughing.

A young man stopped her before she could go any farther.

"Lala Farukh, what is it?" Inaya asked her older brother. She went to his side.

"Abu's health has taken a turn for the worse," Farukh replied. "And four more have fallen ill." He turned to Durkhanai. "Shehzadi, I beg your pardon, but you mustn't enter here."

"Are they all right?" Durkhanai asked. "What's the matter?"

"Hay fever, perhaps, due to the changing of seasons," the man responded. It was April, and winter had thawed to spring.

But as Durkhanai visited more villages and homes over the course of the next few weeks, more and more people were falling ill. Until it was no longer merely a coincidence.

It was a concern.

# CHAPTER SEVEN

y the time Durkhanai made it back to the palace after another round of visits to the villages, she was weary and sad. Another village riddled with illness. First foreigners, then the Kebzus slaughtering the soldiers, and now illness and a very upset people? The past few weeks had been brutal. She needed a hug and a miracle.

"Dhadi!" Durkhanai called out to her grandmother. She rushed to her and was enveloped into a firm hug.

It was enough to fuse some of her heart together for a little while.

"Yes, gudiya?" her grandmother asked, holding Durkhanai's face in her hands. "What's upset you, my dear?"

Durkhanai sighed. "Dhadi," she said. "Everything seems to be going wrong, and it's hardly three weeks since the ambassadors have arrived."

"What now, janaan?"

"The villagers are uneasy," Durkhanai explained. "They don't like having foreigners in our home."

"Ah," Dhadi said. "Nor do I, but I have been negotiating with them, trying to see what advantages we can gain from their arrival. It is at least buying us some time to avoid war."

"Have we gotten any closer to finding out who was behind the summit attack?" she asked. Dhadi waved her off.

"You don't worry about that, chiriya," she replied. "Your Agha-Jaan is handling it."

"But Dhadi—"

"That is enough, Durkhanai," she said, voice stern. "I told you it is being handled, so it is being handled."

"There is an illness spreading through the villages, too, Dhadi," Durkhanai added. "When can we send medicine?"

"I am aware, and I have begun distributing it," Dhadi replied. "But there is not much, so we must be circumspect. Priority goes to the families of soldiers."

Durkhanai frowned.

"Don't worry," Dhadi said, tapping the crinkle between Durkhanai's eyebrows. "Your Agha-Jaan has been Badshah for nearly fifty years. All will be fine. Don't fret about a thing." She smiled and pulled Durkhanai close before motioning her out the door.

As Durkhanai turned to leave, though, her grandmother said one last thing.

"And Durkhanai, janaan? Do steer clear of that Jardumi ambassador," Dhadi said, voice sweet, but there was no mistaking the command. "It does not bode well to be so closely associated to foreigners."

"Bu—" Durkhanai stopped when Dhadi's eyes sharpened. "Yes, Dhadi."

"Now, go, my pretty little princess. Calm your heart and your thoughts."

Durkhanai tried, but her heart would not be calmed. As she walked to her library, she wondered why Dhadi would forbid her from seeing Asfandyar specifically. Dhadi had no qualms with Durkhanai spending time with the other ambassadors. If anything, Dhadi had *encouraged* her to be hospitable to them!

Perhaps it was because Asfandyar was the only male ambassador? It made sense that Dhadi would forbid their acquaintance on those grounds, but being forbidden from something only made Durkhanai want it all the more.

She was never forbidden from anything. It was one of the perks of being the beloved princess. Her every wish and want was granted.

Frowning, she stood before the window in her private library. Then, there was the matter of the illness. Surely, Dhadi would arrange for more medicine to be procured. Then what of the evidence? Dhadi said Agha-Jaan was handling it, but he was preoccupied with fortifying the eastern border against the Lugham Empire.

Durkhanai wanted to obey her Dhadi—to not worry about any of it—but she couldn't quite convince herself.

Which is how she found herself seeking out Naeem-sahib. She rode her beloved horse Heer to the estates on the periphery of the palace compound where many of the noble families had their homes. The Yusufzai estate was closest to the palace and was thus a short ride. She was led into the house and into a receiving room, where an elaborate chai spread was quickly set up for her.

She sipped her tea, waiting. She did not have to wait long.

"Shehzadi, to what do I owe this immense pleasure?" Naeem-sahib asked, joining her. He lowered his head in respect, and she nodded, acknowledging him. She did not rise from her place.

He smiled, his black and gray beard wrinkling in the folds of his face, eyes warm. Durkhanai had always liked Naeem-sahib. He was a clever tribe leader and was fiercely loyal to the Miangul family.

But he was the most powerful noble and was well aware of the fact.

He sat across from her.

"I wanted to speak with you about the illness that has been spreading recently," Durkhanai said, smiling sweetly. "I hope it is not proving too detrimental to the village people?"

Naeem-sahib was one of the three provincial governors within the S'vat state. He managed the tehsil directors who controlled the villages within the province. The tehsil directors in turn managed the jirga councils which were made up of the villages' elders from each family.

His forefathers had been the head of his tribe for centuries, and the Yusufzai clan had consistently maintained a system from which all tribespeople have benefited. They were good farmers, had sturdy craftsmen, and had a natural talent for dealing with people. They were a wealthy, versatile, and powerful tribe.

Naeem-sahib had personally cultivated the respect of every other tribe leader, and they were almost as loyal to him as they were to the Badshah, though the two always went hand in hand.

Marrying Naeem-sahib's eldest son and heir, Rashid, was probably the most auspicious match she could find. It would unify their clans even further and bridge the nobility with the royal family twofold.

"You bring up an important subject," Naeem-sahib said, stirring sugar into his chai. "It is something I have been contemplating myself. Seeing as the Badshah is preoccupied with the wars and the Wali busy with the ambassadors, I may as well discuss it with you."

Durkhanai straightened. While she did not enjoy being a last resort, at least Naeem-sahib thought her capable—even if only in regards to domestic affairs. "Please do."

"I am finding that the illness is taking its toll," he said. "The workers are not able to accomplish as much as they once were."

Durkhanai nodded. "I feared as much. What can be done to aid those in need? Perhaps a redistribution of resources and skills between clans?"

Naeem-sahib shook his head. "This idea has been brought up before, but clan members do not like working for others for no apparent benefit. While *I* can understand and appreciate how sending a Durrani farmer to a Wazir field while a Waziri mason comes to fix Durrani homes will benefit the community at large, unfortunately, the people do not wish to participate unless there is some advantage to them personally."

"I see."

"What we need is more medicine, properly distributed."

"The medicine is . . . being tested for accuracy," she improvised. "I assure you, distribution will be swift and soon."

"It must be sooner," Naeem-sahib insisted. "The farmers are angry—they are threatening to leave their work until their families are cured, which is understandable, Shehzadi. I have tried to raise the issue at the palace, but no one has heard my concerns."

He paused, collecting his thoughts.

"I, as well as the other tribe leaders, have tried to keep the people calm, but they are understandably upset, particularly with the onslaught of foreigners in the capital. We don't want any riots or protests on our hands, do we?"

Durkhanai blinked. She had not expected a threat, however subtle. She had thought she would have a polite conversation with Naeem-sahib, learn what she wished to know, then be on her way.

"I understand, Naeem-sahib," she said. "And I assure you, the medical staff is working as hard as they can. I will speak to the villagers—reassure them."

Naeem-sahib let out an irritated noise, unconvinced. "If the Badshah does not do something and soon . . ." His voice trailed off.

"What then?" Durkhanai would not allow him even to insinuate discontent with her grandfather. When Naeem-sahib did not reply, she continued in a low voice. "I would advise you not to question the Badshah. Not now. Not with everything else going on—when you know his attention is elsewhere for understandable reasons. One may misinterpret it as purposeful."

Naeem-sahib's eyes widened slightly, face stunned and frozen. Then he lowered his head.

"Of course, Shehzadi," he replied. "That was not my intent."

He stepped back, and she nodded.

"Abu!" Rashid's voice called as he entered the room. He froze when he saw Durkhanai, then quickly lowered his head in respect. He joined them, and Durkhanai smiled sweetly at him. He looked away, cheeks pink.

"I have been looking for you, Abu. It is good you are here, as well, Shehzadi," Rashid said. "The women from the Nurzai family refuse to work until their men have been healed. Many others are saying the same."

They were in the eve of the second of two seasons—Manay. The crops of this season—maize, rice, jute—were to be sown in June and July, then harvested from September to the end of October. But with many people ill, already not all the lands were being sown. With these protests . . .

"Shehzadi, this is what I was speaking of," Naeem-sahib said with a sigh. "Something must be done."

And it was his final glance toward her that warned *or else*.

Durkhanai wanted to punish him for that glance alone, the barbarism within her boiling, but she bit her tongue. Though he respected her, Naeem-sahib was clearly not willing to back down either.

"Of course," she replied, voice curt. "I will take my leave."

Durkhanai would have to attend to this matter, as well, and the sooner the better.

"Let me walk you," Rashid offered, smiling brilliantly at her.

They walked together to the stables, where Heer was waiting for her.

Free of Naeem-sahib's observant gaze, Durkhanai let out a sigh. She clenched her jaw, pinching the bridge of her nose. Taking in her worry, Rashid frowned.

"Shehzadi, what's wrong?" he asked, voice hesitant. They had never been alone together before. He seemed nervous. He readied Heer for her, then handed her the horse's reins.

"Your father is discontent," Durkhanai said, voice weary. "As are some other tribe leaders. And at a time like this, we must all be united, more so than ever. We cannot show weakness to the ambassadors."

"Don't worry," Rashid reassured her. "I'll handle my father, and the other nobles will fall into line. I'll manage them."

"You would do that?" she said, genuinely touched. But her voice was extra sugary sweet, and she batted her lashes just in case.

Rashid looked away, laughing nervously. "Yes, of course."

She touched a hand to his arm, and his cheeks burned red. "Shukria, Rashid," she said, drawing close, waiting to feel something.

"Of course, Shehzadi," he said, offering her a sweet smile in response. "Excuse me."

As she watched him go, she realized how steady her heartbeat was. She told herself this was what mattered: stability, comfort, surety.

And yet.

She returned to her palace, thoughts turning. Something needed to be done. Perhaps there was nothing she could do for the villages just yet, but there was another matter she could try to attend to.

Durkhanai went to find Zarmina and Saifullah and found the latter in the halls.

"Saifullah, I was just coming to find you," Durkhanai said. "I was hoping we could call for tea with Rukhsana-sahiba from Teerza. Perhaps find out a little more about her . . ."

"Sorry, dear one, but I must attend to something," Saifullah said. There was a letter in his hand, but it was not addressed to anyone. Before she could ask, Saifullah began walking again. "Do try Zarmina! Not like she's ever up to anything."

Durkhanai felt unavoidably hurt by the brush-off, but she redirected her steps all the same. Zarmina was in her room, reading a book of poetry.

"What's the matter?" Zarmina asked, closing her book. "You look prepared for war."

"I wanted to call for tea with Rukhsana-sahiba. She's the only ambassador with whom I haven't spoken personally. Will you join me?"

Zarmina nodded. Durkhanai grabbed parchment and wrote a note to Rukhsana-sahiba to invite her, followed by a word to her maids to prepare her sunroom with a chai spread.

"Let me just get ready, and I will meet you there," Zarmina said. Durkhanai nodded, going to her room. While she dressed, the maids wove her hair into a complicated braid. They fixed her dupatta in place with her crown, and she replaced her walking shoes with silk khussay.

Zarmina, too, was properly ready when she entered, her dark hair twisted into a simple updo, her simpler clothes exchanged for an embroidered gharara and kurta. The maids followed her in with fine porcelain plates of samosay and biscuits and chicken patties.

They waited.

And waited.

Somebody arrived at the door. Durkhanai straightened her stiff back, but it was just a messenger with a note. The note was from her Dhadi.

*Rukhsana-sahiba is priorly engaged and cannot join you for tea.*

Durkhanai crumpled the paper and tossed it aside. Zarmina quietly went to read what it had said, then sighed. She came to take Durkhanai's hands. "There will be more opportunities."

Durkhanai frowned. "I need to do something, *now*."

"You look tense, jaan," Zarmina said. "Perhaps what you need is rest."

For once, she felt uncertain of what to say. She considered telling her cousin about what Naeem-sahib had insinuated and the refusal of the people to work without medicine. But while Zarmina was family, there was a distinct separation between their roles, and thus, a distinct separation between their loyalties. Saifullah had shown as much already.

Durkhanai did not wish for Zarmina or Saifullah to doubt her grandfather's rulership. Nor did she wish her visit to the nobleman to come across as purposeful meddling, taking things a step too far from assuaging the villagers' worries to direct action to address it.

No, perhaps she should not bring it up until she had discussed it first with Dhadi.

"The illness in the villages is only getting worse," she said, able at least to divulge that much, "and the people are not getting the medicine they need." Durkhanai rubbed her temples.

"You worry too easily. I am sure Nano has things under control," Zarmina said, referring to the Wali. "She has dealt with far greater challenges."

Durkhanai bit the inside of her mouth. "Yes," she said. "Of course."

"Come, let me recite you some poetry to soothe your mind," Zarmina said, leading her to the couch and picking up a book from the table.

But even after an hour of beautiful lines, Durkhanai was not content. If anything, she felt more aggrieved. She knew there was another she could seek out, but Dhadi's warning rang in her mind.

She ambled through the halls, stopping by a rose-scented room filled with candles to sit on a jhula, a large, wooden swing that hung from the center of the ceiling. The seat was hand carved with floral motifs and large enough to seat two, perhaps even three, so she had to reach quite a bit to hold onto the sides. The chains holding the swing up were entwined with leaves and flowers, giving the effect of twisted branches.

Slipping off her khussay, Durkhanai pushed off from the ground, the cold marble a quick press against her feet before she was swinging. She threw her head back, her long hair falling behind her. She closed her eyes, swinging back and forth, back and forth, until her heartbeat steadied once more.

But she could not steady the melancholy spreading through her.

It was with sadness that she retreated to her private library, leaning on the windowsill and staring out at the mountains. A crow cried in the distance.

A little time later, in the last place she'd expect someone, she had a visitor.

# CHAPTER EIGHT

"Am I interrupting?" a deep voice asked.

Durkhanai's heart caught, but she refused to turn from her spot in her private library, her favorite place to slip away to think. She stood before one of the highest windows in the palace, overlooking the lush valley below. She heard footsteps padding across the rug as he approached, but she did not move.

She reminded herself that he was a foreigner. One her grandmother forbade her from seeing. In the three weeks that had passed, she hadn't talked to him much. She had been far too busy—perhaps *intentionally* too busy—with visiting villages and cataloguing the new illness sweeping through them.

Despite how large the marble palace was, she had seen him often in passing, and even if they didn't speak, they always shared a glance and a nod of acknowledgment. Sometimes a smile, even, or a smirk.

Once, however, she saw him thrice in the span of a day, and on the third occasion, she couldn't help but laugh. Something about him made everything turn bubbly, like she'd downed champagne.

"Ambassador," she had said, feigning surprise. "Are you following me?"

"Shehzadi," he had replied, feigning equal surprise. "Perhaps it is you following me."

"Need I remind you, this is my palace?"

Neither had stopped walking, merely slowed their respective pace. He had laughed as he passed by, and the way he looked at her—she couldn't get it out of her head.

He was charming, and she was optimistic. She was a rosy-eyed fool, but oh, did the rose smell sweet.

She could sense she was being silly, but she didn't mind. Even though she should have. If the ambassadors weren't here, she could return to focusing on the wars and the villagers' well-being rather than spying. It was why she had not sought him out.

So, in that moment when Asfandyar finally sought *her* out, as she had somehow sensed he would, Durkhanai refused to acknowledge him. He came and stood beside her. Still, she did not turn.

"Not interrupting, then?" he asked again. She could bear it no longer. She looked at him; her response, an indifferent glance. He looked casual, with the sleeves of his kameez rolled up, the top button undone.

He nodded, turning to lean against the window. As he did, he slipped his pakol off, unfurling his curly hair.

Durkhanai regarded the valley once more.

"Gham ki shaam lambi hoti hai," she said, more to herself than him. *The evening of despair is long.*

"Magar shaam hi toh hai," he said. *But it is only an evening, after all.*

Durkhanai looked at him. He smiled softly, and tears pricked her eyes. It was one of her favorite lines of poetry. How had he known?

She felt inexplicably seen, as though he'd carved open her chest and rather tenderly touched her heart. She wished to tell him, to somehow touch back, but she was afraid of ruining the sudden intimacy.

She did not care if it was forbidden. She would not turn him away.

"You haven't been here much," he said, breaking the silence, the comment too plain for the moment. A jolt ran through her; she was taken aback. He was looking at the hat in his hands, not at her. She furrowed her brows.

"I've been occupied," she responded. "How did you come across this place?"

"A spy never reveals his secrets," he responded with a smile. "Another tip for you to learn, though, I won't ask you to reveal the secret of your hidden mountain trails for eavesdropping."

He was teasing again. She glared. She didn't want to talk about herself. Perhaps it was time for him to feel bare.

"How did your parents meet?" she asked suddenly, changing the subject. She had wondered for some time now.

His entire face crumpled.

"Does it matter?" he snapped, jaw set.

"No," she snapped back. "It doesn't."

She shouldn't have asked. She shouldn't have wanted to know him. She needed allyship from him, not friendship. *Want* had no place here. As Dhadi had so pointedly reminded her.

Asfandyar sighed, looking at her guiltily.

"I'm sorry for snapping," he said. "It's just that I'd rather not give anybody the opportunity to further torment me for my mother's race."

Durkhanai appreciated the honesty. "That's fair." Perhaps allyship and friendship were one and the same after all . . .

"Qismat ka kehl hai sara," he said, voice soft. "A woman from Dunas, and a man from Jardum. It was improbable, impossible."

"And yet."

"And yet." He smiled.

Durkhanai, the hopeless romantic, wanted to ask more details about their backstory but didn't want to seem too interested.

"They must be proud of you," she said instead. "So young and accomplished. I'm sure many would kill to have gotten the chance to come to Marghazar as ambassador."

He sighed, running a hand through his curls. "A few years ago, Abu died in the war against the Kebzus, and Ammi died shortly after from grief," he said. "I never knew somebody could die from grief, you know, but after Ammi—I understood."

Durkhanai gasped. "I'm sorry." He was an orphan as well, and while she'd never known her parents, making their absence perhaps a little more bearable, it seemed he had lost his parents after years of love.

Asfandyar shrugged, but his voice was cloudy when he said, "It was a long time ago." He cleared his throat, confident and easygoing once more. "Now, will you tell me why you're Princess Pouty today?"

Her lips quirked. "There is some sort of sickness spreading through the villages. I've visited a few in the past weeks, and the people are falling ill in a manner most alarming, especially considering it's near summer."

"You have medicine here in the palace, don't you?" he asked. "Why not distribute it?"

"I asked, but we do not have much."

"Perhaps what you are looking for is hidden from you."

"I have access to everything," she said, voice icy. "So if you are trying to imply my grandparents are hiding something from me, you are wrong."

"Perhaps you aren't looking in the right places," he said, unbothered by her thorns. "The palace is huge, after all. I doubt you've searched every nook and cranny."

"If you have something to say, say it."

"I would check a cupboard in the corridor east of the infirmary," he replied casually.

"And how exactly would you know that?"

"You've been busy; so have I," he said with a shrug.

She wanted to pout, then remembered how he had said to not let every emotion show.

It made her want to pout even more.

"Why are you here?" she asked instead. "Hoping to manipulate information out of me?"

"I doubt you have any," he replied easily. "I'm here to find evidence of my own, and truth be told, the more I see, the less I am convinced Marghazar was behind the summit attack."

The way he said it made it seem like an insult.

"Don't think we are cunning enough?"

"Precisely. The attack was immensely nuanced and had to have been carried out by somebody who knew the area meticulously— your lot never leave your lands."

Not that she needed Asfandyar's approval or his help, but Durkhanai was glad he believed in Marghazar's innocence as well.

Besides, he made a good point. Plus, he had been at the summit—he had witnessed the attack. She had been racking her brain for the past month for ways to find proof of her people's innocence but had come up with nothing.

In just a minute, Asfandyar had already provided her with more information than she or anybody she had asked could have ever come up with, because he was right—she and her people didn't leave their lands. Eavesdropping on Palwasha-sahiba had been a failure. Calling for tea with Rukhsana-sahiba had been a failure.

She had no clue about any of the details. This was a problem.

"Then who do you reckon was behind it?" she asked. "And why are you telling me this?"

She held her breath.

"Despite your sharp tongue, you may be the only person in this blasted tribe with any useful information beyond what I've been able to find myself. I've spent the past few weeks without any success—I figured we might be able to help one another."

"And why would I help you?"

"For the same reason you would help yourself: You don't want war between our tribes, nor do you want peace. The sooner this dreadful matter is closed, the sooner we can both go back to our people and our lives."

"So, you're proposing we . . . what? Work together?"

"The enemy of my enemy is my friend," he replied with a shrug.

Interesting.

"I'll consider it," she replied, turning to go.

"Durkhanai," he called. Something tickled in her tummy upon hearing him say her name.

"Hmm?"

"It's good you're worried," he told her, voice earnest. "About your people, I mean. It means you care. So don't give up on them." He smiled. "They adore you."

"Thank you," she said, and she meant it.

It felt good to talk to him. Unlike everyone else, who told her not to worry, Asfandyar took her seriously. It was only this that compelled her to search where he had told her to.

She found the cupboard he spoke of easily, but it was small and held only a half-empty medicine cabinet. Durkhanai almost gloated, but for the sake of her people, she checked the other corridors. Nothing.

She returned to where Asfandyar had suggested. This time, she looked closer.

The medicine cabinet wasn't flush with the wall.

She leaned around the side. Sure enough, it was a cover. She pushed the light cabinet over, and it glided easily, revealing a door that led to a massive room.

Rows and rows of medicine vials. They were labeled differently, for different things. Different colors and consistencies. She opened one, and it smelled strongly of cardamom.

"Fitteh mu tera," she whispered. "Goddamn him."

He was right.

Which also meant her grandmother had hidden the truth from her.

Durkhanai could understand her grandparents keeping her at a distance with the ambassadors, but she had always thought they trusted her completely when it came to her people. It was why she was so meticulous about meeting with them.

Dhadi always praised her for the care she showed the villagers. Agha-Jaan always said she was performing her duties most diligently.

Yet, they had kept this from her. They did not truly trust her in this, either.

The sense of authority she had crumbled. Perhaps all it really had been was a falsified sense of authority to begin with. Just enough information to make her feel as though she knew everything, when in truth, she knew very little.

It hurt.

And it didn't make sense. Why not give out all the medicine they had?

Durkhanai wanted to ask her grandmother outright but stopped herself. Perhaps Dhadi would hide the medicine again, and then it would be of no use to anyone.

But why hide it at all? Durkhanai was sure Dhadi had a good reason, but she wouldn't risk it by bringing it up, not at such a critical moment for the people down in the villages, not after what Naeem-sahib had implied. Her grandparents might not take her seriously on these matters, either, and then she would fail the very people relying on her.

And how had Asfandyar known?

Maybe Gulalai and Saifullah were right: Asfandyar was dangerous.

Right then, she needed to focus on the medicine. She needed clarification.

"Doctor-sahiba," she called, peeking her head into the head doctor's office. The doctor immediately got up and lowered her head in respect, touching her fingers to her forehead.

"Shehzadi," the doctor responded.

"Doctor Aliyah," Durkhanai said. "There is an illness spreading through the villages. Would you be able to locate some medicine for me?"

"The Wali has informed me," the doctor replied. "We are already working on finding the proper medicine and distributing it. Don't fret, Shehzadi."

"Yes, but I would still like to see where the medicine is held." She paused to clarify. "Rather, which exact medicine will be used."

"We are still modifying the precise concoction. No doubt the Wali would not wish to worry you." Doctor Aliyah reassured Durkhanai with a confident smile. "Now, if you will excuse me."

She left before Durkhanai could press further. It felt like a ruse. She left the office with a pout. She had found medicine but didn't know what to use, and Doctor Aliyah was only prescribing through Dhadi.

She needed to take matters into her own hands. She was the princess after all. She remembered the villagers' sadness, their fright, and it was all she needed to devise a quick plan.

She peeked through the infirmary, plucking a young doctor in training from the room. He was a year younger than her with crooked glasses and frazzled eyes.

"Yes, Shehzadi?" he asked, blinking quickly. She gave out an exaggerated cough, melting her face into one of pain.

"I don't feel so well," she told him. "I think I have a fever."

She leaned against the wall dramatically, closing her eyes and moaning. It had the desired effect; his face crumpled in despair.

"I will alert Doctor Aliyah immediately!" he assured her. Durkhanai caught his arm; gave it a squeeze. The boy froze.

"No, don't," she told him, coughing again. "I'd hate to be a bother."

He looked like a scared kitten.

"Why don't you just bring me the medicine I need?" she asked. He blinked at her, swallowing hard.

"Me?" he asked. She nodded.

"I would be *so* grateful," she replied. Durkhanai batted her eyelashes for extra effect.

"Right away, Shehzadi," he said. "Would you please tell me the symptoms again?"

"Fever, cough, fatigue, and sore throat," she told him. He nodded.

"Wait here just a moment, Shehzadi," he said. He disappeared and returned with a little vial of medicine.

"Put this in warm milk with turmeric, and drink it in the morning and evening for three days," he told her. "With Allah's blessing, you will be healthy once more."

"Jazakullah khair," she said. "Your princess salutes you."

The boy smiled shyly, and Durkhanai didn't even feel a little bit guilty as she walked back to her rooms.

On the way, Asfandyar crossed her path.

"Princess, did you find what you were looking for?"

"Indeed, I did," she replied.

He nodded, smug. "What are you going to do now?"

"Don't worry about it," she told him, smiling to herself.

# CHAPTER NINE

"You really are predictable, you know that?" Asfandyar told her not four hours later.

Durkhanai scowled. The instant she'd lit a candle in the medicine cupboard, he appeared, casually leaning against the wall. With his bedroom eyes and sleepy sighs, he was even more insufferable.

To make it worse, he smirked like it was his profession.

"Khuda ke liye," she muttered. "How long have you been standing there like a lunatic?"

He rolled his eyes.

"Just long enough to think about how satisfying it would be to catch you," he said, grinning now.

"Don't gloat." She pushed him to the side and began reaching for the medicine vials. She placed them into the leather bag she had brought which already had little handwritten instructions to be given out with the medicine. She'd spent all evening writing them out.

Asfandyar shook his head at her.

"Well? Are you going to help me or not?" she asked.

"Do tell me what your plan is," he replied, looking at her satchel. "You're going to, what? Steal medicine and walk around the villages in your absurd night attire, handing it out?"

Durkhanai's mouth fell open as she pretended to be offended. In truth, she was relieved he had caught her. She hadn't wanted to do this alone anyway, and now, she could bully him into helping her. And he seemed looser at night. Friendlier even.

"First of all," she started, "it's not stealing because, as I must continuously remind you, this is my castle! Two, this is not absurd night attire!"

Durkhanai looked down and realized that perhaps her argument had been lost. She wore slippers, baby pink silk shalwar kameez, and a palachi shawl wrapped around her shoulders.

He raised his brows at her.

"*Maybe* this is slightly inappropriate," she conceded. Especially considering how thin these clothes were; she could feel the curvy outline of her body against the silken fabric, and from the way Asfandyar looked at her, he clearly could, too.

"*But,*" she continued, pulling her shawl tighter, trying not to smile, "the people need medicine, and I have medicine to give them. Now, are you just going to stand there, or are you going to help me?"

She pouted for good measure. He rolled his eyes and snorted.

"I'll help, but only because you're entirely hopeless without me," he said. "You're welcome, by the way. Maybe this will convince you we really ought to be allies after all."

He gave her a grin and took the bag from her hands. Which was lucky, since it was getting heavy. At least all his muscles weren't just for show.

"Acha, zaada mat bano," she told him. "Don't get ahead of yourself. But thank you, nonetheless."

"Of course, Shehzadi," he said, giving a dramatic bow.

"Are you done?" she asked. "We ought to get going soon."

"With the dramatics? Never."

She gave him a pointed look.

"Before we go, you're going to need to change," he pressed. "That outfit is much too distracting."

Durkhanai raised a brow. She could have sworn she saw Asfandyar ears turn the same pink as her blouse.

"To the public, of course," he stuttered, clearing his throat. "Pink silk? It's a sure way to be found out."

She bit back a smile.

"Go on!" he insisted. "I'll meet you in the library in ten minutes." Asfandyar put his hands on her shoulders and steered her toward the door.

"Acha! Kya hai? I'm going," she said.

But his hands did feel lovely on her shoulders, especially through the very thin silk. She was beginning to appreciate her night attire much more.

*Don't be ridiculous*, she told herself. It must be the late hour. Her thoughts were getting out of hand.

When she reached her room to look for something to wear, she realized she had nothing that wasn't absurd or ridiculous attire for clandestine night outings. How inconvenient. After rummaging around for some time, she finally found a cotton lawn sleeping outfit, but even that had chikankari embroidery on it. She slipped the chaadar across her head. At least she was able to find a woolen loi. The thick shawl would cover her mostly. She put on her riding shoes and headed out but not before checking her braid to ensure she looked as beautiful as she always did.

"Hai Allah, you take forever," Asfandyar said when she entered the library.

"Am I at least less distracting now?"

Asfandyar didn't respond, just shook his head at her.

"Let's go," he said. "We haven't much time before fajr, when the villagers will be awake. What was your plan of escape?"

She had one, but it included using the secret passageways that connected from her room. She wasn't stupid enough to show Asfandyar, and he must have realized something along those lines.

"Don't worry," he said. "Meet me by the stables."

She raised a quizzical brow. "How will you get out of here?"

His response was a cocky grin. "Spy, remember?"

How infuriating. "Asaman se uth'reho? Why do you walk around like you're God's gift to mankind?"

"You think I'm God's gift to mankind?" he responded, brows raised, clearly pleased.

She rolled her eyes. "*I* don't think you are. *You* do," she clarified.

He shot her a wide grin, unconvinced. "See you on the other side," he said with a wink.

As she made her way through the passageways, Durkhanai knew this was all a bad idea. It was dangerous to be going out at all, and thricefold as dangerous to be going out with Asfandyar.

Especially if she was caught.

Firstly, she couldn't be caught with a man in the middle of the night. Secondly, her people hated the ambassadors—any foreigners—and if she was seen with one, it would be doubly worse.

But she needed the help, and he was willing and—she trusted him. She didn't know why, but she did. It was a gut feeling.

Perhaps he really could help her—beyond just the medicine, but with finding out who was behind the summit attack. Time was ticking, and she was so caught up with checking in on her people and trying to quell their discontent that she'd hardly had any time to continue her investigation. After all, the attempts she had made on her own to investigate had come to nothing, and he himself had admitted he could use her help, too. This might be a good way to show him her gestures were sincere.

She knew the Badshah was searching vehemently, but he was preoccupied with the borders and the Lugham Empire. And the Wali was busy negotiating with the ambassadors and trying to buy more time. It was up to Durkhanai to exonerate her land, whether her grandparents realized she was capable of that or not.

But she seriously doubted herself when she tripped on a branch, snapping it loudly in half, and Asfandyar shot her a withering glance.

"Do be a little louder, Shehzadi," Asfandyar whispered. He offered her his hand, and she pushed it aside.

"Go to hell," she hissed back.

"But then, what would you do without me?" he replied cheerily.

"Be immensely happy."

"You break my heart," he said, holding both hands to his heart, wincing dramatically.

"Uff, taubah!"

She tripped again and swore. This time when Asfandyar offered his hand, she took it. As he grabbed her hand, she saw his gaze catch on the family crest ring she always wore on her third finger. He seemed to recognize it for an instant, then his face was masked yet again.

This was the second time.

Before she could wonder, Asfandyar pulled her along. He was as strong as the river's current, and they began the hike down the mountain in comfortable silence.

When they arrived, the village was quiet. Thankfully, the nights hadn't gotten so hot quite yet, so the people were soundly asleep inside. In the more humid nights, the people pulled their charpai outside, sleeping under the open sky. Tonight, the courtyards were empty.

"How do you want to do this?" Asfandyar asked.

Durkhanai smiled. "With grace," she said. "Watch and learn, spy."

Durkhanai recalled which homes held the ill and went to the one closest by. Most of the village structures were open-doored, which made her work simpler.

Silent as a mouse, she slipped into the kitchen area, which was separate from the main structure of the home. She pulled a small vial from her satchel and set it down beside the ghara—the clay pot used to store water. It was the first place people visited in the morning.

From the smaller purse inside the satchel, Durkhanai pulled out a rolled piece of paper. It held the instructions for the medicine and a little note signed, *from a friend.*

Heart beating quickly, she slipped out.

"See?" Durkhanai whispered, going back to where Asfandyar was waiting on the street.

She was euphoric off of not getting caught and of what she had accomplished; the good she was spreading. It felt like a splendid game.

"That was the good work of a spy," Asfandyar admitted, impressed.

"I don't know what I am," she said offhandedly, laughing just a little.

"You're amazing, that's what you are," he said in earnest. "Knowing just who needs the medicine and coming out to personally deliver it to each of them . . . I confess, when I first caught you in the cupboard, I assumed you'd pass medicine vials to a messenger to deliver. But what you are doing . . . it is amazing."

"That I am," she agreed, flipping her hair.

So they went on.

Durkhanai recalled which homes needed medicine, and she slipped little medicine vials into their kitchens while Asfandyar stood watch. They worked in easy silence, a quick and nimble system. It wasn't long before they ran out of medicine.

The time was getting close to fajr, when the people would wake to pray before dawn. They had to get back before anybody noticed their absences and before anybody could see them arriving.

They began the hike up, both lightheaded from exhaustion and giddy from what they had accomplished.

As they grew closer to the palace, they neared a wide, gaping amphitheater built into the mountain. In the moonlight, the empty seats shone as if waiting to be filled. The dirt at the base was smoothed clean, yet it was so easy to imagine a lion bursting forth; it's roar echoing through the mountains.

"Is this where tribunals are held?" Asfandyar asked.

"Yes," she replied. Though she didn't say so, she knew from her grandparents' stories over the years that the massive arena was centrally located to the surrounding villages for good reason. There could be no spectacle without the presence of thousands.

"You don't find the idea entirely uncivilized?" he asked. "It is why people call the Marghazari barbaric after all."

"It is our tradition," she replied. She did not take offense. She knew her people could be brutal and exuberant, perhaps steeped in old traditions some people occasionally argued should have been shed decades ago, but they were strong and fierce and true. They were hers.

The trial by tribunal was one of the traditions that had given the Marghazari people their notoriety.

The rules of the tribunal were simple: The accused was brought before two doors, completely identical. The accused was then given a choice to decide his own fate; to pick the door. Behind one door was a cruel lion. Behind the other was a kind lady, or a kind man, whichever the accused preferred.

If the accused was guilty, the lion would rip him to shreds. If the accused was innocent, he was to marry the lady.

Perhaps to outsiders, it seemed uncouth and unreasonable, but to them, it was tradition and truth.

"Besides," she said, the hint of a smile on her face. "Are we not a barbaric people?"

He tucked a stray curl behind her ear, his voice low as he said, "I dare say you are."

He was too close. He seemed to realize the same moment she did. He took a step back.

"Your hair smells like coconut oil," Asfandyar remarked, wrinkling his nose. "It's horrid."

The moment was broken.

"Excuse me?" she balked. She opened her hair from its braid and tossed it in front of his face. Asfandyar pretended to gag, and they both laughed.

"Aren't you tired?" Durkhanai asked him, yawning. He was wide awake.

"I don't sleep much," he admitted nonchalantly.

"Why not?"

He paused, maybe because nobody ever asked, or maybe because he was wondering if he should tell the truth or lie. "I have nightmares."

She frowned. "Why do you have nightmares?"

He let out a sigh-laugh, so she laughed, too, brows knitted in confusion.

"What?" she asked. "You can't offer such a response and not expect curiosity in return."

He ran a hand through his hair and kept it there, his fingers twisted at the roots. All the mirth vanished from his mien; he was nearly about to cry. Her heart knocked against her chest as he said, voice broken, "My best friend passed away when I was seventeen. So, I have nightmares about her."

"Oh," she breathed. "I'm so sorry you had to go through that."

And she didn't know what else to say. How truly awful and wretched. With one glance at him, one would never guess; he was always smiling and laughing, teasing and playful.

"Life is lived through love and loss."

"That it is." She hadn't expected him to shift from banter to meditation so seamlessly, but it was genuine.

Perhaps it was the night or the fatigue, but she felt open around him—a cloudless sky.

"Thank you, by the way," she told him. "For coming along and helping me. It was honorable of you to help people who aren't your own. Perhaps an alliance with you wouldn't be so bad."

"Was that a compliment?" he asked, mouth agape with fake shock. She shoved his arm lightly.

"A half compliment," she responded. "Don't get ahead of yourself in flattery."

"Still," he responded, holding his hands to his heart. "A half compliment from the princess. I shall cherish this memory for all of time." But then he added quietly, "Truly, Shehzadi, the honor was mine. And besides, all the people of this world are my own, regardless of tribe."

Durkhanai's heart felt full as the soil after rain, flowers on the verge of blooming. She had never spoken thus with a man, and perhaps it should have felt more awkward or intimate, or strange even, but Durkhanai just felt at ease. Comfortable.

They arrived back at the palace.

"Well, good night," she said, though neither made any moves to leave.

Asfandyar smiled and bowed dramatically. "Good night, Shehzadi," he exaggerated.

Durkhanai tried her best to give him a straight face, but she couldn't hold it. She giggled, then giggled again. He was laughing now, too, and she couldn't seem to stop.

"Shh!" she said through her laughter, waving her hands to quiet him. "Everyone's asleep!"

And before she could stop herself, she bridged the space between them and covered his mouth with her hand. Asfandyar's laughter slowly fizzled out against her palm. He stilled, and she realized just how close they were.

Durkhanai swallowed.

They were much too close to be appropriate, even if she hadn't been a princess and he a foreign ambassador. She was close enough to see the long eyelashes framing his hooded eyes; each curl that unfurled from beneath his pakol.

Durkhanai dropped her hand but couldn't seem to move away, despite knowing she should. This close, she had to look up at him, and he was gazing down at her. He was heavenly warm against the cool night, the space between them a perfect cocoon.

*One more second,* she told herself.

She took a deep breath.

And stepped back.

Durkhanai cleared her throat, biting her lip. She looked up at the stars, away from Asfandyar, intent on distracting herself from the burning on her hand where his mouth had been.

The night sky was awake; throbbing and pulsing with a thousand glittering stars. It took her breath away, frightened her with the grandeur. It seemed impossible, like a dream thing come alive—a being on its own. An angel, a monster, something that would swallow her whole, and she would let it, willingly, gladly, if only to catch the glimmer of beauty for a second more.

This is what is meant to be mesmerized, astounded. This was brilliance made real, a thousand diamonds shimmering in the black velvet cloak of night, crystal and clear.

"Look," she whispered, tilting her head further back as if to drink the night sky. "It's breathtaking."

"Indeed, it is," he said. But when she looked, he was staring at her with a soft expression. She bit her lip, nervous all of a sudden. She expected him to look away, flushed, but as usual, he had no shame whatsoever. *Besharam.*

"What?" she asked. She had meant to sound irritated, but the question came out softer than she intended. She bit her lip.

His lips curved in a half smile, but he said nothing, just kept staring. She felt like he was stripping her bare with just his gaze, though it never traveled past her eyes.

The blacks of his eyes were glistening like the night sky.

"What?" she said again, though this time, she couldn't quite keep the quiver from her lips.

"Nothing," he said, shaking his head and smiling.

She wanted to devour the smile from his lips with her own.

"I agree," she said, cutting off her thoughts. She cleared her throat. "We should work together to find out who was behind the summit attack." She swallowed. "So you can go home, and we can both go on with our lives. Allies?"

She put her hand out to shake, and he did. His fingers brushed against her palm. A shiver ran down her spine. Asfandyar lifted her hand to his lips.

"You should rest," he said, kissing her palm. "Sweet dreams."

He turned and went, and she was left standing there, watching him go.

# CHAPTER TEN

*T*he next day, Durkhanai felt more settled than she had in weeks. Though she was tired from being out for most of the night, there was satisfaction that came from doing good work. And now, her mind was clear enough to consider investigating who was behind the summit attack.

After breakfast, Durkhanai went to find Asfandyar. However, on the way, she ran into another.

"Shehzadi Durkhanai, I'm glad to have found you," Rashid said, smiling sweetly at her. "May I join you?"

When she nodded, he matched his strides to hers. "I wished to speak with you about a most curious matter. Last night, it seems medicine was distributed in a village. Some sort of guardian angel placed them in the homes of the ill, along with instructions. I was wondering if you knew anything about it?"

Rashid looked at her with wonder. He was thinking it might have been her. She could divulge the secret to him and earn his favor, strengthening their bond from acquaintance into friendship.

As princess, it was Durkhanai's duty to always think of her people first. But she couldn't help but think about last night, how fresh it still was in her mind.

The stars in Asfandyar's eyes.

She saw him as clearly as though he were right there. She wished to reach out, to hold a hand to his face as she had the night prior; feel his beard against her palm.

She shook her head to clear her thoughts.

"That is wonderful news!" she said to Rashid, forcing surprise into her voice. "But I must confess, I know nothing about it. Perhaps a local physician expended their own resources to do so."

Disappointment flashed across Rashid's face.

"So . . . it was not you?"

Durkhanai released a little laugh. "How I wish it was, but I'm afraid I was asleep here in the palace. Surely, you would not expect a princess to sneak into the night like a miscreant, handing out medicine?"

"No, I suppose I would not," Rashid said. He opened his mouth to speak again, but Durkhanai did not want him to ask too many questions, to be too curious. She could not have Dhadi finding out she was the so-called "guardian angel."

"I must go now," Durkhanai said, touching his arm. "But I hope to see you again soon."

She walked away from Rashid and toward another. Asfandyar was in the courtyard, staring at his reflection in a fountain. He stood so still, staring. She wondered what he saw. She nearly asked, but the moment she approached, the pensive, sad expression he wore was swiftly exchanged for one of amusement.

"Shehzadi Durkhanai, to what do I owe this pleasure?" he asked, smirking.

"Ambassador," she said, trying to keep her voice level. She reminded herself that the only reason she was working with Asfandyar was so that he could leave; it was a necessity.

And once he was gone, she could focus on Rashid more. Her inevitable engagement.

"You look well," he said, looking her up and down. "I take it you got a good night's rest?"

But the way he said made it seem something unscrupulous, something she wouldn't want others to overhear. She gave him a pointed look.

"Enough small talk," she told him. "We must focus on finding evidence. Let's go to my library—we must be discreet."

"I assure you, Shehzadi," he said with a wink. "I can be quite discreet."

She rolled her eyes but couldn't help being amused.

They walked toward her library, but as they did, Saifullah and Zarmina approached.

When they saw her with Asfandyar, an identical look of concern crossed the twins' faces.

"Ambassador," Saifullah said, giving Asfandyar a nod.

"Where are you two headed?" Zarmina asked Durkhanai, eyes worried. Durkhanai didn't want to lie, but she knew her cousins wouldn't understand the truth, either. Knew they would try and stop her, thinking she was being a fool. But she could handle herself and her people.

"I'm just loaning the ambassador . . . a book," Durkhanai replied with a smile.

Neither of them believed her, but they let her go. Zarmina gave Durkhanai one final glance that said, *we will discuss this later.*

"You don't lie easily," Asfandyar noted, when they were out of hearing range.

"I try to avoid it whenever I can," she replied.

They walked in silence the rest of the way until they arrived at her library, which was quiet and serene, as usual. Thoughts spinning, Durkhanai boiled down to one solid theory: that the Kebzu Kingdom was behind the attack. She told Asfandyar as much.

"What do you think?"

In the past few weeks since Gulalai first proposed the idea to her, Durkhanai had been considering it, and it made sense.

"It is plausible," Asfandyar replied. "But who would have given the Kebzu Kingdom the information?"

"And why? Who would risk their Wali's life in such a manner? That's what I can't figure out." Durkhanai paused. "But since you were there and you know most of the walis and their advisors, I figured you would have a better idea."

Durkhanai pulled out a piece of paper and pencil, sitting down in front of Asfandyar.

"Walk me through the events of that day," she said, ready to take notes. "Any detail, anything that could be useful."

"All right," he said. "Well, it was held in Teerza—at the Wali's mansion. The four walis were there—from B'rung, Jardum, Kurra, and Teerza—as well as two to three advisors each. So, about fifteen people total, I would say. We all sat in a large room with great big windows. As people were arriving, we were discussing casual things with one another."

He paused, trying to remember.

"Then, the Wali of Teerza quieted us all down, telling us to take our seats once everybody had arrived. He began distributing papers—there was an excitement in the air. We knew it wouldn't be easy, but it could be something worthwhile."

Asfandyar stopped, swallowing.

"And then the explosion. It seemed to come from everywhere, all at once, before the Wali of Teerza could even speak. I was thrown across the room, but the fall was softened by other bodies. When I opened my eyes, the room was full of sulfur and smoke, dust and debris. As I looked to my side, I found the Wali of Teerza with glass lodged throughout his body, blood flowing across his skin. He was already dead.

"I stood, inspecting the wreckage, and saw the Wali of Jardum, arm decapitated. A large mass of stone had fallen and crushed her body. I had regarded her as family; she was a good friend of my father's, and after his passing and my mother's, she had always treated me like her own."

He closed his eyes, face contorted in pain.

"I didn't even get to see her face," he whispered, then stopped, no longer able to speak.

Durkhanai hadn't realized how gruesome it had been. Nor did she consider how painful it would be for him to relive the memories of that day—after all, he could have been among those deceased or severely injured.

And people he had known—colleagues—had been among the casualties.

"I'm sorry," Durkhanai said, voice small. "I didn't realize . . ."

"It's all right," he replied, opening his eyes. He cleared his throat. "The attack—it just reminded me of the fronts."

"You were a soldier? But you're so young." She couldn't keep the shock from her voice.

Asfandyar shrugged it off.

"I was in a bad place then," he said. She wanted to ask him more, but he continued on before she could. "What I don't understand is why a zilla would have informed the Kebzu Kingdom. Unless nobody did and the Kebzu Kingdom has spies of their own?"

"No, I don't think they have spies," she replied.

The entire affair was immensely secretive. In Marghazar, only she and her grandparents had known about it, and Asfandyar had mentioned before that only the walis of the zillas and their most trusted advisors had known about it. Of which, he was one.

Durkhanai wanted to ask how he managed to become a senior advisor at such a young age—he was only nineteen after all. And while Gulalai and Durkhanai were both seventeen and eighteen and in similar positions, they were blood of the walis.

But those were questions for another time.

"Who is benefiting from this situation?" Asfandyar asked.

And suddenly, it hit her.

"What about B'rung?"

Durkhanai had written them off initially—as had Gulalai—because they were usually ignored and seen as irrelevant.

But they could have orchestrated the summit attack in order to gain Marghazar's favor and gain a strong ally as well.

Durkhanai recalled how her grandmother, the Wali of S'vat and person dealing with negotiations, had been spending quite some time with the B'rung ambassador, Palwasha-sahiba.

B'rung was Marghazar's neighbor in the south and shared a border. Could the Badshah be considering annexing B'rung into Marghazar? It would explain why Palwasha-sahiba was being so amiable with the noblewomen during the mountain walk. The Badshah could be contemplating such a thought in order for more resources, but more importantly, for fortifications against the Lugham Empire in the east, which he was determined to defeat once and for all.

But if that was the case, her grandparents would know B'rung was the informant and thus behind the summit attack, no? Wouldn't they tell her?

They wouldn't.

Just as they had withheld the medicine, they could be withholding more information. They didn't tell her everything which meant that Durkhanai had to find out the truth for herself. Then figure out what to do about it.

"What are you thinking?" Asfandyar asked. "I can see your mind working."

"I'm thinking it was the B'rung zilla that informed the Kebzu Kingdom about the summit—after all, hadn't they been eager for this negotiation period with the Badshah? And their wali hadn't been killed; barely injured."

"You're right," Asfandyar agreed, recalling the day. "B'rung wasn't too interested in unification, either. They seemed to have been bullied into attendance."

"There's our lead," she said.

"You know what this means, don't you?" Asfandyar said, eyes gleaming. "Time to spy."

Durkhanai made her way to the ambassadors' wing, Asfandyar on her tail. Palwasha-sahiba should have been at a meeting with the Wali of S'vat, if Durkhanai was correct—which meant, this was a perfect time to snoop through her belongings.

But she froze right before turning the corner.

Asfandyar looked over her shoulder and swore.

Palwasha-sahiba was out, but her servant was still there, tidying up.

"We'll come back in a little while," Durkhanai whispered. They both turned to leave, but their path was blocked by a cane.

Durkhanai's eyes traveled the length of the cane until they met the person wielding it.

"What's going on?" Gulalai asked, voice sweet. She looked between Asfandyar and Durkhanai; how close they stood, how guilty they looked to have been caught. Gulalai narrowed her eyes at Durkhanai, giving her a look.

"Gulalai, do me a favor," said Durkhanai. "Distract that servant over there."

"Pardon me?"

"I need to go to Palwasha-sahiba's room," Durkhanai said. Gulalai looked to Asfandyar to see if they were being serious, and he nodded.

"And why would that be?" Gulalai replied. "You do know B'rung is Kurra's ally, don't you? And Asfandyar-sahib—are you forgetting B'rung is Jardum's ally as well?"

Durkhanai pulled Gulalai to the side, lowering her voice so Asfandyar wouldn't hear.

"You want your alliance with Marghazar, don't you?" she whispered. "Time to prove your loyalty."

Gulalai considered this, her fingers tapping the jeweled handle of her cane.

"Fine," she conceded.

Durkhanai grinned, squeezing Gulalai's arm. "I won't easily forget this, Gulalai."

"I would hope not."

They went back to stand with Asfandyar, and Durkhanai nodded at him. They stood to the side, watching as Gulalai approached Palwasha-sahiba's room, looking around to create a diversion. Just then, the servant came out of the room, carrying a mop and a bucket of water, heading down the hall.

Durkhanai swore she saw Gulalai sigh.

Then, she dramatically bumped into the servant, sending the bucket of soapy water tumbling. Gulalai shrieked as water spilled over her, then made a show of slipping and pulling the servant down with her.

"What have you done!" Gulalai cried. "Are you blind? Guards, help me!"

And while everyone was distracted, Asfandyar and Durkhanai slipped into Palwasha-sahiba's room.

"Quick, we won't have much time," Durkhanai whispered. They headed toward the attached office in the back of the room, where there was an empty desk, a bookshelf, and little boxes.

They split up, rummaging through the boxes and the papers, trying to find something, anything. She found letters from family members and other sorts of things, but nothing important, until Asfandyar whistled to get her attention. He held up a box.

"Locked," she said.

He grinned, coming toward her. Before she could ask precisely what he was doing, he lifted a hand into her hair. A shiver ran down her spine, involuntarily moving her closer to him.

He held up a pin.

"Just one moment please, Shehzadi," he said, his nimble fingers going to work at picking the lock. He eased it open in no time. She gave him a light round of applause.

"Impressive."

He gave a slight bow.

They began sifting through even more papers until Durkhanai's eyes fell on correspondence signed by the Wali of B'rung.

"I found something," she whispered. Durkhanai unfolded the letter to begin reading, but just as she did, her ears perked.

They heard voices approaching.

"Hide!" Asfandyar whisper-shouted, closing the box and putting it back where it belonged.

"Wait! There's something here."

She scanned the words—reading quickly—the words barely registering. But what she understood was the Wali of B'rung writing that the ambassador must use this opportunity in Marghazar or it will all have been for nothing.

What will have been for nothing?

Before she could read more, Asfandyar grabbed her hand, dragging her into the connecting changing room just as the door to the room opened.

Durkhanai swore under her breath as she heard Palwasha-sahiba yelling at her servant. Behind them, she could hear Gulalai speaking as well. The voices came closer, louder and clearer, as Durkhanai and Asfandyar scrambled for somewhere to hide.

"Here," Asfandyar said, as he saw a traveling trunk. When he opened the lid, it was empty, all the clothes unpacked. Without another word, he climbed in.

"Come on," he said.

Durkhanai looked behind her. The voices were coming closer.

"It's okay," he said, voice gentle. He was sitting with his back pressed against the side of the trunk, legs spread open. With one hand, he held open the lid of the trunk, and he offered his other hand to her.

"Fitteh mu tera," she muttered, taking his hand. She climbed in, sitting in front of him, but it was a tight squeeze—her legs wouldn't fold. She pressed her back against him, bending her limbs as much as they could, and Asfandyar lowered the lid of the trunk.

He held it open with one hand, leaving a crack of light and air in. They were pressed together, and the trunk was suddenly very, very hot as she realized how close they were.

"Why are your legs so long?" she hissed, trying to separate herself from him. They were tangled together, every muscle of his chest pressed into her back.

"Why are *your* legs so long?" he hissed back.

But in the heat and the dark, claustrophobia spread across her chest—a constricting feeling that made her whimper. She breathed in short bursts of air, trying not to hyperventilate.

"It's okay," Asfandyar whispered, voice gentle. His free arm untangled to come around her. She clutched his hand tightly, felt his bones crush between hers.

"It's all right, I'm here," he murmured. "Shh, it's okay."

Just then, the voices came close enough for Durkhanai to tell they were in the changing room. Heart beating fast, she prayed they wouldn't be found.

She and Asfandyar both froze, not moving a muscle, their limbs cramped and strained.

"Gulalai-sahiba, I'm so sorry for my servant's clumsiness," Palwasha-sahiba was saying. "Here, take this shahtoosh shawl as a token of apology."

"It's no problem at all—thank you so much!" Gulalai answered, voice high. "Come now, won't you join me for tea in my rooms?"

"Yes, of course," Palwasha-sahiba replied.

"And bring your servant as well!"

The voices were growing distant now, and Durkhanai released a breath she didn't realize she was holding when the room finally fell silent once more.

"I think they've gone," Asfandyar whispered. The trunk creaked as he eased open the lid, revealing the empty changing room.

"It's okay," he said, stroking Durkhanai's hair with his now free hand.

She hadn't realized she was still clutching his other hand.

"Yes," she said, clearing her throat. "Shukria."

Fresh air kissed Durkhanai's cheeks as she stepped out, and she sighed with relief, stretching. It was then she remembered she still had the letter from the locked box.

She read it carefully, then handed it to Asfandyar for inspection.

"Yes, this makes sense," Asfandyar replied, reading about B'rung's need for roads. "I have been there before, and B'rung is exceptionally hilly, which makes the land highly inaccessible. Even within the zilla, roads are underdeveloped, and there is no proper system connecting the villages to the main cities."

The letter continued to describe how Marghazar had such impeccable infrastructure—if Palwasha-sahiba could negotiate for Marghazar to aid B'rung in the building of roads, they could negotiate something for B'rung to give something in return—something the Badshah couldn't refuse.

But it didn't say what exactly.

As they snuck out of Palwasha-sahiba's rooms, one thing was sure: The B'rung zilla was immensely suspicious. They could have been the ones to inform the Kebzu Kingdom of the summit, inciting the attack.

All she needed was proof.

# CHAPTER ELEVEN

*A*djacent to investigating, Durkhanai got into the habit of slipping out some nights to hand out medicine with Asfandyar, trying to reach different villages each time. During the day, she tried to note which homes housed the ill, and they would do as much as they could in the little night they had. They would send one another letters to check if the other was awake, then head out. One night, it rained, so they stayed in the palace, but they sent letters back and forth for hours.

Asfandyar was always awake.

They had an easy alliance, an even easier friendship, and she started to look forward to that time with him, when nobody was watching, and they didn't have to pretend or worry. He didn't have to accompany her, but she suspected he enjoyed that time as much as she did.

Soon, Durkhanai became addicted to the game of it all.

It felt like gambling: the thrill, the risk, always on the edge. She pushed and tested the boundaries each day, waiting to see how Asfandyar would react. They had an easy rapport, and for every nudge she sent, he always nudged back.

Durkhanai had to keep reminding herself she was only working with Asfandyar out of necessity. To exonerate her people and avoid war.

But it was getting harder to convince herself.

So, she focused on the ambassadors other than the wry one from Jardum—starting with Gulalai.

"Your help with Palwasha-sahiba is something I will not easily forget," Durkhanai said at their first opportunity to talk privately. Their alliance was now set in stone, and Durkhanai would repay the favor in kind whenever she could. Until then, she asked Gulalai to trust her—she didn't want to discuss the theory about B'rung until it was confirmed. After all, B'rung and Kurra were still allies.

In return for that trust, Durkhanai sought out an opportunity to speak to the Wali of S'vat. She wondered if her grandmother would know anything about B'rung and a link to the summit attack.

There was a breakfast feast that jummah morning. Durkhanai got ready early, knowing that Dhadi would be the first in the great hall.

She was right.

"Dhadi," Durkhanai called as she entered. They were the only ones there other than maids setting the table with finishing touches of fresh flowers and lit candles. "How are negotiations going so far?"

"They are going well, janaan," Dhadi replied, distracted. She pointed to a server. "The chakore should be on the *right*, not the left." She turned back to Durkhanai. "Nothing to fret over." With a smile, she went to straighten one of the place settings.

"I can speak to some of the ambassadors if you would like," Durkhanai offered, trailing behind her. "You must be so terribly busy."

"There's no need for that, gudiya," Dhadi replied, caressing her cheek. "I suggest you focus on what you do best, which is caring so lovingly for your people."

"I'd like to try my hand at negotiating, Dhadi," Durkhanai said, voice sweet. "Perhaps I can talk to Palwasha-sahiba?"

"I said there is no need," Dhadi said, voice stern. She gave Durkhanai a pointed look.

"Yes, Dhadi."

"You are staying away from that Jardum boy, as I instructed?"

Durkhanai nodded. "Of course," she replied, tummy turning at the lie.

"Good. Now, you go on for the breakfast feast." Dhadi kissed her cheek. "I will arrive promptly."

Durkhanai was dressed for the occasion, stacks of gold chudiyan on her arms, gold jhumkay hanging from her ears and a matching necklace on her neck. Fresh mehndi covered her hands, and a dupatta was draped across her head, falling down to one shoulder. Honey wisps of hair framed her face, and as usual, she was the pretty little princess.

Durkhanai went to stand between Saifullah and Zarmina in front of their chairs, the seat across from her empty until Asfandyar swooped in and pulled it out. His dimples made a brief appearance.

"Did you see that?" Zarmina whispered. Durkhanai's heart caught.

"See what?" she asked innocently.

"Rashid was coming to sit across from you, and Asfandyar took his place."

Durkhanai truly hadn't noticed until Zarmina pointed it out. "That's . . . strange."

"Immensely so," Saifullah said. He gave Asfandyar a withering look, and Durkhanai elbowed him.

"Zara sambhal kay," she told him. "Relax."

"We need to focus on other things," Zarmina whispered.

"Hush now, you two," Saifullah said, looking at Asfandyar. He wasn't paying attention to them—or at least, he was trying very hard to make it look like he wasn't paying attention.

"Hello, friends," Gulalai said, taking in the empty slot beside Asfandyar. He gave her a respectful nod, which she reciprocated. Durkhanai wondered what the alliance between their zillas was like. Whatever it was, the two ambassadors seemed comfortable around each other.

A quick jab of jealousy pricked her, and it only grew when Asfandyar spoke.

"Shirin says salam, by the way," he said to Gulalai. "She hopes you received the dried apricots she had sent over."

Durkhanai furrowed her brows. She did not like him taking another girl's name. Gulalai seemed as discontented by the exchange as she was.

"Those were from her?!" Gulalai said, cheeks coloring. "I'll have to discard them, now."

"But you love dried apricots," he said.

Gulalai made an irritated sound. "Yes, what a pity."

Durkhanai wondered what their relationship was: Asfandyar and Shirin's; Asfandyar and Gulalai's; and Gulalai and Shirin's.

She didn't have time to think further. The Badshah had arrived with his wife by his side. Everybody lowered their heads in respect and sat after the Badshah had taken his seat. Durkhanai looked straight which meant looking directly at Asfandyar.

He looked her up and down, giving her the "wah, bhai" head bob. She could read it clearly: He was pretending to be impressed by how extravagantly she was dressed, especially in contrast to how he saw her for the long hours of night. She responded by raising her chin in an *I know* fashion, ignoring his sarcasm. He shook his head with a little downturned smirk. In just a little over a month of knowing him, she could understand his expressions like it was their own private language.

The servants brought out plates of crisp parathas, glistening with ghee, accompanied with eggs spiced with red pepper and sautéed with long, thinly cut onions. Then came the fried puris, served with a yellow potato curry and an earthy chickpea curry. The Badshah began to eat, and the rest of the court followed.

After eating, when everyone began to disperse, she noticed who paired off, and most interestingly of all, Asfandyar remained alone.

It was strange, for he clearly knew how to navigate a crowd. He looked . . . lonely.

Walking on his own, looking out the window, hands clasped tightly behind his back.

And Durkhanai knew she must have looked like that, in the months Zarmina was away from court and Laila Baji was busy in her own home and her grandparents were more king and queen and she had everybody to call her people but nobody to call her own.

Loneliness had different shades—different scents and flavors.

She somehow felt that she understood his.

"Durkhanai, what are you doing?" Zarmina said, grabbing her arm. Durkhanai hadn't even realized, but she was about to approach Asfandyar before Zarmina held her back.

"What?" Durkhanai responded, playing it off. Zarmina shook her head.

"Janaan . . ."

"What?" Durkhanai feigned innocence.

"Don't act. I saw the way you two were looking at each other. He is our enemy; you must remember that. There's a reason Dhadi forbade you from forming too close an acquaintance with him, but do you listen? No."

"Is he, though?" Durkhanai sighed.

Zarmina gave an exasperated sigh.

"I'm sorry," Durkhanai said, taking Zarmina's hands. "Let's leave it."

"No," she replied. "You always see the best in people even when there is none to see. But you must understand: Marghazar will never accept a foreigner. *Especially* when Naeem-sahib has already set his eyes on you for his son. You know I want you to be happy, but you must use your common sense."

That was the problem: She lost all sense when it came to Asfandyar.

"He is an enemy to our land," Zarmina said sadly. "Don't forget that."

But Durkhanai didn't see him as an enemy to her. How could he be an enemy to her land?

They were one and the same.

"You're right," she said, not wanting Zarmina to worry. "I'm sorry for being prickly and unpleasant."

Zarmina shook her head. "No, stop. I'm sorry for being harsh—I'm just looking out for you, you know. I don't want you to be made a fool of."

"I won't," Durkhanai said sharply.

Tears suddenly stung Durkhanai's eyes. She felt entirely misunderstood and like she never would be understood.

"Oh, Durkhanai," Zarmina said, voice soft. "I just don't want to see you get hurt."

Durkhanai nodded, waving her off, trying to ignore the contradictory truth: that she was a chubby crybaby but hated being treated as one.

"Zarmina, stop bothering our dear cousin," Saifullah said, coming to join them. "Come, Durkhanai, let's go riding. It has been so long."

She went with him outside, toward the stables. The mountains were greener now, plush fields of velvet, and the weather was quiet and beautiful, only a little cloudy. The warmest months of the year always took too long to arrive, then left so quickly when they did. Durkhanai couldn't see too far into the distance anymore, but the strong and solid mountains remained constant and sure.

They saddled up and began the ride. Her horse, Heer, seemed apprehensive today, and maybe she was reflecting it off of Durkhanai's own body language. Durkhanai forced herself to relax.

"What did Zarmina say to upset you?" Saifullah asked after some time.

"Nothing, bas vasai," Durkhanai replied quickly.

Saifullah sighed. He wasn't saying much, and although he had always been quiet, this was an added layer of silence. Even when he had difficulty communicating, she could always understand the emotions on his face, the thoughts in his mind.

"Is something the matter?" she asked. "I've hardly seen you."

"You've been too busy," he muttered.

"Sorry?"

"I've been busy," he said, clearing his throat.

"With what exactly?"

He gave her a pointed look, and here, with the mountains and sky as a backdrop, she realized suddenly what a man he had become, a thick beard covering his face. And something deeper: dark circles under his eyes, something somber and sad in his expression.

"I've been watching the ambassadors," he told her. "Learning. Contemplating." He gave a pause, deciding on his next words. "Trying to save our people and our land."

He sounded bitter, almost accusatory.

"If you want to say something," she said sharply, "just say it."

He looked at her, gaze heavy. "Do you think perhaps the Badshah is wasting his efforts? Against the Lugham Empire?" he asked, voice hesitant. "That perhaps he is being blinded by vengeance at the cost of his own people."

"How could you say that?" Durkhanai asked. "Everything Agha-Jaan does is for his people."

"Yes, but intentions and actions do not always align in their purity."

Durkhanai furrowed her brow. Where was this coming from? Saifullah had never been so discontented before.

"Forget it." He smiled at her in a way that said she would never understand.

Durkhanai felt like she was disappointing him, somehow, but she couldn't tell how. Before she could prod him further, he rode ahead, leaving her, heart stinging. She could have caught up, but she didn't.

She just watched the distance between them grow and felt a greater distance in what she knew and what he was telling her.

The feeling only grew that evening when she was wandering her marble halls and found Saifullah suddenly slipping out of a narrow hall. She was far enough away that he didn't see her, though he did look around to make sure he hadn't been caught before hurrying along.

Durkhanai approached where he had come from and realized how he had suddenly appeared: He had exited one of the passageways. Perhaps it was a coincidence, she told herself. But she thought about where that passageway led, specifically, just in case.

The clearest path from there led to the eastern part of the palace, where many of the rooms for guests were.

It was also where all the ambassadors were staying.

Durkhanai didn't understand. Hadn't he said he'd been busy? What exactly did that mean? She told herself she would ask Saifullah about it later—find out who he had gone to see or what he had gone to do.

For now, she saw her grandmother approaching and met her halfway.

"What are you up to, meri jaan?" Dhadi asked, kissing both her cheeks.

"Mm, just wandering," Durkhanai replied, cuddling into her grandmother's side. "What about you?"

Her grandmother gave a dramatic sigh. "Tumhe toh pata hai. Work never ends. I'm off to see Doctor Aliyah and discuss medicine distribution."

Durkhanai stilled. Was that a pointed comment?

"Oh. Good." Durkhanai forced an innocent smile. "How is that going?" She bit the inside of her mouth. She hoped nobody had noticed the missing vials. Or if they had, that they would not suspect her.

"We are giving priority to those families with their men on the front," Dhadi explained. "While more medicine is being made." She paused, looking at Durkhanai intently. "It is a very meticulously set up system."

One that Durkhanai was interfering in. Durkhanai swallowed. "Good idea."

What would she say if Dhadi asked about the "guardian angel?" She had lied to Rashid, but she did not know if she could do the same with Dhadi, or even if she could do it plausibly.

"I know you do not understand why we are not distributing it all immediately," Dhadi said. "But you must trust that we know what we are doing."

"Of course, Dhadi," Durkhanai said, hoping she did not look as guilty as she felt. "I understand."

"I am glad that you do." Dhadi smiled. She reached over and pinched Durkhanai's stomach. "Do I need to have Doctor Aliyah send you more vitamins? You're too thin."

Durkhanai let out a startled cry. "Dhadiiii," she replied with a pout. "I am more than healthy."

"I'll have the cooks make you halwa drenched in ghee, that'll do you good," Dhadi replied, unbelieving. "And I won't hear anything more."

"Acha, okay, Dhadi," Durkhanai agreed, releasing a little laugh. Her grandmother looked at her closely. Heart beating fast, Durkhanai called on every ounce of willpower she had not to look away—doing so would surely raise Dhadi's suspicions.

Instead, Durkhanai smiled reassuringly. Dhadi pinched her cheeks, dark eyes warm.

"Acha, chiriya," her grandmother replied. "Now I'm off. Go, gudiya, continue your wandering. Let your heart lead the way; you'll find what you're looking for eventually."

Her grandmother left her to attend to some important matters, not taking Durkhanai along with her.

She released a long breath. Durkhanai pressed a hand to her heart, trying to steady its rapid beating. Guilt needled through her to be deceiving her grandmother, but what choice did she have?

Taking measured breaths, Durkhanai went to the window. The wind sent her open hair into a frenzy of honeyed curls around her face, and she let it, inhaling the fresh air.

A little while later, another joined her.

He rested his hand on the sill beside her legs, and she noticed his beard had grown in longer. The setting sun made his face glow golden, his eyelashes casting long shadows onto his cheeks.

He said nothing. Neither did she.

They just kept one another company, and any unpleasantness she had felt that day drifted far, far away. Zarmina's worry and Saifullah's disappointment, it all faded away, like clouds after losing their rain.

Asfandyar turned to look at her, and when he smiled a soft smile, her heart felt full, like she had just drunk the sweetest cup of chai on a cold afternoon.

She had read about love: the all-consuming kind. She had always been in awe of it, sort of like it was magic, almost like it wasn't real. And she so desperately wanted it to be real.

Later that night, standing on her balcony, the night air was a warm embrace. May brought with it the sweet and endless days covered in a soft rose gold sheen. Leaning on the railing, a sigh escaping her lips, Durkhanai wondered.

She wondered and wondered and wondered, looking up to the stars, sprinkled across the horizon like raw sugar, and she plucked them from the sky, let them melt in her mouth.

If she stuck out her tongue, would it be stained gold with starlight or navy from the night sky?

# CHAPTER TWELVE

*A* few days passed without any further leads regarding
Palwasha-sahiba. Then, while Durkhanai was taking
a stroll, she noticed Palwasha-sahiba and Rukhsana-
sahiba engaging in what seemed to be an intense debate. Palwasha-
sahiba seemed tense, listing to one side as she spoke past her stutter.

As Durkhanai neared to listen in, Rukhsana-sahiba noticed her
presence. The pair quieted.

"Shehzadi," Palwasha-sahiba said, voice sweet. The ambassadors lowered their heads with respect, waiting for her to pass.
Durkhanai was long out of hearing range when she turned and saw
they had begun talking once more, Rukhsana-sahiba angry and
Palwasha-sahiba frustrated.

It made sense.

B'rung most probably did not want to be allies with Teerza and instead wanted to be allied with Marghazar, which would rightfully upset Rukhsana-sahiba.

But Durkhanai was merely theorizing. To learn more, later that day, she went to Rukhsana-sahiba's room. It was a little rude to come unannounced and uninvited, but this was her palace. She would not be ignored again.

"I've called for kava," Durkhanai said, smiling. Rukhsana-sahiba looked up from her desk, where she was reading through correspondence.

"Shehzadi," she said. "I must say I am in no mood for tea at the moment."

"Then perhaps you will keep me company."

Without waiting for a reply, Durkhanai made herself comfortable in the seating area of Rukhsana-sahiba's room, motioning for the maids to bring the green tea in. A maid poured her a glass and stirred in sugar. With a resigned sigh, Rukhsana-sahiba came and joined her, nodding to have tea poured for herself as well.

"And to what do I owe this immense pleasure?" Rukhsana-sahiba replied, sitting across from her. Her lips turned upwards, but it was a poor attempt at a smile. Rukhsana-sahiba was a middle-aged woman, face slightly wrinkled, but her dark brown eyes were sharp.

"I just thought we'd chat," Durkhanai replied, fingers warming from the teacup. "I'd like to know if you knew anything about the tragedy of the summit attack—the sooner we find the true culprit, the sooner this awfulness of war threats can cease."

"Tragedy?" Rukhsana-sahiba repeated. She blinked. When she spoke again, her voice was steel. "Do not sit here and pretend to understand my grief, Shehzadi. You did not see the blood of your brother staining his dreams."

So, the Wali of Teerza had been her brother—that ruled out Teerza being involved in any way.

"Though you may not trust me at my word, I truly am sorry for your loss," Durkhanai said, voice gentle. "We are not your enemies. I assure you. We wish to discover who was behind that egregious attack just as much as you do."

"Your honeyed words will have no effect on me." Rukhsana-sahiba shook her head. "Perhaps, instead of attempting to wheedle information from me, you should be a good little Shehzadi and focus on your people." Rukhsana-sahiba's expression sharpened. "I hear whispers of unrest because of the wars against the Luhgams in the east and the Kebzus in the north. A shame, really." She smiled, then sipped her kava.

Durkhanai pressed her teeth together. This again, with the joining of tribes into a united nation. Even united, Marghazar would be barely stronger and probably, inversely, would be weaker from carrying the other zillas' weight.

"It is a thing to consider," Durkhanai said, trying not to be hostile. It seemed the conversation was over. She stood, telling herself to give Rukhsana-sahiba a chance. A united nation was Teerza's main objective. Of course she would be pressing for it, even now.

Despite how antagonizing Rukhsana-sahiba was, Durkhanai still wanted to believe she was good at heart. Durkhanai tried to see it from her perspective. Rukhsana-sahiba was just looking out for her people, same as Durkhanai. Plus, the Shehzadi was young and impetuous and spoiled in her eyes. It must be difficult for an older woman to speak to a teenager.

"Khudafiz," Durkhanai said, taking her leave. Rukhsana-sahiba nodded, lowering her head in respect. Only when Durkhanai reached the door did she offer her parting words.

"If only Marghazar had allies in the other zillas," Rukhsana-sahiba said. "If we were all united as one nation, we would be undefeatable."

Durkhanai did not turn. She left without another word, mind spinning.

Spent from the meeting, Durkhanai went to visit her people, expecting the love she often received.

But today, something was different. Something was buzzing, like bugs around spoiled meat—they lingered but did not attack.

Until somebody broke the silence.

"Would unification be so awful, Shehzadi?" a young woman, Shazia, asked her. Durkhanai saw the mother give her daughter a warning glance, but Durkhanai smiled to let them know it was all right.

"Would it not make us stronger to fight our wars?" Shazia continued.

"We are going through a troubling time now, Shehzadi," her father added, emboldened. "My three sons off to war with no news of return, and Shazia ill a few weeks ago. We were among the lucky who were blessed with medicine mysteriously in the night, but what of all those who were not so blessed?"

"I understand your qualms," Durkhanai replied. "But we have *always* been against the unification of the zillas into one nation. It would only spread our resources even thinner than they already are."

"Yes, but the times are changing," he replied. By then, a few of the neighbors had joined in to see what Durkhanai would say.

They regarded the Shehzadi with something that flavored strongly of disillusion.

"Would it be truly so horrible to consider it, at least?" someone said.

"The Badshah did not even attend the summit meeting," someone else added.

"Why not hold another, just to give it a chance?"

"The wars against the Luhgams in the east and the Kebzus in the north have lasted too long."

"If Marghazar had allies in the other zillas, if we were all united as one nation, perhaps we could defeat those imperialists once and for all!"

Nobody was being outright accusatory, but she heard the undertones of vilification directed toward the Badshah.

She had heard those words before—from Rukhsana-sahiba. Had she been speaking to the people, planting these seeds of discontent? The people were distressed enough, and if Rukhsana-sahiba was meddling . . .

"I will speak to the Badshah," the Shehzadi coaxed. "We have not ruled out any options, and we will do what must be done."

Even as she persuaded the public toward contentment again, Durkhanai knew the creation of a united nation wasn't just a horrible idea, it was impossible. Waving off her anger at Rukhsana-sahiba's manipulation, Durkhanai considered the situation logically. Even if the summit had not been attacked, Durkhanai doubted the five Walis would have come to agreement on a single thing.

Joining with them would only hold Marghazar back, tie them down, and anyway, the other four zillas would never reach accords. It would merely be a struggle between the four leaders over the immense power of so many people, such a vast stretch of land.

Marghazar only ran so smoothly because the decisions ran through one main person—the Badshah. Throw in four more different opinions and a united nation would be taken over by imperialists before it could even celebrate its inception.

But there was only so much Durkhanai could say. The people would not understand. Disheartened, she made her way back to the palace. Durkhanai went to her grandmother's courtyard, which connected her wing to her husband's. There, she found Agha-Jaan and Dhadi soaking in the sun; Agha-Jaan reading a book and Dhadi's lips moving as her fingers rolled over a tasbeeh.

"How is my little Shehzadi faring?" Dhadi asked, smiling sweetly. Durkhanai gave a dramatic sigh. She sat by her grandmother's feet and laid her head on Dhadi's lap.

"Kya bataon," she replied. "Some people are determined to see us as the villains, no matter how I explain it."

"You mustn't worry, meri jaan," Dhadi replied, unbothered. "The villain of one story is the hero in another."

Durkhanai had learned this long ago. It all boiled down to perspective. But she had never considered her family being the villains in any version of any story.

"I don't want people to think of us as villains," Durkhanai said.

"Oh, gudiya," Dhadi said, stroking her hair. "Someone must be, in the end."

Agha-Jaan opened his eyes, his gaze warm on her. He reached into the fountain and sprinkled water onto her cheek. Durkhanai wrinkled her nose, smiling.

"Sometimes, that someone is us," the Badshah said. "Don't you remember when you were a little girl, so small you could sit just on my one knee, and you would sniffle and cry whenever we stopped you from doing anything at all?

"Did we not look like the villains then, in your small little mind, when we told you not to go too close to the mountain's edge or not to near the roaring fire or to head into the rushing stream?

"You would pout and fuss, seeing us only ruining your fun, not knowing we were only doing what was best for you," the Badshah said. "That is what it is to be a ruler: to be as the parent—sometimes good, sometimes bad—but always, *always* doing what is best for those who you love."

She still remembered how indignant she would become whenever stopped from doing what she pleased; how furious. It could have been something so small as not being allowed sweets too close to dinner, and she wouldn't speak to Agha-Jaan, suddenly a tyrant, for a whole twenty minutes.

Durkhanai would just stand there, arms crossed, pouting, until she was given her way.

She supposed it was similar with the people; they didn't understand the nuances of everything occurring, so they could not comprehend the actions being taken or the decisions being made. Durkhanai wished she could explain it all to everyone, to hold all her people close, but it was infeasible.

They had to trust what she was doing came from a place of love.

"You cannot please everyone," Dhadi reminded her.

"Nor can you befriend everyone," Agha-Jaan added.

But she wanted to. She wished to keep everyone content.

# CHAPTER THIRTEEN

In what had become routine, Durkhanai and Asfandyar slipped away from the marble palace, bags full of medicine, and began distributing at a nearby village. Today's run was a second trip to Kaj'li, her favorite village and thus the first to be receiving a second visit from the "guardian angels."

But as they finished their route, they saw a figure walking through the shadows ahead of them. Face covered, the figure carried a large bag. As Durkhanai crept closer to get a better look, the figure slowed their pace.

"Who is—" Durkhanai started, but her voice was cut off when Asfandyar's hand slipped over her mouth.

"Shh," he whispered, finger to her lips.

He pulled her into the foliage. The figure turned to look over her shoulder, and as she did, her chaadar slipped to reveal her face.

Palwasha-sahiba.

"What is she doing?" Durkhanai whispered.

"We're about to find out."

Palwasha-sahiba walked down a trail. Slowly, Durkhanai followed her, maintaining her distance and shrouding her face with her chaadar, as well. Asfandyar followed suit, masking himself.

Palwasha-sahiba slowed her pace, pausing. She seemed to be inspecting something, but from this distance, Durkhanai couldn't tell what. Perhaps the roads?

Or was she lost?

Durkhanai inched forward, trying to get a closer look, but just as she did, she saw Palwasha-sahiba's entire body tense.

The ambassador began to run.

"Why is she running?" Durkhanai hissed as she and Asfandyar began to run after her. But Palwasha-sahiba was fast and already twenty paces ahead of them.

"Follow me!" Asfandyar said, grabbing her hand.

He cut through the trees, pulling her along with him, and for a moment she doubted him—then she saw; Palwasha-sahiba ran parallel to them on lower ground. Durkhanai quickened her pace, getting ahead of Asfandyar, branches snapping against her arms as she ran.

Until someone intercepted her path.

It was a group of men, and from the look and smell of them, they were drunk.

Durkhanai scrambled to pull her chaadar up to cover her hair and face. As she did, Asfandyar stepped in front of her, breathing heavily.

"Are you the little bandits handing out medicine?" one of the men asked.

Caught up with Palwasha-sahiba, Durkhanai and Asfandyar had gotten sloppy—they hadn't been watching their own backs.

"Not quite," Asfandyar said. His hand slipped into his pocket, and before anybody could react, sand flew into the air. It briefly blinded the men, and a moment was all they had.

Asfandyar grabbed her hand, and they ran.

Their feet beat against the ground, and the sound of the men quickly followed. Asfandyar quickly veered left, pulling her out of the forest and into an alley with him.

"Go on," he told her. "I'll lead them another way."

"No," she protested, grabbing his arm. "We stay together."

"*Go*," he insisted. "We already lost Palwasha-sahiba. At least take the last vial to the child who needs it. I will meet you there when I've lost them."

Durkhanai's face scrunched with anger.

"*No*," she said simply. "Don't try and tell me what to do."

"I wouldn't dream of it, Durkhanai," he said her name with extreme tenderness. "Please. The child needs his medicine."

There was urgency in his voice—and no time to fight. Durkhanai pushed him away from her and ran before she could change her mind, thoughts spinning from Palwasha-sahiba to where she was to deliver the medicine.

The house was a few blocks away, home to a little boy named Mahmud, who spent every free moment he had in drawing little pictures. He was the boy who had drawn her on top of the highest mountain peak, her crown made from the rays of the sun.

When she had seen him last, he was too sick even to play games with his brothers in the streets or to draw anything at all. He had been burning up with fever, his throat and nose clogged with mucus. He'd barely been able to talk. Durkhanai had especially saved medicine for him.

She ran toward Mahmud's home, not stopping to look back for even a moment, just pushing forward.

Until a large man came into her path.

Durkhanai didn't know if this was one of the men who had been chasing them or someone new. She pulled her chaadar to cover half her face, holding it tight around her shoulders with the other hand. Tightening her grip on the last medicine vial, she masked her panic into the appearance of a feeble young woman.

"You there," he said, voice slurred. "What's a girl like you doing out so late at night?"

He was staggering toward her, his breath wheezy.

"I'm just going home," she said, voice quiet and feeble.

"So late?" He kept getting closer. Durkhanai took a step back for every step he took forward. "I've heard of bandits delivering medicine in the dead of the night to sick villagers," he told her. "Might you be one of the guardian angels?"

Durkhanai's heart sank. She only had one left.

"Yes," she told him. "If you tell me where you live, I can bring you some more tomorrow. I don't have any medicine left tonight."

"I need medicine now," he replied. "My wife—"

"I'm sorry," she said, her voice melting. "I don't have any more, but if you just—"

Her voice cut off into a gasp as his rough hands grabbed her shoulders.

"I *need* medicine," he said. Desperation scratched his throat.

"If you just tell me where you live, I can bring you some tomorrow," she repeated, struggling to keep her voice calm.

Nobody touched her, most certainly not so callously. She wanted to claw his hands off of her.

But he didn't know who she was, and perhaps if it stayed that way, he would let her go.

The man shook her shoulders. Durkhanai bristled, swallowing her anxiety. She could smell alcohol on him. He was sick and angry and drunk.

Where was the accursed Asfandyar when she needed him?

But no. Durkhanai could handle this. She must.

"Sir, take your hands off me," she said, her voice icy. There was no need to mask her identity any longer. She would demand the respect she deserved. "As your princess, I command you to back away."

"Princess?" he repeated. "No."

He shook his head.

"You're just a pretty little fool."

He seized her.

Durkhanai barely released a gasp before he had her pushed against the wall, his body pressed against hers. The alcohol on his tongue was putrid in her face. She turned her cheek, her chaadar slipping from her hair. The night cold was sharp to nip on her ears, but his breath warmed her neck. She swallowed her revulsion as visions of Inaya in this same situation flashed through her mind.

"Let me go," she seethed, baring her teeth.

She shoved him as hard as she could, and he stumbled back. Shock and disgust slowed her sense, and she vaguely thought to reach for the little weapons she had hidden into her jewelry, only to remember that she wore none on these secret trips.

Panting, she moved to run, but he recovered just as she did. Arm locked around her waist, he grabbed her from behind and threw her to the ground, as if she weighed nothing at all. Even with a drunkard, her strength was nothing to his.

Her knees broke the fall, but the sudden collapse forced her hands to pitch forward, sending the vial catapulting from her hands. Durkhanai watched it shatter, so simply. Another day Mahmud would stay ill. Another day he would suffer.

Anger filled her chest like ice. Her hands grasped for anything, anything in reach with which to hit him, when suddenly, a hand covered the man's mouth. His eyes bulged, then closed. His body crumpled to the floor, unconscious, revealing Asfandyar behind him.

Durkhanai stood, filled with the sudden urge to kick the man's head, to run her nails over his skin, though he lay motionless. She shook from withholding the urge. There were no roses then, only thorns laced with poison.

Her hands had closed around a broken branch while she was on the ground. She approached, hands raised to strike, when Asfandyar intercepted her path.

"Don't," he whispered. She opened her hands. The branch fell to the floor.

*Where were you?* she wanted to shout, but she couldn't bring herself to say anything.

It didn't matter: Asfandyar caught the accusation in her eyes.

"I'm sorry," he said. "I didn't mean to take so long."

Durkhanai shook as the anger dissipated, leaving only the trauma. She wanted to cry, to scream—anything. Asfandyar came close, tentative, and she threw her arms around him, grip lethal around his neck.

He rocked from the force, taken aback. She thought maybe he wouldn't react at all. But then he grabbed her with equivalent force, his arms encircling her. He stroked her hair, saying nothing, and she was glad. Durkhanai took quick, short breaths, hyperventilating into his neck. She could feel her heart beating like a hummingbird's in her chest and wondered if he felt it, too. Her knees were collapsing, and he lowered her gently to the ground.

An irreversible eternity passed in those few moments.

"Whenever you're ready," Asfandyar finally said, voice hoarse. She knew she would never be. She didn't want to let him go.

She was cocooned against him, face against his neck. Her hands had fallen to rest on his waist, and she was leaning into him.

She felt safe, but Durkhanai knew she must pull away. Just another moment, she told herself.

One more second.

She forced herself away, holding her hands on his chest to steady herself, and looked up at his face, her eyelashes glittering with unshed tears.

"We lost Palwasha-sahiba, too," she said. "Where had she been going?"

"It's all right," Asfandyar said. "We'll keep an eye on her."

As he spoke, Durkhanai noticed a slice on his lip. She reached over to touch the cut. Asfandyar winced, jaw clenched, but he didn't stop her. "Batameez," she muttered, giving him an angry pout. "Getting yourself hurt."

She remembered something. She reached into her bag and got out a little coconut oil balm.

She attempted a smile. His mouth twitched.

"You and your blasted coconut oil," he muttered, but he allowed her to spread it across his lower lip, which was soft as a cushion. The oil melted upon contact, making his lips glisten. There was excess still left on her finger so she spread it across her own lips, her fingers warm.

Asfandyar stood completely still, watching her finger glide across her bottom lip.

He swallowed.

She felt her heartbeat in her ears.

The sweet scent stayed with them as they made their way back. He kept one arm lightly by the small of her back, guiding her, not touching her entirely, but the heat of his skin was close enough to warm her.

When they passed a well, Durkhanai paused to take water. It tasted strange, as though the whole night had turned rancid, even the air sharply sour.

Despite knowing that it was a bad idea, Durkhanai leaned into Asfandyar, feeling his solid chest against her shoulder. His hand fell to her waist, clutching her tightly, and they were joined at the seams.

Durkhanai's heartbeat was violent against her chest, and she was glad for it. She focused on the staccato, rather than the revulsion from before.

They arrived back in the last whisper of night before dawn. This was where they usually broke apart: him to his room, her to her passageways. But that night, she couldn't let him go.

"Will you stay with me for a while?" she asked, like her voice belonged to someone else.

He hesitated, and she thought she saw guilt trek across his face, but then he nodded.

She led him to the passageways, holding his hand, leading him through until they reached her room. In silence that was neither awkward nor uncomfortable, she crawled into bed, wishing he would join, but of course, he did not. Instead, Asfandyar sat down beside her curled legs.

She was glad he was there. Her stomach felt uneasy, her throat itchy with emotion. But when Durkhanai looked up to Asfandyar from her pillow, she was at ease. Less alone. And she wondered how it was possible she had never tired of the view.

He gave her a soft smile and tucked a curl behind her ear, but his eyes were filled with a grief she did not understand. He ran a hand through his hair.

She didn't want him to go but knew he must.

"Rest well, Shehzadi," he whispered.

And then he was gone.

After he left, she scrubbed her body raw. Even after the sun began to slant into the room, she couldn't get his face out of her head. She was addicted to him, somehow.

She didn't love him—she knew she didn't. But she could grow to. She knew she should cut the thoughts and feelings at their inception before they manifested into something too deeply rooted to get rid of, but she couldn't quite bring herself to butcher this sapling.

It was a soft, quiet thing; she felt a tenderness toward it, even if its thorns pricked her from time to time because, oh, did it smell so succulently sweet.

She could get drunk off just the scent.

# CHAPTER FOURTEEN

When she finally awoke, just a few hours later, Durkhanai's mind was spinning.

What had Palwasha-sahiba been doing out so late at night? Why had she run? Her mind was racing with questions and concerns, theories and secrets. Then, it all gave way as she remembered the man from the night prior: the slow and sickening feeling of losing control. Her whole body hurt and ached. Then, her heart melted as she remembered what had come after; the exact comfort of safety that can only come after a sufficient dosage of fear.

Outside, the weather was stormy, on the verge of rain, and hazy even though it was summer now.

She felt a creeping feeling she didn't know how to describe. A haunting feeling.

Durkhanai had something to say but couldn't taste the exact flavor of the words. When she opened her mouth, nothing came out, and maybe she knew what it was, deep down, but she didn't have the courage to bring herself to speak.

Her head was pounding, but she busied herself with investigating.

If Palwasha-sahiba had done all this to gain Marghazar's favor, there had to be some correspondence, some alliance papers, something.

And she knew where they would be.

Durkhanai grabbed a key and slipped into her passageways without another word.

The passageways were dark and cool as ever. It was refreshing; her skin felt too hot. She lifted a lantern for light and began the route she had memorized by heart, her hand trailing along the wall for guidance at every turn, every corner. She had learned these passageways when she had first arrived at court—she knew every room, every entrance, every exit. The Badshah had made sure of it.

For if one got lost in here, there was no saving them.

A pebble skittered behind her.

Durkhanai turned, straining her ears to hear, but—silence.

Perhaps she had imagined it. She continued walking until she felt a shift in the air—the cool current no longer empty. Footsteps echoed behind her.

With a swift movement, Durkhanai pulled the dagger from her side and turned around, holding it up to her follower's throat.

He raised his hands in surrender.

"Asfandyar?" she balked. "What the hell are you doing?"

"Following you, obviously."

She gave him a look.

"Yaar, can we drop the dagger?" he asked, looking down at the tip of the blade that pinched into his chin.

She narrowed her eyes at him, pressing the blade a little closer to his skin. He raised a brow, and she dropped the blade.

"I almost stabbed you," she informed him. "Don't frighten me thus."

"I'll keep that in mind," he replied, rubbing his neck. "Where on earth are you going?"

"Why on earth are you in the passageways?"

"I was coming to see if you were all right after last night," he responded easily. "But since you are wielding dangerous weapons, I can see that you are. Also, you didn't answer my question."

"I'm going to see . . . a friend." It was a poor attempt, but her head was spinning. He gave her a look.

"Right," he replied. "Here I was thinking *we* were friends— allies. But if you are acting suspicious, I must assume Marghazar is suspicious, as well."

"No," she replied. "It's just—I'm actually—I don't . . ." She rubbed her temples and released a sigh. "Fine, you can come along."

He grinned. "If you insist, Shehzadi."

It was just as well. She could use his help in deciphering whatever she found. Besides, two people would be better to investigate in the little time they had before the Badshah would be back from his meeting.

They reached their destination, and Durkhanai pulled a little key out from her waistband. For the more important rooms, the passageways had locked doors, barring entry into the room without a key.

Durkhanai unlocked the door, and they entered the Badshah's private office.

"Try to find anything from the B'rung zilla," Durkhanai told Asfandyar. "Anything to do with Palwasha-sahiba, such as negotiation drafts."

Durkhanai's gaze caught on a painting that rested behind the Badshah's desk. In it, the Badshah and the Wali of S'vat were adorned in finery, as usual, and the Badshah held a baby girl on his forearm between them, the baby's feet sitting in his palm.

Durkhanai smiled. Agha-Jaan always said she was only that small for a few weeks, but he had always loved holding her in one arm.

Durkhanai had been in her grandfather's office only a handful of times, and she had never snuck in before; guilt crept through her, making her dizzy. She put her hand on the table, steadying herself.

She pushed the guilt away—she needed answers.

They began looking around, and she rummaged through some of the books, hoping to find something hidden between the spines.

After some time, she turned to see how Asfandyar was faring and caught him holding her grandfather's seal.

"Don't touch that!" she scolded. It was the Badshah's mark for his correspondence. He dropped the seal and held his hands up innocently.

"Stay focused," she ordered. They continued to read through documents until Asfandyar suddenly stilled.

"Do you hear that?" he whispered.

She didn't, but before she could even react, he rushed toward her. "Someone's coming!"

He grabbed her waist from behind and pulled her toward the bookshelf, hiding in the shadows until they were hidden from plain view. Durkhanai's heart pounded furiously against her chest, but she reckoned it had more to do with Asfandyar's fingers lingering on the bare skin of her waist.

"No one is here," she whispered, taking a step away from him.

But then she heard it, too.

The Badshah and the Wali outside the doors.

Durkhanai pulled Asfandyar toward the passageway entrance, slipping in and easing the door closed just as her grandparents entered.

"This is good," she whispered. "I wanted to be here for when they met later."

Durkhanai left the door open a peak so they could listen. It was impossible to hear once the door closed. They pressed against the wall to catch the conversation. She pressed a cheek against the cold stone, but Asfandyar was warm behind her. She suddenly felt breathless, her feet swaying.

But whatever was wrong with her felt deeper than just his presence. Her head was still spinning. She leaned against the wall.

"Are you all right?" Asfandyar asked, hands falling to her shoulders to steady her.

"Yes."

Durkhanai tried to focus on what the Wali was saying.

"It is confirmed then?" the Wali said. "The Kebzu Kingdom carried out the summit attack?"

"Yes," the Badshah replied. "Read this."

Durkhanai couldn't tell what it was that he was showing the Wali, but no matter. She had been right—it was the Kebzu Kingdom. But they still couldn't provide evidence as to who informed them. Durkhanai continued to listen to the Badshah's conversation, but there was nothing more of substance, and finally, he and the Wali left. When they did, Durkhanai and Asfandyar followed suit and began walking back.

"I didn't get to show you, but I think I found something," Asfandyar said. "It was a negotiation draft: Marghazar would help B'rung in the building of roads if they gave Marghazar a tax in the form of soldiers, I suppose to aid Marghazar against the Lugham Empire."

It was the initial step to annex B'rung into Marghazar. The same thing had happened with Trichmir and Dirgara, when they were smaller zillas of their own, before the Badshah joined them together with S'vat to create Marghazar—a hegemony.

"Hmm. So B'rung is getting a good negotiation with Marghazar after all."

They had a good incentive, then, to inform the Kebzu Kingdom about the summit. Without the summit attack, they wouldn't have had the opportunity to negotiate with Marghazar.

"If B'rung was responsible," Durkhanai began. "Marghazar wouldn't have war, correct?"

"I suppose not," Asfandyar replied. "B'rung would have to pay a price, but only if concrete evidence was found. To avoid war between our zillas, we need something that explicitly shows B'rung was the zilla that informed the Kebzu Kingdom of the summit— only then will Marghazar be exonerated."

"Marghazar won't be blamed for B'rung's actions, even if B'rung did it to gain Marghazar's favor, yes?" Durkhanai asked.

"Precisely."

But how could they get such evidence?

They both contemplated this until Durkhanai had an idea.

"Somebody had to inform the Kebzu Kingdom, correct?" Durkhanai asked. "And I doubt the Wali of B'rung would provide that information in written paper—it would be much too risky. Instead, the Wali must have sent someone to deliver the message."

"If we can get that person here to confess, we would have our evidence," Asfandyar said, finishing her thoughts.

"We could send a letter from Palwasha-sahiba to the Wali of B'rung asking for that witness to come here—we can claim the Badshah wishes to see evidence to prove that B'rung was behind the summit attack before he believes them and forges an alliance?" Durkhanai proposed.

"Yes, but it will take time," Asfandyar replied. "At least five days journey to send the mail and then five days journey back."

There was only one month left. On the first of July, the ambassadors were to leave, and if they were unsatisfied, they would return with armies.

It would never get to that point; if the Badshah had suspicions the ambassadors were unsatisfied, he would have them killed before they could leave, out of spite. At that point, war would already be declared.

The only way the ambassadors were leaving was with a peace treaty.

# CHAPTER FIFTEEN

urkhanai slept through the day, and she woke not feeling the slightest bit rested.

All she could think about was Palwasha-sahiba, Rukhsana-sahiba, alliances, negotiations, wars, threats—everything spinning and spinning. When she closed her eyes, all her body could remember was Asfandyar's skin against hers, their bodies pressed together against the cool stone walls.

But something else nagged at her, too: discomfort and unease. Perhaps all the fatigue of her late nights and worries was catching up to her. Durkhanai wanted to talk to somebody about this all—no, she wanted to talk to Zarmina. But Zarmina would only worry about what a fool Durkhanai was being.

But in the end, she didn't have to say anything; Zarmina came to her on her own.

"You showed Asfandyar the passageways," Zarmina said, voice broken. She stood in Durkhanai's doorway, not coming in.

It wasn't an accusation; it was fact. She was angrier than Durkhanai had seen her in a long, long time.

"How did you—" Durkhanai started, heart hammering. She went to stand, and her head spun from the sudden movement.

"I saw him leaving, at fajr, before dawn," she replied. "I've barely seen you lately . . . and I couldn't sleep after praying . . . so I thought I would come visit—I didn't know you already had a visitor."

"You don't understand," Durkhanai said. Her mouth filled with bile. "Please, come sit with me."

She felt like she was being squeezed into a tiny box. Shame pressed her cheeks red hot like coals sitting on her skin. Zarmina would think the worst, seeing them together so late at night.

"Nothing . . . like that happened," Durkhanai insisted. "We were just discussing something about the illness spreading through the village."

It was a half lie, acidic in her mouth.

But how could she explain? What could she say?

"Whatever it was, you showed him the passageways?" Zarmina asked, incredulous. "You do realize how stupid that was, don't you? The one mode of hidden transportation within the palace—not even everyone in the family knows. You told Saifullah and I only a few years ago, yet you immediately told our enemy? When did you become such a fool?"

"Zarmina, please," Durkhanai said. She was suddenly tired, much too tired. "I don't want to argue."

"You're being nonsensical!" Zarmina said, scolding Durkhanai as if she was a child. "You're so distracted, and you've become obsessed with Asfandyar. People are beginning to notice, and rumors—"

"Enough about rumors," Durkhanai responded, rubbing her temples. "I've done no one harm, who would spread rumors about me?"

Zarmina shook her head. "You still don't know how the world works. This could ruin you, not only as a woman but as the princess."

"I know what I'm doing."

The people knew the truth about her, just as they always had. Who would believe such filth? She was confident nobody would believe it, and if they did, somebody would defend her, just as she defended her people.

"You don't understand," Zarmina said. "Asfandyar is the most important ambassador. You haven't been paying attention, but Saifullah and I have. Jardum is our biggest threat. They are the most favored zilla. They haven't even been negotiating—since clearly their ambassador has been occupied—and they've just been watching.

"They are friends with everyone. It's said Jardum is the middle, the ally that gets goods for the other zillas, the one that gets things done. And it's said Asfandyar knows everyone, everywhere. He's so young, and there are many rumors about how he got such a position so quickly, but some say he works for a man—"

"That's enough, Zarmina," Durkhanai said. "Don't treat me like a child."

"You're acting like a child!"

"Zarmina," Durkhanai warned. "Enough."

"I've tried to be patient with you, but you aren't seeing sense! The only reason he is here is to gain an advantage," Zarmina said, exasperated. "And advantages are not gained but *stolen* from the powerful. We are the most powerful: your crown and your land and your people."

"He isn't like that," Durkhanai tried to say. She didn't want to think he was. She believed in him.

"When the negotiations are finished, he will leave here," Zarmina reminded her, eyes sad. "And you will never see him again."

"I *know*," Durkhanai insisted, but Zarmina wasn't finished.

Zarmina shook her head, turning to leave. She stopped, turning back to say one last thing before she went, her face cold.

"When you are left standing alone at the end of the day, I wonder if he will be enough for you."

---

Durkhanai fell ill that evening.

She felt it coming all day, but that evening after maghrib, she laid down and couldn't seem to get up. When a maid came to find her for dinner, she found Durkhanai's skin burning with fever.

Of course the entire palace was thrown into a frenzy. Durkhanai was visited by doctors and told what to do: here, change into something warmer; here, drink this medicine; here, lie down and rest.

"Of course you've gone and gotten sick," Zarmina fussed, irritated. "Batameez."

Durkhanai knew Zarmina was worried, and she squeezed her hand. It was the language of sisters, and they were versed in it well.

"Don't worry," Durkhanai said. "I'm fine."

"Yes, I am sure she is," a voice said. They turned to find Gulalai entering. She was shaking her head, exasperated.

"Durkhanai, you're too much," Gulalai said dramatically. "Is this all a ruse for attention because I haven't had chai with you lately?"

"Why, of course," Durkhanai joked, voice faint. "You're such a horrible friend, I hardly see you. I had to do something."

"Yes," Gulalai sighed. "Well, I surrender! I'll be more attentive, I promise. Now hurry and get better soon."

Gulalai reached over and squeezed her other hand. They were both sitting by her legs, and while it was nice to have them so close, Durkhanai was beginning to feel hot.

Sticky.

Saifullah noticed from his seat by her bedside.

"Give her space," Saifullah said, shooing Zarmina away. "You girls and your incessant need to constantly be glued to one another."

Zarmina made a face at him but did as she was told. She and Gulalai found seats on the opposite end of her bed, by her feet.

"Better?" he asked quietly. She nodded.

"Thanks, Lala," she said. She rarely used the word of endearment for brothers; he smiled.

But there was something rooted deep below, something growing. An emotion she couldn't understand. She recalled the passageways, his strange behavior. Even now, how he couldn't properly look her in the eye.

"What is on your mind?" she asked him. He looked distracted, averted.

"You're a good princess, Shehzadi," Saifullah said, hand gentle on her hair. She smiled up at him and saw that he looked . . . sad.

"But?"

"But you are untested, untried," he told her, voice lowering. "What if the Badshah were to do something you disagreed with? Would you defy—"

"That's enough," she said, shaking his hand off. "Agha-Jaan knows best, always."

"Yes," Saifullah said, agreeing with her, but she saw he wanted to say something more and didn't know how.

He looked hopeless, as if her incorrigible attitude toward her grandparents was a source of despair. But she didn't understand. In this, they had all always been resolute.

Durkhanai suddenly felt severed from something vital, the blood between her and Saifullah ebbing.

"Saifullah—" she started, but he cut her off with a smile.

"You are not feeling well," he said. "You must rest."

She wished to broach the subject once more, to mend whatever had been broken, but suddenly, everybody in the room lowered their heads in respect as the Badshah and the Wali entered together.

The Badshah wore a navy blue jacquard sherwani with an elaborately embroidered shawl; the Wali wore a periwinkle silk gharara and kameez with a jacquard dupatta that matched the print of her husband's sherwani.

On the outside, they were every bit a king and a queen, but their faces were simply her grandparents.

They were worried for her. While they kept their composure, Durkhanai could tell from their pinched expressions just how much her illness had affected them.

"Chalo, chalo," Dhadi said, ushering everyone away. "Come, let our Shehzadi rest."

"But Nano—" Zarmina began, but with a harsh glance from their grandmother, she was silenced.

"Go, now," Agha-Jaan said. "Durkhanai needs rest."

Zarmina, Saifullah, and Gulalai rose and exited without another word.

"Dhadi, Agha-Jaan, aren't you busy?" she coughed. "I know you must have dozens of appointments for the day."

"How could you say such a thing!" Dhadi held a hand to her heart. "Our Shehzadi is sick, and we are too busy to tend to her? It cannot be." She shook her head. "No, we are here with you."

"Yes, jaani, we are here with you," Agha-Jaan said. He came and sat beside her, his face tense with worry.

She wrapped her arms around his neck, felt his beard scratch her cheek. A sob rose in her throat. It was strange: Her grandparents were always around, but she realized she had missed them amidst the stress and struggles of the past few weeks.

He lowered her back onto her pillow and planted a soft kiss on her forehead, holding her small face in his large hands, just like he used to when she had first arrived, when she was a little girl.

She imagined, to him, she still looked so small, despite the more than decade that had passed since that time.

"Meri jaan," he said gently. "I knew visiting the villages so often would come to this. You are too devoted, at your own detriment." Her grandfather smoothed her hair. "Tell me exactly which village you visited, and with whom you interacted with. We will trace this illness and punish whoever it was that gave you this illness."

"Agha-Jaan, it is no one's fault," she said, voice thick. He was just fussing, but he shook his head.

"Gudiya, I cannot bear to see you like this," he said, holding her hand. "But we can discuss that later. You must rest now and get better soon. Doctor Aliyah is preparing the medicine for you, and I've told the cooks to make you something nice."

"Here, drink this now," Dhadi said. She called a maid forward, who brought a teacup full of turmeric milk to Dhadi. Her grandmother brought it toward Durkhanai, who made a face.

"Not dhoodh haldi," she whined.

"*Mhm*," Dhadi clucked. "If you don't drink this, how will you get better?"

"Dhadi," Durkhanai whined.

"Chalo, meri jaan," Dhadi said, and there was no stopping her. Durkhanai drank the milk, wrinkling her face like she always used to. But she drank the milk too fast, and it went down the wrong way. Durkhanai began coughing, making a terrible wheezing sound.

"Maids! Water, now!" Dhadi called, voice panicked.

"*Now!*" Agha-Jaan roared. Durkhanai's eyes filled with tears from the coughing, but she saw how frightened the maids were when they rushed in with water and washcloths, then ran off before they could be scolded.

"There, there," Dhadi soothed, rubbing Durkhanai's back.

"Drink," Agha-Jaan ordered. "Slowly."

He held the cup of water to her mouth, and she drank. The wheezing subsided, and she fell back onto her pillows, catching her breath.

"Uff," Dhadi fussed. "You cannot be left to take care of yourself, that much is clear."

"That is why we are here," Agha-Jaan said, squeezing her hand tight. She nodded, smiling sleepily.

"Meri bachi," Dhadi replied, kissing her cheek. "My little girl."

Dhadi stayed with her, taking care of her like she used to when Durkhanai was too small to take care of herself. Despite how busy Dhadi was, she stayed, more grandmother than wali. Dhadi tucked her into bed that night, wrapping her in shawls and blankets, then sliding in beside her.

"Tell me a story," Durkhanai asked, already drifting asleep.

"Once upon a time, in a very olden time, there lived a king . . ." Dhadi began.

Listening to her grandmother's voice, bundled up warm and tight, Durkhanai was safe. She was taken back to when Dhadi had devoted all her attention to making her feel at home in the summers and after she moved into the palace for good. Durkhanai had refused to be taken care of by nannies, always asking for Dhadi, who would oblige whenever she could. It wasn't easy being the queen or a mother, but Dhadi tried her best.

The next morning, she awoke to Dhadi sitting on a chair by the window, reading the Quran. Warm sunlight streaked through the window, shining onto her grandmother's face. Durkhanai felt like she had been transported to a memory from long ago.

"Good morning," Durkhanai said, stretching. She still felt horrible. Her entire body ached and quaked.

"Ut'gai, meri shehzadi?" Dhadi said, coming over. "You're awake."

She smiled and planted a kiss on Durkhanai's forehead, blowing softly on her face.

"You freshen up," Dhadi said. "I'll call for breakfast and your Agha-Jaan."

Durkhanai did as she was told, and it took much of her energy from her, even with the help of maids. When she came to her drawing room, she found breakfast had been spread across the table, and her grandfather was sitting, waiting for her. She bent down to kiss him on the cheek.

"Assalam u alaikum, gudiya," he said in greeting.

"Walaikum assalam," she greeted back, offering a smile. But by the time she sat down for breakfast, wrapped in a shahtoosh shawl to keep her warm, she was exhausted.

She wanted to crawl back to bed, and Dhadi must have guessed as much because she shot her the Grandmother Look. Dhadi set a plate in front of her full of yogurt, fried eggs with runny golden yolks, and a crisp paratha glistening with ghee.

"You must eat this entire paratha," Dhadi instructed. "I've had it made with extra ghee, so you can get your energy back."

Durkhanai opened her mouth to protest and Dhadi only sharpened the Grandmother Look.

"Yes, Dhadi," Durkhanai conceded, beginning to eat.

The food was delicious, but Durkhanai hardly had an appetite. She could barely swallow a few spoonfuls of sweet yogurt. She was scheming a way of getting out of eating it all when Dhadi reached across the table to pour herself more tea.

"Agha-Jaan," Durkhanai whispered, nudging her grandfather when she thought Dhadi wasn't looking. She gestured to her leftover paratha, and her grandfather chuckled. He nodded, and she discreetly slid her bread onto his plate.

"I saw that," Dhadi said, sipping her chai. Durkhanai laughed.

She *had* missed them.

Even though she always saw them and nothing had changed, really, it hadn't been just them in quite a while. She missed being a little girl . . . sometimes.

"How are negotiations with the ambassadors going?" Durkhanai asked. "Is everything—"

"Nothing about that, gudiya," Agha-Jaan cut her off. "You mustn't worry."

"So you don't have to get back?" Durkhanai asked. "I'm sure you are terribly busy. I can manage on my own."

"Nonsense," Dhadi tsked. "We have nowhere to be but here, with our granddaughter."

"You used to not even eat if it wasn't with us," Agha-Jaan reminded her.

"Oh, how you would fuss!" Dhadi added.

"Do you remember the first summer you came?" Agha-Jana asked. "Just to visit, when you were four or five, I believe. I hadn't seen you in a year, and by Allah how much you grew!"

"Itni moti," Dhadi recounted, laughing. "So chubby and fat."

"Aur kitni shararti," Agha Jaan added. "So mischievous, always running around, keeping us all busy."

"Hai, you gave us such trouble," Dhadi said, shaking her head. "You wouldn't listen to any of the nannies or maids, so I had to take care of you myself. And you would only sit to eat if it was in your Agha-Jaan's lap."

"And even then, you would feed *me* one bite, *then* eat one yourself," Agha-Jaan said. She remembered it, vaguely. Sitting on Agha-Jaan's lap like it was her personal throne.

How patient they had been with her, indulging even when she was at her brattiest.

"And you insisted on bathing down in the creeks whenever it got too hot and sunny," Dhadi recalled.

"Those were the happiest days," Durkhanai said, smiling at the memories. When it was just them three. It felt like another lifetime. An entirely different world even.

Bathing in the creek always made her feel more at home, rather than the elaborate bath and maids that always awaited her in the palace. Down in the creek, the water was always deliciously icy, straight from the glacier, and Agha-Jaan would hold her in his arms. She remembered being so small but so safe.

"But once, the current was too strong," Agha-Jaan said. "You got carried away."

"Ai, januman," her grandmother winced. "Don't talk about that. My heart still breaks just thinking about it."

"But you saved me," Durkhanai said. "I remember swallowing gulps and gulps of ice water, eyes burning, and then I was in the sun again."

Agha-Jaan had held her so tight, covering her entirely. She remembered she hadn't even been afraid, not even under the torrent—she had known Agha-Jaan would be there, no matter what.

"I would never let anything happen to you," Agha-Jaan said firmly. "It was true then; it is true now. You mustn't ever worry."

# CHAPTER SIXTEEN

ne week passed in illness.

One week full of sleep and medicine and home remedies. A week of Dhadi in her bed and Zarmina by her side and Saifullah checking in.

One week without seeing Asfandyar.

He hadn't come to visit, not even in secret, which he could have. Durkhanai gathered her courage to go see him. She had a feeling he would be around, somewhere close by. If she knew him at all, he would be in her library. One night, when she was alone, she made her way there, on the edge of her private wing. She felt something pulling at her, nudging. Someone had once said that love without intuition was not love at all.

And she was right. Asfandyar was moving to leave as she neared the windows.

"Ambassador," she tried to tease. "Are you following me?"

She offered a soft smile with all the energy she had.

He sigh-laughed, rerouting to walk beside her. "Why, of course," he replied. "Where to next?"

"Surprise me," she dared, raising a brow. He smiled, but his eyes were sad.

Durkhanai suddenly felt that she had missed something. She hated to be asleep when everyone else was awake. She could tell something was wrong, but she didn't understand what, as though they were suddenly communicating in a dialect she didn't fully understand. She could understand the emotion but not the meaning or the context.

Asfandyar wasn't saying anything. He sat down, resting his head in his hands. She wondered if the concern was for her health.

"I'll be good as new soon," she told him.

But no, it seemed to be something deeper. He looked like he wanted to say something—guilty almost. Like he'd broken her heart. Or like she'd broken his.

He looked up at her, and his face was entirely too raw.

"I don't understand," she said finally, catching his eye.

"Sometimes we see what we want to see; sometimes we see the truth," he said. "But only if we are lucky are the two the same."

She still didn't understand, but he didn't elaborate. She wanted desperately for things to be okay between them. Something had happened.

"Have you noticed any strange behavior from Palwasha-sahiba?" Durkhanai asked, trying to bring them both back to their alliance. "In case she goes out again. We must find out what she was doing—who she was meeting."

Asfandyar shook his head. "Nothing. And no word from the Wali of B'rung yet, either, I assume?"

"Nothing." Durkhanai had told the postage officer to inform her first if any mail came for Palwasha-sahiba and to bring it to her before alerting her of its arrival. But nothing had come.

"Time is running out," Asfandyar said.

"I know." She felt like a river flowing toward a waterfall: inevitable, uncontrollable. They had just two weeks left to find out who was truly behind the summit attack, and while they were getting close, it wasn't enough.

They needed proof. But Durkhanai's mind was spinning.

"I went to Kaj'li and visited Mahmud," Asfandyar said. "He's doing better. I sent him your regards."

She wondered why he had done something so deeply intimate, something that tethered them together. She knew she should admonish him for being so public about their friendship, or whatever it was between them, but sick and sleepy, she couldn't be bothered anymore.

"And the rest?" she asked. "I have the privilege of medicine," she added. "But many don't, so you must still go out and distribute without me."

She needed her people to be strong if war truly was coming. Asfandyar nodded again, but he was like a wilted flower—lifeless.

Durkhanai hadn't realized how much she had missed him. He was sitting on the seat in front of her, head bowed.

Suddenly feeling reckless, Durkhanai held him against her.

He hesitated for a moment, resisting, but then he sighed. She felt the energy seep from his skin as his arms came around her legs. He rested his brow against her belly, his nose grazing the soft skin above her waistline.

She was dressed but felt completely undressed, her limbs turning to liquid.

Durkhanai swayed slightly. Asfandyar caught her arms, looking up. The contact was broken.

"You've overexerted yourself," he told her. "Are you feeling faint?"

She nodded. He offered her his arm. Wordlessly, they walked back to her room. A guard gave her a strange glance, but she was so disoriented, she barely waved him off. Asfandyar led her to her room, then waited by the door, unsure.

"Aaj jaane ki zid na karo," she whispered. "Don't go."

He led her into bed, piling her blankets on top of her. She wanted so badly to sleep but felt she would miss something pertinent if she did.

"I'm supposed to drink that," she said, seizing onto the excuse to point out an orange-yellow liquid in a teacup. She made a face.

It was turmeric mixed into warm milk and cardamom, mostly probably also mixed with other home remedy spices. Asfandyar brought it to her, and she shook her head.

"No," she said, pouting. "It tastes horrid."

Asfandyar gave her a face, and she turned her cheek, knowing she was acting like a child. She wanted to see if he would indulge her, and though he ordinarily wouldn't, today he did.

He sat down on the corner of her bed. "Drink," he said. She turned her cheek further away. "Tch, Durkhanai."

Her name on his tongue sent a shiver through her. He put an arm over her legs for balance, curving his face over to meet hers.

"Mm-mn," she whined. He shook his head at her.

"It isn't so bad," he said, taking a sip. He wrinkled his nose. "See?" he said, but the word was a grimace. She giggled.

"Fine," she replied. "But you have to drink it with me."

"All right," he conceded.

Asfandyar brought the teacup to her lips, tipping it into her mouth. As the taste hit, she scrunched her nose, making a face, but he didn't move the cup back. She put her hand over his on the cup, pressing down hard, and drank.

"Your turn," she said, wiping her lip with her thumb. Durkhanai watched as he turned the cup to put his lips where hers had been. Not breaking eye contact over the cup, he drank.

Durkhanai suddenly felt very hot, especially under all the wool blankets and shawls. It was June, and the weather had only gotten hotter and hotter.

But she suspected it wasn't the weather.

He handed the cup back to her, and she mirrored his action, turning the cup. Feeling dangerous, she put her lips where his had been and drank the rest.

"Well done," he remarked, standing. "Now rest. You're so drugged, you won't remember any of this when you wake."

He leaned forward and kissed her forehead. When he pulled back, he gave her a soft smile.

"Your hair smells like coconut oil," he murmured.

"I'm sorry," she said, eyes closing. "I forgot the scent drives you mad."

"No, Durkhanai," he whispered. "*You* drive me mad."

# CHAPTER SEVENTEEN

No matter how much time passed after that, how her health improved, how many baths she took, she could feel Asfandyar like a ghost. He was etched into her skin. Her cheeks still flamed remembering his brow against her belly, his lips against her forehead. And she ached for more.

Perhaps what she felt for him was pyaar, in which case, there was still hope; for while pyaar was a lovely affection, it was not so deep-rooted that it could not be exhumed.

So, perhaps this was heavenly intervention, why she hadn't seen him, why they kept missing each other. And it wasn't fair, her heart insisted resentfully, to want him and not have him. But it was an unholy thing to even think.

Is this what love did? Turn one unholy? It was the only word she could use to describe this: the shift in her mood, the aching, the desire, the wanting—him, him, him.

For now, the only thing in her grasp was the shadow of love—long and slanted and faint—but she knew it was not far from the actual shape of love, knew it was not far from the love that would inevitably come.

And then she saw him.

She saw the instant he saw her.

But he didn't turn, just walked straight ahead, jaw clenched.

Durkhanai didn't understand.

Perhaps he hadn't seen her, she thought. He hadn't turned after all—but, no. She knew his body language. He had seen.

He was ignoring her.

But why?

Perhaps it was just this once, she reasoned, but the next day, the same thing happened.

And suddenly, she wasn't running into him anymore, as they usually did. Before, it had almost been like they had each other's schedules memorized, so it was understood they would see each other, even just for those brief moments in passing, after her morning walk, or before the jamaat gathered for Zuhr salah.

It felt like he was staying away from her, somehow.

Why?

Durkhanai got her answer when she was summoned to her grandfather's private chamber. Agha-Jaan stood by the window, his back to her.

Dhadi sat on a chair sipping chai.

"Somebody has made it known throughout the villages that the palace is harboring an abundance of medicine without distributing," Dhadi said without preamble. "And now the villagers are splintering with rage at the crown at a time that we must all be the most united."

"Who?" Durkhanai asked, heart beating fast. "Who told?"

Who had even known? As far as her grandparents were concerned, *she* didn't even know—though she suspected they had caught on to the full truth now.

"That Jardumi ambassador, of course," Dhadi replied, shaking her head. Durkhanai's heart stopped altogether. For a moment, she didn't believe Dhadi.

"Are you—" she began, but Dhadi held up a hand to stop her.

"You're doubting me now?" Dhadi asked, eyes sad. "Yes, I am sure."

"How—"

"You think we didn't notice the missing vials?" Dhadi said, shaking her head. "I know all that goes on in this palace. I warned you to stay away from him; in fact, I remember expressly forbidding it."

"Why didn't you say anything?" Durkhanai replied, heart wilting. "Or stop me?"

"Jaani, we wanted you to feel like you were doing something to help. Delivering a few vials is of no consequence, so long as you were discreet." Dhadi sighed. "But you weren't careful; you trusted someone who was not to be trusted. Now, everyone will have noted the unfair distribution. Bevakoof ban'gai. Naeem-sahib is already vexed by the slow distribution—the people already up in arms to stop working in protest—and now this? It's made matters worse, *especially* considering Naeem-sahib has already expressed interest for you to marry his son."

Rashid—Durkhanai had nearly forgotten about him.

She should have been more careful, especially when Naeem-sahib had already expressed his discontent with her.

She'd been distracted.

Dhadi's face hardened with irritation. "You've made a mess. And now we must fix it. Durkhanai, when will you learn to stop acting like a child and more like a future queen?"

Agha-Jaan finally turned to look at her. The disappointment in her grandparents' countenances stung sharper than a thousand knives. Agha-Jaan remained silent, face stony. He never had the heart to yell at her or discipline her in any manner, but his presence confirmed that he agreed with his wife.

"When you treat me more like a future queen and less like a child," Durkhanai said, voice icy. "You always tell me not to worry and don't involve me in anything. I asked you about the medicine, in the very beginning, but you brushed me off. I had to take matters into my own hands. That is what a future queen does: look out for her people and their health."

"No, bachay," Dhadi replied. "You must be strategic. You cannot act on every whim and emotion your heart sends running through your veins. You must think."

"But, Dhadi, why not just give the medicine out?" Durkhanai asked, exasperated. "Why must you use everything as an opportunity?"

"Because that is what the Badshah must do," Agha-Jaan responded, no longer silent. "You want to be treated less like a child? Fine. You must stop deluding yourself into believing the problems of this world can be solved so simply, that you can give something in return for nothing."

Her throat clogged. Agha-Jaan had never been so stern with her, only Dhadi had ever been. Her eyes stung with fresh tears of frustration.

"No more pouting," Dhadi scolded. "Henceforth, we will treat you as a queen, and you must behave as one. Think twice before meddling. Quell the people's qualms, the unrest that has been growing. You don't want to be a pretty little princess anymore? Fine. Then stop acting like one."

# CHAPTER EIGHTEEN

urkhanai didn't realize how heartbroken she would be. How much her heart would pinch and ache. She couldn't believe she had been a fool, that everyone had been right. What good it had done her to believe he was better than he truly was.

What hurt the most was how wrong she had been. She had valued their friendship, and there was no bigger sin than disloyalty. He had sold her out.

And she never wanted to see him again.

Durkhanai convinced herself she was fine, heart cold, and it lasted only as long as the stretch of time when she didn't see him. But then she ran into him on her morning walk.

Seeing him felt like she'd chewed on glass.

Durkhanai tried to walk past him quickly, avoiding eye contact, but he intercepted her path.

She leveled a glare at him, and he swallowed hard, his hand running through his curls.

"I need to talk to you," Asfandyar said, eyes desperate. His face was full of raw emotion. She could read him like a book, still, but she didn't understand all the words. Everything inside of her felt singed; she tasted her charcoal heart in her mouth.

She wanted to spit it out.

"There is no need," she said calmly, feeling savage. "You will always be alone."

He stopped in his tracks, and she walked away, her back straight as steel, chin high.

She finished her hike, taking measured breaths through her nose, letting out the steam. She passed a little creek, and inside, the water was stone gray, like liquid cement. And suddenly, being outside reminded her of that first hike, so, so long ago now, when the ambassadors had first arrived.

It made her sick.

She kicked a rock into the water, watched it splatter.

Durkhanai went back inside the palace, her mood more bitter than karelay. When she went to her rooms, she found Gulalai sitting on one of her couches, reading a book, her cane resting beside her.

"I've been waiting for you," Gulalai said, not looking up from her book.

"If you tell me I told you so, I'll cut out your tongue and wear it as a necklace," Durkhanai seethed. She plopped down beside Gulalai, arms crossed, face sour.

Gulalai put her book down.

"Hai Allah! Come now," Gulalai tsked, shaking her arm. "Don't pout."

Durkhanai shrugged her off, face scrunched. Her eyesight was foggy from emotion. She wanted to do something terrible or painful or horrible, but she didn't know what.

"Bas bohat hog'ya," Gulalai said. "That's enough!"

Durkhanai was attacked by a pillow to the face.

"Hey! Ye kya batameezi hai?" she snapped, picking up a pillow and retaliating. She hit Gulalai hard.

"Ow!" Gulalai exclaimed. She hit Durkhanai again, ensuing a mini battle. They hit one another, and Durkhanai had to curl her fingers into the pillow to avoid actually hurting Gulalai, who had no fault in all this.

Durkhanai tackled Gulalai, smushing the pillow into her face, and she found that it was upending all the toxic energy within her—it felt good. They were both laughing.

But as she hit and hit Gulalai, her breathing getting deeper and deeper, she felt something unravel inside of her. Tears sprung into her eyes, and she told herself it was from the pillow blows, though she knew it wasn't. The pillow was knocked from Durkhanai's hands.

She pushed Gulalai onto the plush sofa.

"Ah!" Gulalai laughed. She mirrored Durkhanai's actions, but rather than pushing her, she threw her arms around Durkhanai and tackled her into the cushions, falling on top of her.

Gulalai squeezed and squeezed. They laid in silence, clutching one another, hearts beating in tandem.

"Okay?" Gulalai whispered. Durkhanai nodded.

She was anything but okay, yet she still rose.

"You're right," Durkhanai agreed. "Enough dramatics."

Durkhanai had too much going on to be worried about a stupid boy. She had to continue her investigation, with little under two weeks left until their three months were finished.

And still no word from the Wali of B'rung yet.

Without proof, war was inevitable—and with the illness lowering the people's ability to work and weakening the general public, her people were in no shape for war.

"Now you can focus on the people and civil unrest," Gulalai said. "Rather than being distracted."

"I wasn't distracted," Durkhanai snapped, even though she knew she had been.

"Acha, acha," Gulalai said. "You weren't." She bent over to pick up her fallen book, and as she did, a letter fluttered out from the pages.

"Oh, your—" Durkhanai started, reaching for it.

"No!" Gulalai intercepted the letter. Durkhanai stilled. Dread coursed through here.

"Gulalai, who is that letter from?"

"No one." Gulalai waved a hand nonchalantly, but there was no mistaking the color flooding her cheeks. Embarrassment? Shame? Regret? What was it?

How well did Durkhanai *really* know Gulalai? Could she trust her?

"Hai Allah." Gulalai's shoulders sunk. "I can see you doubting me." She sighed. "Very well, here it is."

Durkhanai quickly scanned the letter and saw it was from Shirin, the Wali of Jardum. But there was nothing official about the letter. Rather, Shirin seemed to be . . . teasing Gulalai.

"I didn't realize you were friends," Durkhanai said, trying not to smile.

"We're not." Gulalai made an irritated sound. "Now, I have an idea to cheer you up!" She grabbed Durkhanai's hands and pulled her along into the drawing room. "Let's call for tea! Nothing like chai and samosay to lighten one's mood. You sit right here, and I will be back!"

Gulalai disappeared, leaving Durkhanai alone to her treacherous thoughts.

She didn't understand: She knew he was bad for her and—yet.

And she couldn't even turn to anybody. Not Zarmina or Gulalai or anyone because they had all warned her from the beginning, from the first star that had sparkled in her eyes, they had warned her, told her to stay away from him, told her he would ruin her.

And here she was, ruined. With nobody to blame but her own wretched, cruel heart.

*Ya Allah, help me, please, help me.*

A knock on the door interrupted her thoughts.

"Yes, come in," she called, wondering why Gulalai had bothered knocking when she had just left. But when the door opened, she realized why.

It wasn't Gulalai.

It was Rashid.

"Assalam u alaikum," he said. When she returned the greeting, he sheepishly lowered his head. Pink tinged his ears. *Oh, Gulalai.*

Just what she needed to solve her boy problems: another boy. Excellent.

"Gulalai-sahiba said you wanted to see me," Rashid told her.

"Yes," Durkhanai improvised. "I had some . . . matters to discuss. Will you join me for tea?"

"I would love to," Rashid replied, offering a sweet smile. He joined her at the table, and they both sat.

Rashid reached for the tea.

"I can do it," she offered.

"I insist," he replied.

He poured tea into her cup, asking how much sugar she would like. She allowed him to pour it into her cup and stir, then watched as he did the same for himself. He then moved onto the various little finger foods.

Ordinarily, Durkhanai would put whatever she liked onto her own plate, but she was amused by how endearing Rashid was in his efforts to be a perfect gentleman and impress her.

He was nervous, she could tell, and it was made further evident when he accidentally dropped his napkin to the ground.

"Oh," Rashid said, reaching down to pick it up. Durkhanai watched curiously as he did so, and, just as she suspected he would, hit his head on the table on his way up, causing tea to spill from his teacup.

She refrained from sighing.

"I'm terribly sorry," he said, embarrassed, moving to clean up the mess. He gave a surprised sort of laugh, but she saw the quick knit of his brows, the frown tugging at his lips.

"No, don't worry about it at all," she said, offering her sweetest smile. It was at least nice, she supposed, to have a boy be a fool for her, rather than her being a fool for a boy.

"Yes, well, what did you want to discuss?" he asked, after cleaning the mess. There was a pile of tea-stained napkins lying to the side. The silk tablecloth was stained as well, though she hoped not beyond repair.

"I just wanted to . . . converse with you," Durkhanai improvised. "To be certain all was okay with your family."

His was an important one, allied to the Miangul family for generations.

"How thoughtful," he responded, genuinely touched. "My sister is doing much better now, shukria."

"That's good to hear," Durkhanai replied. She had no idea what he was talking about but assumed his sister had gotten sick. "How did she get ill?"

"She teaches Quran in the villages some days, so we believe she contracted it from there, though she didn't touch anyone or anything, so we aren't quite sure how," Rashid explained.

"Ah," Durkhanai responded. "I hope she recovers soon."

"And how are you feeling?" Rashid asked. "I heard you had fallen ill as well. I had wanted to visit but didn't want to bother you."

"That's so sweet. Thank you for asking," she replied. "I am much better now. I was bedridden for some time, but I got to catch up on some readings, so it proved fruitful."

"You'll have to recommend me a good book," Rashid said. "I haven't read since I was a schoolboy, but I see all the books you have gathered here in the palace and wonder."

"Yes," she replied. "I would recommend . . ."

And they continued on, the conversation pleasant and uneventful and comfortable and unstressful. Durkhanai was at as much ease as she was speaking to Saifullah.

As Rashid went into great detail explaining something, Durkhanai vowed to herself to stop being distracted. Rashid had been in her heart, she reasoned, long before Asfandyar had stolen his way in. She made the intention to later rip all the letters from Asfandyar that she had kept—but she knew, with a sinking feeling, that ripping him from inside of her wouldn't be so easy.

But Rashid could help with that—he was the tribe's golden boy. Marrying him would secure the loyalty of the strongest clan, and it would strengthen ties between the royal family and the nobility.

It was what a queen would do, not a silly girl.

"You support me, don't you?" Durkhanai suddenly asked Rashid, eyes soft. "You believe I am a good princess?"

"I do," he responded firmly. "As do the other noble families. Even with this whole business with the medicine—I understand why the Badshah would wait to distribute it all. Why he had prioritized the soldiers' families. The other noblemen will come to understand, as well. You mustn't worry, Shehzadi."

"You're sure, aren't you?" she asked. "I'd hate for my own people to not believe in me."

It was a pretense. She was exaggerating her own worries to prompt Rashid into helping her. With his family's backing, the other nobles wouldn't dare raise any brows toward her.

Guilt riddled her for an instant, but perhaps this was what diplomacy was: using people. Was the fault hers for manipulating him or his for being so easily manipulated?

And the Wali had said she had to act more like a queen. Maybe this was what it was. Durkhanai knew she was easy to love, that people fell at her every extravagant whim and excessive command.

Rashid fell just as easily.

"If you'd like, I can talk to the other nobles and reassure them," Rashid offered.

"You would do that?" she asked, voice timid.

"Of course," he said with a smile. "Anything to help."

"Shukria," she said, relieved. "I appreciate your support greatly."

"Don't worry, Shehzadi," he said, fondness in his features. He really was too sweet.

"With you by my side, there is no need to," she said, smiling. He ducked his head in embarrassment.

"Well, I'll be off," he said. "Thank you for chai. It was lovely."

"Of course," she said, watching him go.

After he had gone, she let out a breath. Too dense with decorum, she took off some of her jewelry, swapping her heavily embroidered organza dupatta for a simple chiffon one. She left to find Saifullah, aching to be outside.

She found him in his room writing a letter.

"Saifullah," she said, standing in the doorway. "Come walk with me."

"All right, Shehzadi," he replied. She approached, and he casually folded his paper in half, covering what he had written.

"Come," he said, standing up.

She peered over his shoulder. "What are you writing?"

"Oh . . . just a letter to Ammi," he replied hastily. "Nothing important."

"Send Nazo Phuppo and the children my love."

"I will," Saifullah said, not meeting her eyes. "Let's go."

*Strange.*

The weather was warm enough that neither of them needed their chaadars, but they still shivered involuntarily from the mountain air. They began walking through the dense trees, dark green, arching over them, with only little pockets of sunlight peeking through.

"You were the one distributing medicine to the villagers, weren't you?" Saifullah asked, after some time had passed.

Durkhanai nodded. "Was it stupid?" she asked. "Or selfish, maybe. I just wanted to do something to feel like I was helping, but now everybody is angrier than ever."

"I understand," he replied. "I just wish you had told me. I could have helped, you know. I may not be an heir, but I am not useless."

Durkhanai frowned. "I've never thought you useless. I'm sorry you've felt that way, Lala."

"It's all right," Saifullah responded. "Your heart is in the right place. You did what was right, even when Agha-Jaan and Nano couldn't."

"Don't say that," Durkhanai said. "You know Agha-Jaan always does what is best."

"Does he?" Saifullah whispered.

She furrowed her brow. "Why are you questioning him all of a sudden? Has something happened?"

Saifullah sighed. He was closing off again, like he didn't know how to speak with her anymore.

"I'll tell you soon, Durkhanai," he finally said. "It's nothing to trouble over now."

She wanted to ask more but knew he wouldn't budge until he was ready to. The stubbornness ran in them all. And he didn't look worried more than just . . . sad. Or perhaps guilty.

They passed a little creek, and the water looked like blue-gray marbles, looked like glass. If she looked close, she wondered what her reflection would show. But she did not go near, out of fear.

Neither did Saifullah, she noticed.

"Saifullah," she said, remembering. "I saw you leaving the passageways once. What were you doing?"

"Just familiarizing myself with them," he told her easily. "In case anything happens. I haven't been in them much."

"Oh . . . okay," Durkhanai responded. She didn't know if she should believe him, but what reason did she have not to?

But in case *what* happened?

"I'm surprised you even noticed. You've been distracted lately," Saifullah told her. "You . . . haven't been seeing things clearly."

"I'll be better."

"Zarmina will be glad to hear that," Saifullah said.

"Glad to hear what?" a voice behind them said. When they turned, Zarmina stepped up to join them, looping her arm through Durkhanai's. "I heard you were out here, so I decided to see to it that you weren't having any fun without me."

"How could we have fun without you?" Durkhanai replied with a laugh.

"Fret not, little one," Zarmina said, patting her head. "I am here now. And I heard Dhadi gave you a scolding?"

"She did," Durkhanai sighed. "I need to start acting more like a queen."

Neither of them gloated; they just nodded in agreement. Durkhanai was glad. At the end of the day, family was the most important thing. The one constant, the people she could always depend upon. There was no bond stronger than blood, nothing more sacred. She had lost sight of that, but no more.

"Will you help me?" she asked them.

The twins didn't need to exchange a glance. It was understood.

"Of course," Saifullah sighed.

# CHAPTER NINETEEN

hile Durkhanai waited for word from the Wali of B'rung, she focused on her people. The next day, Zarmina and Saifullah accompanied her to the villages for the day. They made their way to the stage in the center of the village, where the people were already gathered in preparation for her visit. Zarmina squeezed her hand, and Saifullah nodded at her.

"Salam! As many of you may have heard by now," Durkhanai began, voice strong. "There are rumors going around that the palace has withheld medicine distribution. I have come to tell you this is only half-true, and there was a reason for it."

"But, Shehzadi, *why* withhold the medicine at all?" a young woman asked. "When so many of us had fallen ill?"

Her voice was not accusatory, merely confused. Durkhanai wished she had the answer to her question, but it was a solution she herself had been searching for.

"It was necessary," Durkhanai said, voice compassionate. "When medicine is made in such large supply, there is easy room for error—for impurities. We wanted to make absolutely sure the medicine was right before sending it to you all—wanted to make sure it would help you rather than make you feel worse. We only risked it for the sickest among you, when it was better to try something than nothing."

Guilt nudged her insides, but she told herself this was necessary. This was no time for the people to be losing their trust in the Badshah or their Shehzadi. It was better for them, anyhow, not to know all the gory details.

What good would knowing do? Durkhanai knew, and all it had done was leave her even more confused. But she had blood binding her to the Badshah; her loyalty would never waver. She could not guarantee the same for the people.

"I assure you," Durkhanai said, projecting her voice loud and clear. "Now that all the medicine has been tested and prepped, relief efforts will be intensified. I will personally work to bring about the swift recovery of all those afflicted."

They spent some time in the village, talking to the people, and by the time Durkhanai made it back to the palace, she was in desperate need of chai and a warm bath. Her heart raced with apprehension as she walked her halls, hoping to and not to run into Asfandyar as she often did, but she hushed her thoughts.

This was her palace. She did not need to avoid anyone.

Durkhanai made it back to her room with her head held high and freshened up for court. She swapped her lighter, traveling jewelry for heavier sets. She changed out of her shalwar kameez into an emerald green zardozi lehenga choli, the long skirt trailing behind her as she walked toward the courtyard.

"Shehzadi!" a voice called. She turned to see Rashid catching up to her.

"Come, let's sit," Rashid said, eyes glittering. "Rest—you need to take care of yourself."

Durkhanai smiled fondly, easing into the soft comfort that Rashid's company brought. He felt so familiar, like a warm shahtoosh shawl wrapped around her heart, keeping her snug.

"So, how has your day been?" Rashid asked as they sat on a bench by the flowers.

Durkhanai considered this and the wonder of him asking such a simple question. Something soft melted inside her as she regarded him, and a smile tugged at her lips.

"My day has been all right," she said. "How about yours?"

"I read that book you recommended to me," Rashid said. "It was quite good, though, I don't know how you manage to read such fictitious stories."

"They're extraordinary fun!" Durkhanai said, defending her books. "Isn't it wonderful to be lost in a story, to lose sense of time and place?"

"Lose sense of time and place?" Rashid repeated, a smile tilting his lips. "Are you sure it's reading you're doing and not smoking opium?"

Durkhanai laughed loudly, surprised by his humor. "Yes, I am quite sure!"

She made a face as if to be offended, but she couldn't help but to continue to laugh as Rashid laughed as well, clearly proud of himself for such a quip.

Then, Asfandyar entered the courtyard and hesitated when he spotted her. She could feel him looking at her, noticing her with Rashid, the two of them alone.

Durkhanai grinned at Rashid, looking through Asfandyar like he wasn't there at all. She was ignoring Asfandyar completely—but she could not ignore the way her heart began to ricochet, a sudden jolt going through her that made her feel a thousand times more alert, a thousand times more awake.

"Rashid-sahib," Asfandyar said quietly, bowing his head in respect. "Shehzadi."

All he did was acknowledge Rashid, who bristled uncomfortably. Both boys were quiet for a few heartbeats, and while she expected it from Rashid, who was usually quiet and shy, it was new behavior for Asfandyar.

For once in his life, he had nothing to say.

She refused to react; she stayed quiet, as well. When Asfandyar continued on, leaving them alone, Rashid let out a short breath through his nostrils, but Durkhanai's heart was beating uncommonly fast. She told herself it was rage; she was still furious with him. She didn't understand why he would tell the people about the medicine without consulting her first, without even telling her.

*But she had been sick and preoccupied; perhaps he hadn't gotten the chance? Or he knew she would advise against it, and he needed it to be done. Maybe he knew it would force a quicker distribution plan. But then why hadn't he mentioned it on that occasion they met in the hall . . . ?*

Durkhanai cut off such thoughts—there was no need to be making excuses for him. If he had wanted to explain himself, he would have.

Just then, Gulalai entered the courtyard. She was passing Asfandyar, who was on his way out, and the two stopped for a moment to talk. Durkhanai couldn't hear them, but when Gulalai laughed, she felt a sharp twinge of jealousy cut through her.

What was she laughing about? She frowned to herself, but forced her face to remain neutral as Gulalai approached.

"Kya chalra hai?" Gulalai asked, sitting down beside Durkhanai. "What's going on?"

Durkhanai let Gulalai link her arm through hers.

"I'll let you girls enjoy your time together," Rashid said, bowing his head.

"Khudafiz," Durkhanai said. Gulalai waved enthusiastically, watching him go.

The instant he was gone, Durkhanai turned to find Gulalai wiggling her brows. "So, how was your tea time yesterday?" she said with a devilish smile.

Durkhanai smacked her arm. "Batameez! What a lousy friend you are! Setting me up!"

"Lousy!" Gulalai repeated, appalled. "Is that how you thank me for arranging one-on-one time for you and Rashid? Your future fiancé? I reckoned I would speed things up. Maybe there will even be a wedding before I go!"

She clapped her hands, excited.

"Bakwas band karo," Durkhanai pouted. "You know it is not in my control. I will marry when my grandparents decide it, and to whom they decide."

It was an excuse. Her grandparents loved her too much to force her marriage.

"Yes, yes," Gulalai said. "And they will have great qualms with you marrying the most important tribe leader's son, will they? Someone whose lineage has been linked with yours in camaraderie for centuries?"

"Gulalai," Durkhanai whined. She didn't want to talk about it or even think about it.

"What?" Gulalai asked, confused. "I thought this was what you wanted?"

Durkhanai didn't know anymore.

As more time passed, she became even more confused.

Throughout the week as Durkhanai waited for proof, she actively spent more time with Rashid. First, because the closer she was with him, the better her relationship with the Yusufzai clan and, by extension, the other nobles would be.

And second, to see if the strange feeling in the pit of her stomach would go away, but it didn't, and she couldn't understand it.

He was well-mannered and respectful and adoring and comfortable. She felt calm around him. They had an easy friendship with clear boundaries. Everything was always exactly in its place, no wrinkles, no crinkles.

Unlike with Asfandyar—she couldn't help to compare—with whom her heart was always racing, with whom she was always on the edge, nudging and being nudged.

Why didn't she love Rashid? It made perfect sense for her to. Everything about him was precisely what she needed, precisely what was good for her.

So why didn't her heart catch on him? She didn't understand. It infuriated her. What a treacherous heart she had. Before, when she had known that maybe they would end up together, the idea of him excited her.

But ever since Asfandyar had been introduced, it was like Rashid ceased to exist. What a cruel heart she had.

How could she keep turning back to Asfandyar, the one who was the worst possible choice for her? Her people would never accept him. All they ever did was bicker. They were both cold and cruel and proud. Ice did not melt ice; fire did not extinguish fire.

Why was this so? What a wretched, wretched heart she had.

Perhaps she could grow to love Rashid. She had held him in her heart for so long, she should still give it a try. It would be so easy, seamless, and everyone would be happy. He was the son of the most important tribe leader. Their union would be most auspicious.

And maybe in the end, it wouldn't matter if she loved him or not because she loved her people, and if this was what was best for them . . .

Durkhanai shook her thoughts away. There was no use agonizing over something that was so far away, when there was so much else going on.

Something she was reminded of the next morning when a messenger knocked on her door at dawn.

"Shehzadi, I have the mail you had requested I keep an eye out for," he said, handing her a letter. It carried the seal of the Wali of B'rung.

"Shukria," she said, dismissing him.

This was it.

And with hardly any time to spare. In three days, their deadline would be over. If the ambassadors truly decided to declare war on behalf of their districts, the ambassadors would be killed on the spot—and no matter how angry she was with Asfandyar, she didn't want to see him killed. Or Gulalai for that matter.

Heart pounding, Durkhanai grabbed a knife, easing open the seal to reveal the letter inside.

It was a short letter, one that she read quickly. Then read again just to be sure.

The Wali had no idea what "Palwasha-sahiba" was mentioning. They were innocent.

But if it wasn't B'rung who told the Kebzu Kingdom about the summit, who had?

# CHAPTER TWENTY

*A* celebration was called for that jummah.

Durkhanai didn't know how her grandparents could be arranging such a banquet when they were all on the cusp of war, but it was the fiftieth year of the Badshah's rule.

To celebrate, feasts were sent to all the villages, boxes of sweets distributed to every home. In the marble palace, a great banquet was held. A canopy was spread over the courtyard, from which fresh flowers and hanging candles dripped down.

The floor of the courtyard was covered in mirrors, reflecting the flowers and candles, creating double the effect. The courtyard opened into an open field, where the flames of candles glittered on pillars and great big bonfires filled the skies. The aroma of firewood was thick in the air, mixing with the charcoaled smell of grilling meat, freshly slaughtered that day. There were tables upon tables of drinks and platters of food: golden and red dishes of biryani, stacks of chapli kababs with mint chutney, rows upon rows of mutton roast.

In the background, folk singers hummed low songs, in tune with the rubabs and dhols.

Everyone was dressed in their finest for the celebration, and Durkhanai spared no preparation; she wore a heavy peach lehenga, intricately worked with silver and gold zardozi, with a matching peplum gown. Her hair was braided and twisted into an updo, fashioned with little pearls. She wore a seven-pronged string of pearls around her neck—Dhadi's—which hung lower than the gold-and-kundan choker that sat on her collarbone.

"Meri jaan, you look splendid," Dhadi said, kissing Durkhanai on both her cheeks. Dhadi herself was a sight to behold, her hair twisted into a simple updo with a gold and pearl set adorning her ears and neck. She wore a deep pink peshwas gown with a delicately embroidered shahtoosh shawl hung delicately on one shoulder: elegant and regal as always.

"Tumhari beti hai na," Agha-Jaan said. "She is your daughter after all."

Dhadi grinned, clearly pleased.

"Woh to hai," she said, self-appreciating. "That is true."

"Agha-Jaan, how can you be so calm?" Durkhanai asked, voice low. "Our three months are finished tomorrow, and we still haven't exonerated Marghazar from the summit attack."

All the time and effort Durkhanai had spent in the past weeks investigating had been for naught: the B'rung lead was a dead end.

The Badshah and the Wali exchanged a private smile.

"Don't worry, janaan," he told her.

"Don't you trust your Agha-Jaan?" Dhadi said.

Durkhanai did, but there was a creeping feeling spreading within her. If they had evidence, why hadn't they told her?

"Come, now, let us address our people," Agha-Jaan said before Durkhanai could argue further. Dhadi and Durkhanai followed him to the front of the room, standing up on the incline of the hill.

The Badshah motioned for one of his attendants to quiet the crowds. The crowd's chattering came to a halt, all eyes turning to the Badshah.

"Thank you, my dear family and friends for joining me in this celebration," the Badshah began. Durkhanai looked to her people: her cousins and aunts and uncles, the nobles and family friends, all the people she had known her whole life—her family.

She felt safe, secure.

"This year marks the fiftieth of my rule," the Badshah said. "A rule that I, as a young boy, could have never imagined. As the third and youngest son, I was never meant to inherit this crown—never meant to inherit these lands or these people.

"After the Luhgams ruthlessly slaughtered my family—my father and my brothers—I had no choice but to take this position. I had been full of grief and rage, just a young boy, then. But I am eternally thankful for the open arms that embraced me after my coronation—for all of *you*, who welcomed and supported me, who made me into a king worthy of its subjects.

"A king is only as good as its people. Marghazar's success comes not from me but from all of you, who work hard every day, who live in peace and kindness and tranquility."

The audience clapped, as did Durkhanai, feeling proud and full of love.

"One final toast, to the one without whom I would be nothing," Agha-Jaan said. He turned to the woman by his side—to his wife. Dhadi smiled fondly, eyes moistening with tears.

"Allah has blessed me with a life partner who is more brilliant than a thousand suns," Agha-Jaan said. "Without you, janaan, the world would know no beauty, no peace, no joy. I am eternally indebted to you.

"May Allah bless you with a life longer than mine so that I do not know how lifeless this world would be without you. May He bless you with infinite health so that I may see your shining smile every day. And may He grant you endless happiness, for mine is bound to yours."

Agha-Jaan lowered his head in respect to Dhadi, the only person in the entire world he would offer the gesture to.

Forty-five years of marriage, and their love had only grown stronger and stronger, like the tree whose roots sunk deeper and deeper into the earth as the years passed. Durkhanai yearned for a love like her grandparents'—one of adoration and respect and understanding. Agha-Jaan and Dhadi were made for each other.

Her eyes involuntarily turned to Asfandyar, and she noticed he was looking intently at her grandmother, something in his eyes she couldn't recognize or place.

"And now, for a surprise," the Badshah said. Durkhanai watched as Marghazari soldiers brought forward a bloodied man, his face beaten, one of his eyes swollen shut.

She gasped along with the crowd when they realized who he was.

A Kebzu soldier.

His uniform was matted with blood and dirt, but they could all recognize it nonetheless.

"I bring before you proof that Marghazar was *not* responsible for the egregious attack on the summit meeting held in Teerza all those months ago—it was the Kebzu Kingdom!"

The soldier fell forward on his knees. Durkhanai glanced across to the other ambassadors to assess their reactions. Gulalai's eyes were hard with vindication, while Palwasha-sahiba had a hand covering her mouth. Durkhanai could not find Rukhsana-sahiba.

"In these past three months, I have spared no resources in investigating, and finally I found this spy, trying to flee our lands—speak now! Tell the people what you confessed to me."

"It is true," the soldier spat. "The Kebzu Kingdom ordered the attack on the summit to keep the tribes weak—an alliance would threaten us. I'm the one who arranged for a deadly explosive."

"And how did you know about the summit?" the Badshah asked. "It was secret information."

"We have spies everywhere," the soldier seethed. "Why should I give away who they are?"

The Badshah made a disgusted face at the soldier, shaking his head, before addressing the people once more. "Rest assured, this despicable being will be dealt with—as will the Kebzu Kingdom. But for now, rejoice. War between our tribes has been avoided!"

The Badshah and the Wali both grinned as the audience began a round of applause, but something did not set right within Durkhanai. It all seemed too easy—too neat. Something was off, and as she looked to the crowd, her eyes involuntarily falling to Asfandyar, she could tell he felt the same.

They exchanged a glance, but she looked away.

Whatever the case, the matter was now closed—Marghazar exonerated, war avoided. She did not know how willing the ambassadors would be to believe this evidence, but even if they had doubts, doubt alone would not suffice for further action. Asfandyar would be heading home now.

It was what was best—for her, for him, for her people. She had to put this entire ordeal behind her.

"Now, enjoy the banquet!" the Badshah declared.

The music started again, this time louder, a quicker beat, and slowly people began to dance while others dispersed toward the food or toward small gatherings of friends.

Durkhanai joined the crowds. As a force of habit, she found herself searching for Asfandyar, but she immediately pushed the thought from her head. He was leaving, she reminded herself.

So instead, she focused on Rashid, who was making his way to her side.

"You look lovely," Rashid said, upon seeing her. He wore an embroidered gold and white sherwani, accented with his own pearls. Slung across his hip was a bejeweled sword case.

In the candlelight, with his beard grown out, he did look quite handsome.

Durkhanai regarded him closely, waiting to feel something . . . more. A spark, something sharp—but instead, she felt like an unlit fuse.

"Thank you," Durkhanai replied, smiling sweetly. He handed her a goblet full of mint lemonade.

They made their way to the center of the gathering, talking about here-and-there things without much substance. He asked what she had read lately, she replied, and had he read anything new? The answer was no, he was too busy with work and his father, though he didn't elaborate.

Durkhanai mentioned something about the people, but he steered the conversation away, not wanting to talk politics.

They made their rounds, stopping to chat with the other noble tribe leaders, saying hello, how are you? But even then, it was nothing that caught Durkhanai's attention; she was distracted . . . bored. Durkhanai kept waiting for the feeling—the knife-in-her-gut, the fire-in-her-chest, the electricity-in-her-veins—but it never came.

There was nothing outright boring about Rashid, but her eyes kept subconsciously searching for someone else.

"Shehzadi!" Rukhsana-sahiba drawled, greeting Durkhanai, kissing both her cheeks. The other ambassadors were with her, even Asfandyar, and they were all so . . . cozy.

Such great friends, which was vaguely threatening but more so outright strange.

She wished everyone would just be upfront instead of all this pretense and suspicion and confusion.

"What a splendid banquet! Marghazar has been most welcome," Rukhsana-sahiba drawled. "And what a lovely surprise! At such perfect timing as well—one more day and we would have all had war!"

"Yes, well," Durkhanai started. "The truth always reveals itself one way or another."

"Such a pity for us to have to be leaving soon," Rukhsana-sahiba continued. "We have learned a great deal about Marghazar's people during our time here, and they are a boisterous bunch. Tragic really, though, about the illness—the workers are spread so thin."

Durkhanai opened her mouth to respond, but Rashid was quicker.

"The people are having a swift recovery, but thank you for the concern," Rashid said, smiling. "The people of Marghazar are resilient. A little sickness cannot keep them down."

Durkhanai knew he was speaking from a good place, being diplomatic, but she could answer for herself and her people. She narrowed her eyes, and of course, Asfandyar noticed.

She ignored him.

"Let us hope," Rukhsana-sahiba said with a laugh.

"If you'll excuse us," Rashid said, his hand hovering by Durkhanai's back to guide her away. She resisted eyeing his hand— not in front of the ambassadors.

They went their separate ways, and she caught Asfandyar sending her a glance over his shoulder.

Her heart squeezed tight.

"How are your tribespeople doing?" Durkhanai asked Rashid, forcing her attention to him. "Have most of them truly recovered from the illness?"

"Yes, alhamdulillah," he replied. "Thank you for asking. And you're not feeling worse or anything, are you?"

"No, I'm fine," she said. "And the people, have they eased back into working? Are they no longer discontent?"

"You don't have to worry about the people," Rashid said. "You are a good shehzadi. They adore you."

Durkhanai tried not to frown. She knew it was coming from a good place, but she didn't need him to coddle her, as well.

"Right," she replied, not pushing. They continued their chatter, making their rounds, and Durkhanai soon caught glances on her. People were giving her extra glances, and she wondered why.

Even Naeem-sahib was giving his son a pointed look.

Then she understood. She had been by Rashid's side all evening, and he had been by hers. And at a gathering such as this, staying so close could easily be interpreted as meaning something. Even Asfandyar kept glancing her way, frowning.

At the very least, being with Rashid was making Asfandyar jealous.

The thought entered her mind and left in a flash. She paused. How despicable she was becoming—or perhaps she always had been awful.

"Excuse me," she told Rashid. "I just need some . . . fresh air."

"Are you all right?" he asked, concern covering his countenance. They were already outside, what more fresh air could she need? But there were too many people.

"Yes," she said with a forced smile. "I'm perfectly fine, thank you."

In truth, she wasn't. She felt scrambled inside, her emotions skittering this way and that. But she knew one thing for certain at least—finally some clarity—Rashid deserved better. She found her way to the edge of the courtyard, toward the end of the mountain face.

Durkhanai leaned her back against a tree, letting the music and chatter die away behind her. Taking a deep breath, Durkhanai looked out to the stars, waiting for the wind to pinch her skin.

But it was almost July. There was no breeze. It was hot, much too hot.

She was suffocating from the heat.

# CHAPTER TWENTY-ONE

urkhanai began her walk back to the gathering, and as she did, she overheard Rukhsana-sahiba, loud as ever, speaking to a group of people.

"Yes, the plants in Teerza are truly astounding," she drawled "Such variety! There are so many teas and medicinal herbs." Her voice lowered. "Even something to slip to another if they're bothering you too much, if you know what I mean."

Rukhsana-sahiba winked, laughing along with the others. Such talk was ordinary among the nobles; they all kept their own personal arsenal of little plants and potions, just in case. Durkhanai herself knew how to poison people with at least thirty different plants, each with varying effects.

They were hidden on her person at all time: hidden little packets in her jewelry or sewn into her clothes or clipped into her elaborate updos. Just in case. She had never used any.

But from the way Rukhsana-sahiba talked, it was clear this was common in Teerza.

It got Durkhanai thinking of how she herself had fallen so suddenly ill, how everyone had. Maybe, just maybe, it hadn't just been ordinary sickness—but poisoning.

Illness hadn't spread so far and so fast in a long, long while. Was it a coincidence it had occurred now, just after the ambassador's arrival?

How *had* she gotten sick?

Durkhanai recalled that night, how she had interacted with no one but Asfandyar. The bandits had been there—but they hadn't been ill, and neither had Asfandyar.

She had assumed she had gotten it from the man who had attacked her—he had been coughing—but she had scrubbed her body raw that night, and besides, she had only been near him for a moment.

*What else?*

Durkhanai pressed her mind to think, searching blindly for details in the memories of that night, despite the sharp pain that slit through her to think of how Asfandyar had comforted her, how he had brought her home. His arms around her . . .

She brushed the sensation away. There was something missing.

How did illness spread? How could it have spread so fast amongst the people? It almost seemed deliberate, a cruel punishment sent from Allah—but, no. It wasn't arbitrary enough. No one in the palace or court had fallen ill except for Durkhanai, and that was only because she had strayed.

And Rashid's sister but that was also because she went down to the villages to teach.

Durkhanai tried to recall the pattern of the illness, how it had spread from the top of the mountain, the villages closest to the palace, then further down. And even in the village, it seemed to be the workers who were getting most ill, not the women who stayed at home with their little babies or the older men who spent all day cooking.

What was it?

And then, clear as day, she remembered a detail: the water from the well.

Anxiety struck through her heart like lightning, spreading through her veins, filling her and filling her. *No.* Durkhanai pressed her fingers into her throat, felt her pulse thrum furiously.

Durkhanai tried not to run back to the main throng of the gathering, but still, her steps quickened into something close to a jog.

Of course, the moment she entered, Rashid found her.

"Feeling better?" he asked, voice concerned. Durkhanai nodded, distracted, looking around the room.

"Rashid, do you know where your sister is?" she asked, scanning the crowds.

"Hala?" Rashid asked. "Come, I'll take you to her." He took her hand. Durkhanai obliged, not even noticing how easily she gave her hand to him until he was already pulling her along through the crowds and it was too late to withdraw. What had gotten into Rashid? Always so prim and proper, careful not to even bump shoulders with her, now suddenly holding her hand in his? A creeping feeling spread across her chest, but there was no time for that now.

"Hala!" Rashid called. "The Shehzadi was looking for you."

Hala lowered her head in respect, but even she noticed her brother's hand with the princess's. She was a pretty girl with the same wavy brown hair and warm hazel eyes as her brother. "What an honor," she replied.

Durkhanai shone her brightest smile. "Come, take a walk with me."

She slipped her hand out of Rashid's and looped her arm through Hala's.

"I'll find you after," Rashid told her, trying to give her a bright smile to hide his downcast countenance.

Durkhanai smiled in response but made a point of moving out of hearing distance. "How are you doing?" she asked Hala, trying to remain calm. She did not need to alarm anyone, not when all she had was a suspicion.

"I'm well, Shehzadi, shukria," Hala replied. "And how are you? Is everything well?"

"Yes, thank you so much for asking," Durkhanai replied. "I was ill some time ago, but alhamdulillah I have recovered."

"Yes, I had heard," Hala responded. "It is good you are better now. I was ill myself."

"Yes, Rashid told me," Durkhanai said. "Strange, no? The illness seemed to have come from nowhere, yet so many have been afflicted."

Hala nodded. "Yes, strange indeed. I had gone down to the villages to teach the Quran to some children, as I try to do often, and suddenly I woke up ill a day or so later."

"You didn't happen to drink water from one of the wells, did you?" Durkhanai asked, voice low. Hala slowed down, surprised.

"I often do, of course."

Durkhanai didn't say anything more.

"But it couldn't have been something in the water," Hala said, confused. "The water in the wells comes from underground springs which provide freshwater from the melting glaciers."

"Right," Durkhanai said, shaking her head nonchalantly. She smiled. "There is no way for the water to be contaminated."

The concern left Hala's countenance, and she relaxed once more, laughing nervously. Durkhanai stopped walking, leaning forward to kiss Hala's cheeks.

"I must attend to the other guests," she said. "Please, enjoy the festivities. Make sure you eat the chapli kababs, they are exceptionally delicious today."

Durkhanai took her leave, trying not to run, to remain calm. Her mind was running in a hundred directions, leaves fluttering away from different branches, all being pulled in different directions by the wind. What if it hadn't been a natural illness—what if someone had been contaminating the water at its source, poisoning it?

With four foreigners and their servants in her lands, it wasn't unfathomable.

Durkhanai's blood boiled just from the thought, and she tried to calm herself, but the storm inside would find no peace. She needed to leave, immediately, before she caused a scene—pulling the ambassadors out and interrogating them, or worse, running her nails across their skin. Durkhanai passed by delicate vases perched on pillars and wanted to knock them over, spill all the flowers inside and carry the shards like blades.

But she kept the barbarism at bay—she controlled her emotions. She needed a plan.

Durkhanai was on her way out of the courtyard when she realized the gathering had gone quiet, eerily so. Even the music had died down, and voices had lowered to whispers. Durkhanai turned, not knowing what to expect—but it certainly wasn't Asfandyar.

He was standing in front of the Badshah, his head lowered in respect. With a nod from the Badshah, Asfandyar turned, addressing the audience. She finally looked at him: He was dressed in crisp white shalwar kameez with an embroidered sherwani, his curly hair half out of his pakol. His eyes were sharp, jaw determined.

"I have an announcement to make," he said, his strong voice carrying.

Even though he was across the space, she could hear him as clearly as though he were standing right next to her, talking directly to her. She felt his gaze on her, even from so far away.

She stared at him openly, waiting. The people quieted, and a figure subtly began to make its way toward the back of the crowd. Then, an instant later, the figure was gone—disappearing like a shadow into the night.

"After the beloved Shehzadi fell ill, I began to investigate where the illness could be coming from," Asfandyar said.

At her own mention, Durkhanai's heart seized painfully—*the beloved Shehzadi*. It was language everyone used—daily—but from his mouth, it felt like a tantalizingly soft kiss to her cheek.

"I have found the springs to be poisoned by a plant found commonly in Teerza," he said. "When the leaves have been dried, then soaked in water for two nights, they release a toxin—it is this that has caused the illness spreading through the villages. It is this same plant that I found in Rukhsana-sahiba's room."

Durkhanai was right.

Blood rushed through her ears. She curled her hands into fists, resisting the urge to run. There was only one thing keeping her in place, and it was Asfandyar's face.

Though he was far away, she saw his intent. He was speaking to the crowd, but his eyes were focused entirely on her. She could read his expression, as simple and clear as a children's book.

He had done it for her.

# CHAPTER TWENTY-TWO

*D*urkhanai ran.

Before anyone could react, she ran through the crowd, past the shocked noblemen, past her furious grandfather, a confused Asfandyar.

She ran through her marble halls, past guards, hitching up her lehenga, heart pounding, feet thumping. Her heavy gold earrings bounced up and down, her chudiyan chum-chum-ing up and down her wrists. She ran toward the stables.

There wasn't a moment to be lost.

She grabbed her chaadar and threw on her riding boots.

"Shehzadi, you mustn't leave at this hour!" a stable boy cried, trying to stop her.

"I must," she said, grabbing Heer and wrestling the white horse out of the stable. She adjusted her chaadar, covering herself, and with a sturdy kick, Heer was off.

She needed to warn her people.

Wind whipped through her hair, upending the chaadar that covered her face, and her eyes burned, but she couldn't stop.

How could she when she knew what was causing the illness? She had to stop it. She had to do *something*, anything.

Her people.

She rode far and fast, down the mountain, toward one of the villages, Kaj'li. Ignoring the sudden bite of the night, anxiety propelling her forward, Durkhanai had only one thing on her mind: to warn her people.

It was much too dark for her to be out riding, and alone, but she was sure the guards were following her. If she listened close, behind the rustling trees and the wind, she heard hooves riding not too far behind her.

How stupid she had been all this time!

Not to realize that the water had been poisoned. How else would illness spread so far, so fast, and remain undetected? She had been so focused on everything else . . . and now her people were paying the price.

"Nobody drink the water!" she cried, when people entered her line of sight. The village homes of Kaj'li shone with moonlight, some lit with the glow of lanterns.

"Shehzadi!" a man cried, recognizing her from her garb. "What are you doing here, and at this hour!"

"Isn't the Badshah's celebration tonight?"

"Is everything all right?"

"What has happened?"

The villagers' voices all mingled together, confused, concerned, apprehensive, worried. They began to gather, upon hearing the Shehzadi was in their presence. It was late—well past the Isha prayer, and many rose from their sleep to greet her.

A man handed her a torch, which she held up. The fire warmed her flushed cheeks. Durkhanai straightened her back, waving her hands to quiet the people down.

"Please, you must listen to me carefully," she shouted, projecting her voice so the gathered people could hear. "Nobody drink the water! It has been poisoned."

"Poisoned!"

"In our own lands! Our home!"

"But who would do such a thing?"

"It was those cursed foreigners! The Badshah should have never let them into our home!"

The people's voices buzzed into a frenzy, raising in frequency.

"I assure you all," Durkhanai cried, "the Badshah will be swift in punishment to those responsible for this." She trod carefully along the path, making eye contact with as many villagers as she could, exuding sincerity. "But for now, it is my duty to warn you. The instant I heard the news, I rode out to you—I do not want to see any more of you ill."

The people's rising riot began to ebb, understanding and appreciation in their features.

"Jazakullah khair, Shehzadi!" somebody cried. "You have saved us!"

The others began to cry in agreement, thanking her.

Durkhanai knew it worked like this: one minute rioting, the other, eternally thankful.

If only they could stay grateful . . .

Her thoughts were interrupted by the sound of horse hooves and a voice calling her name. Her entire body seized.

"Durkhanai!" Asfandyar cried, riding to meet her. She turned her cheek, not wanting to look at him, afraid of what she would show, of what she would say.

"The foreigner!" a man cried. "Was it him who poisoned us?"

"Did you hear?" one said, voice accusatory. "He calls our Shehzadi by her name!"

The people began to buzz once more, anger and hatred filling the air.

"No!" Durkhanai cried, voice strong.

Despite how irritated she herself was with Asfandyar, she didn't want others to question him. She couldn't help but defend him, even if he didn't deserve it.

"It was not him," she assured the people. "This is the man who discovered the source of the illness that has been spreading. Had it not been for him, we would have remained ignorant to the cause of this illness! We must thank him for his vigilance in uncovering the truth."

She saw their doubt, the questions in their eyes to see their Shehzadi defend the foreign ambassador. Saw the people glance between her and the handsome Asfandyar and raise their eyebrows, wondering.

"Why would he do such a thing?" somebody asked. Durkhanai herself did not know.

She gave him a look, and finally, he spoke. "Because I care for the people of this land. I could not in good conscience let such information go untold."

The people's voices dwindled down to murmuring, which was sometimes worse, for she couldn't understand what they were saying, what they were feeling.

But it didn't matter. She was here with a purpose.

"I implore you, send a rider to the neighboring villages, and have them send one to their neighboring villages," she said, gathering their attention once more. "Send word that the wells have been poisoned and that nobody should drink directly from them. Take the water home and boil it first. That should clean it of impurities."

Given their orders, the people began to disperse. She saw to it that a rider was sent in the directions of the neighboring villages, further down the mountain.

Villagers came to offer her chai, but she refused them. She couldn't stomach anything until she knew her people were safe once more.

As she gave orders and spoke with the townspeople, Asfandyar trailed her like a shadow, watching her. He didn't interrupt or intercede; he let her do her work. She was comforted by his presence, to know somebody was by her side in all this.

With the work done, at least for the night, Durkhanai said her goodbyes and began her ride back to the marble palace.

"Did you see my guards following?" Durkhanai asked Asfandyar, finally speaking to him. She wondered where they were. Not that there would be any use in them looking for her now that she was on her way home.

"Yes, but we diverged paths," he replied. "They went east, to Dhok-Alfu, I believe that is the main commercial village? I traveled west, guessing that you would be here."

"And how did you guess that?"

"This was the first village we visited to distribute medicine," Asfandyar replied. "And the one you visit the most; you have close relationships with many of these villagers, so I just figured . . ."

"Right," Durkhanai said, cutting him off.

She both liked and disliked being so known by him. She nudged Heer forward, but Heer had other plans. She went to nuzzle against the horse Asfandyar rode, and it was then Durkhanai registered which horse it was.

It was Heer's mate, a strong horse with a chestnut coat and a thick black mane. Ranjha was well known for his affection for Heer. The two horses had been raised together, and Durkhanai had grown up riding both, though, she preferred Heer.

"You had to take this horse, didn't you?" she said to Asfandyar, glaring.

"What?" he replied. "I've taken quite a liking to him."

She reminded herself she was angry with him for more than simply taking her second horse and debated on what to say next.

Until a raindrop plopped onto her forehead and decided for her.

Durkhanai swore.

"Follow me," she said, striking Heer with a kick to get her going. She made a sharp cut to the left where a small village would be coming up in about a fifteen-minute ride. In the meanwhile, the occasional raindrops turned into a drizzle, which quickly became a downpour.

Sure enough, just as they were beginning to get soaked, they reached a stretch of farmland. They rode into the farmhouse, seeking shelter from the storm pouring away outside.

Chickens squawked in apprehension at their arrival. Other farm animals were fussing due to the rain, so she quieted them, calmed Heer, and got off. These storms were unpredictable. They could be stuck there all night.

Even longer if there was a landslide.

Durkhanai settled Heer and went to the open mouth of the farmhouse, leaning against the frame. The roar of rain bombarded her ears, the air filled with sweet petrichor.

Tentatively, Asfandyar did the same, standing on the opposite end of the frame. He watched her wordlessly.

After a few moments passed in silence, Asfandyar took a few steps forward and offered her his woolen loi. She still said nothing, turning her back, further soaking from the rain blowing into her. Even under the roof of the farmhouse, there was no relief.

"Durkhanai, take it," Asfandyar coaxed, bringing in front of her again. She ignored him. "Tch, chanda," he said, touching her shoulder.

Her heart warmed at the term of endearment, but she gave him a dirty look, throwing his hand off of her. He held his hands up in surrender.

"Your face is florid," Asfandyar informed her, tapping her nose. Durkhanai fixed him a withering glare, then pressed her hands to his solid chest and pushed him from under the canopy into the rain. He gave a yelp, almost falling, then rushed back under the canopy, hair dripping.

"Happy?" Asfandyar asked, shivering.

Finally, she smiled, taking the shawl from him. The instant she wrapped the scratchy wool around her shoulders, she was warm. Drier, even.

"Quite," she replied, twisting her lips. He held a hand to his heart, pretending to be shot by an arrow.

"Ah, Shehzadi, you break my heart," he said, wincing dramatically.

"Shut up," she snapped, the smile gone. "I'm still furious with you."

"You should be," he said, giving out a long sigh.

"Nothing else to say?" she snapped. She took a step toward him, wanting to fight.

He looked away, scratching his neck. He opened his mouth to speak, then shut it again. Face contorted, he looked . . . heartbroken.

Like she had broken his heart, somehow. She couldn't explain it—he looked . . . raw. The anger seeped from her, replaced by a soft tenderness.

"Why did you do it?" she asked, voice neutral: not angry, not forgiving.

He sighed, taking the peace offering.

"To force the Badshah into spreading the medicine faster and farther," he said. "When you were sick, the people were getting worse, and I couldn't do much alone. Besides, even together, we had hardly made a big difference."

A plausible explanation.

"Why do you care so much about my people?" she asked.

"Ever noble, no?" Asfandyar replied with a half-laugh, all empty-arrogance and self-deprecation. She frowned. "You can doubt me, but people are people," he continued. "I don't want to see anyone suffer."

"You should have told me."

"You're right," he said. "I should have told you. I'm sorry."

"Hmm."

She wondered if she should believe him.

He *was* here now though.

"It's why I found out what was causing it, if it's worth anything," Asfandyar told her. "I knew something strange was occurring; illness doesn't spread so fast, all of a sudden, especially not in the mountains in the summer, not like this. And then I got to thinking . . ."

"So, you did all that because you're a good person?" she said, giving him a difficult time. Asfandyar shook his head, shrugging, not even bothering to agree.

"No, I'm not," he said. "But sometimes I try to be."

And he looked at her in a way that said: *Sometimes for you, I try to be.*

But he didn't say it, and Durkhanai told herself she was imagining things now. Her heart was like clay, always molding to different shapes: angry and sharp one instant, soft and watery the next. She couldn't hold being angry with Asfandyar anymore.

"Right," she said, wrapping the loi around her tighter. "And you thought you'd be the hero, chasing after me with a loi and all would be forgiven?"

Finally, Asfandyar grinned.

"It worked, didn't it?" he said, raising his eyebrows at her. She rolled her eyes but couldn't help her laugh. How horrible. She detested him, truly.

What an unholy, insufferable—but she couldn't finish the thought. She couldn't finish the idea because she knew the blame was all hers. "Zyada mat bano," she said. "Don't gloat."

"Besides, I wanted to speak with you," Asfandyar said innocently. "Did you ever receive word from the Wali of B'rung?"

"I did," Durkhanai replied, frowning. "But it was a dead end— the Wali didn't know anything."

"I suppose it doesn't matter now," Asfandyar responded. "The Badshah provided his evidence—the matter is closed. We've avoided war, and I'm sure after wrapping up some negotiations, we'll all be heading home. Back to our lives."

"I suppose."

But Durkhanai couldn't shake the feeling that there was something more.

"Did you recognize the soldier at all?" Durkhanai asked. "He would have been there, that day, right?"

"No, I didn't recognize him—he must have been in the background, hiding."

"Doesn't it all seem a bit . . . clean cut to you? Something doesn't feel right."

Asfandyar considered this. "I agree, but what else can be done?"

"I have half a mind to interrogate the soldier myself," she said, voice trailing.

"Well, why don't we?" he replied. "After this blasted thunderstorm ends—we go back and see this through."

"And how do I know you won't use that information against me?" Durkhanai responded.

"I really am sorry," he said, eyes suddenly intense. "For everything. I won't betray you again."

Asfandyar drew nearer, true guilt on his expression.

"It's all right," Durkhanai replied. "You are forgiven. Allies once more?"

She put her hand out to shake, but he shook his head instead.

"Friends," he said.

She smiled.

"Friends."

They stood in silence, staring at the rain as it poured down, washing away impurities as it did.

Durkhanai turned back to see how Heer was faring. The mare disliked the rain and was looking out apprehensively. Durkhanai reached over and stroked her white mane, making comforting noises, before doing the same for Ranjha.

"I cannot believe you've been riding my horse," she grumbled.

"Technically, *Heer* is your horse."

Asfandyar joined her, his fingers brushing against hers on Ranjha's mane. Durkhanai shivered. "Ranjha is your spare."

"Still."

Asfandyar shrugged. "He took a liking to me." He neared the horse, stroking his mane. "Isn't that right, Ranjhu?"

Ranjha nuzzled against Asfandyar, but his nose sniffed toward Asfandyar's bag, where something glittered in the moonlight.

"Shh," Asfandyar whispered, but it was too late. Durkhanai snatched his bag.

"Sugar cubes!" she cried, holding out a handful. Ranjha immediately licked them from her hand. "That's cheating!" Durkhanai crossed her arms. "It doesn't count."

She expected Asfandyar to laugh. She expected him to tease. What she did not expect was for his face to suddenly grow serious, his eyes glittering with moonlight. The downpour of rain was thunderous in her ears.

"Love is love," he said, voice low. "No matter how it started, what I feel is true."

She didn't understand.

# CHAPTER TWENTY-THREE

*H*eart beating fast, Durkhanai turned to go farther into the farmhouse, away from the spray of rain at the opening.

She looked over her shoulder to catch a glimpse at Asfandyar's silhouette but saw instead that he was watching her go.

Then she was tumbling.

In the first instant, Durkhanai was stunned: she never tripped.

Then, sharp pain cut into her hand. She let out a cry.

"Durkhanai!"

Asfandyar was by her side in a moment, skidding onto the floor beside her. Durkhanai immediately cradled her hand to her heart, but Asfandyar reached for it to look.

"It's fine."

She had cut her hand on a farm tool. The wound was bleeding, and she knew he hated the sight of blood. Knew it made him recoil.

Warm blood spilled onto her chaadar, soaking lightly onto her chest.

"Durkhanai," he said, voice woolen, and she looked up to see his face was pale.

But more than that, his countenance was covered in raw emotion, and his eyes—they spilled all his secrets. The way he looked at her—it took her breath away.

She knew what it meant.

Asfandyar cleared his throat, focusing on her hand, which she refused to show him. Suddenly, she wanted to cry.

"You're never clumsy," Asfandyar said, confused. "You're exhausted."

"I'm fine," she insisted, but her voice was thick, and tears spilled onto her cheeks. Her legs were tired from riding. Perhaps that was it.

"Durkhanai, you're crying," he asked, even more worried. "Does it hurt that badly?"

"No," she said, wiping her cheek on her shoulder. "I'm not crying."

It was just her emotions, dripping out. Perhaps sometimes the heart needed to be wrung dry to keep a person from drowning.

Durkhanai refused to meet his gaze until he finally pulled her face close to his.

"Please, let me see," he said, voice gentle.

She gave him her closed fist, and he carefully pried it open. The release of pressure caused a fresh flow of blood, and the open air made her gasp with sharp pain.

"Okay?" he asked, hesitant. She nodded, sniffling.

"I have such unbelievably low pain tolerance," she informed him, trying to act blasé.

They both inspected her hand. There was a gash running from beneath her pinky finger, across her palm, and down to her wrist. She saw the open gash and felt nauseous. Blood stuck under her nails and dribbled down her wrist in rivulets.

She looked away.

"One second," he said, getting up. "Keep your hand closed, like it was before."

She did as she was told and watched as he grabbed a bowl and ran to the mouth of the farmhouse, holding it out to the open sky to fill it with water. He returned to her, his arm drenched.

"Give me your hand," he said.

She obliged, and he cleaned it with water. Fresh blood spilled out as the old blood left.

"It's not too deep," Asfandyar said. "But we'll want to cover it."

He bit into the hem of his kameez and ripped a piece of the cloth off. She hadn't even noticed he had discarded his embroidered sherwani and wore the simple shalwar kameez underneath.

Durkhanai put a hand on his shoulder to steady herself as he wrapped the cloth around her hand, clenching her jaw to bite back the ache.

"This might hurt," he warned. She nodded. He pulled the cloth tight, forcing the skin of her wound together, and she took in a sharp breath, her nails biting into his shoulder. "All good."

"Shukria," she said, slightly embarrassed. She let go of his shoulder, and cradled her hand to her chest again. As she did, she felt sticky blood on the bottom of her necklace. With an irritated grumble, she undid the necklace, then undid the rest of her jewelry, too.

Asfandyar got up and returned with a little sack, and she put her gold inside. She could see that he was shivering and that she was being a little selfish with the loi, which had fallen off her shoulders when she had tripped. She picked it up. The loi was made of thick and scratchy wool, the size of a blanket; they could share.

"Come," she said, adjusting the loi so half of it covered her, and the other half hung off her outstretched arm. "The night is cold."

Asfandyar hesitated, a rare show of chivalry stopping him.

"It's okay," she said. "There's no telling when the rain will stop; we'll have to wait it out before we can return."

Asfandyar nodded, moving to sit beside her. He took the other end of the loi and wrapped it around his shoulders, but because he was sitting far away, it barely reached.

"Why are you so large?" Durkhanai tsked.

Asfandyar chuckled. "Apologies, Shehzadi."

"We need to be strategic," Durkhanai said, heart hammering. "Come closer."

When he inched closer, careful not to touch her, Durkhanai moved closer herself, relishing his warmth as she aligned their bodies from their shoulders to their hips to their knees.

Which was probably a bad idea.

But at least now the loi fit, and Durkhanai brought it to wrap across their legs. Instantly, they began to warm, in a cocoon, but Durkhanai's fingers remained frozen. She cradled her hands to her chest, blowing on her fingers.

"Allow me," Asfandyar said, voice low.

Durkhanai hesitated.

"Oh, *now* your shame is stirred?"

"How rude!" Durkhanai balked, bumping his knee with hers. "Are you saying I'm shameless?"

"No," he replied quickly, thinking he had truly offended her. She laughed.

"It's okay," she said. "We're friends, right?"

But Durkhanai felt dangerous, on the edge.

"This is okay," she said, giving him her hands, and she wasn't sure if she was convincing herself or him, but she knew she was fooling neither of them.

He held her hands in his, blowing on them, pressing them tight in his palms, careful of her wound. A shiver ran down her spine. She was holding her breath, her heart beating too fast, too loud, in her ears.

"Better?" he asked, voice close to a whisper.

"No," she said, pulling her hands away, swallowing hard.

Then she remembered something she did to routinely torment Saifullah. Thinking it would lighten the mood, Durkhanai pressed her fingers against Asfandyar's neck, his skin deliciously warm against her freezing fingers.

Asfandyar swore, making a strangled sound, writhing from her fingers, and she withdrew her hands.

"Are my hands too cold?" she asked innocently, grinning.

"Yes," he replied, voice rasped. "That's it."

"How are your hands not cold?"

Asfandyar shrugged carelessly. "One of my invincible qualities."

"Ooh," Durkhanai replied. "People do say you're star-touched. It's how you've become so successful so quickly."

"Not because I'm the Wali's whore?" Asfandyar teased, referencing their first meeting. Durkhanai grimaced, covering her face.

"I really said that?" she groaned.

"You really did," he replied, amused by the memory. How far they had come.

"You infuriated me," she said, defending herself. "You do still."

"Don't worry, you infuriate me, as well," he replied. He turned to meet her gaze, eyes soft. "Though I can't seem to mind."

Durkhanai was suddenly acutely aware of all the places their bodies were aligned, separated by thin articles of clothing, and something buzzed through her, sending a shiver down her spine. Her chest felt like it was on fire.

She bit her lip. He was looking at her with wonder, awestruck, like she was something magnificent, something sublime. It was suddenly very quiet. Durkhanai heard his breath. He was so close to her, his mouth a whisper away.

Asfandyar was still, no movement, save for the rise and fall of his chest. Then Durkhanai realized why it was so quiet: The rain had stopped.

Durkhanai pulled back, hand and heart throbbing.

"Time to go!" she said, voice overly cheerful.

She got up quickly, pulling out from under the loi. Trying to steady her heart rate, she walked away from Asfandyar.

As she did, she stepped in a pile of mud, which lodged her khusa and foot. In horrible slow motion, Durkhanai fell forward, landing straight into a wet pile of mud.

Durkhanai swore loudly. "This blasted lehenga!"

She fell back, sitting down, which only made it worse. She was covered front and backward in gross dirt. Durkhanai wanted to cry again, but then Asfandyar began to laugh, and she did, too.

"This isn't funny," she said, trying to pout, but a smile lingered on her face.

"What is wrong with you?" he asked, genuinely surprised. She wished she knew. "Are you sure you didn't accidentally drink wine earlier?"

She reached to hit him with her muddied hand, but he moved out of her reach, squealing.

"Help me up!" she ordered. "Batameez."

"Don't even think about it," Asfandyar warned, offering her his hand. She was thinking about pulling him into the mud with her but recanted, deeming it too cruel.

"Fine," she said, pouting but meaning it. "Just help me up."

She took hold of his hand with her good one, but before she could pull herself up, Asfandyar tumbled forward, falling into the mud anyway. Durkhanai let out a laugh.

"Look who's clumsy now!" she teased, though she suspected he had done it on purpose to make her feel better.

"Clumsy?" Asfandyar repeated, grabbing a handful of mud and running it down her arm.

She cried out. "This is an attack on the Shehzadi!"

She grabbed a handful of mud and plastered it across his chest, up his neck. He squirmed, but they were both laughing, and perhaps they truly had drunk wine accidentally. She felt drunk.

"Shehzadi, you must stop attacking me," he said, straightening his kameez.

"Don't tell me what to do," she replied, shoving him again. He tumbled forward, almost falling, but caught himself before he landed farther into the mud.

Suddenly, he bumped his shoulder into hers. They were acting like children. Because he took her by surprise, the force sent her tumbling.

"Hey!" she pouted. "Don't be so mean to me! I am but a delicate maid."

"You? Delicate?" he repeated, laughing loudly. "That is entirely untrue."

"Yes," she agreed with a smirk. "But it is a mask I like to wear sometimes."

She took his hand and pulled him into the mud beside her.

"Truce!" he cried, lying down. He looked up at her, and now that she had seen it, she would never tire of the way his eyes gleamed to drink in the sight of her. She grinned.

"Come, we should go," Asfandyar said, breaking the silence.

She didn't want to but knew they must. They grabbed each other's arms and helped one another up. Cleaning off the mud as best as they could, they climbed their horses and began the journey back in comfortable silence.

When they arrived at the palace, Durkhanai whispered, "Let's use the passageways. I'll let the guards know I'm home after we're inside. Then we can clean up and go see the Kebzu soldier."

Asfandyar shrugged. "I doubt anyone has noticed I've been missing, anyway."

Durkhanai led the way, walking to a secluded section of the lower gardens to make entrance into the passageways.

She grabbed a torch from the hidden stash on the side, and Asfandyar lit it.

"I'll take you to your room first," Durkhanai said.

"No, no, no," Asfandyar replied, putting his hands on her shoulders. "You've already fallen twice and injured yourself once. I don't trust you to make it back on your own."

Durkhanai rolled her eyes. "Oh, please!"

"I'll drop you off," he insisted, moving her along.

Durkhanai obliged, too tired to argue, and relished in the few moments more with him, the illicit thrill that ran through her with his warm hands on her shoulders. She was filled with barbaric desire.

When they arrived back at her room, however, Durkhanai noticed the light was on.

Curious, she opened her wardrobe and made her way into her room.

"There you are!" a voice said. Durkhanai jolted and saw Zarmina in her bed.

"Zarmina?" she said, incredulous. "What are you doing here?"

"Waiting for you," she replied. "I was worried. Where were you? Are you okay? You're a mess. Did you tell the guards? They've been out looking for you."

"I was down in the village, alerting the people," Durkhanai replied. "I just got caught in the rain for a bit and fell."

"And your hand?"

"Zarmina, it's all right, I'll get it checked come morning," Durkhanai said. She needed Zarmina to go back to sleep immediately. Durkhanai hoped Asfandyar had enough sense to go to his room on his own, but she had a feeling he didn't.

"Why is your face so florid?" Zarmina asked, taking in Durkhanai's flushed complexion. "Don't bother getting enraged over Rukhsana-sahiba right now."

"No, that's not it," Durkhanai said, waving her off. She busied herself with cleaning up, going to her dressing room. She took off her muddy clothes, avoiding Zarmina's curious gaze.

"Did you see Rashid?" Zarmina asked next, gasping. "Is that why you used the passageways to sneak into your own room?"

"No!" Durkhanai said, but she responded much too quickly. Her cheeks burned red, remembering the boy she had been with.

She washed her hands and face with cold water, not removing the edge of Asfandyar's kurta on her hand. When she left her dressing room, Zarmina's face had widened into a shocked grin.

She sat up.

"Chal jhooti!" she said. "You little liar! What were you guys doing? Everyone did see you together all night. But now so late! The scandal! Hai main margai!"

"Zarmina," Durkhanai whined, getting into bed. "Kuch nahi. Let's go to sleep."

"Acha, acha," Zarmina said. "You don't have to tell me, but I can guess."

She wiggled her eyebrows, and Durkhanai pulled the covers over her cousin's face. She hoped Asfandyar had gone from the passageways by then . . .

"Sleep," Durkhanai insisted, getting comfortable herself. "I'm tired too."

"*Someone's* a little exerted!" Zarmina teased, laughing.

"Zarmina!"

"Fine," Zarmina said. "Shabba khair. Goodnight."

Finally, her cousin nestled back into bed, and she was asleep in an instant. She always fell asleep in the blink of an eye.

Carefully, Durkhanai slipped out of bed, going to her wardrobe. She opened the door, brushed her clothes aside, and moved the panel to find Asfandyar leaning against the frame, wide awake. His shawl was around his neck, and he held the ends, giving her a nice view of his throat.

"Rashid?" was all he said.

*Hai Allah.* She waved him off.

"Ja yahaan se—go," she whisper-shouted. "Why are you still here?"

"I thought I'd wait for you," he said innocently.

"Go clean up, and I'll meet you here again in fifteen minutes," she whispered. "We can't very well go down to the dungeon covered in mud."

He nodded and left.

As she changed into more suitable clothes and washed her face again, Durkhanai's thoughts roamed.

She was scared she would do something unholy.

She wished she lived in the stars, in her dreams, where she wasn't alone, but not just not alone, because she wasn't alone, really, she had so many people—but in the dead of the night, she wanted somebody to put his arms around her.

And she kept seeing his face.

Oh, her cruel heart wouldn't stop thinking of him, wouldn't stop tormenting her. She couldn't stop herself, no matter how hard she tried. She imagined a world, an impossible world, where she let herself dream—a world where he loved her, where he was hers.

She was already his.

It was absurd, with everything else going on, absurd how small this was, in the grand scheme of things.

But then, to her, it felt like the most important thing. So, she let herself dream of being in love, and she knew she was being a fool, always the fool, but maybe, just maybe, it could work.

*Let me and my awfully, awfully romantic heart breathe this lilac scented air, sweeter than vanilla and warmer than pink tea*, she thought to herself.

*No*, Durkhanai warned herself. She would not lose her grip.

She swallowed her love like it was a lie and told herself it was lust.

Cleaned up and covered in a shawl, Durkhanai slipped back to her passageways, where Asfandyar was already waiting for her. His face was covered as well.

"Ready?"

They headed down, Durkhanai leading the way. She knew all the routes by heart, and as they made their way to the lowest level, her heart began beating fast with fear. What if the Kebzu soldier told her something she didn't want to hear? What if her grandparents truly had manipulated the evidence? What if there was some greater enemy out there that she hadn't even considered?

Questions flitted in and out of her mind, a thousand scenarios and possibilities.

But it was all for naught.

When they reached the Kebzu soldier's cell, he was already dead.

# CHAPTER TWENTY-FOUR

ith the Kebzu soldier dead in his cell, there was really nothing more Durkhanai could do to find the truth. She had to trust her grandparents—trust they knew what they were doing, despite their suspicious behavior. The next morning when she asked them why they hadn't informed her about the evidence earlier, Dhadi had an easy response ready.

"It was a surprise, gudiya," Dhadi had said. "We didn't want you to worry about that—it was your Agha-Jaan's responsibility."

"We wanted you to focus on the people, and you have been so good at caring for them," Agha-Jaan added.

"Besides, we wanted to give you space to spend time with Rashid," Dhadi said.

While Durkhanai still felt unsettled, she hid her qualms, especially in front of Asfandyar, who she could tell was also doubting her grandparents. But it was one thing for her to doubt them and an entirely different thing for him to express concerns—she was blood.

So as Dhadi finished negotiations with the rest of the ambassadors, who were preparing for their journey home, Durkhanai spent the day in the villages.

It was a welcome distraction.

Durkhanai had always prided herself on never lying, on being honest and blunt always. Of speaking the truth. Not wasting time with deception or misleading others. But when she began to admit to herself how she felt about Asfandyar—it hurt too much.

She couldn't stand it. So she hid, even from her heart. She lied to herself, said she didn't notice him, said she didn't care, said his smile didn't make her melt. Said he was nothing.

When really, he was everything.

She avoided him.

Once, by chance, he stumbled into her view, and the instant she saw him coming from a distance, her heartbeat quickened, and she felt it viscerally: desire nipped and bit, bruised and bled. She ached for him from her teeth to her toes.

Perhaps what she felt for him was ishq, in which case there was still a lingering hope, for ishq was a love sourced on madness, and madness could still pass.

She avoided him, lest she bring herself into disaster. But the cut on her hand and the pain of memories it brought with it would not be ignored.

Durkhanai arranged to meet the people in the villages most affected by the poisoned well. In each village, the story played out in the same way. She would stand on raised ground with Saifullah and Zarmina, the people surrounding them, and their accusatory glances were enough to both break her heart and boil her blood. It took all her strength not to bite.

"I know you are hurt," Durkhanai started. "I know you are confused. I am here to discuss whatever you would like, to answer your questions."

Durkhanai could have sent for the noblemen to handle their tribespeople, but she wanted to do this herself. It would be best coming from a member of the royal family, more personal.

"We call for the ambassador's head!" one man shouted, and the others cried out in agreement.

"This calls for war!" another shouted.

But they could not have war, nor could they have Rukhsana-sahiba's head.

"I understand your grievances. I will speak with the Badshah to ensure proper actions are taken," Durkhanai said, trying to calm the crowds. "Everyone gets their due, in the end. Is our Lord not Just?"

Durkhanai had the faint thought of wondering what she was due, but she refused to dwell on it.

"But when!" someone cried. "When will we have our victory?"

Durkhanai pressed her teeth together. She wished she had all the answers, but she didn't.

"Patience, my dear people. Listen to your Shehzadi, who cares for you and loves you," Saifullah said, sensing her distress. "Believe in her; have faith in her. All will be settled, in the end."

Durkhanai nodded at Saifullah, grateful to have her cousins by her side. They did not say much, but Saifullah helped in coaxing the people to listen to her when they became angry, trying to soften their frustrations.

"I promise you all, proper actions will be taken," Durkhanai told her people. "The Marghazari are just and strong. We will not allow blows against our people to go unpunished. But we cannot have another war, not now! You do not wish to send off your young boys, do you?"

The people mumbled in agreement.

"The Shehzadi is right," a voice cried out. "We cannot have new wars on new fronts. We have no men left."

They settled down for a moment, only to rise up again.

"When will the rest of these wars end?" another voice responded. "Decades have passed, yet still we are stuck in the same place!"

Their concerns were valid. While the crisis of illness had been resolved, the wars still raged on. Too many men were dying at the Kebzu borders, even more so against the Luhgams. They couldn't afford a war against Teerza, not then.

Even if Durkhanai wanted it to make Rukhsana-sahiba pay.

"Have the wars not gone on long enough, Shehzadi?" someone asked. "When will the Badshah relent?"

Durkhanai took a deep breath, turning to Saifullah. Yet he stayed silent when the people stated their anger at the Badshah— he almost seemed to agree with them. She furrowed her brow.

"You know as well as I that the wars will not be so easily won," Durkhanai reminded her people, though now, even she was beginning to doubt the validity of these wars. "If we relent now, we will be reduced to nothing more than a colony in the Lughum Empire!"

But was that the only reason they fought? Or was it for the Badshah's vengeance?

Surely, the Lughum Empire was tired of fighting, as well. Could a truce not lead them both to an advantageous era of peace?

She did not give voice to these thoughts. Instead, she said, "Yet we continue to fight for our freedom—to remain unconquered by the imperialists."

The people continued their grievances, and Durkhanai continued to listen. She wanted to lash out at them, to tell them to stop their fussing because there were enough things on her mind, but she knew she had to be the dutiful Shehzadi, patient and poised.

By the time Durkhanai made it back to the palace after a week of such conferences, she was agitated beyond patience. Feeling scattered and pulled thin, she went straight to the presence chamber, veins thick with emotion, face florid.

Her people were right—Rukhsana-sahiba had to pay for what she had done.

Durkhanai would fight for her people.

She went to find her grandparents. They were alone in the war room. Agha-Jaan stood pensively before a map that covered the expanse of a table. Dhadi stood across from him, shifting pieces on the table.

"What is to be done with the Teerzai ambassador?" Durkhanai asked, stopping at the head of the table. Agha-Jaan did not look up. Dhadi sighed.

"She is leaving today," the Wali replied. "The preparations are nearly complete."

Durkhanai stilled.

"*Leaving?*" she repeated. "That's all?"

She waited for a reaction and received none. Not even her grandfather, so hot-headed, so swift and severe in punishment, had anything more to say. He shifted a piece on the map, then stood back to consider it.

"Agha-Jaan, she *must* be punished!" Durkhanai cried.

"She must," the Badshah replied, not turning to her. "But she won't be. This is the diplomatic solution."

"Diplomacy?" Durkhanai wanted to scatter the entire table's pieces, but she would not lash out as a child would. "The foreign woman who poisoned our own people in our lands goes free without penalty? Why the sudden recourse?"

"Durkhanai, enough," Dhadi sounded tired.

"You're the ones who said you must never give something in exchange for nothing," Durkhanai snapped. "Yet you so willingly give this woman her freedom."

"It is the best option," Agha-Jaan replied, voice hard. He finally looked at her. "Teerza no longer has any good cause to quarrel with us, and for their transgressions, Teerza must send soldiers to help aid in the fight against the Luhgams. And besides, there is no hard evidence against her—just because that plant is popular in Teerza does not mean that is the only place it grows."

"If there is no evidence, then this is the perfect cause for trial by tribunal," Durkhanai said, satisfied with this punishment.

It was, after all, the custom of her people. She didn't care if it was considered barbaric by their contemporaries. She was sure Rukhsana-sahiba would be torn apart by the cruelest lion for her transgressions.

"No. The ambassador had come to negotiate something from us; she will leave giving us something instead," Dhadi explained.

"This is cause for tribunal," Durkhanai argued, her blood still running hot like lava through her veins.

"No," the Badshah replied, voice resolute. "*We* know her to be guilty, but her life is worth nothing. However, with the Teerzai soldiers, we can strike back at the blasted Luhgams and end this ceaseless war."

Durkhanai held her tongue, not saying what she was thinking: that the war with the Luhgam Empire would never end, not even with a few more soldiers.

How far would her grandfather go to defeat the Luhgams? She was only beginning to understand.

There was nothing more sacred than blood, and the Luhgams had filled the earth with the blood of the Miangul family. Retribution was necessary; the Badshah would have nothing less than his revenge in the form of a victory.

The Badshah was growing more and more impatient.

Durkhanai knew she must look at the larger image: to see how the Teerzai ambassador was such a small piece in a much larger game that was being played. But she did not care.

Rukhsana-sahiba had attacked her people. By extension, she had personally attacked the Shehzadi herself.

The matter was settled, yes, but Durkhanai's anger had not.

She would not let it go so easily.

# CHAPTER TWENTY-FIVE

She went to find Rukhsana-sahiba and find her she did.

Rukhsana was in the corridor outside her room, gazing out the window, perfectly calm. She seemed at peace, even, with a cup of tea in her hands.

"No shame in being caught?" Durkhanai spat at the elder woman. Rukhsana-sahiba turned and smiled. She set down her teacup.

"Have you come to see me off, Shehzadi?" she cooed. "Such a shame to leave the frivolous splendors of your marble palace and it's uncivilized people, but I believe the time has come for my departure."

Rukhsana reached for Durkhanai's hands, as though they were friends. Pulling back, Durkhanai clenched her hands into fists.

Anger burned her tongue. She was losing hold of her emotions and felt them cut inside of her. She felt more barbaric as the days went on. She was beginning to feel cruel.

"Don't miss me too much, will you, dear?" Rukhsana said. "I promise I'll visit again soon."

"Bring your burial shroud with you when you do," Durkhanai seethed. "For if you step foot in my lands again, it will be your mangled corpse sent back to Teerza."

Rukhsana tsked lightly. "Oh, darling, come now, don't be so crass. I'd hate to tell the Wali of Teerza how ill-mannered and barbaric the famed Shehzadi of Marghazar is."

"Tell the Wali whatever you please," Durkhanai said, a thought turning in her mind.

She ironed out her anger, forcing her countenance to melt into that of the sweet Shehzadi's. Durkhanai smiled her rose gold smile. "Who do you think people would believe? The old, pitiful ambassador who was unsuccessful in bringing her zilla any goods or advantages? Or the famed Shehzadi of Marghazar, adored by all?"

Rukhsana laughed. "Not so beloved anymore, from what I have heard."

Durkhanai was no longer amused. The anger returned, swiftly. She could only pretend for so long. "You don't know what you're talking about," she replied. But her voice wavered.

Rukhsana caught on all too quickly. "Oh, sweetheart, life catches up to everyone, eventually. Even Shehzadis. Your fall will follow shortly after your grandfather's, if it is not with his, I can assure you that much."

"Shut up," Durkhanai said through her teeth.

Rukhsana leaned forward, her voice dropping to a whisper. "The Badshah's insatiable greed for victory against the Luhgams will be his downfall. Even with Teerzai soldiers, he will die a sad, old man who has accomplished nothing in his long reign."

Rukhsana pinched Durkhanai's cheek, slapping her softly.

"Well, nothing except for raising a pretty little fool."

Durkhanai wanted to tear Rukhsana-sahiba's eyes out, but she needed answers before she did. "Why did you do it?" she asked, anger rising once more. "Because you hate Marghazar for refusing to unify with the other zillas?"

Finally, Rukhsana-sahiba's light-hearted and amused facade broke to reveal grief underneath. Her eyes shone.

"Because I know the truth," she said, voice catching. "That it was Marghazar behind the summit attack—the blood of my brother is on your hands."

"That's absurd—"

"Is it?" Rukhsana-sahiba said, eyes hardening. She did not let the grief linger. It morphed quickly into an anger powerful enough to match Durkhanai's. "The evidence provided was weak, at best, but because the other zillas wish to avoid war, they have conceded." She shook her head. She took in a deep breath, composing herself. When she spoke again, she did so simply. "So, no, I didn't do it because I hate Marghazar—I did it because we *will* have war, and when we do, your people will be much too weak to put up a good fight.

"I can promise you one thing, Shehzadi—you will *never* be badshah."

Durkhanai pushed Rukhsana back, and in one swift movement, she pulled the little dagger out from the back of her gold necklace, where it always rested hidden under her hair by the clasp. It was only small enough for a direct attack. Durkhanai held it to Rukhsana's throat.

All Durkhanai needed was a centimeter, and the knife would plunge into Rukhsana's jugular, but Rukhsana barely flinched. She actually smiled.

Gone was the anger, gone was the grief. She was amused once more, as though Durkhanai was a child playing at being queen.

"Do it," Rukhsana said, unthreatened. "Kill me."

Durkhanai didn't know what she would decide—and then, she didn't have to. A voice called out her name.

It was Asfandyar.

Durkhanai pulled back, the trance broken. The fog of her anger subsided, and she looked at the little knife in her hand. The smooth silver glistened with the light.

"Yes, do go," Rukhsana said, giving her a parting kiss to the cheek. Her voice fell once more to a whisper. "Run along to your whore."

Shocked, Durkhanai stood frozen, unable to react. Rukhsana smiled one last time before disappearing.

"What were you doing?" Asfandyar asked, catching up to her.

Durkhanai was beyond irritated, beyond frustrated, and he only intensified the plethora of emotions running through her. But she didn't want to take her anger out on him. Didn't want him to see this ugly part of her, the semi-barbarism over which she was losing control.

"Nothing," she snapped, turning to leave.

"Durkhanai!" he called her name again, but she did not turn.

She walked away, still buzzing with anger and confusion and *hurt*. She ached and wanted to wipe the smug look off Rukhsana's face. To make her pay for what she had done and her complete lack of remorse.

She acted as though the Marghazari deserved it.

Durkhanai's feet began carrying her someplace without informing her where . . . until she was in the kitchens.

She was perfectly calm, perfectly innocent, not that anyone would question her anyway, when she went to the pantry where they were preparing food packages for a journey.

"This is for the Teerzai ambassador, yes?" Durkhanai asked the boy who was wrapping bread in cloth. He nodded quickly. He stepped back from the table and lowered his head.

"Y-Yes, Shehzadi," he said, not meeting her eyes. Durkhanai looked around and found that no one else was there. She offered the boy a kind smile, then looked at the contents of the package.

"I'd like to ensure our guest is receiving an appropriate farewell," she told him, examining the rest of the food. "How about some more cake, hm? It cannot be said that the Marghazari are stingy."

The boy nodded, quickly disappearing to find more cake from within the kitchen. Hands sure, Durkhanai slipped a finger into her jhumka earring where a little packet of powder was hidden beneath the large umbrella design. Seamlessly, she emptied the powder onto the bread, then spread the remainder into the leather flasks full of water.

The boy returned just as Durkhanai finished wrapping the last stack of bread.

"Everything looks perfect," she assured him, smiling her rose gold smile.

Durkhanai walked away, her heart cold as ice.

Now Rukhsana-sahiba would suffer as Durkhanai's people had.

Durkhanai knew she was being cruel, but she did not care, not even in the slightest.

"Shehzadi!" a voice called. She turned to find a messenger with a letter in his hand. He handed it to her and was off, leaving Durkhanai with shaking hands and a shaking heart.

But when she opened it, it was just from Rashid. He had called for her to come meet with him, which was not alarming at all, until she saw where he said he would be waiting for her.

He would be waiting by the eastern falls and lavender fields.

Durkhanai sighed—she did not want to go—but she could not outright ignore Rashid, especially when his note said he had an important matter to discuss.

She had run off from the banquet. Perhaps he wished to speak with her about what had occurred there.

She prepared and went to the stables, brushing Heer's white-haired mane.

As she brushed, her thoughts roamed to what she had done to Rukhsana's food. Her hands slowed, and Heer gazed into her eyes, as if searching deeply. Durkhanai stared back.

She felt no remorse, only the settling calm that came with a wrong being righted.

"Chalo, Heer," she said. "Let's go."

She mounted, and they set off. Strong winds whipped across her face, Heer's gallops beating loudly against the earth. Durkhanai lost herself in the ride, but it was over too quickly.

She dismounted, straightening her hair and crown. The falls were just as breathtaking as ever. There was a serenity filled by the sound of rushing water, the chirping birds, and the sky deepening into shades of purple and blue. The perfect backdrop for a beautiful memory.

For a moment, Durkhanai wished to stand on the cliff edge, feel the spray of water on her cheeks—but then she recalled why she was there.

"Shehzadi!" Rashid called. His face lit up when he saw her. He had dressed well, which wasn't strange for a meeting with the Shehzadi, but he had never dressed so formally before. He wore a jacquard black and gold waistcoat over his black shalwar kameez.

"Salam," she said in greeting, smiling. She tried not to be nervous, but she was suspicious as to why he had called her to meet him in such a gorgeous and, now that she gave it some thought, such an intimate location.

"Come, let us walk near the falls," Rashid said. He offered her his arm, and she took it. As they walked, she felt his gaze on her. He stopped them too far away for her to feel it's rushing waters spray past her.

"Beautiful," Rashid said, voice soft. She turned to look at him, and his hazel eyes were warm.

She looked away. "Yes, it is," she said, letting go of his arm. "Though not beautiful enough to distract me. You said you wished to discuss a matter of import with me? I thought perhaps it had something to do with the springs these falls provide water to?"

"No, not quite." Rashid smiled. "Though I so admire your knowledge of the land. It is one of the many things I admire about you."

Durkhanai gave him a friendly smile and continued walking.

"Perhaps you wish to discuss Rukhsana-sahiba?" she suggested. "You must be as furious with her as I am myself, but she has taken her leave, and I have faith she will get her due, in the end."

"I am glad to hear it," Rashid said, "though that is not what I had in mind."

He hurried again to her side. Durkhanai lifted a hand to adjust her dupatta, and as she did, Rashid's gaze caught on the bandage wrapped around her wrist. His face crinkled with worry.

"What happened here?" He reached for her. She deflected, cradling her hand to her chest.

"Nothing to fret over, I assure you," she said, giving him a quick smile. "Just a little scratch. Doctor Aliyah gave me a salve that has done wonders. Oh, of course. *That's* what you wished to discuss. The plans for distribution of medicine; now that we have found the source of the illness——"

"No," Rashid interjected. "What I wish to discuss is of more import even than that." He took a deep breath. "I wish to discuss . . . us."

He drew nearer, and Durkhanai took a step back, heart racing.

"Perhaps we should get going," she suggested. "Heer is not a fan of the dark."

It was an excuse, and they both knew it. But Rashid would not be deterred. She could see it on his face. He had mustered up the courage and would not let it pass.

"Wait. I really——" he paused, almost choking on the words. He cleared his throat and pushed forward. "I adore you. I would like to make my intentions clear."

Durkhanai froze.

*Oh no*, she thought. *Oh no, oh no, oh no.*

"Oh," she said aloud. "Um . . ."

She didn't know what to say.

Rashid looked at her with his soft eyes full of hope and adoration. Full of expectation. Durkhanai bit her lip, face blank, not letting any emotions show.

An auspicious match. Guaranteed support. And yet . . . her heart burned bright, a warning.

"I'm sorry," she said, trying to find a coherent thought. "I'm sorry, let me just think for a moment."

Rashid smiled his sweet smile. "What is there to think about?" he asked. "Surely, you must see what an opportune match this could be."

"Of course, yes, but—" Durkhanai fiddled with her fingers. "Can you give me a day to consider?"

Rashid blinked. He had clearly not expected this. "Do you need it?"

"Yes."

His eyes flashed with hurt, but he hid it away. He bowed. "Very well then. I will—" He cleared his throat. "I will take my leave."

He went. She watched him leave. As he did, she waited for regret to seize her, to feel her heart swell. She waited for her voice to call out for him. Instead, she felt—nothing.

If he never came back, her life would remain unchanged.

It was true she had thought she felt something for him before. True that she had seen him as her future husband even. But in the middle there, the more she got to know him—she had been confused. She didn't know if the soft fondness she felt for him was romantic or strictly platonic.

But if she had been confused before, his confession had brought her perfect clarity; she felt nothing romantic for Rashid.

Durkhanai debated his proposal as she made her way back to her bed.

She was a princess. Hadn't she always thought that love would come, no matter who she married? There was no room for romance in the life of a princess; marriage was a partnership, it only required mutual respect and understanding.

But Durkhanai found she wasn't content with that anymore.

Would she feel the same if she had never met Asfandyar? If she were to rewind to a year prior, when all she had ever thought about was Rashid? When she had dreamt of the day he would finally ask for her hand, make it official?

Then Asfandyar had changed everything she had ever known. Shown her emotions and parts of herself she didn't realize were there. And she had forgotten about Rashid. She had realized how much bigger the world was. How much possibility there was for love and for life.

Rashid deserved better than her. He deserved somebody who adored him as he did her, somebody who loved him much more than she would ever be capable of doing.

Durkhanai felt terrible, truly. She didn't know if she had misled Rashid, perhaps to make Asfandyar jealous, or if she had really just been so confused.

But what could she do? She hadn't meant for things to go this far. Durkhanai sat back and wondered if she cut her heart open what it would look like. What color would she bleed?

"Tumhe kya hua?"

Durkhanai turned to see Zarmina had entered the room. Durkhanai sighed into her pillows. Zarmina came and laid down beside her.

"You look terrible," Zarmina noted. She poked Durkhanai's chubby cheek.

"Rashid proposed," Durkhanai said.

"What!" Zarmina exclaimed, shaking Durkhanai's shoulders. Her face was covered in excitement . . . until she saw Durkhanai's face. "I don't understand," Zarmina said. "You've always wanted to marry Rashid. How many times did you wonder and wait precisely for this moment?"

"I know," Durkhanai covered her face with her hands. "I just—I've changed. I don't want that—him anymore."

Durkhanai didn't have to say the rest. She felt Zarmina realize, saw her go quiet. She knew she was being unreasonable. She had no future with Asfandyar. Her grandparents would never accept a foreigner for their princess, least of all the ambassador of a tribe with which their own had such strained relations. Nor would her people.

Deeper than that, Durkhanai knew there was something more. Something her grandparents would never own up to or accept. And it had to do with the color of Asfandyar's skin.

She would be a fool to reject Rashid—perfect Rashid—for a chance with somebody she could never be with. She knew how their story would end. And yet . . .

"Durkhanai," Zarmina started.

"Please, I don't want a lecture." Durkhanai's eyes welled up with tears.

"When do I lecture you? I just wish to understand. Marrying Rashid would only strengthen your standing . . ."

"Please, Zarmina," Durkhanai said, cutting her off. But her cousin would not be deterred. There was genuine worry in her eyes, her voice anxious when she spoke.

"Just listen to me. You must think of your future. Marrying Rashid would secure it! You do not realize—"

"Zarmina," Durkhanai snapped, voice harsh. "I don't wish to hear any more."

Zarmina opened her mouth to speak once more, and it seemed there was something she wished to say that she could not say, for she bit down on whatever words she'd considered pushing past Durkhanai's resistance.

She released a long breath, then sank into the pillows beside Durkhanai.

"There, there," Zarmina said, stroking her hair. "Everything is happening precisely as it must, remember? You always tell me that when things seem awry. All will be all right, janaan, in the end."

When would the end come?

Her head and her heart were at a war like the Marghazari against the Luhgams. Durkhanai called for a ceasefire as she closed her eyes and drifted to sleep.

When Durkhanai awoke sometime later, her room had darkened with the setting sun. She rushed to the window to catch the last glimmer of sunset, but it was too late.

The sun was already gone.

# CHAPTER TWENTY-SIX

Durkhanai had no answer to give Rashid, so she gave him none at all.

There was work to be done, besides. The next time she went to the villages, she brought a small army of the palace's doctors with her. The Badshah would not be happy to learn she had ordered them to come with her, but she had not been happy to be kept in the dark about the Kebzu soldier, either.

"Come, this way," she instructed. She led them to an open area of land outside the village homes. The center of the village would have been more opportune, but it was already congested from the bazaar and the traffic that led to the main roads, which cut up and down the mountain to the neighboring villages.

"Set up the tent here, then we can get to preparing the stalls," Durkhanai ordered. The workers who had accompanied her from the palace got to work setting up the medical station. She had brought three doctors from the palace.

"The stalls are ready, Shehzadi," a worker informed her when they were done. The morning had been productive, and she was glad.

"Good," she said. "Now go to the bazaar and inform the villagers to come for checkups. This stall will be here for the duration of today and tomorrow, and I expect all villagers to be examined."

"Yes, Shehzadi."

He was off, and when he returned, a line of villagers were behind him: old women and small children and young men.

"Please queue in three lines," Durkhanai instructed. "And be patient—you will each get your turn."

Durkhanai stood at the head of the tent, watching and hoping her presence would remind her people that she cared.

"Here, a gift from the palace," she said as the first examination was done. She handed a package of dried apricots, nuts, and beef jerky to the villager. She hoped the small package of food would appease the people.

This entire affair had been costly to the palace, and she knew the Badshah would give her a harsh glance for it when he found out, but Durkhanai would meet his glare with one of her own.

After ensuring things were running smoothly at the clinic, Durkhanai visited the stream where women went to do their washing. Sure enough, there were bassinets of sleeping babies on the side while women were crouched by the water, cleaning their clothes. Their toddlers chased one another around the trees, tumbling and falling.

"Salam," Durkhanai said, smiling. She pinched a toddler's cheek.

The women touched their fingers to their foreheads in respect, setting their washing aside to hear what she had to say.

While many women worked in the fields, those with infants and toddlers stayed home, caring for their children. It was here that Durkhanai called for volunteers: for mothers to perhaps watch their neighbors' children, allowing more women to work. Durkhanai spent an entire day negotiating between families, trying to set up a network for better distribution of human resources.

She worked directly with tribe leaders, her nobles, on other bartering of resources and skills. Some tribes had superb craftsmen, others had efficient farmers.

However, the more powerful clans like Naeem-sahib's had everything.

"Again with this idea—we have no need for more farmers," Naeem-sahib said when she approached him to negotiate. "Nor do we need more women. While overall efficiency has decreased due to the illness, our men are quickly recovering. I am perfectly capable of ensuring my tribe's success, Shehzadi." He paused. "Perhaps you should focus your attentions to more pertinent matters."

He gave her a pointed glance. Rashid had told him then. She would not be derailed by proposals.

"There is nothing more pertinent than this," she replied, meeting his fierce gaze with her own.

But he was right in regards to the other matter. If he had wanted for nothing, what incentive could she give him to help the others who could use the spare hands? And he was right again that this idea had been suggested before but to no avail. He had said that the people were unwilling to accommodate other clans unless it was of direct advantage to their families. Durkhanai knew she had to appease him. And she could do so with something no one else could offer.

"I can reduce the quota of men from your clan going to war," Durkhanai said.

Each clan had to provide a certain amount of men, proportional to their population size, for the wars being waged. It was definitely a bad idea to give favor to some, one the Badshah would abhor, but what else was there to offer?

Naeem-sahib paused, considering the offer.

"With fewer men going to war, you have more hands for the fields," Durkhanai continued. "You can thus take some women out of the fields and have them watch the children of your neighbor's tribe."

Durkhanai used a similar tactic with some of the other tribes who weren't hit as heavily by the illness. Following Naeem-sahib's lead, other tribe leaders agreed as well.

But it wasn't the end of trying to settle things in the villages.

"When will the ambassadors leave?" somebody asked her at one point.

"When negotiations have been settled," Durkhanai replied. The man sighed in response, almost rolling his eyes.

"Problem?" she snapped. He immediately stood straight, stammering.

"No, no, Shehzadi," he said, lowering his head.

Durkhanai noticed this throughout the villages; the people were being . . . strange around her. Like they knew something she didn't. It made her feel bitter, quick to snap at anyone with even the slightest changed tone of voice.

She did not respond well to anything short of adoration.

It was the same, day after day, for weeks while Dhadi continued negotiations to ensure the ambassadors left to never return.

Durkhanai visited the various villages of her mountain, and everything seemed to be in chaos since Rukhsana-sahiba's departure. Durkhanai barely had time to do anything but reassure her people, to calm the rising war cries and the discontent.

At the very least, the calls for unification had died out, though they had been replaced by the zealous push for the foreigners' departures.

The ambassadors had all extended their stays to further discuss negotiations and draft a consolidated peace treaty. Rukhsana-sahiba was gone. That was one less person to worry about, supposedly Durkhanai's biggest concern.

So why didn't Durkhanai feel safe in her own home?

Rukhsana-sahiba's words haunted Durkhanai: *you will never be badshah.*

Somehow, July had tumbled into August, the summer and the heat fleeting to soon welcome the crisp bite of autumn and the inevitable freeze of winter.

Everything was slipping between her fingers like sand grains falling to the wind, and the tighter she held on, the faster they fell. Almost like she was losing control over everything.

She had a creeping, haunting feeling that tasted bitter in her mouth and raked against her chest like frustration and anger. She found herself continually walking with a clenched jaw, hands curled into little fists.

The light and sunshine of summer was fading much too fast.

The haunting feeling in her gut came to fruition one day when she arrived back at her palace.

"Shehzadi, the Badshah and the Wali await you in the presence chamber," a servant told her.

"Khairiyat?" she replied. "Is everything all right?"

"There is a messenger with news," the servant replied.

She went, and sure enough, there was a messenger in the presence chamber, waiting for her, to tell her the news. She could tell from her grandparents' faces that they already knew.

"Agha-Jaan, what is it?" she asked.

The creeping feeling filled her lungs, making her feel like there were little bugs crawling across her skin.

The Badshah motioned to the messenger to relay the news.

"Rukhsana-sahiba has passed away," the messenger said.

Durkhanai drew a breath. She recited the prayer for the deceased. "Inna lillahi wa inna ilayhi ra'ji'oon. What happened?" She held her hands together tightly.

"When the Wali's people came to meet the ambassador by the border, she had fallen ill," the messenger told her. "A few days into their travel, she quietly passed in her sleep."

"And the treaty?" Durkhanai asked. She immediately grimaced at herself—a woman had *died*—but she needed to make sure her people would be all right, that they would not be harmed because of this.

"The treaty is still valid," the Badshah said. "Rukhsana-sahiba passed from natural means. The Wali of Teerza has no reason to quarrel with us."

The messenger nodded, taking his leave, and Durkhanai was alone with her grandparents. Heart hammering, she recalled her last encounter with Rukhsana-sahiba, how the woman had taunted her, how furious Durkhanai had been—how impetuous.

But Durkhanai hadn't meant to *kill* her, just cause her pain through the illness, for a few days, perhaps. To make her suffer, to make her understand the pain she had caused Durkhanai's people.

She must have sprinkled too much of the powder. Tears filled her eyes.

Durkhanai had killed her—*no*.

She held her thoughts at bay, blinked the tears away. She hadn't meant to; it wasn't her fault.

Death came to all.

Durkhanai excused herself, holding her head high and back steady as she walked out of the presence chamber. It was only when she was out of their sight that she ran, lifting up her gharara, face scrunching in the prologue of a sob.

She ran to her room and shut the door, breathing hard.

Durkhanai ripped off the necklace and jewelry weighing her down, throwing off her dupatta and tiara. The gold clunked against the marble floors, a cacophony of sounds as she pulled the pins and braids from her hair, letting the hair fall loose.

She couldn't breathe.

Durkhanai ran out to her balcony, leaning her body on the railing. From here, she could see nothing but mountains—her mountains. She steadied her breathing, tried to steady the blood rushing and gushing through her veins.

Guilt flooded through her. She felt sinful in the private space between Allah and herself, but Durkhanai pushed those thoughts away, shoved the feelings from her heart. She could sense she was being unreasonable, stubborn even, but she would be what she needed to be.

Durkhanai was losing her grip, becoming more and more volatile. More barbaric.

Cutting off Durkhanai's thoughts, her wardrobe doors opened.

Her heartbeat quickened the instant Asfandyar's shadow entered her sight; it ricocheted against her ribs further when she saw his face. She knew what she felt for him was otherworldly, but what she couldn't quite figure out was whether it was from heaven or hell.

All she knew was that they were bound together: as inevitable as an exhalation.

"Was it you?" he asked without preamble, out of breath.

"I don't know what you mean," she said, clearing her throat. She tried to iron out her emotions, but he caught her fumble.

"Durkhanai," he sighed, coming close. "What have you done?"

Her patience thinned; she did not need him to make her feel more guilty. "She deserved it, after attacking my people," she said, voice steel.

"And you're god now, are you?" Asfandyar responded, pinching the bridge of his nose. "What is this madness?"

"An attack against my people is an attack against me," she insisted, but she was losing her resolve.

She was losing her grip.

"All people are my people," he replied. "Durkhanai, just as the lives of your people have worth, so do the lives of everyone else. One life is not worth more than another just because of the arbitration of tribe or family."

She knew she agreed with him, to a certain extent. But she didn't want to be lectured, least of all from him. She didn't need to be reminded of his goodness. Her heart was hardening more and more, and all she wanted was him.

It was the stubbornness rising within her, one she had not felt since she was a child. She was trying so hard to fix things for everyone, but no matter how she pushed, some things would not bend.

She could not let him go. But she could not have him, either.

She didn't know how to handle it—this struggle. She knew she should dampen the stubbornness and soften her edges, but she didn't want to.

She was too emotional, too volatile.

She needed this energy or she was afraid she would go numb. It felt as though all her life she had been asleep, and only recently had she been woken. She was afraid to fall asleep again.

"You should leave," she said, voice hard.

"Why?" he asked. "Because I'm right?"

"You cannot be right," she snapped. "Not for me." She was a match about to be struck.

"Durkhanai, don't—" he began, voice soft, and she could not bear it.

"Rashid has proposed to me," she said, voice full of fire.

Asfandyar went still as stone. Finally, he had nothing to say. He studied her face, eyes blazing. She was breathing hard, her hands curled into fists.

"Congratulations," he finally replied. "Don't forget to send me an invitation."

Her nails bit into her skin, but before she could say anything else, he left without another word. Her heart hammered with anger and a thousand and one emotions more.

She didn't understand, didn't comprehend if he was bad for her, wrong for her, impossible for her. Was it her instinct and self-preservation pushing him away or pride and arrogance? She couldn't understand it.

Why was her heart caught on him? Why did her heart keep turning to him, even as she tried to walk away? Even as he walked away? Oh, wretched, cruel thoughts. How horrible they were to her.

Durkhanai knew she would never marry Rashid, yet she still hadn't told him. Judging from Naeem-sahib's comment earlier, Rashid must have been anxious for a response.

Chagrined, she could sense she was being a coward, prolonging the inevitable. She had pondered over the softest way to approach the situation, but enough was enough.

She had wondered if problems really didn't go away if they weren't addressed. She had been determined to test it out, but no more. Rashid deserved a response. She went to get Heer, intent on riding to his house. But when she neared the palace stables, she found there was no need. Rashid was there in the hall, heading in the same direction.

"Rashid!" she called. He turned. When he saw her, a bright smile covered his face.

"Shehzadi!" He walked toward her.

"I need to speak with you," she said.

"I was just going riding with my father." He cast a glance over his shoulder. His father stood in the distance, watching them. "Perhaps we could have chai together afterward?"

Why wasn't Rashid the one she loved? Durkhanai cursed her wretched heart.

The sight of the nobleman almost changed her mind, but—no. She had to choose herself. She deserved more, and so did Rashid.

"It will only take a moment," she said quickly.

Rashid stepped closer. Durkhanai took a breath.

"I appreciate what you said," she told him. "But I do not feel the same. I cannot accept your proposal."

"Oh," Rashid said. His face slackened, contorting with confusion. He shook his head. "I don't understand. Is it not opportune? Have our families not discussed this very idea?"

"It is, they have, but I cannot." Durkhanai hoped he would understand, not press her for more details. "I do not wish to marry merely for political gain."

"But I thought . . . you asked me for help." His usually warm eyes had lost their sunlight. "I spoke to all those noblemen on your behalf."

"You are to head your clan one day," she responded. "Surely, you were not being amiable to the other noblemen solely for my sake?"

"But I thought—"

"Rashid, please," she said. "I am sorry if perhaps my actions misled you. I do consider you a good friend and an even greater ally. I sincerely hope this unpleasantness will not ruin the bond our families have shared for generations."

"You cannot care about that," he said, voice bitter. "Not when I am trying to strengthen that very bond, and your response is to callously reject me."

"I do care, which is why I think we will be better suited as allies than husband and wife. I am sorry, Rashid, but I cannot offer you more. I will leave you now."

Without waiting for a response, Durkhanai set off. She released a long breath. She knew this would have consequences, but she could not lie. She did not wish to.

Durkhanai had negotiations to handle. She was tired of waiting. Until now, the Wali of S'vat had been handling everything. The Badshah, too focused on his wars, could not be bothered and nor could the Shehzadi, too focused on the people—but no more.

The people had asked her when the ambassadors would be leaving. Durkhanai would give them a response.

She went directly to Gulalai's room. Her friend was sitting, writing a letter.

"Come with me," Durkhanai said, plucking the pen from Gulalai's fingers.

"Durkhanai, what's the meaning of this?" Gulalai asked when Durkhanai grabbed her hand.

"Trust me," Durkhanai responded, bringing Gulalai along until they reached the presence chamber. Durkhanai threw open the doors, walking in with Gulalai at her side. The Badshah and the Wali watched carefully.

"Ambassador," the Wali nodded her acknowledgement. "Durkhanai, jaani, what is it?"

"Kurra's ambassador is leaving, and she will return with one hundred horsemen to aid Marghazar in her war against the Luhgam Empire, as Teerza has provided soldiers." Durkhanai declared. "When the ambassador returns, she is welcome to an extended stay here as my guest. I pledge my loyalty to her as a friend, as she has pledged hers to me."

Durkhanai took everyone by surprise, including herself. Gulalai balked. The Wali was surprised, but they all waited for the Badshah to respond. Durkhanai's grandfather regarded the young girls carefully, showing no emotion, no reaction, until finally, he nodded.

"One hundred and fifty," he replied. "We make no written commitment to Kurra, and the pesky matter of the summit is truly settled, never to be brought up again."

It was a bad deal, in truth, and Durkhanai was entirely dependent on Gulalai to trust her. And while Gulalai was her friend, she was also an ambassador and daughter of the Wali of Kurra.

Durkhanai waited with bated breath to see if Gulalai would agree to the terms. She turned to her friend. Gulalai tapped her fingers on her cane, her nails clicking against the jewels, face pensive.

It would need to be enough. Perhaps this was how long-lasting alliances began: with nothing but trust.

Finally, Gulalai turned to look at Durkhanai. Her brown eyes were warm.

"One hundred and twenty-five," Gulalai responded, voice sure.

"Done," the Badshah said.

And thus, the oath was made.

"Bring me the contract, and you will have my word on paper allowing your stay in exchange for the horsemen," the Badshah told the Kurra ambassador. "When everything has been finalized, you will bring me those horsemen and continue your stay here, as our guest."

"Yes, Badshah," Gulalai replied, bowing her head in respect. Durkhanai saw Gulalai's lip quiver ever so slightly.

"Ambassador, you are dismissed," the Wali said. "Durkhanai, stay a moment, will you, gudiya?"

Durkhanai nodded, turning to Gulalai.

"Wait for me," she said. Gulalai nodded, then exited the presence chamber, leaving Durkhanai alone with her grandparents.

"We do not allow foreigners in Safed-Mahal," the Wali said. "You know that, Durkhanai. These months have been an exception, due to the circumstances, but let's not make it a habit."

"I trust her," Durkhanai replied, keeping her voice cool. "And I think it's time we change some traditions. How else will we progress?"

She sounded like a libertarian, she knew, but perhaps it was time.

"Durkhanai, janaan—" Dhadi began, but Agha-Jaan cut her off.

"I think it is good Durkhanai is taking charge," he said. "The deal is not so horrible. With those horsemen, we can strike the Luhgam Empire hard. Good work, gudiya."

Durkhanai smiled. She knew the Badshah would see only his wars and would question nothing more. He was getting old, too old, and she felt a little guilty for using his greed against him, but if she was to be the Badshah, she would need to learn how to be a queen.

"Very well," Dhadi said, eyes sharp. Durkhanai could sense Dhadi wished to say something more, but because Durkhanai had gained Agha-Jaan's favor, Dhadi withheld. "That's all then."

Durkhanai bit back a smile, satisfaction coursing through her. Her grandmother had challenged her to be a queen, and that was exactly what Durkhanai had done.

Dismissed, Durkhanai went outside and found Gulalai waiting. She leaned against her jeweled cane, frowning.

"You could have warned me," Gulalai said, clearly cross.

"You're right," Durkhanai said. "I've been in a mood. I'm sorry. I sort of thought of it just then."

"It's all right," Gulalai replied. She gave a long sigh. "My father won't be happy with these terms, but I will convince him. Durkhanai, you know this isn't the most auspicious negotiation for my people."

"I know," Durkhanai replied. "But you can trust me. We will lay the foundation of a life-long friendship and alliance in the coming months, and though it will not be written explicitly on paper, I swear my loyalty to you as the future Badshah of Marghazar. I swear it to Allah."

It was a powerful oath, one made to their Lord. Breaking it was damning. Durkhanai had not sworn to many things in her life. It was a sacred act, as sacred as blood.

"At the very least, my father will appreciate you keeping me as a guest here for longer," Gulalai said. "But Durkhanai—be warned. The Badshah's greed for victory is alarming, not only to me but to the others as well. It seems he is losing sight of anything else. You wouldn't want anybody to take advantage of the situation."

"Is that a threat?" Durkhanai asked calmly.

Gulalai laughed. "No, my friend. A warning. As your ally, I find it pertinent to tell you." She held Durkhanai's hands. "And I am glad to be going home only to return. We will continue our misadventures when I do."

Gulalai winked.

"Go now, draft that contract," Durkhanai replied with a laugh. "I have more matters to attend to."

And she did. Durkhanai went next to the ambassador from the B'rung zilla, Palwasha-sahiba, who Durkhanai understood now to be there only to barter some sort of legitimate advantage.

B'rung was a small zilla, sharing a border with Marghazar in the south. Over tea, Durkhanai listened to the ambassador's grievances, and the main problem seemed to be that the B'rung zilla was largely inaccessible due to exceptionally hilly terrain.

"I went out some nights to inspect your roads," Palwasha-sahiba said. "I've found them to be quite extraordinary."

So that explained why she was out that night.

"If Ma-Marghazar could aid in the construction of some roads," she continued, closing her eyes when she stuttered. "B'rung would be most grateful."

Durkhanai tested the same technique she used with Kurra's negotiations and found that both Palwasha-sahiba and the Badshah were immediately compliant. He was willing to do anything for soldiers, his insatiable greed guiding him.

Gulalai was right; the Badshah seemed ready to do anything for more troops against the Luhgams. She knew how badly he wanted to win this war, but he was becoming rash.

He wasn't seeing things clearly, clouded by emotion.

But they had successfully negotiated with three zillas, which left Durkhanai with one more: Jardum.

But that was a matter for another day. For the time being, Durkhanai was spent, mentally and physically exhausted. She went back to her rooms and took a long, steaming rose bath, but even as she cooled off, clean and warm, she could not quiet the anxiety within her. There were a thousand emotions running through her veins, and she squeezed her eyes shut, curled her hands into fists, doubling over, breathing hard.

That night, she dreamt of him.

When she awoke, Durkhanai felt him everywhere.

She couldn't catch her breath, couldn't stop her heart, beating so fast against her chest, she thought for sure it would burst, leaving her a bloody mess. She squeezed her legs tight and pulled them into her chest, curling into a ball, trying to contain this explosion. But it would not be contained.

She wanted to feel his skin on hers, and just the idea was enough to raise her heartbeat to dramatic rates. What an unholy thing she was, thinking such unholy thoughts. She was to remain untouched until marriage, but she couldn't help thinking of all the ways she would let him touch her.

It was dangerous to think such things, but she couldn't stop. She felt drunk off the thought of him, and it was a liquor she never wanted to lose the taste of, drugs she never wanted to lose the habit of. There was madness growing within her, the junoon that came only with ishq.

She wanted to scream.

She didn't understand; she knew he was bad for her and—yet. How could her heart do this to her? She couldn't wrap her mind around it, this revolt of her heart's, this incessant attention and adoration for someone that would bring no good.

That was the worst part, maybe. That she knew nothing good would come from this but she still caught on him. She was absurdly in love with the idea of love, and there he was, a perfect vessel to carry those hopes. There he was, a perfect stature of distraction and aimless, indistinguishable delight.

So she did the only thing she could—she prayed: prayed for her heart to cease this adoration and affection, to cease this love.

She prayed for salvation.

# CHAPTER TWENTY-SEVEN

urkhanai could only prolong the inevitable for so long.

All the ambassadors had reached negotiations and agreements. The only ambassador left was the one from Jardum: Asfandyar.

She could talk to him about anything but this. Because she knew they would settle upon an agreement easily and quickly, and then, having done his job, he would leave.

So she avoided bringing it up, like the coward she was. And she so hated to be a coward. All she could think about was Asfandyar and how close he was to leaving. She was barely bothered when she was summoned to her grandparents.

"Durkhanai, what have you done?" Dhadi asked, confused. "Why did you turn down Rashid?"

"Bas," Durkhanai said with a shrug. "I just did."

"But, gudiya, I don't understand," Dhadi said. "I thought you two got along well—I thought you had grown to find him suitable."

"He is a good man," Durkhanai said. "Kind, sweet, respectful. But I cannot marry him."

"Why?" Dhadi asked. "Meri jaan, we won't force you. I just wish to understand."

"I just don't want to," Durkhanai said. She didn't know how else to explain it. Knowing her grandmother would pester her to no end, Durkhanai went to Agha-Jaan's side.

"Agha-Jaan, I don't want to marry him," she pouted.

"Janaan, now is a good time for a wedding," Dhadi said, trying to coax Durkhanai and her husband. "The nobles are upset with the villagers, and a wedding could unify them all. *You* could unite them all: the people's Shehzadi, the most precious of precious things."

Durkhanai shook her head. When she had made a decision, it was final. Agha-Jaan at least understood as much.

"Let the girl go," he said, calming his wife. "As if that boy is the last man left in Marghazar. We will find someone else, someone we are all happy with."

Even as he said it, Durkhanai knew it was impossible.

"I'm going then," Durkhanai said. She reached over and kissed both her grandparents on the cheeks.

She left the room, then heard her grandmother follow a moment later.

"Durkhanai, look at me," Dhadi said, voice gentle. She tilted Durkhanai's chin up until she met her grandmother's green eyes. Dhadi furrowed her brow. "I do hope you have not grown attached to another." Her eyes sharpened. "Especially when I expressly forbade you from associating with him."

Durkhanai tried to keep her voice steady as she lied. "No, Dhadi, there is no one else."

"Oh, Durkhanai," Dhadi tsked, voice sad.

Durkhanai looked away.

She couldn't bear the disappointment. "Please, Dhadi," she said, voice fogged. "I am tired. I wish to rest."

"My little fool." Dhadi sighed. "Go then."

But there would be no rest for her.

Then Durkhanai, like anyone in crisis, grabbed a glass full of mango lassi and sat on a windowsill, gazing out at the mountains, thinking and aching.

After some time, Asfandyar found her, and she wondered how it was that he always did. He should have made a profession out of it; he could be her Royal Stalker. She wanted to tell him as much, to tease him, but instead said nothing. She had no heart for humor at the present.

"What grief lingers on your tongue, Shehzadi?" he asked, and just hearing his voice, she forgot why she was angry with him.

She responded with a sigh, sipping her mango lassi.

Asfandyar sat beside her, looking out at the view. "The mountains never change," he remarked, and she didn't have to tell him that was why she loved her mountains so much. It was why he had said that in the first place.

Sensing he wasn't getting a reaction from her, Asfandyar held out his hand for her drink. It was natural to hand it to him, but she watched with a pounding heart as he held it up to the light. Her lips had left a red stain on the rim. He rotated the glass. Eyes focused on hers, he pressed his mouth against where hers had been.

Her stomach lurched. Her heart beat quickly, much too quickly.

He lowered the glass. A bead of red blossomed across his lips like blood.

Swallowing hard, she reached a finger toward his mouth to wipe it, but he caught her hand. Held her cold fingers to his warm face.

"Leave it," he whispered, voice rough. "I like having you on my lips."

She felt like she was standing on a cliff, a step away from falling.

"That is hardly—proper," she choked.

His eyes were molten. "I never said it was."

She watched him go, walking around with her lipstick on his mouth, leaving her feeling starved.

Durkhanai continued to sit there for hours, watching the clouds move, watching the sun dance across the sky. She watched the birds and wondered what it would be like to fly. The sun set the sky ablaze, and she felt the same.

Asfandyar found her still there much time later, this time staring at the stars, eyes alight with wonder. She hugged her knees close to her chest, resting her cheek on her knee.

"Did Rashid really propose?" Asfandyar asked.

Durkhanai nodded, still looking at the stars.

"Does he love you?" he asked, voice quieter. "You deserve to be revered."

Durkhanai nodded again. She did not look at him.

"What . . . What response did you give?" he asked, voice faltering.

"What response do you believe I gave?" She finally turned to look at him.

Seeing him standing there, so close, she wished to seize him as she seized everything she wanted in life, but in love, it could not be so. Though she was tired of not saying what she meant, she was too stubborn and proud to be the first one to say it.

Asfandyar ran a hand through his curls, and they bounced back in place.

"Truly, I don't know," Asfandyar replied. "You've become so difficult to read."

"Yet I can read you like a book," Durkhanai replied. His eyes burned, hope flickering within the endless shades of black.

"Then you know," he told her, voice low. "Surely, you must know."

"Know what?" she asked, feigning innocence.

"Durkhanai," he pleaded. Her name in his mouth sent a shiver down her spine.

"Know that you would wish me well in my marriage?" she replied, sitting up. She was annoyed now.

Asfandyar sighed. He was exasperated, his mien tense.

"Do you enjoy tormenting me?" he asked, voice sharp. "I'm genuinely curious."

"Yes," she snapped back, standing. She glared at him, and he glared back. She felt volatile and knew he felt it, as well. He clenched his jaw, trying to grind words out of his emotions. He looked away and released a measured breath from his nose. When he turned back, his face was open.

"Let me try again," he said finally. "I'm inexplicably drawn to you."

"Many people are," she responded. She knew she was pushing him, but she couldn't bear it any longer: the weight of unspoken things between them.

"You're impossible," he groaned.

"I am," she replied. "Is that what you've come to tell me?"

He stood still as stone. She wanted to yell at him, to shake some emotion from him, but she stood just as stoic.

"Khudafiz then," she said, turning. "Goodbye."

Her face crumpled the instant her back was to him, but she forced herself to begin walking away. One step in front of the other . . .

"Wait," he rasped, his voice woolen. "Don't go."

He caught her hand and drew close enough that she could feel his body in the space behind her. She could almost feel his heart beating like a hummingbird against her back.

Somehow, she knew this was the moment.

The final fall.

She could stop it, but she didn't want to. He sunk his teeth into her heart, and she let him.

"I lay myself bare before you," he whispered, his nose grazing her jaw. "What fabric is your heart cut from? Is it silken and soft? Velveteen and plush? Woolen and thick? Whatever it is, cover me with it."

His arms had wrapped around her waist, encapsulating her. He pressed a soft kiss to her neck, and the world turned to starlight.

She couldn't breathe.

"Main tera, main tera," he said, his voice silken. "Entirely, *completely*—I am yours."

She had waited so long to hear the truth made clear, for some sort of evidence and proof, but now that it was finally here, she was frozen. She knew once she turned, once she responded, she would no longer be able to hold back.

Tears pricked her eyes. Her position, her duties, her people, her family, her grandparents—they flitted into her mind for half an instant, but all she knew was him.

Finally, she spoke the truth she had known for weeks.

"I am yours," she whispered.

She found the courage to turn, still in his arms. Between them was a whisper of space. She raised a shaking hand and held it to his face, felt his beard against her palm, just as she had imagined so many times. But her imaginings hadn't been close to reality: the weight, the blood, the bone of him. Her pinky brushed beneath his jaw, and she felt his pulse, running wild like an animal's. Closing his eyes, he pressed his mouth into her palm.

"I tried to stay away from you. I really did, Durre," he said. "But I couldn't resist."

Durkhanai bit back her grin. "Durre?" she whispered. "No one's called me that in ages."

"You don't like it?" he asked.

"I adore it," she said. She looked into his eyes. "And I adore you, Asfi."

He grinned into her hand.

"Asfi?" he repeated. "You're the only one I would ever let get away with calling me that."

"Kasam se?" she asked. "Do you mean it?"

"Teri kasam," he replied, eyes earnest. He swore it on her.

His hands were resting on her waist, and she wrapped her arms around his neck. Snuggled against him, she was safe, at ease, suspended in the eye of the storm raging on around her.

Here, there was peace.

"Durkhanai," he said against her hair, voice gentle but tentative. His body tensed against her. "I need to . . . to talk to you."

"Mm," she sighed into him. "Not yet."

She could tell whatever he had to say was important, and she didn't want to ruin this. She wanted the peace to last a little longer.

"I think you should know," he said, pulling back. She searched his eyes, saw how distraught he was, how torn. He didn't want to tell her but knew he must.

"Please," she told him, voice soft and coaxing. "Let's just have tonight. Whatever it is, tell me in the morning. I just want to spend a little more time with you."

"You don't understand," he tried again, but he was losing his resolve. "There are things I haven't told you—"

Durkhanai didn't want to listen.

"Shh." She covered his mouth with her hand. "Tomorrow."

"Durkhanai—" he sighed.

She could tell, somehow, that whatever he had to say would change things forever. That she would hate him afterward, and she didn't want to hate him. Not yet.

She just wanted the night, before the inevitable happened. She knew it was a bad idea, knew it would change nothing, knew it would only make things more difficult.

But she couldn't help it. She was too selfish, too self-indulgent to resist.

Behind Asfandyar, she watched stars glittering in the sky.

"Tomorrow," she insisted. She felt like she was on the top of the bell tower, overlooking the entire world, heart hammering, wind whipping against her skin.

He opened his mouth to speak, once more. But before he could, she pulled his face down to hers. She kissed him.

He didn't need a moment to recover; he kissed her as though he'd been waiting for this moment for days and it was finally here. His words evaporated on her tongue, engulfed by something deeper.

There was nothing more important than this.

# CHAPTER TWENTY-EIGHT

*T*hey kissed each other raw.

His mouth on hers was like stars melting on her tongue: molten and sugary sweet. She seized his kurta, pulling him closer, insatiable, and his hands ran down her back, one snaking under her leg.

Overcome with desire that nipped and bit, that bruised and bled, she wanted all of him. She could tell he did, too. Her hands knotted into his hair, his glorious curls, and his grip on her tightened.

"Durkhanai," he gasped, pulling back.

"Why did you stop?" she asked, feeling starved.

Breathless, he put his hands on her shoulders to steady himself—and to hold her back.

"Someone will see."

"I don't care," she whispered, biting his lower lip. A soft sound slipped from his throat, and she caught it on her tongue, her mouth sliding over his again. He pushed her hard against the wall, and the cool marble sent a shiver down her spine.

*So this is what it feels like to fly,* she thought.

His lips roamed, marking little kisses on her jaw, down her throat. He inhaled her scent, then released a sigh.

"You can't imagine how many times I've wanted to do that," he said. "You smell so sweetly of roses."

She extended her neck for him, and he closed his eyes, breathing her in. He pressed a soft kiss to her throat, right where her pulse beat.

She swayed, unbalanced.

"We really ought not to," he said, withdrawing, but his eyes were dark. They were both drunk with desire.

"Is that so?" Undeterred, she kissed him again, open mouth skimming across his skin.

"Do not tease me with your savage little teeth," he begged. He stepped away, serious, and she pouted.

"Since when are you so shareef?"

He smiled. "You've made a noble man out of me."

Her pout deepened. "No fair."

"I want to do what is honorable."

She knew this wasn't, knew she should have shame and be shy, but she didn't care in the slightest. This was a sin she would willingly drown in.

"Won't you touch me again?" she asked. Batting her eyelashes at him, she took a step toward him, and he groaned, taking a step back.

"Stay away from me, woman," he said, raising a finger.

She held her hands up innocently. "I won't do anything. I just want to be near you, or is that too much to ask?"

He gave her a suspicious glance, but held out his hand for her. She grinned, grabbing onto it. A man's hand in hers—it felt so strange yet so true. Like he had always been meant to fit right there, at her side.

Was it meant to feel this easy? This comfortable?

They walked together, and Durkhanai only pulled away when they passed a rose-scented room. She ran to the jhula, sitting in it's center.

"Come, push me!"

He laughed, that glorious, rich laugh, and came behind her. As he did, she tilted her head back, smiling up at him. Even upside down, he was beautiful.

His gaze trailed down her face to her lips, then down her long, exposed neck. His fingers grazed her collar as he pulled a stray curl from the skin.

She shivered, tilting her face up. Her lips parted, aching for a kiss.

"Do not tempt me," he groaned, looking away. Releasing a long sigh, he trailed a hand through her hair, so softly she had to still to feel it.

"Why don't I sit with you?" he said, voice purposefully bright and nonchalant. She laughed out loud at that, then made room for him.

He sat beside her, filling the space perfectly. She held onto one side of the swing; he held onto the other. In the middle, she wrapped a hand around his arm. He rested his hand on her leg.

She looked at him, he looked at her. At the same time, they smiled. Overcome with bubbly joy, Durkhanai hugged Asfnadyar's arm, feeling the corded muscle as she leaned her cheek on his shoulder. His chest moved with withheld laughter.

"Together?" he asked.

They kicked off at once, swinging and swinging together, fused at the seams.

"Where to now?" she asked, as the swing slowed. Asfandyar gave her a mischievous glance but said nothing, only began leading her toward the east wing.

When she saw guards farther down the hall, she released his hand. Immediately, she felt cold.

As they passed, Durkhanai ignored their strange glances at her. She knew it was reckless, but oh, didn't she deserve just one night? She was young; she wanted to feel free.

Durkhanai followed Asfandyar. He checked to make sure the coast was clear before quickly ushering her into a room.

His room.

"And you were worried about me!" she exclaimed. "Not so shareef after all, hm?"

He laughed in response.

"My intentions are pure as the snow that caps the heavenly mountaintops, Shehzadi," he told her, grinning. "I have only brought you here because it is the last place anyone would look for you."

"Mhm," she replied, unconvinced. "Sure."

"Get comfortable," he said, sitting down on a chair. "You can leave whenever you please."

She would never leave, she thought, as she undid her dupatta and crown.

She undid her hair next, pulling out the pins and undoing braids until her unruly curls fell in a cascade down her back, brushing against her hips. Asfandyar watched her, eyes skimming the length of her. She then took off the rest of her jewelry: the heavy gold jhumkay on her ears, the jewels around her neck. Her chudiyan made a soft chum-chum sound as they slipped from her wrists, leaving her skin bare. The only thing she left on was the Miangul family crest ring, which always sat on her right ring finger.

Finally, she undid the buttons and ribbons that tied her embroidered cloak-gown around her body. Beneath, she wore a satin slip and trousers.

"What are you doing?" Asfandyar choked. He had been watching her carefully until then.

"What you said: getting comfortable," she replied, wiggling her brows at him. He turned to look the other way, a blush spreading across his cheeks.

*This man, too!* She had never seen him shy before.

He sensed her noticing and got up to get something from his wardrobe. He handed her a folded shawl just as she released the weight of her gown from her shoulders.

"Wear this," he said, not looking at her.

"No, thank you," she replied politely. She took it and tossed the shawl onto the bed. She took a step closer, and his gaze raked over her body. He looked away again, clenching his jaw tightly.

His dimples made a brief appearance before disappearing again as she stepped toward him, crossing her arms.

He finally looked at her, biting back a laugh.

"Come on," he said, voice sweet as he got up to offer her the shawl once more. "You'll get cold."

A smile was playing on both their lips; it felt like a great game. This time, Durkhanai pretended to consider it for a moment before tossing it aside again.

"If I get cold, I have you to keep me warm, Asfi," she said, winking. This time Asfandyar laughed, a wide grin engulfing his face. The same grin covering hers.

"Who are you?" he asked, eyes full of wonder. She stepped close to him and put her arms around his neck. He did not look away.

"Yours," she replied. "As you are mine."

He kissed her nose, and she wrinkled it in response, giggling.

"I'll sit here," he said, untangling her arms from him. He went to sit on the chair across from the bed. "You sit there."

He pointed to a chair on the far side of the room.

"Mm, I'll sit here," she said, sitting in the adjacent chair. She pushed the chair closer to his, holding back a laugh. Asfandyar responded by scooting his chair away. Durkhanai fake pouted.

"No fun," she told him. "I told you I won't do anything."

"Chal jhooti," he said, laughing. "Liar."

"True," she said, grinning, and she went to sit on the armrest of his chair. She leaned close to him, inhaling his scent, and pulled his face close with her index finger.

"But since when do you follow the rules?" she teased.

"You'll be the end of me," he muttered, looking at her lips. She grinned and planted a kiss on his cheek.

"Acha, Asfi," she conceded. "I'll behave myself."

She went and sat on his bed, wrapping the shawl around her shoulders before settling in by his pillows. The bed smelled of him: sharp spice and wood and fire.

"What now?" he asked. Durkhanai shrugged. She didn't need anything more. She could sit there and stare at him all night and never tire of it.

"Are you hungry?" he asked.

She shrugged. "I can always eat."

"Then let's go."

"Now?" She sat up. "We'll get caught!"

"Trust me," he told her. He grabbed her hand. She adjusted her shawl to ensure she was properly covered, then they were off.

They tiptoed around her palace, and Durkhanai felt like a child again—hiding in crevices so the guards wouldn't see as she and her cousins played games and stole treats from the kitchens. It isn't that they would have gotten into any big trouble, then, but it had been the thrill of the game, the adrenaline rush.

With Asfandyar's hand in hers, the adrenaline was thricefold. He ran a finger across her palm. They could hardly contain their giggles as they dodged guards and finally made their way to the pantry where Asfandyar pulled out two gorgeous mangoes.

"Something tells me this is not your first time here," Durkhanai accused. Asfandyar shrugged innocently.

"Pagal," she muttered, biting back a smile. *Crazy person.*

"Tera liye," he replied with a wink. *Only for you.*

They both sat on the floor, waving away fruit flies. Asfandyar grabbed a knife and began to cut the mango into slices, offering one to Durkhanai first. She shook her head.

The ripe fruits were small and orange, imported from the South. Durkhanai could tell from the smell and texture that they were anwar ratol.

Which meant Asfandyar was eating them wrong.

"Why did you cut it in slices?" she asked, shaking her head.

She took another mango and instead, began pressing it between her palms, turning the fruit soft on the inside as it tore from the peel. Asfandyar watched curiously as she ripped the top nub off with her teeth and spit it out, leaving an opening in the peel.

It was immensely unladylike, not at all what the Shehzadi should act like, but it was how Durkhanai had grown up eating mangoes in her valley.

With the top ripped off, the mango was ready to be eaten. She put the opening into her mouth and sucked the sweet fruit, pushing it up with her fingers.

Swallowing hard, Asfandyar watched her mouth. Juice dribbled down her chin, and he caught it with his finger before she could, trailing her jaw.

He sucked his finger, mouth spreading into a slow smile.

"The barbaric Shehzadi shows her truth," he said, eyes dark.

Durkhanai licked her lips and grinned. She grabbed another mango and put it in his hands, putting his slices to the side.

"Your turn," she said. He regarded the fruit, then gingerly pressed the mango with his forefingers. She tsked.

"You have to *feel* it," she told him, coming closer to show him. "Coax the fruit from its shell."

She put her hands on top of his on the mango, his knuckles pressing into her palm. With the hard curve of her hand, she pressed his hands into the mango. The fruit gave way under the pressure, softening. Together, they massaged the fruit, his hands warm beneath hers. Durkhanai reached down to bite the mango nub, giving it to him to finish it off.

"Like this?" he whispered, teeth grazing the skin. She nodded, and he gently peeled an opening, eyes on hers. She held her hands atop his once more to push the fruit into his mouth. His eyes widened in surprise. Then, he laughed.

"Delicious," he said. "What a hidden wonder."

A bead of juice trailed down his throat, disappearing down his kurta. She wanted to lick his skin clean. Her cheeks burned.

"Give me some," she said instead. He brought the sweet fruit to her mouth, feeding her, and the skin was still warm from where his mouth had been.

After they'd eaten, he held her face in his palm, ran his mango-wet thumb across her cheekbone; his caress as loving as the summer's breeze. She leaned into his hand and searched his eyes. He was studying her, memorizing the shape of her face, noticing all the details she was sure no one would ever see.

She wanted to kiss him again.

Durkhanai wished she could vocalize this feeling, this great swelling in her heart, like the rivers after the rain, like the wells surging with water, like the earth absorbing sunlight. But she said nothing, and neither did he, too afraid to tarnish the purity of the emotion by inaccurate words.

Instead, they went back to his room and exchanged stories. She told him about the valley; he told her about the ocean. He was surprisingly just as soft and gentle as he was sharp and harsh. Just as she was.

Though duties of her role had made her sharper, just as his best friend's death had made him darker.

Durkhanai mused over a long-forgotten dream of hers where she returned to the valley and lived a simple life with the women who raised her. They would lie under a thousand and one stars, listening to the leaves rustling, and there would be nothing more than the beauty of a simple life.

Asfandyar mused about a similar long-forgotten dream of his, where he returned to the ocean and lived a simple life with his mother's tribe. They would lie under a thousand and one stars, listening to waves rising and falling, and there would be nothing more than the beauty of a simple life.

The hours passed, and not once did Asfandyar ask her when she was leaving. He had gotten comfortable, too, discarding his waistcoat and stiff day shalwar kameez for a plain black sleeping suit. The buttons at the top of the kurta remained undone, showing off the long column of his throat, the bend of his collarbone.

Durkhanai had no plans to leave, not even when sleep began weighing down her limbs.

"Rest," he told her, seeing her yawn. He stood from his seat, and she reached for him. He bent over to pick her up, and she wrapped her arms around his neck as he lifted her to bed. She settled in.

"Come, lie with me," she responded, lying on her side. He had gone back to sit on the chair across from her, self-control filling the distance between them. But it was getting late; she could see he was tired, too.

"All right," he said, voice low. He came and laid down beside her. They lay facing each other. Candlelight filled his face with shadows; she wanted to reach out and touch the fan of his eyelashes. She touched his cheek. His skin was like velvet; she couldn't stop running her hands across his face, his arms, his neck.

"Tell me another story," she said, half awake. She would never tire of his voice.

"Once, when I was six . . ." He began another story from his childhood, and Durkhanai let the solid sound of his deep voice carry her toward sleep.

"Durre?" his voice was soft sometime later, tentative. "Are you asleep?"

She shook her head lightly but didn't open her eyes.

"I'll blow out the candles," he said. The bed shifted as his weight was lifted, and the soft glow of the candlelight disappeared from the room.

Durkhanai opened her eyes, adjusting to the dark, as Asfandyar came back to bed. The room felt colder without the flames, and she reached a wandering hand toward him. He caught it and held it to his chest. She unfurled her fingers, stretching them to the bare skin at the open collar of his kurta. His heart beat beneath her fingertips.

"Come close," she coaxed.

He did, and she reached for his arm, laying it across her waist. He was so warm.

He caught her hands and held them against his heart. She counted each beat in tandem with her own. He pulled a hand up to his lips, kissing her palm.

"I want to suck on the sunlight of your skin," he whispered, his teeth grazing against her wrist. She was liquified. "Everywhere, everywhere."

"What's stopping you?" she asked, breathless.

"Go to sleep," he whispered. "Or I'll forget my chivalry."

"Who's asking you to be chivalrous?"

"Dewaani." He shook his head at her. "Crazy."

Insatiable, she put her hands around his neck, pulling him closer.

"You'd make a sinner out of the noblest man, Durre," he sighed, kissing her neck. "And I am not noble by far."

Durkhanai grinned, holding him close. She liked this power she had over him, for she knew the power he had over her. It was fire and fire, equally burning, equally passionate. He ran his hands up her arms.

"Your skin is soft as rose petals," he said, half asleep. "But I know the truth of your thorns."

"Do they prick you?" she asked.

"Mhm," he murmured with a nod against her. "But I don't mind. I've never beheld anything so sweet."

They laid together, his head buried in her chest, and she ran her hand through his curls, cradling his head.

"If this is a dream, do not wake me," he sighed.

And soon, he was sound asleep, perfectly at ease as though she was always meant to be there, his personal pillow.

Something she couldn't place surged through her to see this man vulnerable in her arms. He was a large man, tall and solid, but with his arms wrapped tightly around her torso, his lips and cheek against her breast, he was hers entirely.

As he slept, Durkhanai was still half-awake, and she used what little cognizance she had left to dream and imagine a world where his dreams came true and so did hers and they were both happy and they were together, forever. She dreamt that this night was not an anomaly, but a truth that would last for the rest of their lives.

Durkhanai wished she could stay there, in his arms, forever.

Maybe she could, her heart hoped as she drifted toward sleep. Perhaps everything would work out in the end. Perhaps her grandparents truly loved her enough to accept Asfandyar. Sure, things would be a little bumpy, a little difficult, but it would all work out in the end. Then, she would have the rest of her life with him, the rest of eternity.

Yes, everything would be okay.

But the words tasted acidic, like a lie.

# CHAPTER TWENTY-NINE

*W*hat tasted more of grief than broken dreams?

What more of sorrow than a ruined tomorrow?

When she awoke, Asfandyar's arms still around her, Durkhanai was thrust back to reality. She felt a hand around her heart, squeezing and squeezing until all the blood burst out, leaving a limp muscle, once alive, now dead.

Only then did she rise, unraveling herself from him. She allowed herself one last glance to memorize his countenance: the curled eyelashes framing his closed eyes, the soft pout of his sleeping mouth. She would pay her weight in gold to kiss him again, but some things were too precious to be bought so easily. It would only make things harder. What she felt for him was mohabbat, in which case there was no hope, for mohabbat was a love that penetrated every bone in the body, every breath and every heartbeat.

She knew how this story ended. Her grandparents would never accept him. They had no future together.

So, dragging her protesting heart along with her, she slipped away.

Durkhanai locked herself in her chambers, barring all visitors, feigning acute illness. She could not even muster the strength to say goodbye to Gulalai, who would be leaving, too. Durkhanai did not want to risk speaking for fear of what she would say if she did.

She gave the guards strict instructions not to open her doors for anybody, not even her grandparents, who would be too busy with preparing the ambassadors' departures to quarrel with her.

Everyone knew once she had made up her mind, Durkhanai was impossible to persuade.

So, she was left alone.

She sat in silence, watching the world revolve on its axis, the slow crawl of time as the sun trod across the sky, until finally, sunset approached and even passed and brought the cool veil of night across the sky.

Only a little longer then.

She need only wait through the night. Come dawn, he would be gone. No longer a threat and never having confessed whatever secret her instincts told her she did not want to hear.

Things had gone successfully, she reminded herself. War had been avoided. Marghazar was still in power. They had negotiated things from all the ambassadors. Durkhanai should have been happy.

But all she could think about was Asfandyar, how she would never see him again.

Out on her balcony, alone and still, looking out into the inky night sky, Durkhanai told herself in the grand scheme of the universe, this was a minor inconvenience. It would pass, as all things did.

How could the stars be so bright tonight? She felt she could see every star in the universe, but her heart had ceased glowing in tandem with them.

Just a few more hours. Her grip on the marble railing tightened.

She desperately hoped Asfandyar wouldn't come, lying to herself.

*You cruel, insatiable girl,* she seethed to herself. *You're never satisfied, you're never happy. What am I to do with you?*

Why was love a punishment? Why had Allah given her a heart if not to use it? Durkhanai wished she could shake herself from this trance, but even as she thought it, her heart cried in protest. She never wanted to lose this feeling, however wretched, however beautiful. Perhaps the memories alone would be enough to sustain her.

Durkhanai was frozen, numb.

Until she heard a noise from within her wardrobe.

Somebody had entered through the passageways. Perhaps she had left the door unlocked on purpose.

*I hope it's Zarmina,* she told herself, even though her wretched heart was singing, *I hope it's Asfandyar, I hope it's Asfandyar.*

It was him.

She felt his body slide into the space behind her even though they did not touch. Durkhanai did not turn either. She did not want to see him. Did not want him to see her. It would only make it more difficult.

She had let her heart flow, but all it had done was drench her in blood. She could not afford any more blood loss.

He came to her side, and she turned her cheek, not letting him see.

"Safe travels," she said, voice blank. "May Allah bless you with a long and healthy life."

"Durkhanai, please," he pleaded. "I'm not here to say goodbye."

It took all her strength not to turn.

"You are leaving," she said. "Farewells are in order. So khudafiz. Goodbye, Ambassador."

Durkhanai leveled her voice as much as she could. She was still as ice, thrice as cold.

He was still there.

"*Go,*" she said, trying to keep her voice cruel. But she knew he heard it waver.

"Durkhanai—" he began.

Oh, his voice. It sent a crack through her ice cold heart, a shiver down her stone-still spine.

"Leave!" she snapped.

Her voice was angry, but it wasn't directed at him; all the fury was directed toward herself. She held her breath, trying to contain herself. She was an arrow pulled too taut, a whisper away from being released.

She wanted so badly to yell at him.

*How could you do this to me*? she would say. *Don't you know how much it hurts? Do you understand what you've done?*

But all she could manage was, "Please. It hurts."

"I know," he replied, miserable. "Durre, *I* know. But please, can't we talk?"

"I have nothing to say," she told him. She knew she was being unfair, but she didn't trust herself. "Please go before I do something I regret."

"Durre, please—" he began. Tears filled her eyes.

"*Please* leave," she pleaded. "I can't bear any more."

"How can I let you go?" he asked. "I taste you in my lungs every time I try to breathe."

"Please," she said. "I don't want to hurt anyone."

"But you would hurt yourself?" he countered, reaching for her. She pushed him away from her. "That's enough."

"You promised you would listen to me come morning," he said, voice frantic. "But you left me; I haven't seen you since." He paused; she saw how difficult this was for him. "Please, Durkhanai, let me tell you everything, if only for you to understand, if only for you to be safe. There are dangers here . . ."

"Dangers? The only danger here is *you*." She took a staggering breath. "You've infected me with something terrible, and now you are leaving. You are leaving to *never* return."

"Leave with me," he suddenly said, grabbing her arms. His eyes were crazed. He didn't look like himself, so replete with desperation. But she felt it, too, coursing through her. "Run away with me," he said, breathless. "We'll never be accepted by court. Let's run. I know I haven't been completely straightforward, but— just hear me out. I'll tell you everything, anything . . ."

He was rambling, but she wasn't listening anymore.

All she knew was how despicable she was. She was considering it, considering betraying everyone she loved. She pushed him away from her.

"You want me to leave my people? My family? For you?" she repeated.

"I know it's unfair of me to ask, dishonorable, even," he replied. "But I'm too selfish to let you go. Stay with me." He dropped to his knees, taking her hands. "Be with me for eternity, in this life and the next."

While the proposition seemed genuine, there was true fear in his voice. What dangers did he think she would be vulnerable to if she stayed in her home?

She could not contemplate it. She was too furious with herself because she knew there existed a part of her heart that would do it, that would leave everything for him.

She had no honor, no loyalty.

"We can start anew," he told her, eyes full of hope. He held her hands tight.

She pulled her hands from his grasp.

"If you loved me, you would never ask for such a thing," she snapped. "You think I would leave my family, my crown, and my kingdom—for what?" She laughed a mirthless laugh. "To run away, with *you*? Don't forget your place, Ambassador.

"You were an illicit thrill, a reckless little phase, but nothing more," she said, voice entirely indifferent. "You can't imagine it has been more, can you? Oh, then you are as much a fool as anyone else. And here I had higher hopes for you."

"You're being cruel," he told her, clenching his jaw. He stood, drawing near. "Don't lie, not to me, not to yourself."

He saw right through her.

"I am cruel," she snapped. "I am cruel and wretched and awful. Haven't you realized it by now?"

She pushed him back, but he stayed in place, an immovable wall.

"How else would you describe a princess willing to leave her people and her crown for her own selfish reasons?" Durkhanai's voice cut off in a sob.

She wanted to run with him. She wanted to stay.

She couldn't do both.

"I am cruel," she whispered, turning away from him. The wind whipped through her hair. Asfandyar slipped into the space behind her, his arms wrapping around her torso. He kissed her neck so softly, she thought she would melt.

"You aren't," he whispered back. "You are kind and quick and clever and genuine. You are the night sky full of infinite stars. You are wonder and beauty, and I am in eternal awe of you."

Oh, why did he have to say such things?

She felt him pause against her skin, waiting for a response. She wanted to tell him the same, that he was kind and honorable and noble, that to her, he was as glorious as the mountains she called home and thrice as comforting.

But she couldn't.

He needed to leave, or she would never let him go.

The words choked her, waiting to be released, but she couldn't.

He needed to leave.

Before she did something unholy.

Before she did something horrible.

"Leave," she said, voice calm. "Or I will call my guards and inform them you've made an attempt on my life, in my court. You will be executed come morning."

"You wouldn't," he said, voice clouded with disbelief.

"I would," she said, walking toward her doors.

He reached for her hand, but she pulled it away and instead reached for her door.

"Don't do this," he pleaded, but he began to back away, toward the wardrobe and the passageways.

"Goodbye, Asfandyar," she said. The tears fell.

She pulled open her doors.

Before the guards could look, Asfandyar was gone.

# CHAPTER THIRTY

urkhanai woke in a cold sweat as the adhan for fajr rang through the air. Asfandyar was leaving soon. She had been too cruel. He hadn't deserved it. He was leaving. She would never see him again.

She would *never* see him again.

Durkhanai couldn't stand to let him go in such a manner. Breathless, she took out a pen and paper and began to write. There wasn't enough time.

She told him the truth: uninhibited, raw, messy, beautiful. She loved him. She could admit it now. Perhaps he already knew, but she needed to tell him; she couldn't bear the burden of a truth untethered. Even if she never saw him again afterward.

Feeling light, Durkhanai slipped into the passageways, navigating to find his room. She needed to give it to him herself, too afraid of it falling into anybody else's hands. This letter was evidence of her sin. It was damning. She shouldn't have taken the chance, shouldn't have written it, but she didn't care.

She was tired of running.

The words were for him and him alone, and she would deliver them.

It was nearly dawn. Asfandyar would be preparing for travel after the morning prayer. He wouldn't be in his room. She would just slip it into his kameez pocket and disappear. Perhaps he would read it only when he was on the road. Perhaps ten years from now, he would look back and remember and smile at the memories.

Perhaps.

She slipped into the passageways, running her hand along the cold cement walls. Dripping water echoed behind her, mingling with the sound of her sure footsteps. She fingered the letter in her hand, smelled the ink. She pressed a final kiss to the paper as she arrived at Asfandyar's room.

But by the door, she found a little box full of letters.

Biting back a smile, Durkhanai reached down and picked out a little note. She recognized her own handwriting. The notes looked worn, like they had been opened and closed many times.

Durkhanai knew she should do what she came for and leave, but she couldn't resist.

Pressing down on the bruise of her heart, she picked up the box. She unfolded the letter on top, recognizing her own slanted handwriting from the night it had rained. They hadn't been able to go distribute medicine, but they had exchanged letters deep into the night.

She ran her fingers along the words, thinking of what a rosy-eyed fool she had been.

But the box felt strangely full as she carried it to his bed and sat down. She didn't remember writing so many letters to him.

Then she saw handwriting that wasn't hers.

Her first thought was that of jealousy; that he already had a lover. But the truth was much worse.

She read the letter at the top, the most recent, she assumed, and she didn't understand—not who it was from or what was going on. But somebody was giving Asfandyar orders; somebody was growing impatient.

Durkhanai saw that the letters were from two people: one outside, one inside.

The one from within gave him tips and tricks.

*Durkhanai is overly emotional . . . she has never hated anyone in her entire life . . . she is young and foolish . . . she is naive and silly . . . Durkhanai enjoys being right . . . she is stubborn and childish . . . too easily trusting . . . her favorite line of poetry is . . .*

And the advice went on, saying how she was a princess doted on by all but one who craved someone to challenge her. The pretty little princess who wasn't taken seriously and thus craved responsibility. The Shehzadi whose greatest weakness was her family. How she was overly emotional and could be reckless and barbaric and frivolous and much too easily trusting—and on and on.

Asfandyar had been sent to distract her.

He had been sent to make her fall in love with him, so he could make a fool out of her. And suddenly, things began to make sense: how he was always there, always finding her, always knowing what to say.

Somebody had given Asfandyar the blueprints to Durkhanai's soul, and it had to be somebody close to her.

Close enough to know her almost as well as she knew herself.

But who could betray her thus?

Durkhanai felt stripped bare in front of a laughing crowd, but no matter how she reached for clothing, she could not cover herself again. Somebody close to her, somebody who *knew* her and knew her well had been feeding Asfandyar information, telling him about her. She thought she recognized the handwriting, but she couldn't quite place it, but that was irrelevant then.

All she could think about was how everything between her and Asfandyar had been planned. It had been mechanical, all of it.

But for what?

Then she saw.

The letters from the outside, giving him orders, telling him secrets. Describing where medicine would be, how the passageways worked, the ins and outs of the palace. How the people would react to certain things, but the Shehzadi would be too distracted to notice, too enamored to care.

And all of this to keep the Shehzadi busy as Asfandyar ran his own investigations—to prove Marghazar was behind the summit attack. The letters told Asfandyar where to look, and when it seemed they couldn't find anything concrete, the letters told Asfandyar all he had to do was get the Badshah's seal—the evidence could then be forged.

But who could have known such intimate details? Nobody had ever left Safed-Mahal.

Worse still, she had fallen directly into Asfandyar's trap. She had led him to the Badshah's office. She had shown him precisely where the seal was.

Durkhanai recalled that day—how they left together, so he couldn't have stolen the seal right then. But then she remembered how he had pulled her waist when he thought someone was coming—he must have stolen the key at that time, while she was distracted, then gone back to steal the Badshah's seal.

What a fool she had been.

Then her gaze caught on a few lines.

*Marghazar will splinter with civil unrest, and faith in the Shehzadi will drop due to her association with you.*

So it had been deliberate. All of it a ruse.

But why? He risked himself as well, and for what? But men were hardly blamed in such situations. She remembered how quick Rashid had been to assume her requests for help was more of a romantic gesture than a political one. She doubted Asfandyar cared what her people had to think of him.

Heart hammering, Durkhanai kept reading.

*All you need now is a public display of affection to ruin the Shehzadi. The people won't love a whore for a princess.*

So, that was what this was.

Just then, Asfandyar walked in.

He froze, seeing the letter in her hand. Durkhanai laughed, not looking up.

"And here I thought my love letter to you would have been the first," she said bitterly. "You didn't tell me you had a lover already, somebody you were making a fool of me for."

"Durre—" he began.

"Who is it?" she asked, voice curious. It was an eggshell thin covering of the scrambled mess she really was inside.

"Wakdar," he replied simply.

She blinked. "Wakdar was my father's name."

There was truth in his eyes. "You're lying," she said simply. She took a step back. She refused to believe him, but she remembered a worn cloth doll, how she had been told it was a secret gift from her father . . .

*No.* It could not be.

Very calmly, she gathered the letters back together again, aligning all the papers. She put them back where they belonged, her entire being covered in a thick layer of ice. She would show no emotion.

She would say nothing.

She had to leave. Her heart felt like an emptying blood bag.

"Wait," Asfandyar said.

And she did. Despite herself, she stopped in her tracks, back to him.

Everyone had warned her, she remembered. They had warned her to stay away, not to fall, not to be fooled.

But she couldn't have understood then. She couldn't have known until after, when the hurricane was through and she was left to deal with the aftermath.

*What was so addicting about him?* she wondered. *What was so intoxicating that she just couldn't let him go?*

Even then, she couldn't let him go.

"Don't go," he pleaded. "Let me explain."

"You're lying," she said simply, turning to face him. "My father died the night I was born. Poisoned. Killed."

"I'm not," he replied. He pulled something from his pocket and dropped it into her palm. It was a chandi silver ring, the same ring that sat on her right ring finger, the same that sat on her grandfather's and her grandmother's.

The family crest.

It wasn't possible . . .

"Why are you here?" she asked, voice breaking. He fell to his knees. Her bones felt too heavy in her body, too thick, like instead of liquid, her blood had turned to stew.

"For you—because I am yours, entirely," he vowed, reaching for her hands. She snatched her fingers away before he could touch them, cradling her hand to her heart, trying to contain the explosion.

"No," she said, shaking her head, trying not to cry. "*Why did you come here? To* Marghazar?"

"I told you," he responded, eyes blank, voice empty. "I'm a spy."

"For who?"

"Wakdar," he replied.

Her father.

"Why? Explain." She tried to stay calm.

"I am indebted to him," Asfandyar replied. "I owe him my life, my blood. He swore he would exact revenge on the Badshah, and I swore I would help him."

"My grandparents," she said, chest tight. "My family, my blood. You know they are most beloved to me, beyond anything and anyone, yet you speak so casually of exacting revenge on them? *Why?*"

"They broke my heart," he finally said, voice quiet.

"And you broke mine," she snapped. "Are you happy now? You are just as wretched as your enemy."

"There is much you do not know," he said. Her heart had burned to ash, leaving nothing but the seared black bones of her ribcage, echoing emptiness.

What could be worse than this?

"The Badshah has allied himself with the Kebzu Kingdom," Asfandyar continued. "It was him who told them about the summit."

"Impossible," Durkhanai said, but she wasn't so sure.

"It's why I'm here," Asfandyar explained, voice thick with self-hate. "I've been distracting you, stirring civil unrest, as Wakdar prepares."

"Prepares for what?" Durkhanai asked, filled with dread.

She had to warn her grandparents.

"Durkhanai, please, sit down, let me explain to you—" he began, but she held up a hand to silence him.

"I don't *want* to sit down," she hissed. "You need to tell me exactly what is going on right now. Starting with *why?*" Durkhanai's voice broke, and she hated herself for it. "Why did you do all this? You said you owe Wakdar your life, your blood, but *why?*"

"I killed one of his own," he replied.

Durkhanai stilled. One of his own—that would make whoever it was one of hers.

"*Who?*" she seethed. Asfandyar looked miserable, but he had to tell her.

"His daughter," Asfandyar replied finally, voice quiet. "My fiancée."

# CHAPTER THIRTY-ONE
*Asfandyar's Tale*

"She was my best friend," Asfandyar began.

Suddenly, he was no longer nineteen, but fifteen again, falling in love for the first time. Back in Jardum, the song of his childhood played around him, memories unfurling to the distant melody.

Naina had been around for as long as he could remember, with her startling blue-green eyes and freckles and the dimple on her right cheek. She was of another noble family, so it was said, but Asfandyar learned the truth when he got older—that his father, the great General Afridi, had crossed paths with Wakdar Miangul at the frontlines. Wakdar had saved his life from the Luhgam Empire, and it was because of this that Wakdar found sanctuary with Asfandyar's tribe. So Wakdar joined the Afridi tribe, and nobody had the standing to question Asfandyar's father. No one had questioned him when he married a Black woman, either, because it was Asfandyar's brave father who kept his men alive at the frontlines.

They all owed him their lives.

So Asfandyar grew up with the pretty green-eyed girl as his neighbor. He and Naina grew together, but Asfandyar always knew she was different—not their blood, even though she was raised just as he was. She was half, for her father was different. He stayed indoors, and if he ever did make an appearance, his face was cloaked, hidden in shadows.

There were rumors, of course, of who the mysterious man was, but Asfandyar, only a child then, did not care. He only cared about Naina, his best friend.

They grew up chasing peacocks—trying to find the most beautiful feathers—and played in the stream and told each other scary jinn stories at night. An innocent time.

For a boy of seven, this was love.

Then, they grew a little older, and Asfandyar's father passed in the war, and his mother shortly after. Asfandyar went to live with his chacha, and sadness followed him wherever he went until the girl with the blue-green eyes brought him a peacock feather she had saved for years.

For a boy of twelve, this was love.

Then, Asfandyar began to grow from a boy into the strange creature that preceded manhood. He began to chase chickens and break their necks, began to throw little daggers into trees as target practice. He began to fight in the streets when his chacha was asleep, and it was Naina who would sneak out in the middle of the night with a wet washcloth and clean his wounds, scolding him, always worried but always curious to know if he had won. He always did.

For a boy of fifteen, this was love.

Then, Asfandyar went to war, and he watched his brothers and his people die, so easily, so callously. When he came home, he was a changed man, and Naina had become a woman. She understood the haunted look in his eyes, for she had seen the same in her father's. She knew not to push, just to be there, solid, sure, alive.

For a boy of seventeen, this was love.

By then, Asfandyar knew enough of the world to seize it the moment he could. He gave Naina his mother's gold bracelet, the bangle Mama had given him for safekeeping before she had left him. Asfandyar went to the man whose face always remained cloaked and asked for his daughter's hand.

The man refused.

But his daughter would not take no for an answer. She did not eat for three days and three nights, and her father relented in the way that fathers do for their daughters. Naina always said it was because her father had witnessed what separating love did to people and did not want his daughter to experience the same.

Asfandyar was seventeen; Naina was fifteen. Too young, too naive, too bright-eyed. They were fools, but they were fools in love, so they did not notice, or they did not care.

It was then that Naina had confided in Asfandyar—told him that her father was actually the crown prince of Marghazar, to be the next Badshah. Asfandyar had always known Wakdar had come from some faraway place under strange circumstances—he hadn't realized just how strange. Wakdar had run from Marghazar because of how barbaric the Badshah was: too strict, too severe. His parents had caused him great pain. Which was why he had sought refuge in Jardum, where he had remarried and had Naina.

But after Naina's mother passed away, her father became sad. Tragic. Haunted.

"Perhaps if we reunite him with his parents, with his home, he will be able to heal," Naina suggested, hope burning bright in her green eyes. She had such a big heart.

"I'm not sure," Asfandyar replied. What had he known then?

"I can't bear to see him so lost, Asfi," Naina had said. "Please?" She pouted. "For me?"

What had he known then save for his love?

In secret, Asfandyar prepared for the trip. One quiet night, he and Naina snuck away, embarking on the journey with nothing but a little silver ring in her hand as evidence of her lineage. It was the Miangul family crest, and Naina was sure it would grant them entry into the famed Safed-Mahal.

"I can finally meet my grandparents!" Naina had exclaimed, excited. "Can you believe it? I wonder how they will be."

They were both young and optimistic and naive and foolish. It was a long journey, but finally, they reached the mountains of S'vat. Reached the edge of the capital city, where they were stopped at the gates at the base of the mountain.

Nobody could enter; nobody could leave. It was how they kept their land and their people pure, they were told. Only those from their own tribes were allowed in.

"I am from the Miangul family," Naina said, holding up her hand to show the ring on her index finger. It was too big on her. "I have come to meet my grandparents."

The guards led them in, granting them entrance, only to lock them in a prison cell just on the other side of the gates. They waited a day until the guards finally returned, and even then, Naina remained confident, poised.

"They are my family," she kept saying. "My blood."

Until Bazira Miangul, the Wali of S'vat herself, came. She was silent as stone. Naina looked nothing like her.

"Dhadi!" Naina had cried, smiling. The Wali bristled but did not react except to motion for the guards to bring the pair out of their prison.

It was the Wali's eyes: Asfandyar knew right then that they were doomed.

He had seen disgust before—he was half-Black, after all—but never like this.

"Naina," he whispered, hoping to shield her from this, but it was too late.

"How dare you enter my lands?" the Wali asked calmly. "Claim to be my blood?"

"I am Wakdar's daughter," Naina said, quick to explain. Asfandyar remained quiet. "I am your granddaughter."

There was a crack in the air as the Wali slapped Naina. Shaken from the force, Naina tumbled to the ground. Asfandyar reached for her, but he was held back by guards. He watched in horror as the guards lifted Naina, too, holding her up.

"I have one granddaughter," the Wali said calmly. "She was birthed from the mountains. She has no father as I have no son."

"Please," Naina said, lip trembling. "Just listen to me."

The Wali slapped her once more.

"Do not interrupt," she said. "You have insulted me by claiming to be my own, by claiming to be my granddaughter's equal. You are *nothing* like her—she is pure, you are not. She belongs, you do not."

"Where is your hospitality?" Asfandyar cried out.

"You are not my people," the Wali replied. "The Marghazari never return, for they never leave—certainly not a Miangul. If they ever dared, they would lose their status and their lineage—they would lose their blood. The penalty for such treason is death."

"Okay, all right," Asfandyar said, trying to keep his voice calm. "I apologize—we both do. With your permission, we would like to go home now."

The Wali shook her head, face cold.

"Please, let us go home," Asfandyar pleaded then, too frightened. He cast a frantic look to Naina and saw the crippling fear in her eyes—but worse was the grief of rejection. "We won't say a word to anyone. It'll be as though we had never come. Just let us go—have mercy."

"Kill the girl for her false claims to my family," the Wali had said, without batting an eye. "Send the servant back as a warning to the man who claims to be of my blood." She turned and met Asfandyar's eye. "There is your mercy."

The guard holding Naina lifted his sword to her throat.

"No!" Asfandyar cried, struggling to break free. "Send her back. Kill me!"

"I will send you back so you remember," the Wali said. "And because a servant can never be a threat."

"What about a tribunal?" Asfandyar argued, fighting against the guards holding him. "Your barbaric tribunal!"

The Wali just shook her head.

"Please, please! Just send her back, let her live, kill me instead—"

Asfandyar turned to Naina to find that she had gone quiet, face sad but resolute.

"Asfi," she had said, voice so soft, her final caress. "I love you."

And before he could say it back, she dragged her own throat against the sword.

"*No!*" he screamed.

She sacrificed herself, taking her own life—not giving the Wali the satisfaction, ensuring that Asfandyar would live.

There Asfandyar stood; a coward, motionless, unable to do anything but watch in horror as his beloved's body crumpled to the ground, blood pouring from her throat like a waterfall—rushing, ceaseless, unforgiving.

He failed her; it was his sacred duty to protect her, and he failed her.

Everything burned inside of him: grief, rage, despair. And the Wali didn't even flinch.

"A shame," she had merely said with a cluck of her tongue. "If the girl's blood hadn't been tainted, she would have made a proper Miangul. Tell the man who claims to be my son to never near these borders again. Show him this girl's corpse should he wish to test me."

And then she left without another glance.

Asfandyar had cried the entire journey home, Naina's rotting corpse haunting him the entire way. He couldn't stand to look at her lifeless face, yet he couldn't tear his eyes away. So he would stare instead at the little ring that had caused all of this: the Miangul family crest.

Finally, he made it home, guilty and ashamed, traumatized and angry. Hopeless.

He had thought Wakdar would kill him right then and there, and secretly, Asfandyar had wished for it—wished to be reunited with Naina in the Afterlife. But Wakdar had stood completely still as Asfandyar recounted the events.

Asfandyar himself couldn't stop crying; it had been his responsibility to take care of Naina, to ensure she didn't get hurt, and like a coward, he had returned with her corpse.

"I swear my life to you," Asfandyar said that night. "From this day forth, my life is yours as penance for the life of your daughter, who I had sworn to protect. I failed her. I failed you. From this day forth, my life is yours."

"From this day forth, you have one purpose," Wakdar had said calmly. "You will fulfill my revenge."

They began planning. It was not enough just to slaughter the Badshah and his wife; they would take their land, dishonor and humiliate them, and take all that the Mianguls held dear—then, and only then, would they kill them.

So Asfandyar became ambassador, through Wakdar's connections, and the rest of the story unfurled.

"I swore," Asfandyar finished. "We swore to Allah that we would avenge Naina, that we would have our revenge."

Asfandyar watched Durkhanai as he told her all of this; watched the shock and grief and horror. She held her hand to her chest, and he felt his own heart respond in reaction to her emotions.

He loved her, in truth. He would run away from all of this with her, run away from his oath to Wakdar and his oath to Naina. Damn his word, damn his revenge. He would start anew with her.

But there was no point in those thoughts now. Durkhanai would never have him. Yet, Asfandyar couldn't help but imagine him and her, living under the stars, a thousand miles away. He would tell her the stories his own mother once told him, and they would be together, for eternity.

He thought about when Durkhanai had first kissed him, which seemed a lifetime ago now, and how afterward he had pressed a finger to his bottom lip and found it to be swollen, tender to the touch. Delicately, he had run his tongue across it, and, even though it hurt, he couldn't quite bring himself to stop.

He could almost taste her on his lips then, and he couldn't help himself.

After Naina, Asfandyar had thought he would never love again—that he couldn't.

How cursed was his fate.

It nearly made him laugh.

# CHAPTER THIRTY-TWO

"*You* *demon*," Durkhanai seethed.

He stood there like a wilted flower, head bowed. She wanted to strike him.

"Why are you telling me this? Are you trying to turn me against my family?" She shook her head. "How will you benefit? Just as you care about your people, I care about mine." Her nails bit into her palms. "I won't let you harm them."

"*You* are my people," he pleaded, reaching for her.

"Stop!" she shrieked. "*Stop* lying to me."

He opened his mouth to speak again, but she cut him off.

"You have no honor," she said, shaking her head. "You are worse than a thousand curses." She meant every word, and it astonished her, her own cruelty. "I *hate* you. I wish we had never met, I wish you had never been born."

She shook with emotion, but the rage quickly gave way to grief because, oh, hadn't he warned her?

Hadn't he told her from the very beginning that he was a spy? Hadn't he told her he had lost his best friend? The clues were there all along.

She was just too blinded to see them.

"I believed in you," she said, voice breaking. "I saw good in you, despite what everyone said. And this is what it got me—it serves me right for being a fool."

She was losing her mind.

"Durre, please," he pleaded. "I—I love you."

"Why should I believe you?" she said. "Why should I believe anything you said? If your tale is true, my grandmother *murdered* my half-sister. Yet, if your tale is true, why did she not recognize you? Why risk coming to the palace once more?"

"She did not see me as a person, Durkhanai," Asfandyar said, voice low. "Please, just think for a moment."

Durkhanai shook her head. "No, you are a liar and a spy. I don't believe you. You don't love me."

"I do, *please*, just listen to me," he reached for her, but she pulled away.

"Shaam hi toh hai," she said, voice empty. "It'll pass."

It tasted acidic, like a lie.

But her mind was spinning to what she had read before all this—to Asfandyar stealing the Badshah's seal.

"Why did you steal the Badshah's seal?" she asked, fear creeping through her. "What did you do?"

Asfandyar swallowed.

"It was part of the reason I was sent here: to create evidence that proved Marghazar was behind the summit attack," he replied.

"But Marghazar wasn't—you would falsely indict my grandfather?"

"How can you be so sure he wasn't?" Asfandyar countered. She shook her head, and he went from her side toward his desk, rummaging through papers until he found something.

"I wasn't sure either . . . at first," he told her. "But Durkhanai—with the Badshah's seal, I forged a letter from him to send to the Kebzu Kingdom, written as if from the Badshah, inquiring about the summit attack. Just like we did with Palwasha-sahiba."

"Stop," she said, putting up a hand. "Please stop." She didn't want to hear this.

"Do you want to know what they sent back?" he asked, offering her the paper. "They sent back thanks: appreciation to the Badshah for alerting them of the summit."

"What?" she whispered, dumbstruck.

She took the paper, and before reading it, folded it in half to inspect the seal. It looked real, but how could she believe it was not a forgery? As if reading her mind, Asfandyar pulled something from his pocket.

"Check the seal," he said, handing her another letter. I found this in your grandfather's office, as well. It is from last year, discussing a temporary ceasefire in the northeast mountains during the avalanche. Surely, you will remember it and know that this is not a forgery, either."

Durkhanai recalled the instance. She could not allege that this second letter was a forgery, for she had been present when Agha-Jaan had read it for the first time.

She put the seals together, and they matched perfectly.

"Now read the first letter," Asfandyar said. Her hands shook, but she held the page up, reading.

*To the Badshah of Marghazar,*

*You inquire as to whether we took due course of action in regards to the summit of your neighboring leaders, to which we respond that we responded adequately. While it cannot be said that we are friends, for the war that still rages on at our shared border, the information you provided me was surely that of camaraderie. The enemy of my enemy is my friend, and in informing us of the summit meeting and its location, you have earned what you have asked . . .*

Durkhanai could not read further. She felt sick.

The Badshah had orchestrated the attack on the summit.

All this time, she had stood up for her crown, thinking them to be innocent when in fact, it was they who were guilty. She had assured Gulalai and everyone else that Marghazar was blameless, that they would never do such a thing.

She had racked her brain searching for the truth—and here it was: so simple, so hideous.

Of course it was them.

Wasn't Marghazar the one with the most to gain from all this? The one zilla left unscathed? The one most threatened by the other zillas' unification?

"Durkhanai, I'm sorry," Asfandyar said. "I don't want war any more than you do, and now, nor do I wish for anything to happen to your grandparents, simply because I know how much you adore them, whereas just a few months ago, I would have killed them both on sight without a second thought. They spared Naina no mercy, and for that, I would have spared them none—but for you, I would spare them anything."

His hands were tight fists. She could see this was costing him greatly to say. He would not lie, but she did not want to believe him, did not want to imagine her grandmother as a murderer, though she could not have said it surprised her entirely. The Wali was ruthless when it came to protecting her family and her people.

"I don't understand." She shook her head. "What do I do with this?"

"You cannot in good conscience let them continue their rule," Asfandyar said. "Not after what they've done."

"You want me to . . . overthrow them?"

"If you publicly condemn their behavior, stating you had nothing to do with it, and banish them into exile, there could still be a chance at peace," he told her. "After learning of this alliance, no one will accept your grandparents' leadership. But if you make it clear you had no knowledge of such actions and punish the Badshah and Wali for their transgressions, the people will naturally turn to you. It won't be easy—but you could do it, Durkhanai. You could convince the village people and the noblemen. It is your birthright. You would be the Badshah."

Here was the truth in front of her—grotesque and cruel.

What Asfandyar said made sense. She could come clean to the people, condemn her grandparents' actions, avoid war, and take her place as Badshah.

But she couldn't overthrow her grandfather. She couldn't banish them to shame, undoing everything her grandfather had worked tooth and nail for in the past fifty years. It would ruin their legacy, their memory. It would be a permanent stain. She couldn't be so disloyal to her blood. Despite all they had done—the Kebzu alliance, killing Naina—Durkhanai could not forsake them in such a manner.

She took the paper in her hand and ripped it to shreds.

"You have no evidence," she said, voice flat.

Asfandyar was silent in return.

She needed to leave.

"*Wait*," he cried, grabbing hold of her. "You don't understand. I swore my life to Wakdar, after Naina—we both swore to Allah we would avenge her. And yes, I had been sent to spy on you, and it was a ruse, but as I got to know you, I—" He stopped, holding her tight.

"Durkhanai, I love you. I never thought myself capable of any emotion so strong after Naina, but you've opened that part of me once more. I love you."

"I don't believe you!"

"Teri kasam, Durkhanai, I love you," he said, swearing it on her, but his words meant nothing. "I *love* you."

His voice cracked. She shook her head.

"I tried to tell you before anything happened between us," he continued, "but I didn't know how—I lacked the courage—and you've avoided me. You don't understand everything; just let me explain to you, *please*." She had never seen him so desperate. "I decided to run away from my oath to Wakdar after that night in the village, after the farmhouse and the rain. I didn't want to hurt you anymore."

"It's too late," she replied, voice quiet. "It's much too late."

"Please, Durkhanai, I don't want to be the villain anymore," he pleaded. "I just want to be with you."

She couldn't stand anymore.

Her father was alive.

She had a sister, then lost her. Her grandmother had her sister killed? Asfandyar loved her. He was here to cause her grandparents' ruin. Her grandparents, who were guilty.

Durkhanai couldn't understand how all of this was true.

She needed clarity. She needed to think. She needed to *breathe*.

She needed to get away from Asfandyar.

"Please," she said, voice breaking, holding up a hand to silence him. She couldn't bear any more.

Shaking, she approached the door. She needed to speak to her grandparents, to see what was true and what was false, but before she could make it two steps past his room, a slew of guards charged past her.

"What is the meaning of this?" she snapped, a princess once more.

The guards paid her no attention. They went straight to Asfandyar, who was standing motionless, and grabbed his arms.

He didn't even fight.

Something inside of her broke seeing the guards seize him. She knew what this meant.

"Release him," she ordered. The guards did not react.

"As your crown princess, I order you to release this man this instant," she hissed, drawing her full height before the guards. No matter that she was falling apart. She was to be queen of this land— she would have her respect.

"Apologies, Shehzadi," the guard responded, not meeting her eyes. "The orders came directly from the Badshah. This man is to be arrested and stand trial by tribunal."

Tribunal.

The fatal question.

*No.*

"On what charges?" she demanded, heart quickening.

Finally, the guard met her gaze. She saw shame embedded deep, deep within. But even further, she saw disappointment. Lost hope.

A fallen princess.

"For loving you."

*No, no, no.*

"This is absurd," she seethed, but the guards paid no heed. Finally, she looked to Asfandyar; all the fight had left him. "Deny the charges," she snapped, grabbing him by his kurta. "Tell them it isn't true."

She loved him, she loved him. The words burned in her mouth. Oh, what a fool she had been.

"I will never lie to you again," he swore.

She watched with horror as they took him away.

# CHAPTER THIRTY-THREE
*Saifullah's Tale*

aifullah watched as Asfandyar was taken away.

He couldn't help the satisfaction that ran through him, bordering even joy. The only thing that tainted his pleasure was the look on Durkhanai's face. She loved him; he saw it clear as day. How aggrieved she was to see him taken away like the criminal he was. His poor, beloved cousin. What a fool she was.

Saifullah did feel a little guilty, he had to admit. All of this could have been avoided, from a certain point of view, but from another, it was as inevitable as a rainstorm. Yes, the devastation seemed great, but it was only after the rain that the earth could flourish.

It was Saifullah who had informed his grandparents of Durkhanai and Asfandyar's love affair.

"Saifullah!" Agha-Jaan had cried, face florid with fury. "Mind your tongue."

"Do you think I wish to utter such a thing?" Saifullah had replied. "I tell you only so you can stop her. If you do not believe me, send guards to Asfandyar's rooms now. See if he is alone."

Saifullah had been embarrassed to even say such a thing, in truth. His ears had burned with shame at the thought of Durkhanai with Asfandyar at such an indecent hour, and his heart felt scorched with anger. But he had known Durkhanai would be there in the hours before Asfandyar's departure.

Silently, he had hoped she wouldn't, but she had been. It made Saifullah sick, truly, what his cousin had become.

But it wasn't her fault, he reminded himself. It was that accursed Asfandyar who had bewitched her—turned her into someone she wasn't. He had performed some sort of sorcery on her, possessed her.

But in the end, when all of this was through and everything was in order again, she would heal. He would explain it all to her, make her understand everything she did not see, and beg for her forgiveness. She would grant it to him, for they were blood.

Saifullah had hated Asfandyar since the beginning when the boy had first come to his mother and told them his suspicions about the Badshah; Saifullah would have cut off his head then had he and his mother not had similar suspicions about the Badshah's alliance with the Kebzu Kingdom.

The alliance that would lead to the Badshah's downfall.

In exchange for money, Marghazar had been providing soldiers to fight alongside the Kebzus against the Luhgam Empire. It was why the northern frontier hadn't been so heavily threatened by the Kebzus as of late, why so many more garrisons of soldiers were instead dying in the east. But with the Kebzus and Marghazari allied, the Luhgam Empire had pushed back even harder.

It boiled Saifullah's blood that the Badshah would sell his own soldiers, his own people, to fight alongside the Kebzus. Saifullah had felt the betrayal even then, so many months ago, before the summit.

But the attack on the summit had been the catalyst. There was no better time to plant the seeds of revolution his Wakdar Taya had carefully been planning for years. Saifullah's mother, Nazo, had stayed in contact with him throughout, and slowly but surely, they had been plotting.

All they needed was evidence to prove that the Badshah was in charge of the summit attack; it was grounds for war, and when war came, Wakdar would take his rightful place on the throne. But in order to find evidence, they needed somebody on the inside.

It was Wakdar's plan to make Durkhanai fall in love with Asfandyar, to distract her from everything else that was stirring and to destroy her public image. Saifullah knew that despite how clever Durkhanai considered herself to be, she would be a fool for love, trusting a stranger and leading him to create the evidence they needed by stealing the Badshah's seal.

While Saifullah knew of the passageways, he did not have the key to enter his grandfather's study. Only Durkhanai did.

Thus, they had needed someone for Durkhanai to be a fool over. With Saifullah's advice, Asfandyar was the perfect vessel. It was Saifullah who had discreetly written Asfandyar letters all these months, divulging the secret blueprint of his beloved cousin. Though he had hated to do it, he knew it had to be done.

Wakdar and Nazo had a plan, and Saifullah was a dutiful son. There was nothing more sacred than blood, and he owed his blood to his mother first.

When they had concocted the plan, Saifullah knew not to trust Asfandyar—it was why he had kept his identity as the spy within the palace a secret. But the alliance had been made by Wakdar and the Wali of Jardum.

With the forged evidence that the others would believe to be real, war would be incited, which would bring about the perfect opportunity to topple the Badshah and bring forth the treaty between Marghazar and Jardum.

Saifullah's family would take charge of S'vat while Wakdar became the new Badshah. His grandparents would be exiled, and Durkhanai would be pardoned, for it was not her fault Asfandyar had bewitched her. Jardum would receive an ally and all the advantages that came with it: the river and jewels and much more.

Jardum and Marghazar would be united as one. There was no use for isolation anymore. Saifullah was sick of his grandfather's barbaric ways. It was a new world, and they would need to adapt.

Saifullah had hoped Durkhanai wouldn't be the fool, had hoped to soften her fall had she stayed allegiant and resilient, but she had disappointed him—she had fallen for Asfandyar, the foreigner, the spy. It was treason against her people, and treason had to be punished.

It was a bitter pill to swallow, but it had to be done. It was why Saifullah hadn't told Zarmina everything. She wouldn't have been able to bear it. Zarmina knew of the Badshah's alliance with the Kebzu Kingdom, and this was enough to turn her away from him. What the Badshah had done was dishonorable. Marghazar was better off under someone else's reign. It would be enough to turn the people against him.

And they both hated Asfandyar for taking Durkhanai from them, for stealing her away.

Even now, Durkhanai stood there still as stone, watching Asfandyar being taken away. Saifullah came and wrapped his arms around her, brushing a hand through her hair.

"Everything will be all right," he told her.

Saifullah hated to betray Durkhanai thus, but it was for her own good. She was like a little sister to him, and he would protect her. He swore to Allah he would.

When war broke out, if Asfandyar was somehow still alive, Saifullah would kill Asfandyar himself in redemption for the part he played in all of this.

The end was near. They were on the cusp of rebellion.

Only then could they start again.

# CHAPTER THIRTY-FOUR

Durkhanai's world had been ripped apart, and with it, so had her heart.

She wished she could reverse time, go back five minutes, even five seconds—warn Asfandyar, tell him to run far and fast. She wanted to curse fate. Only after Asfandyar was gone did she realize she could not live without him.

Though she wished his tale was a lie, she could not bear to be without him.

"I'm sorry, janaan," Saifullah said, wrapping an arm around her. Durkhanai was frozen in his arms. She did not want to be touched, did not want to be consoled. She wanted to rage.

She pushed Saifullah away.

"I need to go," she mumbled, voice foggy. She bit her tongue, holding back the cry that was rising within her. If she started crying then, she would never stop.

Durkhanai left Saifullah, not stopping to wonder what he was doing there, at that time.

All she could think of were her grandparents. Everything she knew suddenly seemed murky. But how could she doubt her own blood? Surely, everything Asfandyar had said was a lie. Surely, he was trying to turn her against her kin.

But Durkhanai had believed him. Why did she believe him? And if she did, what did that mean? That her grandmother, who had always picked up little spiders from Durkhanai's room and set them free in the outdoors, who had held Durkhanai close to her every night when she had first arrived—she had murdered her own grandchild?

If he was telling the truth, it meant the Badshah had allied himself with the Kebzu Kingdom, and not only that, but he had alerted them to the summit attack. He hadn't officiated the attack himself, but he must have known what would happen.

Head spinning, Durkhanai began walking to her grandparents' rooms. They would be awake for the morning prayer; she would clarify things immediately. There had to be some sort of in between, some space in her heart where she didn't lose all those she loved.

But—wait.

Durkhanai stopped in her tracks, heart seizing with the slow, creeping feeling of shame. It was iron hot on her cheeks, pressing into her ribs.

How could Durkhanai go to her grandparents now?

After the guards had arrested Asfandyar on the charges of loving her—and she had been seen leaving his room in the middle of the night? With what face would she speak to her beloved grandparents?

She couldn't bear the shame.

She couldn't bear to disappoint them, thus. She would have told them eventually, would have made them understand, but there was no use now. All they would see in this circumstance would be her sin.

But she needed answers. And she would have them.

Durkhanai went to her grandparents' rooms. She avoided the stares of the guards, of those who were awake. How had news traveled so fast?

But the tribunal was always thus, for all the people in all the lands came to watch the spectacle.

Her people.

They would all know—what would they think of her? The Shehzadi, fooled by the foreigner, fooled by a lowly ambassador. The Shehzadi who had so easily forgotten her blood and her people, and for what?

For a man. The Shehzadi, the whore.

She had made a mistake; she should have stayed away from him.

Now, she would have to deal with the consequences.

Durkhanai straightened her back, lifted her chin. She could deal with her grandparents and her people. She was the Shehzadi of Marghazar. There was nothing she could not do.

"Dhadi, Agha-Jaan," she started.

They both looked up, gazes blank. The silent treatment. How unlike them. At least for Dhadi, it didn't happen often, for when Dhadi was upset, she would yell and be done with it.

But now, they were so upset, they were looking right through her, like they didn't even recognize her. Her heart constricted.

"Agha-Jaan," she said. She went to where he sat on the bed and knelt by his side. He held a hand to her face, looked into her eyes.

"How could you forget your place?" Agha-Jaan asked, so unbearably sad. "Your people?"

The disappointment and shame in his voice alone made her want to cry. Durkhanai didn't know how to respond.

How could she explain it to a man who had thought of nothing but his people for more than fifty years? How frivolous and spoiled she must have seemed when they discovered her secret. How selfish she was to put them in this situation.

But she wouldn't let her guilt squander her questions. She could supersede her transgression with the knowledge of her father's existence.

"My father is alive," she said, testing them. She waited for them to give her looks of confusion, to ask her what she meant.

She stopped, registered the placid looks on her grandparents' countenances. Realized her stupidity. The fool, once again.

Of course they already knew. Which meant there was truth to Asfandyar's tale.

If her father was alive, that also meant there had been no attempt on her parents' lives the night she was born. Another lie. A story told to cover the truth.

But if her father was alive—where was her mother?

"Where is my mother?" she asked, voice thick with accusation. "Where is she? Where has she been all this time?"

"Meri jaan, come, sit," Agha-Jaan coaxed, pulling her up. "Take a deep breath. You are too excited."

She did as she was told, sitting on the bed in front of both of them, but anxiety was running through her in short bursts, her heart beating too fast, her breathing too fast, everything too much, too soon. She pressed her teeth together.

"My father is alive," Durkhanai repeated. "You said he and my mother were poisoned the night I was born. What is the truth?"

Her grandparents never spoke about either of her parents; she had always assumed it was due to grief. Durkhanai had never known them, so there were no personas to miss, and Dhadi and Agha-Jaan did so well to make sure she never felt her parents' absence, but she had always wondered. She had never asked so as not to cause her grandparents pain, but she should have.

"Did you send him away?" Durkhanai asked, accusatory and angry again. "Why didn't you ever talk about him?"

Dhadi and Agha-Jaan exchanged a sad glance, both sighing. They were conversing without speaking at all, and she felt like a glass wall separated her from them. She felt like a child.

"Gudiya, your father *left* you," Dhadi said, voice breaking. "He left us all. What use is there knowing that the man who was meant to care for you your entire life *willingly* left you alone in this world?"

"But why?" Durkhanai asked, confused, hurt. "Why did he leave me? What reason did he have to go?"

"Because he was a coward," Dhadi replied, holding Durkhanai's hand. "He couldn't handle the responsibilities of being the crown prince, so he ran."

"But—" Durkhanai's voice cut off, confused. "But why not abdicate? Pass the responsibility on to someone else? Like Zmarack Chacha?"

"We had suggested it, as well," Dhadi explained. "But he couldn't bear it. He wasn't strong enough to answer the people's questions or the shame of shirking his responsibilities. Janaan, we tried to stop him from leaving, but his heart was set."

"And my mother?" Durkhanai asked again. "What of her? Did she run with him?"

"After your father left," Dhadi said, but she couldn't manage the words. "Gudiya, your mother killed herself."

"What?" Durkhanai whispered.

Her mother had killed herself. Tears spilled onto her cheeks, and she hastily wiped them away. Durkhanai didn't know how to register such information, but she couldn't succumb to her emotions now. Not when there was still so much to be asked and said.

"So, we told everyone they were both poisoned and sent you away to save you from this truth," Dhadi continued. So, there had been no threat, no assassination attempt. "Now do you understand why we kept this from you? What good would come from knowing your father left you and triggered your mother's suicide?"

"None at all," Durkhanai replied. She was numb.

Her grandparents were right, as usual. And she, the fool.

"But what I would like to know is how you came to know Wakdar was alive to begin with," Dhadi said, curious.

"Asfandyar," Durkhanai replied. She didn't want to say he was a spy for Wakdar because that would be damning; they would kill him immediately. Durkhanai was teetering on the edge of both sides, trying to stay loyal, trying to salvage whatever she could.

*Damn her heart. Damn her love for a pair of enemies.*

"And how did he know?" Dhadi asked.

So, she hadn't recognized him. Asfandyar was right: She didn't see him as a person. Her otherwise sharp-eyed grandmother's sight had been blurred by her own hideous prejudice. Disgust rose in Durkhanai's throat.

"You killed his fiancée," Durkhanai said, hoping it was not true. "My half-sister. Wakdar's daughter."

Durkhanai watched her grandmother rifle through memories until she realized, her face falling into understanding.

"He was there that night," Dhadi said, astonished. "I thought he was a servant." Dhadi almost laughed. "So, he's finally getting the tribunal he asked for so many years ago."

"She was my sister," Durkhanai said. "Our blood. Why have her killed?"

"Oh, Durkhanai," Dhadi said, voice weary. "There are too many things you are still too young to understand. That girl was not our blood. When your father was leaving, we told him he was no longer ours, that our blood had split. He left anyway. And so, that girl was not our kin—she was a *threat*."

"A threat?" Durkhanai repeated. Dhadi nodded.

"Why would she have come, if not to incite a revolution?" she asked. "To lay a claim to the throne—to cause chaos and confusion? She should have known better. She should have stayed away. I did not wish to cause her harm, but we rulers cannot show leniency in situations such as these. We must tear problems out at the roots, or they grow to become weeds we cannot get rid of."

"But . . . you killed her," Durkhanai said stupidly.

"I did, and I am not proud of it. But, janaan, have you never done something you regretted afterward?" Dhadi countered. "How mysteriously Rukhsana-sahiba passed, after the cooks saw you overseeing her food for the voyage."

Durkhanai stilled, defeated. Her grandmother was right.

"I'm sorry, Dhadi," she said. "I understand now."

And she did.

Things were much more complicated than she would have imagined. But there was still the matter of the tribunal. Durkhanai had to stop it.

She had two feasible options. She could act like Asfandyar was nothing to her, prove her loyalty. Seeing that Asfandyar was not a threat, her grandparents could cancel the tribunal. Or, she could show them how much she loved him, fight for him. Seeing how much Asfandyar meant to their granddaughter, her grandparents could cancel the tribunal.

Durkhanai could lie, or she could tell the truth.

It was a gamble either way. Her Dhadi was pragmatic enough to concede given the first option; Agha-Jaan was emotional enough to concede to the second.

So which would she choose?

Durkhanai didn't know what was right, but she knew she was tired of holding her breath, her heart constantly torn between two places.

"Dhadi, I—" Durkhanai stopped.

How could she say it to her grandparents? But she must.

"Dhadi, Agha-Jaan," she started again. "I love Asfandyar. Please cancel the tribunal. *Please*. I love him."

There was the truth, free to fly. A weight lifted off Durkhanai's chest, and she realized just how sweet the words were. Oh, why hadn't she told him when she had the chance?

Durkhanai waited to see her grandparents' reactions. There was no explosion, as she had expected. Instead, her grandparents exchanged a knowing glance, as if they had seen this before. As if this was expected.

"Oh, janaan," Dhadi said. "Of course you think you do. This is precisely why I forbid you from seeing him, yet you did not heed my warning." Dhadi sighed. "You are young. He has bewitched you."

"What?"

"Kala jadoo," Dhadi replied. "He has used sorcery to enrapture your heart."

"No, Dhadi," Durkhanai said, feeling her throat closing with the claustrophobic feeling of being misunderstood. "What we feel for one another is true. It is the truth."

"It is a lie," Dhadi insisted calmly. "He is pretending to love you to make a fool of you. Why else would he fill your mind with these thoughts but to tear you from us? From your blood. How much easier it will be for him to cause our family's downfall with you on his leash."

"No," Durkhanai said, shaking her head. The insinuation filled her with disgust. It wasn't true. "*No.*"

So, this was why her grandparents had reacted so calmly. They believed she had been bewitched, that Asfandyar had cast a spell on her. Surely, it wasn't her fault then but all his.

They didn't believe her, thought her feelings to be a fallacy. Like she was a child with no skill for discernment.

"Did you ever want for anything?" Dhadi asked, eyes sad. "Love, adoration, devotion—anything? Did we not raise you with the utmost care?"

"Dhadi, of course you did," Durkhanai responded, feeling guilty.

"Yet, you still came here with your doubts and your accusations," Dhadi said, voice hurt. "You thought we had sent your father away and done Allah knows what to your mother. You thought me the villain, who killed your half-sister in cold blood."

"No, Dhadi, I'm sorry," Durkhanai said quickly. "I didn't mean to offend you—"

"But you have," Dhadi said. Her eyes hardened. "It is time you learned to be queen, Durkhanai. A true queen. We are tired of waiting."

Couldn't they see she *was* trying? Growing, learning . . . but how could they expect her to be a *true* queen when they did not treat her as such?

"You are tired of waiting?" Durkhanai asked, feeling angry again. "Yet you have told me nothing about the alliance with the Kebzu Kingdom! You cannot expect me to be content tending to domestic affairs with no knowledge of our international relations and political schemes."

Dhadi smiled wryly. "I am sure Asfandyar told you about that. Here you come with your accusations once more."

"But why? What of loyalty?" Durkhanai asked. "Country? Are these not the codes that dictate our culture?"

The tribes were obligated to protect their own lands, not others. And the Kebzu Kingdom had conquered and killed their brethren in the past. How could the Badshah ally himself with one of his enemies, shedding his people's blood for another nation?

"This is necessary," the Badshah explained. "To rid us of the Luhgam Empire once and for all."

And all Durkhanai saw in her grandfather's countenance was the boy of fourteen who had seen his brothers and fathers killed. How it had molded his entire being, sanded and chiseled him down to one purpose, one thought—revenge. He could not see past his own hypocrisy.

"But at what cost?" Durkhanai argued. "At what cost?"

All of their people were dying.

"Whatever the cost," the Badshah told her. "Whatever the cost for the greater good. When I am long gone, I wish for your children and your children's children to live in a world without war. These lives now for the lives of the future. Don't you understand? Can you not see?"

"I do, but, Agha-Jaan, this is too much," she said. "Just as the attack on the summit was too much. Was it really you who alerted the Kebzu Kingdom of the summit meeting?"

"I assume Asfandyar told you this, as well?"

"Yes," Durkhanai replied. "Is it true? And that show of the Kebzu soldier at the fiftieth-year celebration was a lie?"

The Badshah sighed.

"Janaan, there is much you do not understand," he replied. "Perhaps we have kept too much from you but only because you still have such a naive perspective, which is only being confirmed now. Yes, the Kebzu soldier's confession was a lie. But a necessary one to avoid war within our zillas. We cannot handle a triple-frontier war, not now, not when we are so close!"

She knew it.

"As for the summit attack," he continued. "I never told the Kebzu Kingdom to attack the summit. I merely informed them of the summit, clearly stating that we were not participating, so they did not have to worry. I did not tell them the location or the date—that, their spies must have gathered on their own."

"Besides, Allah has a way of making things work out. Now, see with the summit attack: While it was a tragedy, it was also a blessing, for if the other zillas had unified, they would have been strong enough to wage war against us," Dhadi explained. "Which would have been costly, especially when we are sending all our resources to the frontier against the Luhgam Empires. Especially when we are so close."

They had everything planned out, everything explained. All the answers at the ready, calmly explaining things to her as though she was a child still.

Was there anything she had ever known?

*No.* She didn't even know herself anymore.

Perhaps her grandparents were right; perhaps she had been bewitched. She felt hollow. Empty. Alone.

"Why are you telling me this now?" Durkhanai asked. Her voice was quiet, deflated.

"So you understand what it means to be Badshah," Agha-Jaan replied, taking her hand. "Sometimes you must swallow the bitter peel to access the sweet fruit inside. You must let whatever you *think* you feel for Asfandyar go. You must know there is no future for you and him."

"No," Durkhanai said, voice hard. She was full of grief, everything crumbled to dust, heart frozen, but she would fight them on this. "You did not hold Rukhsana-sahiba to trial when she poisoned our people," she said. "You cannot hold Asfandyar to trial for a lesser crime."

Durkhanai couldn't bear seeing Asfandyar sent to trial. Even if she was absurdly angry with him, even if she doubted him, and he had a long way to go before she would trust him again, she didn't want to see him torn apart by a lion or married off to another.

Despite everything, she was his, as he was hers. She would not give up so easily.

"We will not allow for that boy to ruin you," Dhadi snapped. "You are to be the Badshah. You must focus on your duties and your people. They would never accept a foreigner. Already, the people are doubting you due to your association with him. What good is a Shehzadi if she is not loved by her people?"

Durkhanai understood, of course she understood.

Logically, he wasn't good for her. Long term, perhaps it would lead to nowhere but heartbreak, worse than it already had. It was selfish, her love for him, and made her like her father, who abandoned everything for his own conceited reasons. But she couldn't erase how she felt. Despite everything, at least there was somebody who didn't shy away from her thorns; somebody who saw her strengths and her weaknesses and understood her.

Someone who didn't coddle her and took her seriously and pushed her to be better. She liked who she was with him. He made her better. The people would see that, wouldn't they?

Did she not know her people? Better than Agha-Jaan or even Dhadi? It was Durkhanai who visited them, Durkhanai who played with the children. It was Durkhanai who distributed medicine, Durkhanai who quelled their qualms.

She was a queen, whether her grandparents saw it or not. She would not be cast aside.

"You cannot claim I am not beloved by the people," Durkhanai said, voice strong. "You cannot. Not when I have been intimately involved in their lives for *years*, whereas you hardly visit, and even then, just to pass by and remind the people of your presence. You may wear the crown, but it is *my* face the people recognize. Not yours."

"Perhaps," Agha-Jaan said. "But the decision still lies in the crown."

"Which is why you must decide carefully," Durkhanai told her grandparents. "Won't a tribunal result in the war we have so delicately tried to avoid? Jardum will not be pleased."

"That is of no consequence now," the Badshah said, shaking his head. "The other tribes have no quarrels with Marghazar, and Jardum is not strong enough to wage a war on its own. Besides, they will hardly go to war over an irrelevant ambassador who shouldn't have forgotten his place."

"Cancel the tribunal," she insisted again. "Punish him some other way; negotiate something with Jardum. This is barbaric— holding a man to trial for his feelings."

"He has beguiled you away from your senses," the Badshah said, voice hard. "He tricked you into doubting your own blood, distracted and fooled you, yet you still fight for him. He is to be held to tribunal for sorcery, not only his feelings for you."

"No!" Durkhanai cried. "He hasn't done anything! Let him go."

"Word has already been given," the Badshah told her. "It is too late."

"You are the Badshah!" she argued, angry. "You can do whatever you please. You could cancel this tribunal, if you wished it. Just as you said, the decision lies with the crown."

"You are right," the Badshah replied. "But I do not wish it. I wish for that man to be held accountable for his deeds. Only then will you be safe."

"Why do you hate him so?" she cried. Her grandparents exchanged a glance that said she would never understand, and she recalled how the Badshah had called Asfandyar a servant all those months ago, how the Wali had done the same all those years ago.

"You cannot abhor a man for his race," Durkhanai said, but her voice wavered. Who was she to lecture her grandparents? It went against everything she had learned about respecting her elders, but their behavior was not right, either. She steadied her voice.

"It is not the Prophet's way," she added. "It is a sin."

Agha-Jaan shook his head.

"Of course we do not blame him for his color," he said. "But he is a foreigner."

"You cannot detest a man for being a foreigner, either!"

"That is enough!" Agha-Jaan snapped. Durkhanai jolted. "We will not be lectured at by a child."

"He is a liar and a spy," Dhadi added. "He used you and beguiled you from your senses. Surely, you must see that. You must."

She saw it all, but she could not bear to see him go to trial.

"Agha-Jaan, please," Durkhanai pleaded. "Cancel the tribunal. Send him far away. I'll never see him again. Just please don't force his fate thus."

"Sending people away has done us no good," Agha-Jaan replied, shaking his head. "Wakdar was sent away, and look at what it has brought us."

"This is different!" Durkhanai argued, on the verge of tears. She didn't know how to make them understand. "Please, we can trust him. He'll go far away, he'll never return. He'll forget about me and Marghazar and everything. He'll disappear, like a ghost. In a few months, we won't even remember his name."

"Janaan, do not be a fool," Dhadi replied, voice clipped. "What has trusting him gotten you thus far?" She shook her head. "No, we cannot trust him. For your sake, I wish we could, but I am sure he is a spy for Wakdar." Despite Durkhanai keeping it from them, her grandparents had deduced as much. "He is intent on causing our ruination, and we cannot allow that. If he is guilty, he will die. If he is innocent, he will be married and live here, where we can watch his every move."

"Dhadi—" Durkhanai tried again, but the Wali held up a hand.

"*Enough*," she said. "You must be a shehzadi at this moment. Think of your people and what would become of them if we let Asfandyar go and he and Wakdar were to return. If they were to incite chaos. With all that is already happening, your people need you to be a strong princess. To place them *above* yourself. Think of your people."

Durkhanai wanted to cry out in frustration, but she held her tongue. She understood her grandparents' perspective, understood all that they were saying, and she understood Asfandyar's perspective, as well, and to an extent, her father's, but wasn't there a middle that could be reached?

To the Wali and the Badshah, there wasn't.

She was defeated—for now.

But defeated she would not remain.

"I know it is difficult, now," Dhadi said, kissing Durkhanai's cheek. "But one day, you will understand. When you are the ruler, you will understand, janaan, you will."

She said nothing, just stood to leave. Already, ideas were forming in her mind; how to regroup and conquer this subject from another perspective.

"Where are you going?" Agha-Jaan asked, worried.

"To Zarmina's room," she replied, trying to keep the bite from her tone.

She needed to speak with her.

"She won't be there," Dhadi replied.

Durkhanai was filled with dread, and somehow, she already knew why. But she still asked, heart hammering, throat closing.

"Why?"

"Zarmina has been selected to be the lady of the trial."

# CHAPTER THIRTY-FIVE
*Zarmina's Tale*

Zarmina didn't expect everything to happen so suddenly, truly.

Before she knew it, Saifullah had come to her saying that Asfandyar had been taken for trial. Then, she had been taken away to the suite of the lady for the trial.

They had blindfolded her on the way there, and when they'd removed the blindfold, she was in a lushly decorated room with no windows. The suite door was unlocked, but when she reached the end of the hall, the main door was locked. There was no exit.

Zarmina sat alone in the suite now, clean and fresh from a rose water bath. She tried to find some way to call Durkhanai to her, but it was forbidden to interact with anybody, not until after the trial this evening. Zarmina rose, pacing around the room as her wet hair soaked into her shirt. Usually, the trials took place a fortnight after the accusation, but in this case, she knew the sooner the better.

Once Asfandyar was dead, her dear cousin would be safe.

Zarmina had known, since the very beginning, that Asfandyar was a spy for her Wakdar Taya. They needed him to debase Durkhanai to lead to an easier transition of power when Wakdar came.

But of course, Durkhanai had not heeded Zarmina's warnings. She had not merely been distracted and debased. She had fallen in love. It was all Zarmina wished for her dear cousin—love and happiness—but she could not bear for it to be with *him*.

Not when she knew that Asfandyar had caused her Wakdar Taya so much pain by causing Naina's death. Not when she knew that Asfandyar did not truly care for Durkhanai and was only using her.

His feelings for her were false, while poor Durkhanai's feelings were true.

Zarmina could recognize it in her cousin's shining blue-green eyes, could recognize it in her sighs and her smiles: she was in love. Zarmina had hoped what Durkhanai felt for Asfandyar was merely pyaar or ishq, but she knew now that it was mohabbat, and that was a thing that would not be easily extricated.

Not only was it love, but it was *true* love, the kind that brought out the best in her cousin, made her burn brighter. Zarmina had witnessed Durkhanai morph from a petulant, spoiled princess into an insightful, thoughtful queen.

And the object of her affections did not deserve her.

How Zarmina wished it had not come to this. But her grandparents had left her no choice.

Durkhanai thought she knew everything, understood things so clearly, but her grandparents merely fed her enough information to keep her satisfied, serving her pretty little half-truths while the meat of the situation stayed concealed.

Zarmina had only known because of Saifullah. There were no secrets between them, so she had known about the treacherous Kebzu alliance. All this, the Badshah had hid from Durkhanai. He did not trust her, not truly.

Zarmina couldn't bear to see her cousin so underestimated by her grandparents, and in truth, Zarmina had considered telling her everything many times, but she could not diverge from her mother and Wakdar Taya's plans.

It was nearly time. Everything would soon fall into place. And Durkhanai would be safe once more.

Now, the city waited.

Zarmina sat at the vanity. She brushed her long hair in methodical strokes, counting down from one hundred, then counting down again. Outside her suite, she knew the lion cages of all the lands would be searched for the most savage and relentless beasts, from which only the fiercest monster would be selected for the arena.

Ordinarily, the royal family never procured the lady for the trial, but in this case, Saifullah and Zarmina had both insisted. Her grandparents—not knowing Zarmina and her brother were working with Wakdar—relented.

In the rare chance that Asfandyar survived, his marriage to Zarmina would guarantee that Durkhanai would not interfere. She would never ruin the matrimony of her beloved cousin.

Pushing her hair aside, Zarmina fingered the beautiful gold jewelry laid out for her, her fingers pricking at the sharp corners. She pulled her hand away before she drew blood.

Of course, everybody knew by now what the accused had been charged with. He had loved the princess, and neither he, she, nor anyone else thought of denying the fact.

But the Badshah would not allow any facts to interfere with the workings of the tribunal, in which he took great delight and satisfaction. The barbarism had seeped deeply into her grandfather.

Zarmina's gaze went to the clothes set out for the trial: an ornate red wedding outfit with gold embroidery. This was not how she imagined she would prepare for her wedding. Ironically, Zarmina was in the same place her mother had been in so many years ago. Sitting as the lady with a personal interest in the outcome of the tribunal.

But while her mother had prayed for the man's innocence, Zarmina was praying for his guilt.

And truly, Zarmina had only agreed for one reason: to save Durkhanai.

She had a plan.

# CHAPTER THIRTY-SIX

urkhanai took measured breaths, pacing her room. Why would Zarmina agree to this? Was it to spite her? Did Zarmina harbor secret feelings toward Asfandyar? No matter how impossible the thought was, jealousy bristled inside of her.

But no, she would not jump to conclusions, not until she had spoken to Zarmina. But the lady of the trial was always held in seclusion, unreachable. How would Durkhanai reach her? Luckily, Durkhanai knew in which part of the palace the lady was kept. It was knowledge only she and her grandparents knew.

But how would she get through? She sat down, forcing herself to still and think clearly. She ran through different scenarios in her mind, gauging the outcomes. She could order the guards to let her in, but word would surely reach her grandparents, and they would not be happy. They would further be convinced that Asfandyar had bewitched her. Why else would she go to such extremes to speak to the lady of the trial, if not to sabotage it?

No, Durkhanai would need to think of something else.

She would sneak in, dressed as a maid—but her face was too easily recognizable.

She could bribe them? No. Their allegiance was to the Badshah.

Sleeping ointment? No, again. They would be too confused when they woke. It would be too suspicious.

She would need something more.

Then, something turned in her mind. A bud, blooming into shape. Durkhanai smiled. She went to her dressing room. She discarded her shawl and simple clothes. Maids helped her dress. She adjusted her crown atop her dupatta, her chudiyan clinking together on her arms. She straightened her back, lifted her chin.

As she exited her room, she grabbed a little pouch, then began making her way to the lowest levels of the palace, a floor very few even knew existed. It was deep within the mountain and impossible to reach without the specific directions from within the palace. This level was where they kept most of the gold, jewels, important documents, and other invaluable objects.

It was where they hid the lady's suite.

Durkhanai walked to the room, smiling at the guards who stood there. They were young, just as she suspected they would be, because protecting the lady wasn't the most vital job down there.

The younger they were, the easier to fool.

When they saw Durkhanai approaching, they lowered their heads in respect.

"Shehzadi," they said.

"Good morning," she said, smiling sweetly. "I know the lady isn't meant to be interacting with anyone, but as it is my beloved cousin, I have some . . . personal things for her."

Durkhanai held up the bag as evidence.

"And what would be inside?" one guard asked. "We can deliver it to her."

"I'd much rather deliver it myself, thank you," she said. Without waiting, she moved toward the door. Confidence was key.

They did not move to open it but exchanged a wary glance. Durkhanai narrowed her eyes at them. Her voice harshened with petulance. "What exactly is the problem?"

"Apologies, Shehzadi, but we have been given express instructions not to let anyone through," one guard said. "If the Badshah found out . . ."

"If the Badshah found out you were stopping *me* from seeing my beloved cousin on the eve of her wedding, I assure you, he would not be happy," Durkhanai said, eyes hard. "I believe what he would be is *furious*, especially considering I have personal items to deliver. As I already said. And I do hate to repeat myself."

The guards were visibly starting to sweat. "Perhaps, if we could see what was inside . . ." The younger guard started to reach for her bag.

"How dare you!" Durkhanai snatched the bag tightly in her hand. "To even think of going through my belongings!"

"No, no, Shehzadi! That was not our intent at all," the older guard said, hitting the younger guard. "It is only . . . we were told not to—"

"And I'll be sure *not* to tell them you let me in," Durkhanai said. "Your other option, of course, is that I tell them you *did* let me in, to which I am sure you can gauge the reaction. Your decision, boys."

The two guards exchanged a glance, then begrudgingly stepped aside. They opened the doors for her, and she sauntered in. Durkhanai smiled.

"My sincerest thanks to you brave men," she said. They closed the door behind her.

She walked down the corridor, past doors for maids and baths, making her way to the largest room. Durkhanai released an anxious breath, not knowing what would await her on the other side of that door.

Finally, Durkhanai opened it.

"Durkhanai!" Zarmina cried, seeing her. "I knew you would come. Only you can do the impossible."

She hopped off the bed, running to the door to meet her.

"Zarmina, so much has happened," Durkhanai said, voice catching.

"Why did you stray so far?" Zarmina asked her. Suddenly, a hard look covered Zarmina's countenance. Almost as though Zarmina remembered everything in that moment.

"I didn't realize," Durkhanai replied, voice soft. "Zarmina—"

"I told you," Zarmina interjected, voice full of spite. "And now look where we are. You, debased, and me, with the chances of marrying a man I detest."

"Zarmina, why would you do this?" Durkhanai asked, heart hurting. "If he is innocent and you marry him—"

Durkhanai couldn't finish the thought. It filled her with jealousy and betrayal, hot and sticky.

"Don't you see?" Zarmina seethed. "You drove me to this! How else would you realize the severity of what you've done!"

Zarmina chose this. Durkhanai had thought it had been her grandparents' idea as a means to punish her, but Zarmina had chosen this. There would be no persuading her now.

"How could you?" Durkhanai asked.

"How could I?" Zarmina repeated. "Dear cousin, how could *you?*"

Durkhanai turned her cheek, but Zarmina stood in front of her, her hands on Durkhanai's shoulders. "How could you have been so blind? He is our enemy."

"He is *not*. You do not know him," Durkhanai insisted, but she wasn't so sure. Zarmina shook her head sadly.

"He has been our enemy since the moment he stepped foot into this palace," she said. "You just cannot see. Love blinds you. In more ways than one."

"No," Durkhanai insisted. "Zarmina, I had come hoping to convince you from being the lady, hoping we could somehow work together to get Agha-Jaan to stop all of this. But now, I see you are as determined as I am, though on the opposing side."

"I wish it were not so," Zarmina replied. "But yes, I am. You cannot persuade me from this. The trial must happen. It is for your own good. Only then can things be righted."

"But why you as the lady? Royalty is always exempt from being chosen."

"Saifullah chose this," Zarmina said. "I came to agree with him. It's the only way for you to cease your incessant adoration of the man you have forsaken us for."

"Zarmina, do not say such things," Durkhanai said, taking her cousin's hands. "I would never forsake you. You must know that."

"I do now, looking into your eyes," Zarmina replied. "But you have been so far . . ."

"I'm sorry." Durkhanai hugged her cousin. "I'm so, so sorry."

Durkhanai blew out the candle in her heart, allowing the final flame to sputter out in her fist. She didn't know who she was apologizing to anymore, but Zarmina held her close. They were caught in the crossfire, both pierced.

Durkhanai's mind was spinning. She did not know yet what she would do next.

Before she could consider her next move, sudden calm fell over Zarmina's features. She wiped her tears and nearly smiled as she put her hand on Durkhanai's cheek, wiping away her tears as well.

"I know, janaan," she said, voice strong, "that you will do the right thing in the end. You will do right by me, by your family, by your people; by all of us. Which is why I agreed to this—so you could stop it."

Zarmina leaned forward and whispered in Durkhanai's ear which room she, the lady, would be in: the left or the right.

# CHAPTER THIRTY-SEVEN
*Wakdar's Tale*

The night his daughter was born, Wakdar Miangul ran.

While his wife recovered, he ran far and fast. He loved his wife, and he loved his child, but that night he saw neither of them—it would have crushed his resolve, made things all the more difficult. If he had seen her, he would never have been able to leave.

And it was dishonorable, truly, to run as he was, but he had no choice left. If he stayed, he would know no peace until he had slaughtered his parents for what they had done.

The blood was still fresh in his memory, the sight of his best friend being torn apart by the cruelest of lions. Wakdar and Yaqut had been inseparable since birth, and their friendship had grown as Wakdar learned his princely duties and Yaqut rose in the ranks until he became the lead general.

Their friendship had seen happy years and sad ones, long years and short ones. It had even lasted through Yaqut falling in love with Wakdar's sister.

The bond between Wakdar and Yaqut had lacked only blood, which they would have happily spilled for one another.

What their friendship had not survived was the tribunal.

Despite Yaqut's innocence, the door had opened to reveal a lion.

After Wakdar found out from Nazo that the trial had been rigged, he was overcome with rage. His pious father, always going on about the sanctity of the trial, had replaced the lady with a lion. Yaqut didn't stand a chance.

Wakdar swore to exact his revenge, to avenge his murdered best friend.

But how could he?

Against his own parents—the Badshah of Marghazar and the Wali of S'vat—the most powerful people in all the tribal lands? How easy it would be for him to slip into their rooms in the dead of the night. A quick slit to each of their throats.

Painless, soundless. Wakdar could manage it too easily.

But no matter how wretched Ghazan and Bazira Miangul were, they were his blood, and there was nothing more sacred than blood.

He would not raise his sword against them.

So, he had to leave. It was the only way.

He waited until his wife's labor pains began, waited for the marble palace to be in a frenzy, until he could slip away. He couldn't bear to leave his child or his wife, but it had to be done.

He had no choice. He would send for them when he could—he had enough allies to manage it. He knew his daughter would be cared for until then, until he returned for her.

Wakdar had to leave. He couldn't live with the murder of his best friend, who had been like a brother to him. Moreover, Wakdar could not live with who his father was becoming—a man blinded by his vendetta against the Luhgam Empire.

But his parents knew him too well.

"Don't be a fool," his father said the night he caught Wakdar in the midst of escape, harsh face ablaze by moonlight. "Go back to your daughter and wife."

"Kill me if you must," Wakdar replied, resolute. "But I will not return."

So, they were stuck, neither party willing to break the sacred bond between them.

"Beta, please don't do this," his mother pleaded, tears in her eyes. "Do not leave your family."

"I have made up my mind," Wakdar replied, turning to leave. "Khudafiz."

Anger flashed across his mother's face, and for a moment, he did not recognize her. "If you leave now, do not think we will spare your wife," Bazira declared. "Her relation to this family will be severed entirely."

"You wouldn't," Wakdar had replied, ignoring his mother's dramatics. He kept walking. It was this, perhaps, that had forced her to swear to it.

"I swear to Allah I will," his mother said, voice steel.

His mother would never break an oath made to Allah, Wakdar knew. But he had sworn to Allah as well that if he stayed, he would kill his parents for what they had done.

So he was faced with a fatal choice: his wife or his parents?

In the end, there was nothing more sacred than blood.

"Never return," Ghazan ordered. "From this day forth, our blood has split. You are our son no longer."

They had let him go. Wakdar knew, deep down, they couldn't raise a sword against their own son, just as he couldn't raise a sword against them. Despite the hatred between them, they were blood. Neither could expunge one another from their veins.

Or at least, he had thought.

Until halfway through the journey across the mountains when men cloaked in black had attacked him. They were the trained assassins of court. Wakdar recognized their fight.

He slaughtered them and left, leaving his heart in pieces along the path as he did. He worried for his wife, for his child, but he repeated to himself over and over that they wouldn't actually go through with killing his beloved wife, that they wouldn't have the heart to orphan their beloved grandchild, his daughter, the future Badshah of Marghazar now that he was leaving. Wakdar managed to convince himself enough to leave.

But his mother was a woman of her word.

Thus, his wife was killed that night, as he ran.

He heard later that he had died as well, both poisoned apparently. His heart had ached for his daughter then, but he couldn't send for her, yet.

His parents knew him too well and had hidden her away, someplace impenetrable, someplace unknown. He had a guess, but he did not have the resources to go to her, so he had sent her a cloth doll, hoping for then, it would be enough.

Slowly, he built his life up again from the ashes. He gained asylum in Jardum and reconnected with an old friend—General

Afridi. He made connections with the Wali of Jardum who knew the advantages of having the supposed dead Miangul heir as an ally, a man who knew all of Marghazar's workings and secrets.

As the years passed, Wakdar considered many times returning home: exacting his revenge, being united with his daughter. Despite everything—Yaqut's slaughter, the attempt on his own life, his wife's murder—Wakdar could not raise a sword against his parents.

Perhaps it was cowardice or selfishness, but his blood would not be erased.

So, his life continued on.

Slowly, his anger faded, like a snake shedding its old skin, replaced by the new. Wakdar slowly built his connections, built his life. He had another daughter, a jewel among jewels. She became his jaan, his very soul. She was loved by him above all humanity.

In the end, it was her blood that erased his parents'.

His daughter, the most precious of precious things, with a heart spun of gold—slaughtered.

When that cursed Black boy brought his daughter's corpse to him, it took all of Wakdar's strength not to kill Asfandyar on the spot. Instead, Wakdar took the crying seventeen-year-old boy and infused him with his rage, infused him with his vengeance.

He drafted a plan. And Asfandyar became his pawn.

Nazo, his beloved sister, who had kept contact with him all those years, was the first to align with him. She was still bitter from Yaqut's slaughter. Her marriage to another had not erased her love for Yaqut. She was still filled with spite, so many years later, as were her children who were meant to inherit nothing from the Badshah.

And Wakdar knew the Badshah's greed for victory would be his downfall. It would be all too easy to exact his revenge, but he needed to be patient, precise.

So Wakdar waited, biding his time, holding on to the memories of his best friend, his first wife, his daughter. Some days, the grief threatened to take him as well, take him to his beloved, but he resisted—he persisted.

Until, finally, it was time.

He had waited eighteen years—patiently, quietly. But finally, the time was ripe: Asfandyar had sent him the evidence needed to prove that Marghazar was behind the summit attack. With it, Wakdar could convince the other zillas' leaders to join him in war.

The time had come for the crown prince to return home, to claim what was rightfully his: his land, his daughter, and mostly importantly—his revenge.

The blood had emptied from his body. Instead, war was thrumming through his veins.

# CHAPTER THIRTY-EIGHT

*O*nce upon a time, in a very olden time, there lived a semi-barbaric king.

He was the Badshah of Marghazar, a king of kings, with an authority untrammeled by those in his lands. No one had the temerity to question his ways, and half the time, this was acceptable. He was only semi-barbaric, as you recall, and the barbarism showed its way mainly in exuberant fancy. The Badshah, given to self-communing, turned his fancies into facts with only the consultation of he and himself.

One such manifestation of his was the public arena. Built into the mountains, below the marble palace, an amphitheater was made for the entirety of the capital city of Safed-Mahal. It was there that those accused of crimes that warranted public interest went to trial.

The rules of the game were simple: the accused was brought before two doors, completely identical. They masked entirely what was held behind them, and the accused was then given a choice to decide his own fate. Behind one door was a lion, the cruelest that could be procured. Behind the other was a lady, the most kind that could be found.

If the accused was guilty, the lion would rip him to shreds. If the accused was innocent, he was to marry the lady. Instant punishment, instant reward—what better judgment than that made by the Lord?

The appointed hour arrived.

The people gathered from all across the mountain, great throngs piling into the galleries of the arena until all the seats were filled and the overflowing crowds amassed themselves outside the amphitheater walls.

The Badshah sat in his place, the Wali on one side of him and the Shehzadi on the other. In the rows beneath them sat the Badshah's court: his family and the nobles and the ambassadors, who had extended their stay to witness the final fate of one of their own. They sat directly opposite the two doors, those fateful and those fatal portals, so hideous in their sameness.

All was ready.

The signal was given.

From beneath the royal party, a door opened to reveal the lover of the Shehzadi. Tall, beautiful, strong: His appearance elicited a low hum of admiration and anxiety from the audience.

As the young man advanced into the arena, he turned to bow to the king, as was custom, but he did not think at all of that royal personage. Instead, his eyes were fixed upon the Shehzadi, who sat beside her grandfather.

Had it not been for the barbarism in her nature, perhaps the lady would not have come to witness such a horrid event. But the Shehzadi's fervid soul would not allow her to be absent on such an occasion.

From the instant the decree had gone forth to seize her lover to trial, she hadn't spent a second thinking of anything but this event and all the events that had preceded it.

The Shehzadi had done what no other had done—she had possessed herself of the secret of the doors.

And she couldn't stand her options.

The hot-blooded and semi-barbaric princess: She felt her soul burning beneath the combined fires of despair and jealousy. She had lost him, that much she already knew. But what of his fate?

Durkhanai loved him. Despite everything, the truth deep within her core would not be shaken. She loved him with an intensity that had enough of barbarism in it to make it immense and strong.

Durkhanai seemed to be the only one reacting. Around her, the royal family was calm. Even the ambassadors—who had delayed their departure, who she knew objected to such a barbaric practice as the tribunal—wore calm expressions. They weren't the least bit shocked.

It was only Durkhanai who was at war with herself.

On the one hand, she could make a plan for Asfandyar to escape and for her to go with him—but in doing so, she would lose her people, her crown, and her family. She would break her grandparents' hearts, just as her father had.

They would never accept him in court. Running would be the only option. She would be free from all the rules, free as she had been when she was a child, growing in the valley, unadulterated and pure.

They would be together.

On the other hand, she could let him die. This man who she hadn't even known a few months ago. The man she now loved. But what was love? If he were eaten by the lion, all of Durkhanai's problems would flutter away.

It would hurt, of course, but all pain passed, eventually. If he were dead, she would come to terms with not having him, but if he lived, she wasn't sure she could say the same.

They could never be together.

Durkhanai was struck by how much she missed him already. She hadn't seen him, not since he had been taken away. Just a few hours, and already her heart was aching without him by her side. Only a day, and already her lips yearned for his.

She recalled everything that had happened in the hours before his arrest, everything Asfandyar had wanted to tell her while she hadn't given him the chance. And everything he had told her—the knowledge of her father being alive, the betrayal of her grandparents, the mistrust in the crown.

The decision weighed heavily on Durkhanai's shoulders, heavy as the crown on her head. The fatal decision. Was it even a choice when there was nothing more sacred than blood?

Love or blood?

But were they not the same?

Durkhanai wished she had run with him when she had the chance. Now, she stood alone, facing an impossible choice.

She closed her eyes, remembered who she was. She was Durkhanai Miangul, the future Badshah of Marghazar. She was birthed by the mountains and River S'vat.

There was nothing she could not do.

So she stitched her bleeding heart together again. She put her heart in a velvet pouch and tied it tight. Then she put the pouch in a wooden box, and the wooden box in a stone crate, and the stone crate in a marble house. And around the marble house, she molded a mountain. And over the mountain, she poured the ocean.

Thus, her heart was protected, never to be broken again.

She took a breath.

Asfandyar turned and looked at her.

When their eyes met, the haze of faces around them faded away. There was nobody but them, and he saw, by that power of quick perception which is given to those whose souls are one, that she knew behind which door crouched the lion and behind which stood the lady.

He had expected her to know it.

He understood her nature, the determination and stubbornness within her. Even if Zarmina hadn't told her, Durkhanai would have uncovered the truth one way or another.

Asfandyar had complete faith in her.

Then, it was his quick and anxious glance that asked the question: "Which?"

It was as plain to her as if he shouted it from where he stood. There was not an instant to be lost. The question was asked in a flash; it had to be answered in another.

Durkhanai raised her hand and made a slight, quick movement toward the left.

No one but Asfandyar saw her. Every eye but his was fixed on the man in the arena.

He turned, and with a firm and rapid step walked across the empty space, toward the two doors—toward his fate. Every heart stopped beating, every breath was held, every eye was fixed immovably upon that man.

He turned, casting a final glance toward Durkhanai.

There was nothing—no one—in the world but them.

In that moment, she saw the unmasked love in his eyes.

She knew the same love was mirrored in hers.

Then he moved across the empty space, toward a door.

The door on the right.

Which came out of the opened door—the lady, or the lion?

# A PARTING RIDDLE

nce upon a time, in a very olden time, there lived a beautiful girl who fell in love with a beautiful boy. She put her rose gold heart in a rose gold box and gave it to him as a gift. But when the boy opened the box, it was empty.

Was it because she hadn't actually given her heart to him?

Or because she had no heart to begin with?

# GLOSSARY

**Acha:** okay

**Adhan:** call to prayer

**Allah:** the name of God in Arabic

**Anwar ratol:** a type of mango

**Assalam u alaikum:** Islamic greeting meaning "peace be upon you"

**Bachay:** child

**Badshah:** emperor

**Bas:** enough

**Batameez:** ill-mannered

**Besharam:** shameless

**Beta:** son but usually used to mean child

**Chaadar:** a large, cloak-like shawl

**Chacha:** uncle that is a father's younger brother

**Chachay:** plural of chacha

**Chal jhooti:** get out of here, you liar

**Chakore:** a bread basket for roti

**Chalo:** come

**Chanda:** little moon

**Charpai:** a traditional woven bed

**Chiriya:** little bird

**Chudiyan:** bangles

**Dhadi:** paternal grandmother

**Dhol:** double-headed drum

**Dhoodh haldi:** turmeric milk

**Dua:** supplication

**Dupatta:** a long scarf

**Fajr:** the first daily prayer

**Fitteh mu tera:** Goddamn your face

**Gharara:** wide-leg pants with pleats at the knees

**Guddu:** term of endearment for children; doll

**Gudiya:** doll

**Hai Allah:** oh God

**Halwa:** a sweet dish

**Isha:** the fifth daily prayer

**Ishq:** passionate love

**Jaan:** my beloved

**Jamaat:** congregation

**Janaan:** my soul

**Januman:** soul of my heart

**Jazakullah khair:** meaning "May God reward you," said as a sign of gratitude

**Jhumkay:** a type of earrings

**Jummah:** the Friday prayer in congregation

**Junoon:** madness

**Kasam se:** to swear by something

**Kala jadoo:** sorcery

**Kava:** green tea

**Khairiyat:** all good

**Khuda:** God

**Khuda ke liye:** for God's sake

**Khudafiz:** goodbye

**Khussay:** flat shoes

**Kurta:** a long shirt

**Kya:** what

**Lala:** endearment for older brother

**Lehenga choli:** a full length skirt and cropped blouse

**Loi:** a large, woolen shawl

**Maghrib:** the fourth daily prayer

**Main tera:** I am yours

**Manay:** the second season, where the seeds are sown and harvested

**Mehndi:** temporary, decorative skin embellishment; henna

**Meri bachi:** my child

**Mohabbat:** true love

**Meri jaan:** my soul

**Messenger:** in reference to the Prophet Muhammad (PBUH)

**Nano:** maternal grandmother

**Pagal:** crazy person

**Pakol:** soft round-topped men's hat, typically of wool and found in any of a variety of earthy colors

**Phuppo:** paternal aunt

**Puri:** a fried, flaky bread

**Rubab:** lute-like musical instrument

**Sahib:** Sir

**Sahiba:** Ma'am

**Salah:** prayer

**Salam:** shortened Islamic greeting, meaning peace

**Shalwar kameez:** loose pants and a long shirt

**Shareef:** noble and dignified

**Shehzadi:** Princess

**Sherwani:** formal men's wear

**Shikanjvi:** spiced lemonade

**Shukria:** thank you

**Taubah:** to ask for forgiveness

**Taya:** father's older brother

**Tere liye:** for you

**Teri kasam:** I swear on you

**Walaikum assalam:** the response to "Assalam u alaikum," meaning "and peace be upon you"

**Wali:** protector

**Yaar:** friend

**Zilla:** district

**Zuhr:** the second daily prayer

# ACKNOWLEDGMENTS

lhamdulillah. We made it!

Thank you first to the team at CamCat Books for making my dreams come true. To Sue: on that first call, you said, "You can scream now!" and I've been doing just that ever since.

To Cassandra, my wonderful editor. You've taught me so much about craft, and I couldn't imagine my characters in better hands. You brought out the best in me and them, and for that, I am eternally grateful.

Thank you to everyone who went into making this book real: Laura at Marketing and Maryann for a gorgeous book I could hug all day, and Bridget for the copyedits. To Asrar Farooqi, for painting my stunning cover. To Fatima Baig and Areeba Siddique for the preorder art that I love so dearly.

Thank you to my mother and my father, who truly raised me like a princess, showering me with love and comforts, yet always pushed me to stand on my own two feet. I am honored to be your daughter, and I hope I have made you proud. Everything I have accomplished is because of you.

Mama, thank you for being my friend, and Baba, thank you for always making me smile.

Thank you to Zaineb, my vibrant sister. Whenever anyone asks me to think of something I can't live without, I always think of you. To Sameer, for being perceptive and adventurous. To Ibraheem, for being kind and present. I'm proud to be your sister. Even though we don't choose our family, I'm glad I got stuck with you all and we're maneuvering this crazy life together.

To my grandparents, Mimi and Papa, who dote on me so. To Veeta Khala and my cousins Hamnah, Umaymah, Aizah, and the little ones. To Johnnie Mamoo and Faisal Mamoo. To Samina Phuppi. To Madho Khala and Nano and Ahmed Uncle and all my family in Pakistan. To Yasmin Phuppo, for the flowers and chocolates and love. Thank you all for the constant love, laughter, food, support, and guidance. You've taught me that family can be a foundation, from which all else grows. And how I've grown! It is all thanks to you.

To Noor, whose wisdom always guides me. To Mahum, who showed me there is strength in silence. Thank you for all the laughs and pagalpan and besharami.

To Arusa. You are my rock. You are my constant. Thank you for the endless FaceTime calls, for listening to me, for understanding, and for somehow always knowing exactly what I need to hear. I love you more than words. Without you, life would be unbearable.

To Sara, my ray of sunshine. You are my warmth. Thank you for always being so supportive and reading the sloppiest drafts I've ever written and for reassuring me whenever I worried. To Justine, who understands me in ways no one else can. Thank you for always cheering me on. Your constant faith in me kept me going. I love you both so, so much. You are the very best thing to come out of Mt. Sinai.

To Isra, my sweetest friend. Thank you for your kind reminders and for feeling things so keenly with me. I feel seen by you, which is no small thing. To Uroosa, meri jaan. Thank you for always holding me in your heart and making me feel loved and reminding me to be grateful. I love you both so dearly and for the sake of Allah. You remind me to be a better Muslim, which is the very best thing.

To Sadaf, for being loud and proud and teaching me so much about kindness. Your support is a light. To Gia and Sidrah, thank you for all the love and support. We used to be kids, dreaming of what we would do when we grew up, and now we're all grown, and I'm so glad we held on together for the ride. To Murriam and Sabiha and Sara, who are so far away yet still feel so close. To Salwa, Mutahira, Hanaa, and Maria, my gal pals. To Maryam and Sundus, my honorary older sisters. Thank you all for the chaos, the sleepovers, and all the excitement and hype. I love each and every one of you.

To family friends like family: Uzma Auntie, Shana Auntie, Ayesha Auntie, Mona Auntie, and Saadia Auntie, who always showed me so much love and support.

To Yusra and Umaimah, thank you for the outpouring of support and for the laughs we've had along the way. To all my friends on Twitter who have been cheering me on: Sanah, Liya, Siraj, Amna, and Meha. For total strangers, you have shown me so much kindness, so early on. Your support has made all the difference.

To all the friends I've loved and lost over the years: I remember you. Thank you for the memories. I still think of them so fondly.

To my teachers, who have been so instrumental in my growth. To Ms. DePass, Mrs. Wallace, and Ms. Dundas from middle school, for encouraging me and supporting me from the very beginning, when I did not even truly believe in myself. To Ms. Alexander, Mr. McHugh, and Mr. Sallese, for the fun history lessons and widening of my world, and for making high school bearable. To Mr. Markowtiz, for introducing me to "The Lady or the Tiger?". To Professor Sarah Azzara, Professor Brandi So, Professor Jean Graham, Professor E. K. Tan, and Professor Douglas Pfieffer at Stony Brook University—thank you for your wonderfully stimulating classes and only furthering my love for the English language and literature.

Lastly, thank you to the readers, to each and every one of you who picked up this book. This is especially for the Pakistani kids, the brown kids, and the Muslim kids: I hope you felt seen and continue to feel seen. I'm with you. I see you. I hope for a brief period of time, I was able to help you escape the madness of this world and transport you somewhere that is inspired by a country so dear to me with characters pulled from my heart. I hope, too, that you will always choose kindness.

If you can, spare a prayer for me.

# ABOUT THE AUTHOR

*A*amna Qureshi is a Pakistani, Muslim American who adores words. She grew up in a very loud household, surrounded by English (for school), Urdu (for conversation), and Punjabi (for emotion). Through her writing, she wishes to inspire a love for the beautiful country and rich culture that informed much of her identity. When she's not writing, she loves to travel to new places where she can explore different cultures or to Pakistan where she can revitalize her roots. She also loves baking complicated desserts, drinking fancy teas and coffees, watching sappy rom-coms, and going for walks about the estate (her backyard). She currently lives in New York.

**Look for Aamna on:**

**IG @aamna_qureshi**
**Twitter @aamnaqureshi_**
**www.aamnaqureshi.com**

# AUTHOR'S NOTE

*T*he world of *The Lady or the Lion* was heavily inspired by
Pakistan and Pakistani culture. When I first read the
short story, "The Lady or the Tiger?" by Frank R.
Stockton, I was instantly compelled. It is the story of an impossible
decision, with a killer ending, and after first reading it, I couldn't
stop thinking about it.

The short story left much to the imagination, and I found
myself enraptured by the spoiled princess and her forbidden lover.

When I first began imagining the story that would become
*The Lady or the Lion*, I did not consider creating a world inspired
by my own cultural heritage. I had never seen it done before, and
it almost seemed as if I was not "allowed" to do so. Originally,
the backdrop of the story remained a vaguely Western world, just
like many of the other novels populating the young adult sphere.
However, that spring I visited Pakistan, and while most of the time
I stayed in Islamabad, we did take a trip farther north. I loved
the beautiful sights, and as I developed my story further, it struck
me that those gorgeous mountains and lush scenery would be the
perfect background to the story I wanted to write. And it was not

just that—I realized I *wanted* to incorporate the country I loved so dearly into my book.

There weren't any young adult novels I could think of that drew upon Pakistan's beauty and customs, on its food and clothing and culture. When a novel I read even offhandedly mentioned Pakistan or Pakistanis, I was thrilled, as if that simple acknowledgement confirmed my existence. Would it not mean so much more for me to write an entire book inspired by Pakistan?

So basing the world of my novel on Pakistan and Pakistani culture came from a place of love and self-indulgence. Once I began writing, I realized just how much there was to explore. It gave me space to write the story I always yearned to read while growing up, with clever references to dramas, poetry, films, and proverbs, with mention of specific food dishes and types of clothing and familial relations.

While I recognize many of these references are niche, and perhaps many readers will not recognize them, it will be all the more special for those who will. Most importantly, I wrote the book that I loved, and I really had fun writing it.

Unfortunately, most people's perception of Pakistan is stuck in stereotypes. I hope that my book can mitigate those prejudices and show people that the country has a rich history and traditions full of vibrancy and beauty. Through my words, I hope people can fall in love with the culture that I adore so deeply.

# AUTHOR Q&A

**Q:** **What inspired you to write *The Lady or the Lion*?**

**A:** The short story "The Lady or the Tiger?"! I found it so compelling and was desperate to learn more once it was over. I started to think about what I thought of the princess, and the story took root from there. The setting was inspired by my family's home country of Pakistan, which I love to visit, and the culture I am so proud to call my own.

**Q:** **Tell us how *The Lady or the Lion* retells "The Lady, or the Tiger?" and how you put your own twist on it to turn it into something original?**

**A:** The original short story is very sparse in its details and developments regarding the princess. Although the crux of the story centers on her decision, you don't really learn a lot about her, or the way she deals with making the impossible choice between sending her lover to marry another or to death. My novel delves deep into the princess's character, the ambivalence between kindness and cruelty, and provides evidence and little hints as to what choice I think she makes in the end.

**Q: Why did you include so many Urdu words and dialogues?**

**A:** I speak Urdu at home with my family and close friends, and I adore the language. I love watching Pakistani dramas, listening to Urdu/Hindi/Punjabi music, and even reading Urdu poetry (when it's Romanized because I tragically can't read the Urdu script). When I was writing, there were moments when those lines of Urdu dialogue came naturally in my head as a reaction; I decided to add them because I really wanted this book to be specific. Then, there were also some instances where I couldn't find an adequate English word for what I wished to describe, and the Urdu word was exactly what I needed. One example are the different types of love, for which there are separate words in Urdu: pyaar, ishq, mohabbat.

**Q: Do you have a specific writing routine?**

**A:** I try to! When I first get an idea for a story, I usually compile a document of snippets and scenes, then I try to turn that into a cohesive outline, then expand it into outlined chapters, then finally, I tackle the drafting. When I'm drafting, I tend to write the parts I am most excited about first, which is usually the ending (it helps me to know where I am going!). I do not write linearly; instead, I often skip around, then go back to fill in those gaps. It helps me to have a schedule and to set a deadline for myself. I aim to write 2,000 words a day, five days a week, particularly when I am on a deadline. But of course, some days are good, some are bad.

**Q: Who is your favorite character?**

**A:** That's a tough one! I like all the characters in their own ways, but if I *had* to choose, I would say Asfandyar.

**Q: Which character do you relate to most?**

**A:** Durkhanai, because I, too, am a princess. Also because she feels things so intensely, which I can definitely relate to.

**Q: What was the writing process like for you?**

**A:** It took me a few months to draft, then another to do revisions, but before I even started writing, I spent months and months just daydreaming about this story, scenes and snippets flitting into my mind in random bursts. I always had my phone or a notepad on the ready to gather those thoughts before they disappeared. It was like catching fireflies, that sudden burst of light. This initial process was my favorite part, when the story was shiny and new and exciting, full of wonder and potential, and thousands of words still undiscovered.

**Q: Will there be a sequel?**

**A:** Yes, there will be! Which I am sure will make people happy, as they will find out which door Durkhanai sent him to, but another thing to bear in mind is that either way, she'll face tragedy. If she sent him to the lady, and he chose the lion, Asfandyar will be dead. But if she sent him to the lion, and he chose the lady, he'll marry another and live with the knowledge that she sent him to his death. So unfortunately either way, they both lose.

# FOR FURTHER DISCUSSION

1. Which door do you think Durkhanai sent Asfandyar to? The lady or the lion? Use evidence from the text to back your claim.

2. Was the alliance between the Badshah and the Kebzu Kingdom a necessary evil? Why or why not?

3. What are Durkhanai's insecurities? Does she combat them?

4. How do policies of isolationism hurt both the base country and their neighboring countries? Show how this is illustrated by Marghazar and the effects on other zillas.

5. What makes a good match? Are Durkhanai and Asfandyar a good match?

6. What makes a good ruler? Is the Badshah a good king? Is Durkhanai a good princess?

7. The Badshah could have stopped the trial; why didn't he?

8. Should traditions be continued merely for the sake of history and custom, or should they be critically analyzed and discarded if no longer comprehensible?

9. Analyze the usage of the word "barbaric" throughout the text and describe how "barbaric" the Badshah and Durkhanai are.

10. Why did Asfandyar go to the opposite door that Durkhanai instructed?

11. What is a major theme of this novel?

12. Who is the "villain" of this story? Or are there no villains?

13. Should Durkhanai have run away with Asfandyar when she had the chance?

If you loved the lyrical storytelling
and complex family dynamics of *The Lady or the Lion*,
we think you'll also love
*Shadows Over London* by Christian Klaver:

Fifteen-year-old Justice Kasric and her siblings are forced
to choose sides between their mother and father
after a Faerie invasion evicts them from their comfortable life
in London and they discover their magical abilities, which
their parents kept secret from them before the war.

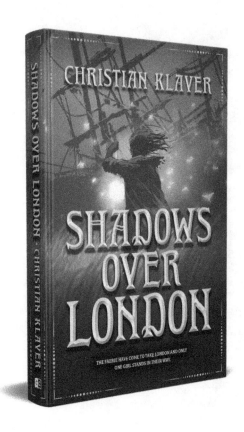

# PROLOGUE
## *The Faerie King*

*S*ome dreams are so true that it doesn't matter if they actually happened that way or not. They're so true that they've happened more than once. My dreams about the Faerie were like that. Most of the rest of England got their first glimpse of the Faerie on the night London fell. But not me. I saw my first Faerie ten years before that, on my sixth birthday.

My name is Justice Kasric and my family was all tangled up with the Faerie even before the invasion.

Because I'd been born on Boxing Day, the day after Christmas, Father always made a grand affair of my birthday so that it wasn't all swallowed up by the other holidays. That's why, long after Christmas supper had come and gone, I stood at the frosted window of my room looking out into the darkness trying to guess what kind of surprise Father had in store for my sixth birthday. I was sure that something wonderful was coming. Maybe a pony . . . or even ponies.

I crept quietly out of my room. I didn't want to wake Faith, my older sister. I didn't see or hear anyone on the top floors, but then I heard movement from down in the front hall. Father. He clicked his pocket watch closed, tucked it back into his dark waistcoat and pulled the heavy black naval coat off the hook by the door. I was sure he'd turn around and see me crouched on the stairs, but he only stood a moment in the shrouded half-moonlight before opening the front door. A cool mist rolled noiselessly past his ankles as he went out.

I was in luck! Where else would Father be going except to feed the ponies? I pulled on my rubber boots and threw my heavy blue woolen coat over my nightgown, determined to follow.

When I opened the door and looked out into the front garden, the mist hung everywhere in soft carpets of moonlit fleece. Father was nowhere in sight, but I could hear him crunching ahead of me.

I paused, sensing even then that some steps took you further than others. The enormity of my actions lay heavily on me. The comforting, warm interior of the house called for me to come back inside. It was not too late to go back. I could return to the rest of my family, content with a life filled with tea settings, mantelpiece clocks, antimacassars and other normal, sensible notions. The proper thing would have been to go back inside, to bed. I remember shaking my head, sending my braids dancing.

I followed Father outside into the still and misty night.

We went across the front garden, past shrubs and frozen pools, and descended the hill into the snow-laden pines. His crunching footsteps carried back to me in the still air. I followed by stepping in the holes he'd left in the snow to make less noise, jumping to match his long stride. The stables lay behind the house, but clearly, we weren't heading there. We lived in the country then, amidst a great deal of farmland with clumps of forest around.

The silence grew heavier, deeper, as we descended into the trees, and a curious lassitude swept over me as I followed Father through the tangled woods. The air was sharp and filled with the clean smell of ice and pine. On the other side of a dip in the land, we should have emerged into a large and open field. Only we didn't. The field wasn't there. Instead, we kept going down through more and more snow-laden trees.

The treetops formed a nearly solid canopy sixty or seventy feet above us, but with a vast and open space underneath. The thick shafts of moonlight slanted down through silvered air into emerald shadows, each tree a stately pillar in that wide-open space.

I worried about Father catching me following him, but he never even turned around. Always, he went down. Down, down into the forest into what felt like another world entirely. Even I knew we couldn't still be in the English countryside. You could just feel it. I also knew that following him wasn't about ponies anymore and I might have given up and gone home, only I had no idea how to find my way back.

After a short time, we came to an open green hollow where I crouched at the edge of a ring of trees and blinked my eyes at the sudden brightness. The canopy opened up to the nighttime sky and moonlight filled the empty hollow like cream poured into a cup. This place had a planned feel, the circle of trees shaped just so, the long black trunk lying neatly in the exact center of a field of green grass like a long table, and all of it inexplicably free of snow. Two pale boulders sat on either side like chairs. The silence felt deeper here, older, expectant. The place was waiting.

Father lit a cigarette and stood smoking. The thin wisp of smoke curled up and into the night sky.

Then, the Faerie King arrived.

First, there was emptiness, and then, without any sign of motion, a hulking, towering figure stood on the other side of the log, standing as if he'd always been there waiting. I'd read enough of the right kinds of books to recognize him as a Faerie King right off and I shivered.

The Faerie King looked like a shambling beast on its back legs, with huge tined antlers that rose from his massive skull. He wore a wooden crown nearly buried by a black mane thick as lamb's fleece that flowed into a forked beard. His long face was a gaunt wooden mask, with blackened slits for eyes and a harsh, narrow opening for a mouth.

Except it wasn't a mask, because it moved. The mouth twitched and the jaw muscles clenched as he regarded the man in front of him. Finally, he inclined his head in a graceless welcome. He wore a cloak like a swath of forest laid across his back, made entirely of thick wild grass, weeds, and brambles, with a rich black undercoat of loam where a silk lining would show. Underneath the cloak, he wore armor that might once have been bright copper, now with rampant verdigris. He leaned on the pommel of a wide-bladed, granite sword.

The Faerie King and Father regarded each other for a long time before they each sat down. A chessboard with pieces of carved wood and bone sat suddenly between them. Again, there was no sense of movement, only a sudden understanding that the board must have always been there, waiting.

They began to play.

The Faerie King hesitated, reached to advance his white king's pawn, then stopped. His leathery right hand was massive, nearly the size of the board, far too large for this task. He shifted awkwardly and used his more normal-sized left hand. Father advanced a pawn immediately in response. The Faerie King sat and viewed the board with greater deliberation. He finally reached out with his left hand to make his move, and then stopped. He shifted in his seat, uncertain, then finally advanced his knight.

I could feel others watching with me. Invisible ghosts hidden in the trees. The weight of their interest hung palpably in the air. Whatever the outcome of this game, it was important in a way you couldn't help but feel. However long it took, this timeless shuffling of pieces, the watchers would wait and I waited with them. With only a nightgown on under my coat, crouching in the snow, I should have been freezing. But I didn't feel the cold. I only felt the waiting, and the waiting consumed me.

Father and the Faerie King had each moved their forces into the center of the board, aligning and realigning in constant readiness for the inevitable clash. Now Father sliced into the black pawns with surgical precision, starting an escalating series of exchanges. Around us, it began to snow.

As the game went on, Father and the Faerie King lined their captures neatly on the side of the board. Father looked to be considerably better off. The Faerie King grew more and more angry, and he squeezed and kneaded the log with his massive right hand so that the wood cracked and popped. Occasional bursts of wood fragments flew to either side.

Father's only reaction to this violent display was a long, slow smile. He took another Turkish cigarette calmly from a cigarette case and lit it. I was suddenly very chilled. That kind of calm wasn't natural. The smoke from Father's cigarette drifted placidly upwards. His moves were immediate, decisive, while the Faerie King's became more and more hesitant as the game went on. The smile on Father's face grew. I watched, and the forest watched with me.

Then the Faerie King snarled, jumped up, and brought his massive fist down on the board like a mallet. Bits of the board, chess pieces, and wood splinters flew out into the snow. Twice more he mauled the log, gouging out huge hunks of wood in his fury. Then he spun with a swiftness shocking in so large a person and yanked his huge sword out of the snow. He brought it down in a deadly arc that splintered the log like a lightning strike. Debris and splinters had flown around Father like a ship's deck hit by a full broadside of cannonballs, but Father didn't even flinch. Two broken halves of smoldering log lay in the clearing.

"Perhaps next time," Father said, standing up, the first words either of them had spoken. He brushed a few splinters from his coat. The Faerie King stared, quivering, his wooden face twisted suddenly with grief. Then his legs gave out and he collapsed in the snow, all his impotent rage spent. He sat, slumped with his mismatched hands on his knees, the perfect picture of abject defeat. He didn't so much as stir when Father turned his back and left.

I couldn't tear my gaze away from the rough and powerful shape slouched heavily and immobile in the snow. White clumps were already starting to gather on his arms, shoulders, head and antlers, as if he might never move again.

# CamCat
## Books

VISIT US ONLINE FOR
MORE BOOKS TO LIVE IN:
CAMCATBOOKS.COM

**FOLLOW US**

CamCatBooks      @CamCatBooks      @CamCat_Books

CPSIA information can be obtained
at www.ICGtesting.com
Printed in the USA
LVHW091542310721
694233LV00010B/344/J